THE WEBS OF VAROK

"The only cause for complaint about Cary Neeper's new novel *The Webs of Varok* is that it has been far too long in coming. It is a follow-up to her breakout novel of 38 years ago titled *A Place Beyond Man*, which was a fine, memorable exemplar of the `70s genre of ecological science fiction. . . . Her new novel is every bit as engaging, multi-layered, provocative, and above all relevant to the times, as the original."

— Frank Kaminski, book reviewer
for Energy Bulletin and Resilience.org

W9-DES-034

"Who knew sustainable economics could be so much fun? Served up with large helpings of adventure and novel romance, the post-growth society of Neeper's complex but completely imagined world on a hidden moon of Jupiter is the setting for a page-turning struggle between the eternal themes of personal accumulation vs. the common good."

— Kathy Campbell, past president,
League of Women Voters New Mexico

"Humans live by myths and stories. In fact, it has been said that the future belongs to whoever has the best story. What better way, then, to instill the idea of a sustainable steady-state Earth than through a science-fiction fantasy? Cary Neeper's *The Webs of Varok* takes on this task with so many alien-imaginative twists, intrigues, and betrayals that the spellbound reader won't even realize s/he's being educated!"

— Professor William Rees,
originator of the Ecological Footprint concept

THE ARCHIVES OF VAROK

In an alternate 21st century Solar System, Earth learns that we have neighbors too intelligent, too nosy, and too near to ignore. . . .

A Place Beyond Man —
How do twenty-first century humans react when they confront similar intelligence residing in "their" solar system? Microbiologist Tandra Grey finds new hope for an ailing Earth and her own future when she makes first contact.

The Webs of Varok —
Tandra has left Earth to learn from the ancient sustainable culture of Varok, with its promise of stability for her young daughter. But a genius with a hidden talent has set her eye on Varok's wealth — and Tandra's alien soul mates. Tandra, the elll Conn, and the varok Orram must untangle a web of deceit to restore balance for Varok and their fragile new family.

With three more titles coming in 2013-14, the five-volume Archives of Varok follows Tandra's family of mixed alien races on quests from Earth to the Oort Cloud, with several stops in-between.

ArchivesofVarok.com

THE
WEBS OF
VAROK

by Cary Neeper

Cary Neeper!
We [can] do this!
6/30/13

Penscript ™
PUBLISHING HOUSE

Copyright © 2012–2013 Carolyn A. Neeper. All rights reserved.

Characters and alien species depicted herein are trademarks of Carolyn A. Neeper. The Penscript logo and calligraphy are trademarks of Penscript Publishing House, LLC.

Publisher's Cataloging-in-Publication
    Neeper, Cary.
        The webs of Varok / by Cary Neeper.
        p. cm. -- (The archives of Varok ; 2)
        Includes bibliographical references.
        SUMMARY: Leaving a troubled twenty-first century Earth behind, Tandra Grey crosses millions of miles of empty space to live with her adopted family on Varok, with its promise of stability for her young daughter. What will it take to make that promise a reality?
        LCCN 2012908441
        ISBN 978-1-62222-000-7 (hardcover)
        ISBN 978-1-62222-001-4 (6x9" trade pbk.)
        ISBN 978-1-62222-002-1 (5.06x7.81" pbk.)

        1. Human-alien encounters--Fiction.
    2. Extraterrestrial beings--Fiction. 3. Sustainability--Fiction. 4. Science fiction.   I. Title. II. Series: Neeper, Cary. Archives of Varok ; 2.

    PS3564.E26W43 2012   813'.54
                            QBI12-600211

First edition
Published by Penscript Publishing House, LLC
San Jose, California.
http://www.penscript-publishing.com

*Dedicated with all my love to my daughters
Tasha, Indra and Shawne, and to my grand-
daughters — Tahvi, Leela, Karis and Allegra — the
inspiration and focus for these renewed stories.
All my love goes with them into a future they
will brighten with ideas full of promise.*

Acknowledgements

My deepest gratitude goes to my partner and husband, Don, and to my daughters—Indra, Tasha and Shawne—and their families, for their loving support and encouragement. They kept the *Archives of Varok* alive and maturing over the years since the first book in the series, *A Place Beyond Man,* was published. They commented gently and honestly on the first versions of the four related books and did some invaluable editing that enhanced the stories of my fun-loving alien friends with their serious messages. Special thanks go to my granddaughter Allegra for designing the mountains in the cover painting.

I am delighted to announce that our shared dream is coming true, for Penscript Publishing House has agreed to take on the entire project. Under the direction of my daughter and editor Shawne Workman, this second book in the series, *The Webs of Varok,* has become a story I believe would make our alien friends proud. It's not easy to catch every inconsistency in content and voice, argument, flow and language options. With expert editing, Shawne helped craft every detail with sensitivity to what I intended.

THE WEBS OF VAROK

A Note to Readers

"Everything not forbidden is compulsory." This socially abhorrent command was written above the entrance to ant tunnels in T. H. White's *Once and Future King*. In the larger context of cosmology and evolution, it becomes a comforting and exciting thought. Our brains are not yet wired to appreciate what an average of 300 billion stars times 170 billion galaxies means. With such numbers, there is probably life we could recognize somewhere out there, with problems we could also recognize.

In *The Webs of Varok*, we humans living on the 21st century Earth are not alone in the solar system. On an undiscovered moon of Jupiter lives an intriguing mix of aliens too intelligent, too friendly and too nosy to be ignored. Their home is called Varok.

Though stable, Varok is no utopia. Nor is it a dystopia. It reflects reality as we humans experience it—and is unlike any current social or political system on Earth.

The kind of economy modeled on Varok was defined by Herman Daly in the 1970s and and is currently summarized by the New Economics Institute and New Economics Foundation in the UK and the Center for the Advancement of the Steady State Economy on steadystate.org. The model suggests humane ways to assure lasting, equitable quality of life on Earth.

Many lives are at stake. If we are not to be found guilty of abdicating responsibility, we must find long-term solutions to ensure human population stability and to reduce the overuse that has led to current massive suffering.

—*CN 2012*

Mahntik's

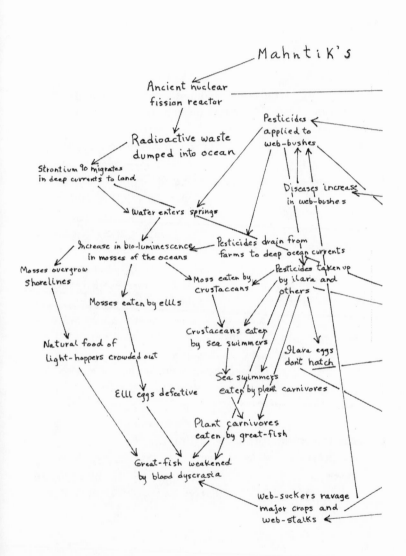

Ancient nuclear
fission reactor

Pesticides
applied to
web-bushes

Radioactive waste
dumped into ocean

Strontium 90 migrates
in deep currents to land

Diseases increase
in web-bushes

Water enters springs

Increase in bio-luminescence
in mosses of the oceans

Pesticides drain from
farms to deep ocean currents

Mosses overgrow
shorelines

Pesticides taken up
by ilara and
others

Moss eaten by
crustaceans

Mosses eaten by ellls

Natural food of
light-hoppers crowded out

Crustaceans eaten
by sea swimmers

Ilara eggs
don't hatch

Elll eggs defective

Sea swimmers
eaten by plant carnivores

Plant carnivores
eaten by great-fish

Great-fish weakened
by blood dyscrasia

Web-suckers ravage
major crops and
web-stalks

Web

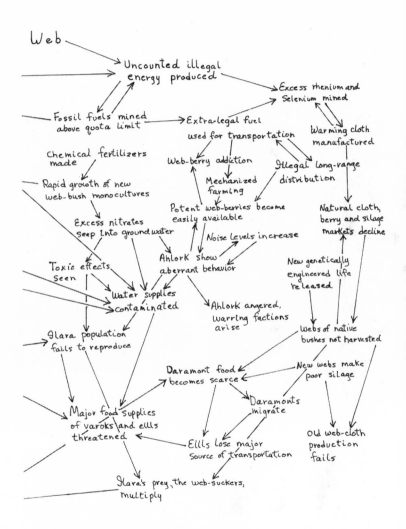

Uncounted illegal
energy produced

Excess rhenium and
Selenium mined

Fossil fuels mined
above quota limit

Extra-legal fuel
used for transportation

Warming cloth
manufactured

Chemical fertilizers
made

Web-berry addiction

Illegal long-range
distribution

Rapid growth of new
web-bush monocultures

Mechanized
farming

Natural cloth,
berry and silage
markets decline

Excess nitrates
Seep into groundwater

Potent web-berries become
easily available

Toxic effects
Seen

Noise levels increase

Ahlork show
aberrant behavior

New genetically
engineered life
released

Water supplies
contaminated

Ahlork angered,
Warring factions
arise

Webs of native
bushes not harvested

Ilara population
fails to reproduce

New webs make
poor silage

Daramont food
becomes scarce

Major food supplies
of varoks and ells
threatened

Daramonts
migrate

Old web-cloth
production
fails

Ells lose major
Source of transportation

Ilara's prey, the web-suckers,
multiply

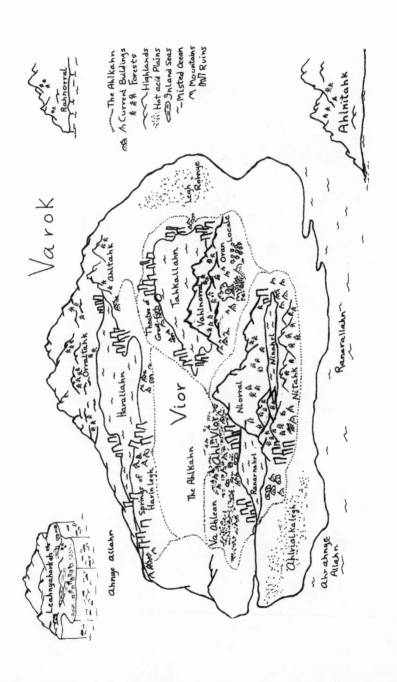

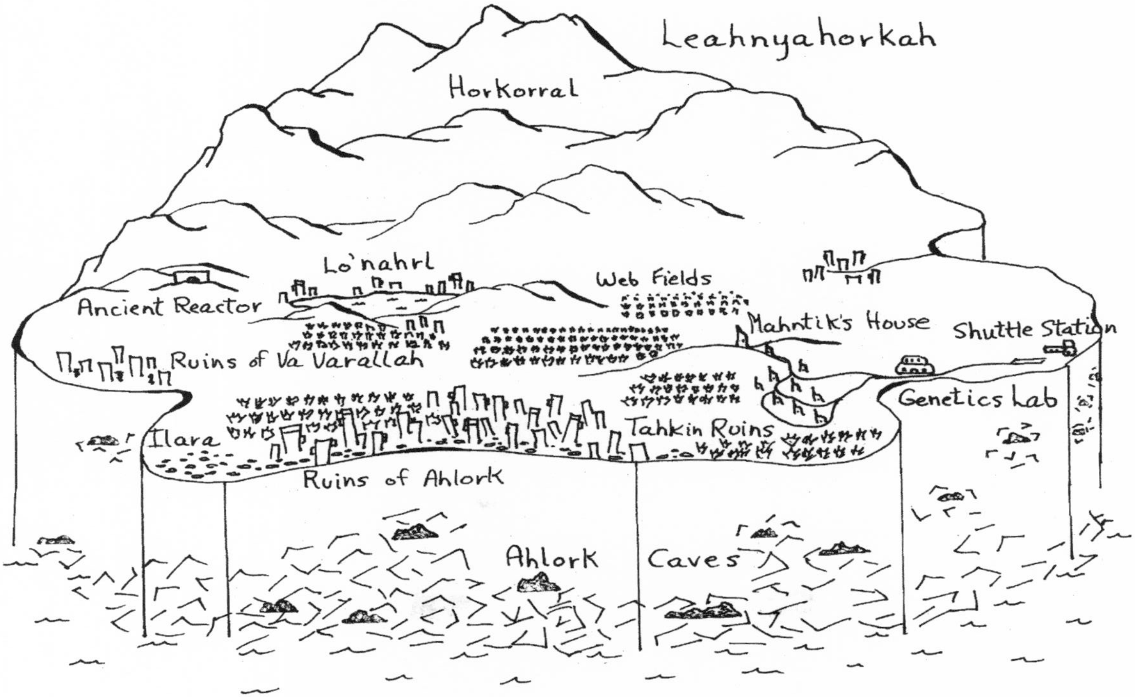

Leahnyahorkah

Horkorral

Web Fields

Lo'nahrl

Ancient Reactor

Ruins of Va Varallah

Mahntik's House   Shuttle Station

Genetics Lab

Tahkin Ruins

Ruins of Ahlork

Clave

Ahlork

Caves

VAROKIAN GAZETEER

AENNAHRL – Lake One
AHLAHNYE – The Source of Mists
AHLKAHN – The Life Line
AHLNITAHK – Forest of Lonely Sources
AHLORRAL (Mt Ahl) – Mountain of the Source
AHLRIALKALEGH – Ahlrialka Plains
AHLTAHK – Forest of Sources
AHL VIOR – The capital city of Varok
AHNYE ALLAHN – The Misted Ocean
AHRAHNYE ALLAHN – Ocean of Deadly Mists
HARALLAHN – The Unbounded Sea
HARINLEGH – Great Desert
HARKAHN – Great River
HORKORRAL – Mountains of Ancients
LEAHNYAHORKAH (L'orkah) – Haven of All That Fly
LEGH ROHNYE – Rohn's Desert
LO'NAHRL – Lake of the Passage
NHA AHLEAN – South Cultivated Lands
NIHRORRAL – Mountains of the Edge
NIHRVIOR – The Edge of Ahl Vior
NINAHRL – Lake Seclusion
NIORRAL (Mt Ni) – Lost Mountain
NIHRRAHN – The High Cliffs
NITAHK – The Forest Alone
NITAHKORRAL – Forested Mountain Alone
ORRAHNORRAL – Mountains of High Winds
ORRALTAHK – Forest of the Mountains
ORTAHK – Forest of the High Winds
RAHNORRAL – Deadly Peaks

RANARALLAHN – Ocean of Nonexistence
RANARNAHRL – Lake of Nonexistence
RUINS OF AHLHORK – City of the Forebears
RUINS OF HARIN – The Unbounded City
RUINS OF TAHKIN – City Near the Forest
RUINS OF VA VARALLAH – City of Western Shores
TAHKALLAHN – Forested Sea
TAHK YE – Forest of Lost Brothers
VA AHLEAN – Western Cultivated Lands
VAHINAHNYELEGH – Brother of Endless Mists
VAHINORRAL – Mountains of Brothers
VIOR – Center of the Winds
VIOR LEGHYE – Central Plain of No Winds
YAT AHLEAN – Eastern Cultivated Lands

Varokian Geographical Words

AEN (āĕn) – one
AHL (ähl) – source, life
AHN (än) – three
AHNYE (änyĕ) – mists
AHR (är) – deadly
ALLAHN (älän) – sea
AHLEAN – (älään) – cultivated land
AV (äv) – two
KAHN (kăn) – life, line, river
IHN (ēn) – after
IN (ĭn) – near
HAR (här) – unbounded, great

HARIN (härĭn) – wide
HORKAH (hŏrkä) – ancient ones
HORK (hŏrk) – ancient
LEAHNYA (läänyŭ) – peaceful place
LEGH (lä) – plains, flat place, endless
LO (lō) – passage
NAHRL (nărl) – lake
NHA (nä) – south
NI (nī) – alone, lost
NIH (nĭ) – after
NIHR (nîr) – edge, cliff
OR (ōr) – wind
ORK (ōrk) – flying ones
ORRAL (ôräl) – mountains
RAHN (rän) – dangerous
RAHNAN (rănăn) – the Mutilation
RANAR (ränär) – nothing, nonexistence
RIALKA (rĕălkă) – young, potential
TAHK (täk) – forest
TAY (tä) – four
VA (vä) – western
VAHIN (vähēn) – brother
VIOR (vēōr) – city, central place
YAT (yät) – eastern
YER (yĕr) – possessive
YE (yĕ) – negative

Prologue

Tandra

I found myself immersed in a living painting. Opalescent blues and tans danced a slow waltz with sheets of lightning behind portly trees, knee-deep in dark, blue-green scrub. Rock and adobe buildings with rounded contours shared nearby cliffs or nestled under huge trees, scattered on the hillsides or clustered near streams and lakes. All sang with a peaceful quiet. Only a few tall figures moved along the paths, spiraling their hands at the occasional rider on wheeled craft. Across broad, rust-hued fields leapt huge rabbits, like shaggy giraffes with smiling dog faces.

"They're daramonts, Orram, aren't they?"

My varok nodded and smiled, raising his chiseled brow without looking up from the navigation panel.

 The vision faded, but the painting was mine now, a part of me.

"Want me to call up some more memories while Conn's still soaking his gills?"

"I'd love it," I said, easing forward to take Conn's usual seat next to Orram.

"Where shall we go?" he asked. "My past is yours for the reading."

"How about interactions with ahlork?"

"I'll see what I can remember. Too bad elll brains are so convoluted. Conn could give us some good memories, but they're not easy to access."

"He's told me about his first encounter with ahlork when he arrived on Varok."

"Oh yes, the ahlork who was applying to the Concentrate." Orram smiled. "Conn took the brunt of Nidok's rage when he was rejected."

"Conn didn't realize he should not offer a comforting word."

"A comforting insult might have fared better."

"Hold that thought," I said.

Orram raised his chin and pulled his mouth into a thoughtful grin. "I was only one Jovian year old when I encountered my first ahlork. I had just started work on calculus at the Concentrate . . ." *sitting outside at a table, a bright peach colored sky . . .*

I felt the pen in Orram's young hand sketching a diagram—no, a graph. Suddenly a small whip encircled his wrist. I felt the grip of an ahlork's prehensile wingtip and heard the strange gargling sound of his rough Varokian words.

"Show me this. Show me this writing, varok."

With his free hand, young Orram pushed five long fingers through his head of silver-streaked bronze hair. *What can I do? The ahlork could slash me if I don't tell him something. What can he understand?*

"Tell me these lines," the ahlork demanded. "What are they meaning?"

"I am learning calculus."

"You learn about warts?"

Young Orram laughed, and for a moment nearly went irrational with comingled fear and bemusement. Quickly regaining control, he said, "No, no. It's your brain that has warts. This is mathematics."

The strangled sound of the ahlork's laugh flooded Orram's memory and filled my mind, overlain with the the crackling of chitinous wing plates as the beast took off from the table.

The sounds faded, leaving pleasant traces that merged with the love I knew was in real time, coming from the deepest blue of Orram's eyes.

"Thank you," I said, as his gaze shifted again to the instrument panel.

"We'll do more later, Tan. Tell Conn to put on a wet-sweater and come back to work flying home. He won't want to miss the swing around Jupiter."

I. A Troubled Homecoming

The soul emerges distorted, unrecognizable,
when actions do not swim
with the good currents nature defines.

—*Leyoon, Great-fish*

BOTHERSOME GREETINGS

Tandra—2051 CE Earth, approaching Varok

"Push off and sail up here, Tandra. You need to hear this."

I didn't like the elll's uncharacteristic dry tone. My soul-brother, the aquatic member of our new family, Conn had not spoken English since we left Earth's moon. Goose bumps surged up my arms.

"We have a personal message from Varok," Orram said. "It's coded 'urgent,' but I'll bet a *kaehl* egg it's not, considering the source." The varok also spoke English, trying his best to sound reassuring.

As I glided to the flight deck, Conn reached back and wrapped my hand in the wide fins between his six fingers. "Where are the kids?" he said. "Are they sealed in?"

"They're fine," I said. "Is something wrong up here?"

Ahead, Jupiter appeared in the ship's main viewing screen, its deceptive beauty roiling with stripes of gorgeous pastel colors.

"We don't need this distraction now." Conn scowled at the maser radio. "We've got the magnetosphere to avoid."

The radio hacked and coughed up a silken feminine sound in Varokian, unlike anything I had heard other varoks produce. "Orram? Mahntik speaking. Welcome home."

Conn's knuckles went bright green, and overtones in Mahntik's voice set off something worse than goose bumps across the back of my neck. The regard, the respect for life, so obvious when I met Conn and Orram, was missing. Now, the two exchanged the kind of look only a varok and an elll on close terms could manage.

"An urgent welcome, Mahntik?" Orram said, rolling his eyes—an expression he'd picked up from our adopted daughter, Shawne.

Mahntik's voice oozed through the ship's speakers. "I am inviting you to L'orkah, Orram, before Global Varok schedules all your time."

Conn glanced back at me. His huge dark eyes flashed with bright green sparks I hadn't seen since our last day on the moon, when human bureaucrats made an empty threat to take three-year-old Shawne away from our mixed family.

"Get off the transmitter, Mahntik darling," Conn snarled. "We've got a ship to navigate."

"Is that you, Conn?" Her words suggested claws, unsheathed.

"My family now includes this rude elll, Conn," Orram interceded, "and the two beautiful humans, Tandra and Shawne OranelConn-Grey. I will share all personal transmissions with them."

"Of course, most messages would normally include your family." Mahntik sounded very different now, almost seductive. "But not this time, Orram. You and I have business of a personal nature."

Orram smiled. "I doubt that, Mahntik." He stretched his long legs under the control panel and let his lean torso sag against his restraints. His smile morphed into a laugh almost edged with pride.

I couldn't believe it. He was flattered—or something I misunderstood from reading his mood. A wave of jealousy crashed over the caution Mahntik's voice had triggered in me. *Who is this person? Old friend? Home-wrecker?* I didn't know all the rules, but I was determined that no one or nothing would disrupt our family.

"I'm sorry I can't accept your invitation Mahnate Tikahn," Orram continued, "but thank you for your welcome. It will be good to be back, if Conn can remember how to nudge this ship into orbit."

Conn pulled my hands to the swirling green lumps atop his head, ignoring the open radio. "I've always wished I could move my sonic melons around a full half-circle, like rhinoceros ears—you know, aim them better, for better navigation under water. Can you wiggle your ears, Tan?"

I smiled and almost laughed. "No, not at all."

"They're gorgeous tiny ears anyway, my delicate human." He raised our hands palm-to-palm, and his temper came down a notch, taking my fear with it. Orram joined Conn's high-five so our family rings clinked together. We made a teepee of our hands—Orram's smooth, bronze and powerful from his youth working the web fields, mine brown and freckled from studying in Earth's sunshine, and Conn's green and webbed for swimming the seas of Ellason.

"Are you there, Orram?" Mahntik insisted. "My invitation is for you alone. Please come here to Leahnyahorkah before you go to the great-fish Leyoon. I have things to show you. I have made great progress with my recombination research at Global Varok's Genetics Laboratory."

"Now that's a first, Mahntik," Conn said. "I never thought I'd hear you say *please*."

She laughed, a real varokian snortful laugh. "You're still too annoying, Conn. I've missed you terribly, but don't come with Orram when he visits me."

The transmission ended, and Conn signaled the elll at the communications console to shut the radio off. Killah knew us well.

"Nice work, my dear elll," he said to Conn. "You're getting as good as Orram at reading Tandra."

"Of course he is," I said.

Our family bonds were working, weaving us ever tighter as a team. Orram was my soul-mate, joined with me in mind, fulfilling his deepest varokian need. And Conn—what can I say about an aquatic biped who can bat his billiard ball eyes like that? As always, he let the air out of my inflated worries without saying anything direct.

Had it been less than one Earth year since we met? Only one year since Shawne and I were quarantined and housed by Elll-Varok Science, schooled, and given work to do on Earth's moon? As a microbiologist working with Killah, I had enjoyed the challenge of studying micro-organisms across species. Our vaccines had worked. We stayed alive, even healthy, when we finally made physical contact.

Then Conn, Orram and I connected in surprising ways as we worked through the differences that defined our species. It took time, but at last I awoke to Conn as the the caring, free-schooling person I could call brother. Orram took a more direct route to my psyche. He was so like us humans, he had to awaken me to his varokian nature. Shawne, then two years old, acted as delightful glue among us three. Though humans share no DNA with ellls or varoks, our brains were wired to connect. We became family.

My full Varokian name is Tandra Oran-elConn-Grey. Oran is Orram's family name. He comes from a long line of distinguished varoks, the dominant bipedal species native to Varok. ElConn refers to the Ellasonian school that raised Conn. Like most aquatic species, he is a master of three-dimensional space, hence a talented space pilot. Grey was my human family name. Was. I have no ties left on Earth.

As family, Orram, Conn, Shawne and I are a legal entity defined by Varokian law, a committed economic unit that creates a secure foundation for social stability on Varok. Forget fertility and other biological constraints. Varok doesn't issue licenses for mating behavior, which is considered none of the government's business. Reproduction is another matter. Both the law and deeply ingrained ethics limit progeny to self-replacement only. Varok's history burned the necessity for population stability onto the genetic imperative of every varokian man and woman. The biological drive for family in varokian society comes from mental, more than sexual, union.

The colorful ribbons of Jupiter's vast storms were still in view, and I wondered what it would take to adjust to Varok—its violent skies, its deep dark in the shadow of Jupiter, its Mahntiks. *Where have I heard the name Mahntik before?* I glimpsed a vague answer in Orram's memory, then he told me.

"Mahntik was a student at the Concentrate when Conn was studying Earth. She's a specialist in genetics, now Director of Genetic Research on L'orkah."

"She talks as if she knows you well, Orram," I said.

He took my hand and placed it on the side of his whiskerless face. "She doesn't know half of me," he said, and his forearm found mine. I noticed, as if for the first time, that our hairless skin was about the same shade of red-brown, but very different in texture. Of course. In the microscope, varokian cells were hexagoal, like some plant cells on Earth.

"What do you think she wants?" I asked.

"I don't know. And I don't know why she assumes I will go to Leyoon. He is *ll-leyoolianl*, one of many great-fish who ply the oceans and lakes of Varok."

"Great-fish," I mused. *Aliens, creatures not evolved on Earth, are supposed to be so weird we humans could never understand them, much less relate. Nonsense. Earth's ocean deeps produce stranger critters than anything on Varok, though the great-fish come close.*

"Of Varok's many intelligent, conversant beings," Killah said, "those most tuned into the complexities of life are the immigrant great-fish from Ellason. Their talent for inspiring awareness among species long ago won the respect of their fellow immigrants, us ellls, as well as the native varoks."

I shook my head in disbelief. "How do the great-fish get such a wide view of things?"

"Two ways," Conn said. "They manage the infrastructure alert system, sensing devices all over Varok that pick up changes in light, temperature, vibration—that sort of thing. They also stay in contact with everyone, create a vast network of ellls and varoks, light-hoppers, and probably ahlork. Even the daramonts go to them with their complaints."

"You may have your answer about the great-fish soon, Orram," said Killah. "Another transmission is coming in now. It's a message from the Council of Species."

Orram put on the headset and let the council's message run its course. He closed with, "I will consult my family," before shutting off the radio.

My eyes met his deep oval blues. They were troubled. I loved this talented giant—his long humanoid body, his face made of angles polished with rounded edges. I sensed that he didn't like what the message implied.

"The Council of Species requests that I accept an appointment as Governor of Living Resources," he said.

It sounded like an honor to me, but Conn burst out with his laugh-like elllonian trill. "Just what you need—a desk job counting all the weird beans of Varok."

Killah was not amused. "The council must have been following your work analyzing the carrying capacity of Earth. There must be new beans that need counting on Varok."

I knew that the councils of Global Varok monitored the entire resource and population inventory, recommending limits to the mining of non-renewables and running auctions for their development, or finding renewable substitutes. When necessary, they enforced quotas, chosen by a two-thirds vote of the sentient populations.

I studied Orram's face. Normally his features could easily be mistaken for human—except for the thought-sensing patch organs behind his ears. I missed the usual look of mischief in his eyes; the smooth planes of his placid exterior hid waves of intense emotion seething beneath.

"I cannot be Governor of Living Resources. My former position as Director of Scientific Operations on Earth's moon does not even begin to qualify me for that job. I have no idea what's been happening on Varok for the last Jovian year. I have been gone too long."

Our fellow travelers gathered at the deck and responded to the news with objections that Orram shrugged off. The varok Junah, the elder elll Artellian and the ellls' first human contact, Jesse Mendleton—all had unquestioning faith in Orram's genius and integrity. They had served under him on the Elll–Varok Observation Base on Earth's moon. All agreed with Conn and Killah, however, that the job as Governor of Living Resources was a bureacratic nightmare, prestigious though it may be.

"Can't you see me climbing into ahlork caves," Orram said, "recorder in hand, asking them how many ilara eggs they had for breakfast?"

"What is your answer, Orram?" Killah asked. "Are you refusing? You've got to make it official."

"I'll answer for you," Conn said.

"You should have the honor, Orram," Artelllian insisted. "You agonized over Earth's dilemma and learned the hardest of lessons—you knew when to back off."

"Oh, that's a good one," Conn said, "as if you'd ever give up on Varok."

"We haven't given up on Earth, either." Orram looked at me, sensing my agitation. "Tandra, tell us what you are thinking."

"I don't know enough to influence your decision, Orram. Would taking this position help us or get in the way?" I felt inadequate to give him the support he needed, and he read it in me.

Earth had given me no experience of what it takes to maintain a robust steady state like Varok's, only book knowledge of selective technology and minimal throughput. "I do need to learn about Varok's steady state in order to provide Earth with an example it could use."

My home planet was imploding with all the stress that overuse, debt, and overpopulation generate, yet my family and alien colleagues watching from Earth's moon had no longer been able to get headlines—not even as fellow natives of the solar system who could help find solutions. We had decided that the best way to make our urgent messages heard on Earth was to demonstrate with living proof—live from Varok—that an intelligent society could live in comfort sustainably, for the long run. I would be the foreign correspondent, reporting with a human perspective.

"We made the decision to leave Earth as a family," I said. "We believed Shawne would be safer growing up in a stable society. I'll support whatever you feel is best for her and for Varok."

Orram held my gaze with well-concealed dismay. "I may not be able to do what is best for both, Tandra. You know that, don't you?"

Approaching Varok

Tandra—moments later

"I'm shutting down the ship's gyros so you can watch Jupiter, Shawne," Conn called to the passenger cabin through the intercom.

I left the control deck, floated to the back of the ship and pulled our three-year-old daughter into my lap so we could watch Jupiter's storms pass below. Where was the warm planet from the home sky of Orram's memory? There the storms were beautiful, but now, seeing them so close and so real, I found them too horrendous to fathom. They made me realize how far from Earth we had come.

None of us liked putting Shawne's health at risk to make this long trip. Her blood—and ours—was pooling. Our bones had lost calcium. We played hard to stay healthy, and to make our three months in space pass quickly. The *Lurlial* felt like an elllonian resort, with its moss-covered walls for snacking, its passenger section designed with plush seats, and its wide viewports. The Elll-Varok ship's closets bulged with musical instruments, puzzles both physical and mental, games of both skill and luck, and educational chips in all the languages of Varok and Ellason.

The trip was marred only by notice from our companion vessel *Ranat* that the varokian astronomer Ahl had died, of natural causes. I grieved for him. He had been a kind mentor at moon base when I applied for a permanent position with EV Science as consultant in human microbiology.

"We will be over Varok soon, Shawne," Conn's voice rang through the intercom. "Keep watch for the tallest mountains on the largest continent. Orserah's house is in a valley full of big friendly daramonts."

A rocky captive of Jupiter nearly the size of Earth, Varok coasted around its host at a comfortable distance outside the planet's magenetopsphere, camouflaged by a belt of ancient dust and debris. The moon's low albedo, about 0.005, made it very faint to human eyes. Its isolation from other moons of Jupiter meant it was missed on Earth's photo missions, Pioneer 10 and 11 and Voyager 1 and 2, which were focused on the Galilean moons.

Tectonic tides generated by Jupiter, along with the rocky orb's radioactive veins and molten heart, supported sulfur-driven life, while Varok's tidal and geothermal forces provided enough energy to drive its more creative varieties of carbon- and oxygen-based creatures. Eventually its prolific life had generated an atmospehere similar to Earth's.

The intercom blared with an elllonian voice. "Would someone tell me what I'm supposed to tell Varok?" Killah demanded. "Now I've got an immigration officer asking questions. Whose replacement certificate is being used for the immigration of the new elllonian tad Da-oon?"

"I'll be right back," I said, undoing my restraints and settling Shawne onto the seat.

"Okay, Mom." She was engrossed with Da-oon, Jesse and Artellian in an electronic game of catch the ilara egg.

"I'll call if she asks for you," the varok Junah said, reading my unspoken question with her patches. "Jesse is up next to be ilara."

Orram was sending the required message as I entered the flight deck. "Immigration notice: Tandra of the Oran-elConn-Grey Family comes to Varok on the deceased varok Ahl's Certificate of Survival. Shawne, the human child, inherits a place on Varok with Conn's certificate. Killah certifies Da-oon as his replacement. Artellian the elll uses his certificate for the human Jesse Mendleton, who will be acting as an official human observer for EV Science. Junah has not used her replacement privilege. No increase in Varok's population results from the acceptance of these immigrants; with Ahl's loss, there is a decrease of one."

Killah closed the transmission.

Orram turned to Conn, his sapphire ovals focused on the elll's narrowed orbs. "We'll soon celebrate Orserah's tenth Jovian year. She'll need help fulfilling her obligations to the land at the Oran locale."

"I'm looking forward to it," I said. "It'll be like my early years on a ranch in Colorado."

"So that's why you are built like a small race horse," Conn said. "If only your face were more horsey, you know, narrower, with a longer nose, like varoks." He turned in his seat, pulled me close with long green velvet arms and enclosed my small nose and cheeks in his wide mouth.

"I know. I know. You like high cheek bones," I gasped, when his dry kiss, or whatever you might call it, let me go. The arms stayed wrapped around me with typical elllonian affection.

Orram sounded serious. "Orserah now has the largest web field there, Tandra. It feeds a sizeable mob of daramonts. And she produces most of the eggs and egg-layer meats for the locale—both ilara and kaehl."

I stroked Conn's head plumes, lifting the red and yellow ones off his eyes, then gently pushed him away. "I love outdoor work, Orram. I don't plan to spend the rest of my life in a biology lab, you know."

Killah turned to Orram with a sarcastic tongue looped over his nasal gills. "The Council of Species has other plans for you, Orram. If you take that job, you won't be much help to Orserah."

Orram's crystal blues focused on Conn, then me. "You both heard the stakes. Should I agree to serve as Governor of Living Resources?"

Conn's eyes relaxed to their largest salad-plate roundness, and his head tilted forward at an angle, daring Orram to read what was in his mind.

"Voice it," Orram demanded.

"You'll get a lot more if you read me," Conn said.

"I don't want to get lost in your brain right now."

"What are you two talking about?" I asked.

"Orram smells a rat on Varok," Conn whispered to me. "They've offered him a chance to be big cheese, but he doesn't like the smell of Limburger."

It was a relief to laugh. I felt grateful for the elll's quirky use of English.

"Varok offers me the honor of a horrific pain in the neck, to borrow another human phrase," Orram said.

"I agree," Conn said. "Do you think the council is asking you to take this job because everything is coming up shiny red web berries on Varok?"

"Something has probably gone wrong," Orram admitted. "The present Governor, Tahl Onaliak, plans to resign. Someone on the council has the wierd idea that my expertise in snooping around Earth will be useful."

"You would not enjoy playing bureaucrat, Orram," I said.

"True," he said, "though I would enjoy roaming the hills, canoeing the lakes—you know, keeping tabs on Varok's living populations."

"Surely, eco-complexity can't be managed so closely," I said, taking him seriously, "only modeled and nudged occasionally. There are too many variables, unknown keystone species in addition to the well-known traps of dealing with complex systems."

"That's all true, but we have to watch for large perturbations, Tandra, and seek out their causes," Orram said, lowering his voice. "To take responsibility for Living Resources would require a total commitment on my part, and more sacrifice than I'd care to ask of this family."

"Sacrifice?" I didn't like the sound of that.

"It means that we might live in Ahl Vior, not at Orserah's house," Conn said. "It could be nice. The ellls at the Concentrate swim a delightful school."

"Then we're agreed, it's not compatible with the life we chose," Orram said, turning on the transmitter.

He radioed his decision to Varok. He explained that he must honor the contract to care for the land and to meet food production obligations at his family's locale. "Collectively, we have many work-hours to share. As a family, we will expand our research and analyze communication that comes from Earth. We intend to continue to present to the human population our recommendations for their gradual conversion to a steady-state." He thanked the Council for the honor. "There will be no further communication until we have landed. Transferring to Port Ahl Vior, Incoming. Orbit attained." He shut off the transmitter.

"Now," he said with a smile, "Enjoy the view, my good farmers. Go behind and be sure all your restraints are secure."

I wasn't fooled. Orram's mind was seething. Soon he would call me into his thoughts, where I would play the mediator between his rational state and his rising emotional challenge.

Conn—moments later

Conn pulsed the fusion amplifiers and teased the ionic propulsion engines, easing the Lurlial toward the remote Jovian moon he had known as home since his youth. Like a banded agate, Jupiter shone in the blackness of space, its image slowly contracting as the ship approached Varok, orbiting Jupiter at a distance of 3.488 million kilometers.

Relax. Unroll your tongue, Conn, my boy. Don't let Mahntik get to you. You can land your family on Varok, and they will remain safe there. Varok could not have changed much in the Jovian half-year since we've been gone. Or could it?

As Varok began to pull the *Lurlial* into orbit, Conn enjoyed his infrared vision of its atmosphere. It shimmered with the continuous sheets of lightning that played against the dancing green, yellow and blue aurorae. The colorful storms encircling Jupiter's huge sphere lit up large slices of the Varokian sky.

Conn loved his adoptive home. Here on Varok he had grown up as a loner and studied at the Concentrate, making his school on Ellason proud of him. Varok's odd collection of intelligent life forms provided good entertainment, and Earth studies filled his dry land time with a serious hobby. The mixed Varokian society could be as steady and true as the course of a running stream, yet any new stone, like the introduction of three alien humans, could shift its flowing patterns. *Who knows what might self-organize with the humans Shawne and Tandra and Jesse Mendleton triggering the complex mini-systems of Varok?*

The thought opened Conn's froggy face into a grin that spread from one side to the other, and his tongue reached up to wet the gills sprouting like wild mistletoe from his trapezoidal nose. *Humans, my loving humans on Varok.* Shawne would be a challenge for Orserah, but she would love the child, and the child would love the pond in Orserah's lodge.

The pond was his watery nest, but piloting the spacecraft was like swimming the deep currents of Ellason's oceans. He played the plasma engines as he would fine-tune his backfin in water. Two meters tall when standing, he had powerful legs that could carry his weight on Varok's lush but twiggy land. Though he preferred to ride the huge daramonts there, he refused to admit that riding was easier than walking on the broad sheets of sensitive web tissue that connected his long toes.

He tried to relax. He didn't like Mahntik and the great-fish contacting Orram. *I doubt they are on the same team.*

Orram joined him at the ship's controls with a questioning look.

"Go ahead and read me," Conn said to the varok in English. "It saves wear and tear on my vocal gills. Why are my hexlines lit up as if I were about to be attacked?"

"I don't need to read you for that—it's Mahntik," Orram said. "She irritated me, too. I'd rather deal with the pythons in Florida. She's some kind of predator."

"She thinks you're cute. Always has."

"Speak Varokian, Conn. How does 'cute' translate?"

"Trust me. It doesn't."

"Trust is a human thing. I can read sarcasm without it—even in that tangle of sensory circuits inside your head."

"We can't fail them, Orram," Conn continued in English, serious. "Tandra and Shawne."

"Ah, there it is. How are we going to protect our beloved, fragile dry-land bipeds from a threat like Mahntik, something that we can't define ourselves?" He turned to look more closely at the elll he had known since their youth. "You know what? I see in you a more basic worry—something about our family not being family in any biological sense."

Conn blew out his lungs and closed his gills in agreement. "Tandra might find it difficult to build a relationship with your son Orticon."

"No more than I will. Tandra and you and I are much closer to Shawne than I will ever be to Orticon, though he shares my genes. Right now I'm more worried about you. Will our family be enough? Or will you need to join the schools of Lake Seclusion, perhaps the larger schools of Tahkallan?"

"I don't think so. I'm too much a loner, Orram." Conn picked thoughtfully at his wet-sweater. "I may need a mate, though. How about you?"

"I'm a varok, Conn, remember? I've got what I need in the mind-link with Tandra. She fulfills all my varokian hormones. It's Tandra who may need a mate."

"Yeah, you may be right. She and I may have more work to do in the sex department."

"We've taken on a bit of a challenge with this family of ours."

"We knew that. All of us knew that, and love trumps it all. Right?"

"Right."

"Swear by my wet-sweater, old pal."

"No need, but sworn—to give your overactive angst some peace."

Woven of the same silver moss that lined the space cruiser's passageways, Conn's wet-sweater kept the elll's pressure-sensitive skin tiles moist and protected the neuromasts, the electro-magneto and ultrasonic receptors in the chartreuse lines between his tiles. Without the wet-sweater, he could not live more than ten light cycles out of water.

"You share five perfectly good, non-aquatic senses with humans and varoks." Orram smiled, turning back to the control panel. "But your hexlines may need some time in the lakes, fizzing and buzzing or whatever your schools do there."

"I don't need schooling buzz, 'Ram. I'm a loner. What I need is varokian patch organs to guess Tandra's mood. When she's in your thoughts, I might as well go suck ilara eggs."

"That's ridiculous. Your empathy is as good as human intuition and any varok's mood-reading," Orram said. "Sometimes you know how Tandra and Shawne feel before I do. Your job now is to let go, let them do their own adjusting to Varok. It might surprise you."

"They won't have trouble adjusting . . . unless Mahntik is after your bod." Conn pushed away from the pilot's console. "You've got to admit it, Orram, my man, if you'll pardon the expression. Something is seriously wrong down there, or the great-fish and our favorite varokian control-freak wouldn't be competing for your attention."

"Mahntik or no Mahntik," Orram said, "Tandra and Shawne will adjust to Varok in spite of us."

Mind Block

Mahntik—moments later on Varok

Two varoks walked in silence, away from the ancient ruins that clung to the southern cliffs of the island Leahnyahorkah, overlooking Varok's Misted Ocean. Mahntik felt sleek and beautiful in her walking tights and tunic, ravenous as a panther on the hunt, eager to consume the varok beside her—Gitahl, with a mind dark and strong, a dangerous but vital thorn on her varokian tree of life.

Words roiled up in the hidden chambers of Mahntik's mind as she tested her companion's ability to read her thoughts: *I can create a shadow world whenever I like, Gitahl, plan my business to grow anything I like, wield economic power to control whatever I choose. No one will ever know. Even Orram will not be able to see into my mind to prove what I have done—if that is what I choose.*

Between the varoks, a questioning mood hovered dense and cold, like the ocean's pale mist far below in the rocks. Mahntik slid open the door to her mind and watched with her patch organs to see if Gitahl noticed any difference. He did not.

Thought-sensing defines all of Varokian society, she thought, setting her mind-block back in place, *but it no longer defines me, does it?*

She laughed and glanced at Gitahl. The laugh startled him, but he said nothing. *He keeps well to himself, and he looks acceptable enough to run a mining project, though I wish he wouldn't wear such a vivid sash around his tunic. I rather like leather on a man.* She saw that he had no idea what she was thinking. Her mind-block must have given her complete protection from his thought-probes, even his mood reading.

The moons Io and Europa shone dimly above Varok's shifting banks of vapor, then disappeared beneath Jupiter's curtain of orange in the lightning-stitched sky. As Mahntik read Gitahl deeply, shamelessly, she saw he was concentrated on her feminine preseaznce. *Good.*

At last they came to the shops and dwellings near the genetics laboratory. They climbed steadily up a steep hill, past a row of stately rock dwellings that stood in geometric patterns amidst peach-colored bushes.

Mahntik wondered how far she should bring Gitahl into her global web business. Probably not far, but she would soon have him trapped. It would not matter what he knew.

On the slope's summit they turned into the stone archway leading to Mahntik's lodge. Its two stories stood high on a rocky shelf overlooking L'orkah's small transport station. An airshuttle from the continent of Vior could be seen making a rare landing.

As they passed through the hand-hewn air lock into the great room, Mahntik read Gitahl's mind. Strange. He was looking at the bare mortared walls, looking for family heirlooms. She read the perception in his mind: *Nothing in this room links Mahntik to the life of Varok or to her past, but what a structure. As old as these hills and built from their bones, as efficient as any varokian structure I've ever seen.*

"This home uses the wind off the ocean," Mahntik said, encouraging his train of thought. "It gathers light from the widest skies in high windows. It's really very well built—vented for deep dark cooling, covered with fireproof roofing, and designed for recycling every element of living. Nothing becomes waste." She focused on Gitahl's thoughts.

She didn't even tear down the old buiding when she moved in here— respected the fact that it was built for permanence. Mahntik knows how to sustain a varok's lifestyle, I'll say that.

Mahntik saw Gitahl shrug away the observation and busy himself with the electronic files at the communications center.

"Satisfy your curiosity, Gitahl, while I pour web juice."

"Do you suppose a juice-dulled mind will be more accepting of your wild schemes, Mahntik?"

"We'll see."

Soon she returned with a tray of cold moth delicacies and steaming cups of an intoxicating drink made from the berries of her genetically enhanced web bush.

They drank in silence. Mahntik captured Gitahl's attempt to read her mood. When he dared to enter her mind beyond mood, he saw her invitation. Mahntik smiled. What he read in her mind both frightened and pleased him.

"So." he said, "You have secured the ahlorks' promise to keep Free-minds at the old power plant and to mine the ruins with the energy they produce. How industrious of you, Mahntik. I will keep a watch on that operation if you like—as long as you have a firm hand on these markets of yours."

"Can you imagine a market run by flocks of ahlork, Gitahl? Even I am not mad enough to allow that."

"Nidok is no fool. He'll stop hauling your web products as soon as the authorities discover what his flock is doing."

"I don't think so. Ahlork already eat too many of the new berries. They couldn't give up their new diet if they tried."

"You are a cruel one, Mahntik." Gitahl's iron-cast expression gleamed with harsh planes as he stared into the fire.

"My cloth is already in production, and my feed-producing strains of web bushes will eventually undercut every other web stalk, berry, cloth and grain market on Varok." Mahntik's voice soared. "Also, I have designed new diseases for ahlork should they prove testy."

"That is more than I care to hear." Gitahl rose to his feet as if determined to leave.

Mahntik pressed on, waving him down. "I have Varok in my hands. My new species of web bush will make me master of Varok within the year. Local distribution indeed. Infinitesimal depletion rates. Selective technology that limits us to a menial existence! Taxes that are graduated so steeply that we innovators are all held in a state of poverty! Orram's Earth people will think us simpletons. We are more advanced than anything within radio contact. I will re-build our technological society in spite of Orram or any other Governor of Living Resources. We will again live like the forebears! It is time to use what we know. Earth knows we exist— finally. Now they will know what we truly are."

"And what if Earth is not as crippled as we think?" Gitahl was cautious. "They know where we are now. Elll-Varok Science—your friend Orram—is in constant radio contact with them. And there are rumors of an Earth launch—more humans coming to Varok."

"Rumors? Orram and Conn can continue blathering to Earth about water conservation. That doesn't mean anything to us. But if humans do manage to get here, we must be ready to snuff them out before Conn can raise a fin."

"Snuff them out? How?" Gitahl's patches strained to find Mahntik's true mind. "Let me be clear. Surely you wouldn't use the diseases you've engineered on humans."

"Why not? I'd use them to keep ahlork in line—even varoks."

"You could never use such a weapon." *What is her full vision?* Gitahl read only bland unconcern, a flat landscape of stark logic. "You can't release germs selectively. Or is it blackmail you are planning?"

"Only if it becomes necessary. You don't understand, do you, Gitahl? The germs are nothing more than a tool to guarantee the control that may be necessary to enable change, to buy compliance long enough for something . . . inventive." Mahntik laughed inwardly, enjoying Gitahl's struggle to stay calm.

He sat down on the hearth's edge, and Mahntik read his direct thought. *How could she propose such things with a mind so placid, so . . . clear?*

"You are mad, Mahntik. How would you target anyone? How would you contain your threat—and keep suspicion away from yourself as a geneticist? If new forms of infectious life are found, the genetics lab will be suspect, and a simple mind-scan will reveal all your plans."

"But I am innocent of any plans, Gitahl." Mahntik said, edging closer to him. "The ahlork do it all, and they are not above stealing germs. Nidok and his flock make deliveries of web seed whenever they feel like it, not when I tell them. I never see the distributors that take my strains of web plants and stalk products. And I have dutifully put all my lovely new germs into the sterilizing pans at the lab."

Slowly, sensing the emotional edge of Gitahl's thoughts, she placed her forearm on his. "Besides," she murmured, "it is all quite academic, Gitahl. I do not fear the deepest mind-probe."

Gitahl moved away so the sensation of touch would not intrude too quickly on his nerves, but his open arms gave him away.

"Come to me now, Gitahl. I have trusted you completely. Perhaps we may yet join our minds." She let the longing in her voice show as she entered Gitahl's thoughts.

Mahntik sensed Gitahl beginning to search deeper through her mind. He saw that she had been reading him, and he began to enjoy the pungent touch of her arm. With growing physical desire, they joined, hoping to trigger the deeper search for identity that could lead to mental union, the consummation varoks desired even more than the physical act.

They lay together as they traced the torturous path of Mahntik's awareness until it led back to her very early life. Her father rose his whip to her as she reached for a second piece of web stalk candy. "Go to the fields and hoe away the climbers if you would have handfuls of candy," the looming presence cried. "But don't you dare rub blisters on your beautiful hands, or get gray mud in your hair."

Her father seemed always to be on the edge of irrationality. "No. Of course you may not have more cloth for another dress. Weave your own cloth. And do it well. I won't have you looking like an artist's waif." His breath stank of fermented juice, his hands stained with paint from the murals he painted for the local architect.

Mahntik was forced to study with few books and no computer, to learn the arts without paint or clay, to perfect her language without tutors, to enhance her beauty with broken combs. Gitahl saw the contradictions—the impossible, double-edged demands and the distorted scars they left in her memory.

They moved on less cautiously, into Mahntik's early years as a student growing up in Vior Leghye. There an intense pocket of anger drew Gitahl like a magnet, and Mahntik urged him on. He saw Mahntik's sister. A neighbor had given the sister new cloth in exchange for her work. *I should have it. It would set off more beautifully the silver strands of my hair. I will have it.* The anger rose to a fury, mindless—

Suddenly, as if he had been struck, Gitahl recoiled from Mahntik. She laughed. "What is wrong, Gitahl?"

"I'm not sure. I feel as if something has fallen between us. As if it something would crush my mind."

"There is nothing between us now. Try again. You were

entering my childhood memories, a quarrel with my sister."

Gitahl focused on his patches, as if to steady them. "I'll start again by reading your mood, while you think of the incident that made you angry. Then I'll see if I can follow your memory to its source. I think we have found a way to begin our consummation."

She thought of the quarrel with her sister, the cruel things that were said so many cycles ago. When she felt Gitahl enter her memory again it was pleasant. She could feel his sympathy like a gentle caress, far more soothing than touch. Perhaps she could become one with him. He was clever. He would know when to leave her alone and when to be by her side.

As she relaxed the portals of her mind, she felt him sink past specific memory to the raw edge of feeling where motivation found roots. He touched jealousy and was groping toward the murderous hate that had sent Mahntik flying with a laser knife at her sister's eyes—when, once again, she slammed shut the window of her mind.

"Aee-e-e-e! Mahntik! You will destroy me." Gitahl rolled away from her, writhing in mental agony.

She laughed again, a terrible laugh. "You see my talent, Gitahl? You see? I am no simple varok."

He sat up, breathing hard, staring at her, trying to read her. She knew he could sense nothing in her mind—no memory, no thoughts of sisters, no recent pleasure—nothing but a blank screen. Gitahl stared in disbelief.

"If you had more pride and less ambition, you would leave me now or murder me," Mahntik said.

"You are telling me that you can do this at will?" he said carefully. "You can block your mind from the probing of anyone, at any level. Is this true, Mahntik?" He probed again, deeply, and saw only the image of his own shocked face, surrounded by emptiness. His mind recoiled.

"You have learned to block your mind?"

"My poor Gitahl. Did it hurt?" She stifled a small smile, then the cold sapphire of her eyes darkened. "But why have I told you? Perhaps no one should know."

"No one will know it from me, Mahntik, will they? You

are a cruel one, indeed. You have forced my retirement from varokian society."

"But we are near consummation, Gitahl." Mahntik showed her longing for him in her face but did not reach to touch him. He did not try to read her thoughts.

"It is no matter to me, as long as we are of one mind," he said. "No one will suspect—unless you indulge your pride again with someone else. I wouldn't if I were you. Unless you give it away, no one will believe that you can block your mind. Every child tries it, and fails."

"It did take some practice."

"Do you realize what this means?" Gitahl reached tentatively for her with his patch organs. "There are no provisions in Varokian law for concealment of fact; and . . . yes. The minds of normal varoks are helplessly open to you. Hopelessly open. Mahntik! My beautiful Mahntik, do you realize—?"

Raw elation overcame them. A thousand scenarios played through their shared minds, a thousand fertile possibilities for the satisfying of any greedy whim, a thousand chances to manipulate Varokian society.

"'A guiltless mind has no need to fear intrusion,'" Mahntik quoted a famous varokian judge. "Without the mind probe, life on Varok would be like Earth, a nightmare of suspicion and litigation." They laughed so long they lost control.

When reason returned, Gitahl spoke as if to himself, aware of the treason they planned. "You are right, Mahntik. Yes. Perfect the art of blocking your mind. It should not be wasted. You are beyond the reach of Varok's law. When your mind proves free of guilt, the authorities must conclude you are innocent. Until it is too late."

"Exactly," Mahntik agreed. "And they will see your guilt."

"Yes, as you planned. I am yours. I will stay hidden, while they write you off as a suspect, until varok has evolved too far to go back. You can manufacture whatever you like, sell whatever you like, distribute it wherever you like. Rebuild the ancient ruins! When varoks have experienced the unrestained lifestyle of the forebears, they will never retreat to the deprivations of the steady state. Varok is yours, Mahntik!"

ELLLONIAN DOUBTS

Conn—on the Lurlial, orbiting Varok

Conn undid his harness and pushed back to the cabin, where Tandra was sitting with Shawne. "Hey, Fruit-juice," he whispered in the child's ear, "we're nearly there." He lifted her with one hand and set her in his lap.

Shawne reached over the elll's shoulder, plucked a handful of the succulent growth covering the *Lurlial's* walls, and stuffed it into Conn's wide mouth. As the elll chewed the moss, the three-year-old played with the stray red and yellow plumes on his forehead, trying to make them stay between the two sonar melons shaping the top of his head.

"Now you can see your new home, Shawnoon." Conn pointed to objects in the ocean far below, making sure both Shawne and Tandra could see. "That large island is the continent Leahnyahorkah. We call it L'orkah; it is where genetics research is done. On the other side are Ahlnitahk and tiny Rahnorral, just now visible over the Misted Ocean. The large continent in the center is Vior. That's where we'll live, in the small locale between three lakes where Orram grew up. Running across Vior is the Ahlkahn—a beautiful, very efficient train, built by Global Varok. We ride it when we need to travel faster and farther than the daramonts want to take us."

"Do some dar'monts really live near Gram-Ors's house?" Shawne asked.

"Indeed they do. They take Grandmother Orserah wherever she wants to go." Conn chose not to tell her how huge the daramonts were, how they could rear up to four meters on their hind limbs, how their great looping strides sent their long bodies into rolling lurches that threw delicate stomachs into knots. Riding them was an art refined by foot-weary ellls.

"I love their faces, Shawne said. "They look like big dogs or rabbits or something, but Artellian says they're almost as smart as light-hoppers."

"I'm not so sure. Daramonts are not very talkative, and the light-hoppers talk too much, so it's hard to tell which is the smartest. Daramonts are a very old species, as old as the ahlork and the forebears."

"Artellian says the forebears turned into varoks," Shawne said, showing off her latest studies, "but the ahlork stayed the same as they were a long time ago. That's why they're so ugly."

"In more ways than one," Conn muttered.

"I'm going to ride a dar'mont when we get home," Shawne said.

Conn's face erupted into a huge smile, and he gave Shawne a lippy kiss on her left ear. "Thanks for that, Shawnoon," he said.

Tandra watched, obviously delighted with his love for Shawne. It brightened her delicate brown face. He cherished that look, cherished the red lights in her long hair. He loved the way she moved her small litheness against his body to look out of the portal, how she had contained her fears to make this huge change in her life.

Orram came toward them from the deck and strapped himself into a seat facing Tandra. "Killah will land the ship at the spaceport near Ahl Vior. What's all this talk back here?"

"Ramram, will you help me catch a dar'mont?"

"You won't have to catch one, Shawne, just ask for a ride—nicely."

"I'll ride those dar'monts," Shawne decided. "But I won't ride any ugly ahlork, and no great-fish."

"I bet you will," Conn said. "The great-fish give the best rides on Varok, even on Ellason."

"I won't. I won't, unless you take me," the three-year-old insisted. "I'd rather ride on wheels."

"Tricycle or noisy shuttlecar?"

"Tricycle."

"Then you'll have to do all the work. We ellls don't have good knees like some humans I know." The elll plucked at the child's knees, and she erupted with laughter.

Killah's voice sounded on the intercom." We have a transmission from the Forested Sea, Orram. It's an acoustic hologram from Leyoon."

Conn felt alarm signals ride through his hexagonal mesh. "How in Hell did Mahntik know he would call? She must have her nosy patches reading deep into someone's brain."

"The great-fish say you must become Governor of Living Resources," Killah said. "They say your experience with Earth makes you uniquely qualified."

"Tell them we'll travel from Orserah's house to the Forested Sea as soon as we can make it over the mountains," Orram said, turning to Conn. "We've got to do mud talk with Leyoon, person to person."

"They say you must accept the appointment," Killah's tone was urgent. "Leyoon won't take no for an answer. They want someone with no investment in current affairs—someone who has seen carbon dioxide out of balance with carbon fixation, water and plant use outpacing recharge and new growth, soil loss exceeding regeneration . . . "

Shock smoothed the varok's face as he struggled to contain the panic that washed over him.

Conn's knuckles went bright green, and his eyes narrowed with frustration. "Leyoon has covered just about all the errors that collapse civilizations—everything but excess births over deaths! What's going on down there?"

AHL VIOR AND THE AHLKAHN

Tandra—moments later

While Conn joined Killah to ease the *Lurlial* toward the spaceport near Ahl Vior, Orram sat quietly next to Shawne and me in the cabin with the others. I felt no joy in him, no anticipation at coming home.

"You look as if Varok were about to swallow us alive," I said.

"Maybe it is. Tan, turn on the intercom over there. Jesse, Junah, let's talk about Varok for a moment. Conn, Killah, is your speaker on? Leyoon says that too much is wrong. The planet's steady-state is broken."

"You can't break a complex system, can you?" I suggested in disbelief. "It has to re-organize around a new principle. This system has given Varok stability for millennia."

"The great-fish said that the economy surrounding Varok's web-plant trade has fallen into the chaotic realm and will not pull itself back into a stable self-organized cycle."

"So something is driving the system so it can't self-correct," Jesse said. "I suspect it's something quite subtle."

"Leyoon may be wrong, Orram." Killah's voice sounded over the intercom. "Chaotic fluctuations don't persist in Varok's local economies. There are too many checks in place. Local price responds in times of stress; businesses can rely on a stable market."

"Unless something like unrealistic low pricing sends an economic sub-system far beyond a critical point," I said. "Maybe that's what Leyoon implied?"

"I guess we'll have to find out exactly what he meant," Orram said, sounding resigned. "As soon as we get our strength back, we'll travel to the great-fish theater in the Forested Sea. I do want you to meet Leyoon, Tandra."

"I would love to go with you, but we'd better not count on it. Shawne and I might have some problems adjusting to Varok's air, the food—who knows what else?"

Orram's eyes rested on Shawne, sleeping beside me. "Leyoon will have to wait until we're ready. Conn and I didn't bring you all the way out here to take unnecessary chances."

"It will be good to relax for a while at Orserah's house," Conn said.

I could sense Orram's mood lift with amusement. "Relax? Not at Orserah's house. It's still the center of the locale established by my family, Tan. Global Varok defines ecological rights, and sets up contract, property and tort laws, but the locales enforce them. Orserah was once judge, as was her father before her. Now she seems content to look after just about everything the locale does. She sees that businesses have local investors or worker-ownership, that the local currency does its job, that the income tax keeps the playing field level. Her favorite hobby has been overseeing the pollution and consumption taxes, especially the tax on excess water usage."

I laughed. "All that and her web fields too."

"The locale offices don't get away with much, I suspect," Conn chimed in from the flight deck. "The Oran locale won't be overproducing webs any more than they're shipping in the latest fashions from Ahl Vior."

"Our locales take pride in their particular styles," Junah said. "They import very little, prefer to create their own goods. They export only enough to pay for the imports they really need. It saves a lot of transportation and packaging costs."

"It's more than that." Killah added a schooler's perspective. "The locales provide a sense of group and place, of personal investment in the land and people. Work hours are shared, so everyone has a job and lots of open time to do creative and volunteer work. The locales compete with each other in their inventive governance, like schools in the larger lakes."

"They also provide for their own parks, libraries, educational schools, and take great pride in their self-sufficiency," Junah said.

"I can't see how such a distributed system could be broken or broadly disrupted," Jesse said.

"This is your tour guide speaking." Conn interrupted from the helm. "We have successfully entered the atmosphere of Jupiter's only civilized moon, the beautiful Varok, and are approaching its largest continent, Vior. Take a moment from your worries to enjoy the rugged ocean shoreline. No, no, keep your seats and restraints! Take a look out the monitor provided for you at great expense by Elll-Varok Science. Soon we will be speeding above the sobering expanse of the hot acid plains. There photoelectric devices designed to trap auroral light or energy from the continuous lightning in Varok's ionosphere cover vast areas. The landscape will soon give way to a lake—the Ranarnahrl. To the north you can see the Ahlkahn. Can you see the train, Shawne? Ages ago it passed through a vast megalopolis. But that was in ancient times, the time of the forebears."

"There it is," I said, pointing toward the screen.

"It's very tiny down there," she said.

The Alkahn corridor was now dotted with independent communities separated by the farmland that supported them. "This country reminds me of the California of the early 1900's my great-grandmother once described to me," I told Orram.

"Except that down there no one owns the land," Orram said.

"No one? No where on Varok?"

"Not now. Land tenants like Orserah hold contracts for the care of the land, its soil, its water, its fauna, and its inhabitants. If I were Governor of Living Resources, I would have to schedule the counts that are made periodically for the mining quotas. They are managed by the region in cooperation with each locale."

"And those who win the bids mine the quotas?" Jesse asked.

"Right," said Orram. "And resources are mined under the supervision of the locales, which have no limits on the laws they can make to protect their local people and the land they tend."

"Not like mining rights on Earth, which trump land owners' surface rights," Jesse said. "Sometimes mining trumps rights to arable soil and clean water."

"I believe Living Resources is safe from such flareups," Orram said. "We would just be counting, watching, analyzing, painting the big picture in case some imbalance needs correcting. Like all the offices of Global Varok, Living Resources is limited to setting long-term goals and identifying extensive problems."

Junah clarified for Jesse and me. "Solutions are left to the locales, thank Harrahn. The larger regional organizations hold the quota auctions and oversee development of high-tech projects like space travel, while metering ocean farming and other multi-locale projects that require lots of expertise or experimentation or technical support—and here we are," she gasped, as the *Lurlial* powered up to make its landing," in the biggest collection of such expertise—my home, Ahl Vior."

Tandra—the Concentrate at Ahl Vior

We made our uneventful entrance into Varokian society at its largest named region, a cluster of locales—a city of 250,000 varoks, 50,000 ells scattered throughout as schools in deep lakes, with a few great-fish in the deepest waters.

After the *Lurlial* settled and passed final checks, we took our places in recovery chairs and rolled out of the space cruiser to greet a sea of brown and green faces gathered for the brief welcoming ceremony inside a great hangar. We made a few comments about the long trip and our pleasure at being welcomed so warmly, but Shawne won the event with her enthusiastic attempts at speaking Varokian.

"I would very muchly like to ride a daramont, if you are pleasing," she said, and the crowd roared its approval with a cacophony of sounds unlike anything we had ever heard.

As the crowd dispersed and we exited the hangar toward the rehabilitation center, I succumbed to a cascading nightmare of unfocused impressions. Lights spilled from the sky in dim waterfalls to an unseen horizon. The flashing and shifting of muted colors obscured the pattern of ill-defined structures that merged seamlessly into a rich fabric of botanical growth. I could hear nothing but a distant mewling and the familiar musical patter of ells speaking Elllonian. The sounds of rushing traffic that I expected of a city were missing. I felt I should whisper so as not to disturb the quiet. A sharp electric smell filled the scene, and I was afraid to breathe, for the gentle breezes carried a disquieting hint of ammonia.

"Ouch. I didn't prepare you well enough." When Orram read my first impressions of Varok, he steeled himself and wrapped his arms around my shoulders. His embrace gave me the reference point I needed. "You have seen my memories of Varok. You know its sights and sounds from all you've seen in my mind, but I couldn't translate for you its raw impact on the senses."

I tried to focus on the view from Orram's mind. It didn't help. "Where is Shawne?" I asked. "Is she all right?"

"She just threw up," Conn groaned from somewhere behind us.

"It's all right, Mom," Shawne said. "Conn's mopping it up." I was never more thankful for Conn's love of children.

The space recovery facility surprised me. Its therapeutic contraptions and electronic monitors lay hidden in a vast park laced
with walking trails and small lakes. Shawne soon grew to love
the elllonian nurses, who sported every variety of head and tunic
plumes. They reacted to her young age and refusal to be separated
from Da-oon with inventive games. "You humans are all elll tads
at heart," they said.

Our physical rehabilitation from space travel passed quickly
as we rotated our duties providing information to Earth and inter-
views for Varok's vast communication networks. We found time
for radio calls with Orserah every light-period.

We humans enjoyed talks meant to orient us to the moon's
oddities, like the changing skies and the occasional bursts of elec-
trons and protons from Jupiter's ionosphere and the solar wind.
Shawne and I enjoyed the enhanced aurorae during irregular
bursts of seven to eight MHz radio noise. When she wondered
where the hot sun had gone, I explained that Varok itself provided
comfortable warmth. Later, she would study at the Concentrate to
understand its source: Varok's internal radioactivity, plate tecton-
ics and tidal effects from Jupiter.

Building our ability to walk in Varok's gravity was not difficult,
for it was weaker than Earth's. We celebrated the gradual return
of blood to feet, worried about subtle threats of headaches and
heart damage, and happily turned off all thoughts of Mahntik.
Time was our good friend as we adjusted to Varok's confusion of
dim light and rare dark.

Sky-hogging Jupiter marched across the sky, the Varokian light-
periods tuned to its changing face. With each rotation of twenty
hours, Varok provided ten-hour shifts of just enough light so we
could manage. Light-periods glowed with something like bright
Earth moonlight, plus the light from constant aurorae and sheet
lightning generated by the five million amp torus that sizzled
between Io and Jupiter. The sun would contribute an additional
three percent when Varok was not in shadow as it made its 42 day
orbit around Jupiter. In shadow and rotated away from the planet,
we could get a reliable ten-hour period of sleep in deep dark.

After many light-periods, our free health passes arrived and we were treated to a final round of vaccinations. As we left the rehab center to walk along the path that lead from the spaceport to the rail station, we were met by Junah's family. In a moment of intense emotion controlled beneath a smooth face and rigid fingers, Junah said goodbye to Orram. She had once hoped they would be consummate mates, linked in mind and body. She left that behind her now to return to her family home in central Ahl Vior, to live the life of a mentor at the Concentrate.

After Junah and her family had disappeared on a shuttlebus down the wheels path, I concentrated on Orram's refreshed impressions of his home planet. The orange and red lights of Varok's wild sky began to order themselves in my mind, but something was wrong, as though someone had painted an unreal picture. Of course. There were no shadows in Jupiter's diffuse light.

We stood on a high mesa overlooking Ahl Vior. It seemed more like an inhabited park than a city. In the distance lay a wide plain framed with distant mountains. Waterfalls of light flooded the scene. Several small lakes dotted the valley, a sign of the plentiful water that allowed the group of locales to grow so large. Small buildings sculpted from rock and clay rose from nearby slopes as if they had grown there. Roofs sported edible gardens, shimmering with collecting troughs and electromotive plates. Many houses were nearly invisible amidst clusters of huge warm colored trees, while blankets of golden succulents gave the urban landscape a pleasant glow.

I was enchanted, drawn to the quiet beauty of this colorful, rich valley. Ellls rode daramonts, and varoks walked at a leisurely pace or rode tricycles loaded with goods. We would get plenty of exercise here. Only once on the winding paths below did I find a small motorized vehicle.

"Hydrogen powered," Orram explained, "probably rented for a long distance journey. Varok has never nurtured a source of fossil fuels, so we have had to do with lower energy sources. Wind, geothermal, tidal changes and water currents are the big ones. Efficiency, of course, is cheaper than all other options."

"And there is a stiff tax for overuse," Conn added.

"Fair warning," I said. "We'll turn off the lights when we leave a room, right Shawne?"

"We travel by Ahlkahn directly southeast past Mount Ni to the Vahinorral junction," Orram said. "There the daramonts of Orserah's fields will be waiting for us."

"They'd better," said Shawne. "I don't like all this walking. I want to ride a dar'mont."

"I'll be your daramont for now," said Conn. His feathery plumes tickled her nose, and she screamed with delight, then grabbed one sonic melon in each hand as he set her down on his shoulders.

At the transport station, Orram pointed out the trim line of the Ahlkahn's long coaches as they threaded their way through the rustic outskirts of Ahl Vior. Briefly the train disappeared, then emerged as it wound swiftly up the twisting grade onto the transport rise. With a soft whoosh of its magneto-levitation suspensors, it came to a halt beside the boarding platform, an incongruous strand of high technology in a pastoral setting.

Many passengers poured from the widening doors: a few ellls, sporting plumes of every shade of green and blue, their faces dancing with bright smiles beneath dark globular eyes. The varoks were dressed simply in hand-woven tunics over narrow slacks, their faces placid—but why so strange? They seemed only remotely humanoid. Their thought-sensing patch organs stood out like ugly warts, obvious behind their ears.

"Those varoks' brains are leaking out," Shawne said. Orram yelped with a rare eruption of delight.

A set of onlookers returned our curiosity and perused our mixed troop, focusing six different shades of blue eyes. Their dark auburn hair glinted with bright streaks of silver above hairless skin that shone like polished mahogany. Was Orram so alien? I glanced up at him, trying to put him in context. I realized with a start that his patch organs were unusually subtle.

"See what you took as family, my *rialka*?" he said. His eyes gleamed mischievously, and he took my hand in his—in a most unvarokian way.

His gesture gave momentary pause to the young varoks. I smiled and nodded to them, acknowledging the trouble they had trying to stay polite, for their curiosity was bubbling visibly from their expressions. A tall varok dipped his head in greeting, with open amusement.

Two ellls raced ahead of us with whooping cheers, and ushered us onto the Ahlkahn ahead of Jesse, Killah, Artellian and Da-oon. "You must be Oran Ramahlak—and this is your human." They spoke Varokian with a tongue tuck not unlike Conn's.

"Where's the human tad? You got her there, eh? Conn, is it? Wouldn't you know the elll of the family would take over the child?"

"And look at you two land critters holding hands," said another. "Not surprising a human could break down the old varokian skin barriers. Good to see you touching, Orram. You'll do wonders for this old planet, human lady. Keep him close."

They swept on down the platform, leaving me choking with laughter. Orram had silently translated as they talked, for my Varokian was still slow.

Conn was furious. "Those ellls must be new to Varok," he said in English. "They haven't got their manners yet."

"I thought they were wonderful," I said, reaching out to stroke the interdigital webs on Conn's hand. "Since when have you worried about manners?"

As usual, the fire of Conn's temper went out as fast as it had flared. He raised my hand, and his long tongue tapped my knuckles. "How are you doing up there, Shawne? How do you like the train?"

"It's okay."

"Can you walk now?"

"I'm okay." She stumbled only once when Conn put her down inside the coach. I was relieved to see her look around, returning the smiles of seated ellls and varoks as if she couldn't befriend them fast enough.

As we searched for seats together, a confusing mix of silent greetings and sympathetic awareness impinged on my consciousness. I realized it must be coming from the seated varoks we passed, through my link to Orram. I was practiced only at reading Orram's mood and focused thought. This barrage of available minds overloaded my brain, already short-circuited by the busy sky and disorienting landscape.

"Orram, I can't handle this," I whispered. "I keep looking for something familiar, and there's nothing, except some of these benches. They help. I think they're for sitting, right?"

"Relax your mind. Don't try to read each mood or impression, especially not literally. Let the varoks' thoughts pass by, like a stream of warm water. You are always at home in that stream of moods and impressions, free to choose one mind as a supporting raft, if you wish."

I focused, and Orram's mind provided that raft.

After walking through three coaches, we found seats for all of us. I shared a bench with Orram. Scattered in irregular groupings about the coach, the soft benches were made of a thick woodfoam that had taken on subtle shapes to fit the more frequent users. Writing desks and game tables, finished with a harder plant material, folded down from the walls of the coach. The thick carpeting was a natural fiber sprayed into a thick mat and left to soften. Most peculiar, however, were the large perches that hung from the ceiling.

"For ahlork," Orram said, "but they rarely ride the Ahlkahn. They like flying long distances."

I put away the hope of seeing one soon. *And just as well*, I thought. *I've already had more input than I can handle.*

The Ahlkahn slid quickly into high speed, and I relaxed into the flood of kind awareness around us. The varoks knew me from our news broadcasts, accepted me as part of Orram, and loved our child for the elllonian qualities they saw in her. *I will never be lonely here, with or without Orram.* The thought surprised me and brought a smile to Orram's face as he read me.

Shawne was trying out a few Elllonian words on two ellls seated nearby. As the train moved into open land, she moved from person to person quizzing everyone who met her eyes. The microbiologist in me went a little crazy with anxiety, but Killah gave me a nod. We had done thorough work checking for cross-virulence in our planets' native germs and undergoing extensive vaccinations. At least he felt confident.

Within a few minutes of rapid travel, the city's continuous patchwork of co-mingled commercial and residential centers, mini-forests, parks, meadows and lakes gave way to the independent locales that made up the heart of Varokian society.

Orram's mind reflected satisfaction with what he saw. The Ahlkahn had not changed since he left Varok for Earth, had not changed much for three thousand Varokian years. He spotted no new construction, very little motorized transport. Varoks walking. Even ellls, though more rode daramonts than risked their webbed feet on the paths.

Surely Leyoon's dire message was an exaggeration. The civilization of the varoks, devoted to selective technology and conservation, had not changed since the adoption of the Rule of Stability in 1947 *ir* (Varokian: *ihn rahnan*, after the Mutilation). The Varok of 4221 *ir* was still a quiet, unhurried place.

"The rights to privacy and quiet are as secure in law as the rights to free expression," Orram told me. "They are as sure as the rights to shelter, pure food, medical support, air, and water. Someone would have to operate far outside the law for Leyoon to give the warning he did."

"You are looking for signs of growth in everything, Orram, as if you were afraid Varok has caught Earth's cancer. Would you take the job as Governor of Living Resources if you thought Varok had changed?"

"I might, but I wouldn't like it. Selfish of me, I suppose. I had my moment trying to help Earth, and I keep asking myself if I couldn't have done more. I doubt that our information dumps will be enough."

"They are all we can do for now, but if you are needed on Varok, Orram, I'll do what I can to help."

After the Ahlkahn left the bucolic farms and shops of the locales near Ahl Vior, it sped southeast toward a broad valley. Still uneasy amidst the ever-shifting patterns of light over the land, I missed the sun, reduced to a bright circle five times smaller than that seen from Earth. In the distance, I could barely make out ruins left behind by the forebears, ghostly silhouettes of tall buildings on the shore of a vast inland sea.

"Those are the remains of mansions and towers that once over-looked the Forested Sea," Orram explained. "Our ancestors had built themselves a lavish civilization. Now the ahlork nest there and make themselves useful by extracting minerals and artifacts."

"Will we see ahlork?" I strained my eyes to catch sight of the lumpish, aerial beasts as we swung past the ruins. Too soon the abandoned buildings shrunk to the size of toy skyscrapers. The Ahlkahn moved into fertile lands fed by waters spilling from the glaciers of Mount Ni. Locales of various shapes and sizes lay well camouflaged in the landscape. I eagerly anticipated Orserah's house, remembering from Orram's memory that it was embraced by an ancient mineral tree, that it blended in tone and quality with the gentle, quiet hills beneath the rocky crown of the mountains called Vahinorral.

"These mountains are familiar old friends to me," Orram said. "They haven't weathered a bit since I was a child nearly five Jovian years ago."

I laughed, knowing he was watching to see if I caught his exaggeration. Varoks recognized the Jovian year as approximately one-tenth of a varok's life span. Jupiter takes about 11.86 Earth years to orbit the sun.

"I'd like to know why so many varoks are riding the Ahlkahn out here near Lake Seclusion," Conn interjected, spoiling Orram's mood. "Ever since we left the ruins we've been taking on passengers."

"The valley has been more populated than the ruins for a long time," Orram quipped.

"But why is there more traffic here than in Ahl Vior?" Conn asked. "I'm serious. Ahl Vior is the major urban center of Varok. In this valley daramonts have always had time to carry varoks, as well as ellls. Something has happened. Look at the size of the locales we're passing. They're packed together like rafts in a flood. The web fields are no bigger than postage stamps. The valley is crowded, Orram."

Just then a clacking and thumping sounded overhead. The electronic whine of the coach doors accompanied rude noises from two squat beings, scuffling with an enraged Ahlkahn official.

"The human beings are not yet adjusted to Varok," the official insisted loudly, trying to keep two waddling, square-faced beasts away from Shawne and me. "They are not for exhibit."

I turned in my seat to watch the creatures. Their stubby torsos rolled from side to side on monstrous talons. Gargoyle faces tilted curiously between the hunched shoulders of the chitin-plated wings folded at their sides. Their wing tips, tapered cones of sensitive flesh ending in whip-like cords of prehensile tissue, rode in a forward position, as if in supplication.

"Oh oh," Conn said to me in English. "Ahlork."

AHLORK ON THE AHLKAHN

Tandra—passing southwest of the Vahinorral

"What strange birds," I said.

"The nearest is a large female," Conn noted. "She's got the bright blue scales."

Under converging brow ridges, her square face, heavily armored, carried a lippy sneer punctuated by two tiny black eyes.

"Better not call them birds," Orram said. "Varok's small avioids don't have such a distinguished ancestry as Earth's."

"No dinosaurs?"

"Not enough heat or light out here. And ahlork are built differently than birds, like tanks with external hard parts."

"Insectoids then."

Orram's sense of fun surfaced. "No, no, Tandra. Bad biologist."

He waved an invitation, and with a clatter of broad, plated wings, the ahlork came toward us, swooping low over two elder varoks sitting nearby. One varok grimaced and ducked ever so slightly in revulsion. The ahlork noticed, circled, and made another pass over him.

I felt a surge of mirth. Orram warned me to stifle it, but the ahlork had already seen my wavering smile. He flapped toward me and landed on my head, then peered down into my tear-filled eyes. I burst into laughter despite the dig of his talons.

"You are nothing more than an elll, with all that shaking and grimacing, First-Human-Being-On-Varok," the ahlork said in abbreviated Varokian. His flapping lower lip was distorted by a long scar that gave him a permanent questioning leer. "We made you crying, I fear."

I answered in Elllonian, trying to remember the ahlork manners Orram had taught me. "I cry for you, plated one," I croaked, "but not out of sadness." I spoke with some difficulty, for the scene played too vividly in my mind—this ridiculous, clumsy creature careening over the crowd of immaculate varoks. To keep himself safe from an overload of mirth, Orram retreated from my mind and gave the ahlork space.

"Please get off my head," I managed to say. "You are very heavy." With that I burst into another volley of chuckles that gave me some relief.

"Get off my human, Nidok." Conn bellowed.

"It's all right, Conn," I said, though the ahlork's talons were threatening to draw blood. "Easy with the toenails—Nidok is it?"

"Conn says my name. I see you are only half mad as varoks."

The blue-plated ahlork standing on the floor spoke in a voice broken with foam. "Surely Earth be beautiful. Not this heap of ruins. Why do you come to Varok?"

"I brought my child here for her health, so we could live in safety, with a future. Basic living rights are protected by law here. No one, not even ahlork, may foul her drinking water and get away with it. Right?"

"Ouch. Too serious, Tan," Conn whispered.

"Wrong," Nidok croaked, rising off my head with a final dig of his talons. "Nidok fouls your stringy hair if Nidok likes. I come from L'orkah to nip ears of your child when I please." The ahlork flapped noisily toward the rear of the coach where Killah held Shawne, wide-eyed and huddling in his arms.

"Stay away from that child, Nidok," Conn warned. He dove through the maze of coach seats after the ahlork, startling passengers as he went.

"You won't stop me, Conn-Who-Gives-Ahlork-Their-Names," the scarred ahlork called, and he settled on a perch near Jesse Mendleton.

Jesse distracted him with a feint and Conn grabbed the ahlork by a wing tip, shouting a stern command in ahlork sounds. Nidok jerked his wing aside, throwing Conn roughly against the coach wall. As Killah ducked away with Shawne and Artellian, Conn looked for another vulnerable spot in the beast's shielded body. With a two-finned grab he locked the ahlork's chitinous wings to his body, and pulled Nidok to the floor.

"Mind your manners, Lop-lip," Conn hissed. "Stay back, Orram. They're drunk."

Conn's announcement brought several varoks to their feet. They converged on the female ahlork, suffering a few scratches in the fray to subdue her. The Ahlkahn official opened the coach door and together two varoks tossed her out of the coach to fly free of the train.

Nidok struggled in Conn's arms, leaving the elll's moss tiles painfully engraved before he broke loose. Conn ducked to protect his face, then rammed into the ahlork's exposed body, throwing him toward the open coach door. I gasped as its wings flexed into a lethal array of chitinous plates.

"Good point! Good point! I give you that one." The ahlork laughed.

It was the strangest sound I'd ever heard from a living beast, something between a gargle and a belch.

"Sober up, Nidok, before you greet newcomers to Varok," Conn growled. "Take your wing-plates off full cock. You are the leader of a good flock. Do not shame it."

The ahlork gazed at Conn for a moment, then backed out of the coach and tumbled into the air to join his mate.

Conn gathered himself off the floor, holding his right shoulder. His wet-sweater was stained with red.

"You're hurt," I said.

"No such luck. Look at this." He lifted mashed berries from his sweater and shuddered. "Those ahlork were drunk on berries. Nidok's lip was smeared with the web fruit."

"Where would they get berries now?" Orram asked. "The harvest is more than a cycle away."

"The ahlork have been harvesting from the new strain of web bush," said a tall varok standing behind Orram. "It produces berries continuously, not only at celebration time."

I felt the stirrings of trouble sharpen in Orram's mind.

"It's a good strain, really," the tall varok explained. "My shirt is made of the fine, soft cloth its web produces."

"I assume this new webbing is an approved strain," Orram said.

"Oh yes, no doubt of that. The new cloth's trademark is well known in the Mount Ni area. See here. This is it." The varok turned up the hem of his shirt to reveal a symbol embossed on the cloth in bold strokes—two stylized Varokian symbols.

Conn's eyes widened, then narrowed with annoyance. "Mahntik!" he exploded, startling the tall varok. "Wouldn't you know she'd be responsible."

"What are you saying?" Orram asked.

"You must have noticed it, Orram," Conn insisted. "Since we left the acid plains, half the varoks who boarded the train were wearing this new cloth. Where did they get it? Mahntik couldn't have fields all along the Ahlkahn. She's shipping a long distance, if its made on L'orkah."

The tall varok frowned and nodded. He spoke carefully. "Whoever is selling this cloth must have had the distribution rights extended. I bought this shirt in the foothills of Mt. Ahl across the Vahinorral, far from Ninahrl."

"How is Lake Seclusion involved?" Conn asked, a suspicious wrinkle in his nasal gills.

"That's where the cloth is woven, I believe," said the tall varok, "from the new webs grown on L'orkah."

"Why would a superior strain of web justify long-distance distribution?" Orram asked. "Web bushes and their berries are not critical for any kind of medication. Couldn't they just import seeds and grow the bushes locally?"

"Face it, Orram," Conn said. "That high-blown geneticist, Mahntik, has pushed her greedy claws right into our backyard. I wouldn't be surprised to find her mark on the ahlorks' berries, too."

Orram turned to watch as the train slid past broad fields. Here and there, a patch of unusually rusty shrubs filled a square in a patchwork of half-tended web bushes.

"Some of these webs haven't been harvested in thirty light-periods," Conn gestured out the window. "We're not seeing an orderly transition from an old strain to a new one. If Mahntik's strain is really better, she should have listed it on available seed lists, so it could be grown locally."

Orram looked out the window in silence, and I watched his mind as the train rushed past broad fields of dead and broken scrub. The webs hung uncombed and uncollected on the bushes. The stalks lay over, broken with dry rot. Slowly the fury growing within Orram turned to cold horror. "Daramonts could never use such stalks as fodder."

"The new strain on L'orkah matures so much faster, you see," the tall varok explained, trying to calm Orram. "The local growers of old strains can't compete."

"There is no reason to waste energy transporting stalk." Orram lost control. "Surely the Daramonts here can eat stalk from local fields. Why are they so neglected? Has no one contracted for the care of this land?"

Shawne began to whimper.

Orram turned to me and fought off his anger with stiffened fingers, then took Shawne in his arms. "My anger is already gone, little one. Poof." He pressed her against his shoulder, as if to keep her from seeing the untended fields. "I will go directly from Orserah's house to the Forested Sea," he said, "and see what the great-fish, Leyoon, has to say."

Conn gave me a silent *yes* with a flick of his long tongue. "He means *see* literally," he said. "Great-fish speak with sculpted symbols. We won't let Orram go alone. He might miss a twist in Leyoon's wet sand."

II. Family Ties

Nothing real can grow forever.

Put a few bacteria in a test tube with some warm soup and watch what happens. In just a few days the population will explode and the food will be gone. You'll be lucky to find a few surviving mutants. Example: the varoks.

—*Tandra's diary, 4225 ir*

ORSERAH'S LODGE

Tandra—arriving at the Oran Locale

At the Ahlkahn station, we unloaded the treasures we had brought from the EV Science Observation Base on Earth's moon. Shawne and I began to enjoy the changing light as Jupiter abandoned Varok's sky. We soon adjusted to the loss of the sun's three percent addition, for the local sources of light grew deeper in tone when in Jupiter's shadow. Near the station we spotted darmonts, their auburn fur shimmering with a rich hint of gold. The Alkahn platform was soon surrounded by a sea of their nodding, furry heads, greeting us with excited snufflings and snorts. Orram translated. Word had spread among the big mounts that the racing elll, Conn, had returned.

"How do we choose which to ride?" I asked Conn.

"Good question," he said. "You do it, Shawne. Pick a daramont for us, then one for your mom and Da-oon. They won't object if you choose."

Our meter-high daughter wandered fearlessly through the forest of knobby knees, looking into their huge Spaniel-like faces. I stayed close behind, wishing Conn would ride with us both. Carefully, slowly, some of the beasts lowered their heads, invitating us to climb aboard.

"Pull the ear of one you like," Conn said to Shawne, wandering off into the mob.

Trust gave me the calm I needed. Conn had to know Shawne was safe with these animals. He had to. I had lost sight of them both.

"I like this one with the chocolate ears," Shawne hollered amidst the snortling.

"Pat his nose, the thing in front of his ears that looks like an eggplant."

"What's eggplant?"

"It's like a shiny purple football."

Silence, for an eternity, then Shawne and Conn emerged above the seething haunches atop a handsome beast. The herd parted so they could join us beside the exit deck. "You take this pretty yellow one, Mom," she said, pointing to a palomino variety at least a foot shorter than the one she chose.

The beauty nodded and lay down, stretching her neck out long and low, so I could mount easily with the elllonian tad Da-oon in my arms. Conn showed me how to slide back along her neck until my legs could grasp her sides.

Jesse busied himself loading a small hydrogen truck Orram had rented to deliver our things to Orserah's house. Killah told the daramonts that his human and varokian companions were weak from space travel and needed rides as much as the ellls. Orram accepted the overtures of a large insistent male he had named Sea Cracker some time in his past. "Hang onto their ears as they get up," he said.

I held my mount's long ears, enclosing Da-oon between my arms, and our mount rose up easily. We lurched along for seven kilometers through fields and orchards. The land glowed with dark colors like late fall in North America—browns and rosy beiges, rich blues and golds, and touches of green. Light-capturing botanic structures, not unlike leaves, consumed the light from the persistent lightning. I knew not to expect plants green with chlorophyll.

As we progressed through the Oran Locale, we passed small farms surrounding a park of ancient shade trees that hovered like loving protectors over a mixed assortment of shops and gardens. Orram pointed out a playground and two schools, a library, a laundry, a sewing center, a silo and a web-processing plant. Plots of web bushes grew mixed with tall fruit-bearing stalks and short plants I couldn't identify.

Across a broad field of healthy web bushes, Orram's mother Orserah stood beside her lodge. A large mineral tree grew as an integral part of the building's structure, supporting the outer porch.

I noticed a big male daramont following our caravan, as he broke into a loping run. He made his way through the web bushes, and, at the porch, invited Orserah onto his shoulders with a nod of his smiling face and a gracious squat. When the aging varok had climbed onto the beast, he stood. His long legs rose and fell with a dancer's precision to avoid stepping on edible plants in her garden.

Orserah's eyes swept over me as her daramont approached mine, and I wondered what she saw, a human woman of slight build and smooth dark hair so unlike the silver-red tresses of the statuesque varoks. I slid off my mount, holding Da-oon in my arms.

"My daughter," she said in the studied English I recognized from our frequent radio conversations aboard the *Lurlial*. "And here is the elll Da-oon, ready to swim the Forested Sea." In response, his tiny fin spiraled upward, imitating the varokian greeting of respect.

"And this is Shawne, on a huge beast with some kind of green creature who has grown fat on moon base omelets."

"Conn's not fat," Shawne said, glancing back at him, then pushing her hand into the air.

Orserah smiled at our child's attempt to imitate Da-oon's fin. My eyes flooded and ran like an elll's. Orserah told me later that my "ripe flower face" blossomed with the most beautiful smile she had ever seen.

"Greetings, Orserah," Artellian bellowed in Varokian, with a grin and nod that shook the dull gold of his age-tipped crown plumes.

"We've come to demand that Varok be paved with channels of water, so that ellls may travel in comfort," Killah added.

The small angles of Orserah's face softened at the sound of the ellls' tuneful voices. "You two were pampered far too long on Earth's moon," she said. "The rigors of walking on Varok should put some muscle back in your toe-fins, Killah. You don't look nearly your age, Artellian. Look at those skin tiles of yours, still green as hopper eggs."

"Has Orticon come home?" Orram called.

"Your son will greet you at the lodge, Orram." Orserah's voice shook with pride and excitement. I couldn't blame her. Orram dismounted and strode tall and elegant through the web brush, his fine auburn hair glistening with sparks of silver. Then he ran the last few yards to Orserah, gave her fair warning with a smile, and caught her up in his arms.

"Yes. Yes. A most unorthodox greeting, Orram. Yes," Orserah

gasped with the intense contact. "Tandra has indeed released your emotions. Oh dear, my dear Orram, I'm going irrational. Put me down or my nerves shall burn out."

"You will have to get used to it, Mother. Your human granddaughter will need some close contact, though she has learned to respect our raw senses."

Conn whispered to Shawne, then, whooping and hollering, urged their daramont to take longer and longer leaps through the web bushes.

"Conn. Stop that, you scamp," Orserah shouted with a smile. "Bring my granddaughter back to me. He'll ruin the locale's best mounts before he's been here three light-periods, Tandra."

I waved him in and was answered with a snorting objection from the mount. Conn obeyed and drew the daramont to a sliding squat so he and Shawne could slide down his back.

"You are teaching your daughter dangerous tricks," Orserah scolded, and was rewarded with a lift into the air that soaked her tunic against the elll's wet-sweater.

"Get away, you horror." Orserah broke with laughter and had a hard time regaining control in her delight. "You're all muscles and moss." She shuddered a little, and Conn let her go. "One cannot stay dry around ellls, can one?" she asked Shawne, and they shared a quick hug.

"Are you really my grandma?" the child asked.

"From now on and always, Shawne."

"Now come meet our good friends," Orram said, "who have come to work with us and our project for Earth." Orram led Orserah to the human man. Standing by the hydrogen truck, he was obvious by the hair growing on his face, a distinction that would serve him well amidst the hairless varokian males. "This is Jesse Mendleton, Mother. He has come to Varok as an observer, but is more likely to become a valuable advisor."

"Welcome to Varok," Orserah said, "Our home is yours, if Killah will let you stay long enough to enjoy it. The officials in Ahl Vior have confirmed your invitation to act as wandering observer of Varokian life. The statisticians want first impressions, they tell me, unedited observations from a human viewpoint. You might as well start with me. Tell them how this old varok strikes you, if you dare."

"They strike me as beautiful and gracious, ma'am," Jesse said. "I have never seen such shining silver hair, and the blue of your gown gives your eyes an azure glow."

"Taciturn hombre, this one, but he knows how to bamboozle old ladies," Conn said in a mix of English and Varokian, "and he doesn't miss a thing."

"I'll remember that," Orserah said, "once I translate what you said. It is so good having you here, my dear friends. Imagine my having a whole new family." She smiled broadly, but I thought I saw sadness mixed in with joy.

"Listen a minute, Conn," Orram said. "Orserah has some bad news. Your patches reek with it, Mother, even more than your worries about Orticon or Leyoon."

With a sigh I soon learned to recognize, the old varok turned to her son. "We have not heard from your brother Orlah for many light-periods. I regret that he is not here to greet you. He has not been at his usual haunts along the Ahlkahn, nor with the ellls of Harallahn. Someone saw him on a road to the genetics lab on L'orkah, but that was nearly a cycle past."

"I see your sorrow, Orserah," I said.

"Thank you, Tandra. Though Orlah's restlessness is my grief, you needn't share it. The web fields will operate without his attention. Very soon you and Shawne will learn many of the tasks required."

"I look forward to working with you, Orserah," I said.

"And I will take my welcome in your fish tank," Conn said, as he re-mounted with a standing leap. "But you can keep everything else. These lands smell of hard work."

"I will find an elll's work for you, Conn, you delinquent," Orserah warned, and she gave his befinned foot a shake, surprising him.

"You must be getting senile," Conn teased. "You've never done that before. Feel good?"

Orserah ignored him, but I saw her smile. "Killah," she called, as the elll rode up to her. "Will you be staying to help

Orram? I understand he has been chosen to be Governor of
Living Resources."

Orram's face went blank.

Orserah stared at him, startled by his reaction.

Killah glanced pointedly at Orram. "I will stay until I know
where Orram needs me," he said.

Orserah's quick patches sensed the situation immediately. "So.
Orram may not be governor after all. Well, never mind. I would
prefer that you tend the fields, Orram. We will bask in your past
achievements and leave you in peace—or do I see a question in
your mind?"

"Not much of a question," Orram said. "Others are more qualified to monitor the living creatures of Varok. I will honor Leyoon's
request and go to the Forested Sea, but not until we are able to stay
upright on daramonts as we cross the mountains."

"Leyoon, the great-fish," Orserah mused. "A dear friend of
Orram's father, Tandra. Leyoon helped him get started when he
served as tutor to the ellls of the southern shore. Leyoon will not
like to wait long for Orram. Come now to the lodge. Let's find food
and rest for you at the house. Hurry, Conn," she said, mounting
her daramont. "Race with me."

"Come on up, Tan," Conn said from atop his daramont's shoulders. "You shouldn't miss this."

I put Da-oon in Killah's arms, climbed up the daramont's lowered back and hung onto Conn's torso under his wet-sweater.

Orserah set Shawne securely between her arms. The beasts
eyed each other, then leapt across the field through the rows of
web bushes.

"Circle the moth colony and the egg layers' yard," Orserah
shouted, "and don't run over the tuber plot."

The daramonts heeded her warning, and we raced to the far
side of the giant treehouse, where an orchard of lush trees grew
tall among scattered clumps of brown, fern-like shrubs that
dripped with nuts and succulent leaves. There the gentle beasts
stopped and knelt low on all fours to discharge us, and Orserah
thanked them for the race. "Only three hoats, my friends. Don't
spoil your forage."

"Hoats are like candy to them," she explained to Shawne. "Come in. I have made a room just for you, though you will have to share it with your uncle Orlah, if he should come home."

As I met her eyes, I felt her surge of grief.

"Later," she said, and the grief subsided.

We entered the house, and Orserah sent Conn off to help Orram and the others unload our gear. She insisted that Shawne and I see every corner of the lodge so we would feel at home.

"My great-grandfather designed the Oran family home to ac-commodate the growth of its integral tree," she began.

Horizontal branches as large as ship masts defined the shape of the porch adjoining the outer walls, which glowed richly with red granite from the Vahinorral. The walls stood thick against chill winds, little changed from the family's first experiments in heat transfer and insulation. Inside, mineral tree timbers divided the sleeping areas from the central hearth room.

Orserah led us deep into the lodge where a small crossing of living branches formed a wonderful hideaway. Large horizontal limbs provided comfortable arms for climbing or curling up with books or for playing imaginary scenes with dolls or working puz-zles. Orserah had studied the rooms of human children on Earth and guessed very well what Shawne would love.

Throughout the lodge, every useable gap where stone met pol-ished timber served as a setting for favorite works of art. Orserah pointed them out—here an elll's water collage, there a varok's frac-tal painting. A great-fish's sand-casting graced a shelf on the most prominent feature in the house, a cascade of red rocks. The rocks served as a heat-storing chimney and staircase that climbed the staunch cliff into which the house was built. A deep pond lay be-neath a water-gathering roof planted with fruiting vines.

The central hearth, capped with metal for cooking, was fired with methane from the waste digester. Nearby, a wet-seat for ellls trickled with a gentle waterfall set into the stonework beside the stairs. Behind the hearth, an isolated room, reserved for study or quiet contemplation, was tucked far back into the rocks.

"The house operates like an independent organism," Orram explained when he joined the tour. "It gulps water and air, consumes lightning and gobbles up the waste of its inhabitants. Then it digests them to replenish the soil, to nurture the methane producers, and to feed the algae and fish that bind the house into a complete bio-energetic cycle."

Across from the hearthstones, the entryway and common room opened into the office Orserah had prepared for Orram. I understood that the data consoles provided access to the central storage banks of the Living Resources Information Center.

With obvious emotion, Orserah pointed out the second communications panel, linking the office by wireless transmitters and satellites to the planetary maser radio linkages with Ellason and Earth. With some excitement, Orserah described the computer she had chosen. "It is the very best pattern recognition model doing cognitive computing, neuromorphic processing they call it, a nice complement to the mathematical computer Orram has owned for some Jovian years. They are both self-aware with many cores, so there is little time-sharing delay."

"You have been most thoughtful, Mother," said Orram. "We will all enjoy such a machine."

"Oh sorry, sorry. I have almost forgotten. An elllonian girl, Lanoll, came from the Resources Center to help set up Orram's office," Orserah said, "but she has already left, sensitive to the fact that Orticon had arrived home from his studies at the Concentrate. He was in no mood to host a stranger."

I wondered if he was in any mood to meet a human step-mother.

ORTICON

Tandra—at Orserah's lodge

As we finished the tour indoors, we heard Conn arguing outside with a young varok.

"Dismount and greet your new family, Orticon," Conn demanded.

"I am late for my astronomy impression. I should not have come here."

"You could have visited us in Ahl Vior. Dismount."

Orticon had no choice. The daramont obeyed the elll and dumped the gangly young varok beside the porch.

"You were recovering. I could not intrude," he said, wiping the dust from his tunic.

"You're full of lame excuses."

"What?"

"Daramont corn."

"What? Speak Elllonian if you can't manage Varokian, Conn."

The daramont took off at a heaving gallop.

"You need to manage respect for your family, Orticon."

"You mean your school."

"You'd better believe it."

Orram had heard enough. He moved past me and disrupted the argument with a hearty laugh. "Going at it already? Since when do we require a formal welcome, Conn? Orticon, go to your studies, if you like. You can meet Tandra and Shawne in person when you are free from information absorption at the Concentrate. Our messages from Earth's moon must have seemed confusing."

"You are too accomodating, Orram," Orserah said, leading me out to the porch. "Orticon, this is Tandra. Honor your father's mind in her."

Orram's son sounded like a young version of his father in tone and bore a stance very like Orram's, but he was nearly as tall and lanky as Conn. He nodded to me with a face frozen in brittle planes and sent us an abbreviated spiral with his right hand.

Conn's irritation with him came through with a wet elllonian hiss. "I found him racing off to Ahl Vior, as if we had an ahlork fungus."

Orticon's face softened just a little at the edges. "You were late getting here, Conn. I must go back to the Concentrate."

"A quick moment then, since you are here," Orram said. "Then off you go."

"I do have questions for you, father," Orticon said, his tone more challenging than curious. "Why have you joined minds with two closed-minded species? Why would they give up the precious gift of a naturally private mind and allow you to abuse their freedom?"

"Orram would never abuse us, Orticon," I said, joining the conversation in Varokian. "Conn and I use empathy and intuition to see that your father does not run away with our minds nor keep his to himself."

Orticon seemed to struggle with my description—or was it his own curiosity? Then he looked away, his eyes as deep blue as Orram's but less grounded. "I must tell you that I have joined the Free-minds, Father."

"Free-minds object to the use of their natural born senses, seems to me," Conn interjected. "I'd give my left sonic melon to be able to read moods."

"We oppose the courts' use of the mind-probe." Abruptly, Orticon turned to face me with a steady gaze that did not avoid mine. "The deep mind probe used in legal proceedings is not natural, Ms. Grey."

"Perhaps I can come to understand that, Orticon. Call me Tandra. My mood and my thoughts are as open to you as I can manage. I would like to learn more about your views."

"Intrigued as I am by my father's experiment, you should know that in my opinion it is too dangerous to bring human beings into this society."

"How are humans dangerous, Orticon?" I turned to Orram, but he seemed honestly puzzled.

Orserah started to speak, but Orticon interrupted. "Please stay clear of my thoughts, Grandmother. I did not invite you into my mind."

"No, you didn't. But I expect your mind to be open to this family, open in a perfectly natural sense of the word. Surely Free-minds don't object to everyday mood reading."

"We object to intrusion into the mind's privacy," Orticon said. "As should any species."

"Humans have analogs in our normal communication," I said. "Varokian mood reading seems to be like reading a combination of human body language and facial expression."

Orticon did not respond.

"Tandra is your father's choice of family; she is my daughter," Orserah insisted. "You can learn many things from her as mother."

"She is a human being. She will be no daughter to you."

"We will see about that." Orserah's voice took on an ominous edge. "She is one mind with your father, Orticon. Do you forget what that means?"

"It means my father has made a mockery of this family."

"You will respect your father's faith in the ancient laws of Varok," Orserah snapped, then regretted her loss of control. "I expect you to be kind, Free-mind or not." She sent a defiant glance at her grandson and opened her hands to me, a gesture of respect. "I am so sorry, Tandra."

"I'm not offended, Orserah," I said. "Orticon and I will find time to talk. I suspect we share some concerns about *Homo sapiens*."

Orticon's face took on less of a cardboard look. "You are right. I have learned that your human history includes violent territorial imperatives. From our own history, we know that overpopulation stress can trigger violence."

"It already has, on Earth," I said.

"And Varok will be invaded," Orticon said. "I believe the human term is *lebensraum*. It is to be expected. A species takes what it requires when its survival is at stake."

"Agreed." I nodded. "But do you honestly believe that humans have the capability to come here and take what they need?"

Orticon looked uncertain, so I went on. "Many humans are struggling to survive. There are enough resources left for the wealthy to make the trip here—perhaps once. That is all. Earth lacks the energy and infrastructure to launch an invasion. Our hope is that Varok will give Earth the knowledge for a more humane existence, free of today's hunger and thirst and genocide. Conn and Orram and I are dedicated to showing humans how Varok has kept the steady state, in spite of the unpredictable aspects of its complexity."

"We will talk later then," Orticon said. "Conn, I need to talk to you. Now."

He urged the reluctant elll up the hearthstones, but not before Conn managed to telegraph his forbearance to me with a quick flick of tongue over nose.

"Peculiar," Orserah said. "Orticon has been difficult lately, but how can I hope to understand him if I am not allowed to read his mood?"

A loud splash, then elllonian laughter from upstairs interrupted Orserah's thoughts. "So Conn can still handle that boy," she said. "Thank Leyoon's faith! Conn must have thrown Orticon into the pond."

Our moods brightened as Shawne and Da-oon found the savory pot of stew warming at the hearth. Next to Conn—who earned the old varok's love with the life-grasping joy unique to ellls—I guessed Orserah would indulge the children. They knew it instinctively and were soon seated at the hearth filling their stomachs.

Orserah waved us all toward the hearth pot. Its contents smelled like a rich stroganoff and tasted even better.

When Shawne and the elll tad had emptied their bowls, she gave them warm cakes from the sweet shelf in the hearth. "Da-oon, come here, my poor dried-out little tad. You are always welcome to use the wet-seat over there by the stairs. Now put on this wet-sweater. We will get you into water soon. Come here to me, Shawne. Orticon is in a bad temper, and Conn is being a good father by schooling with that boy. We had better leave them alone for a while. I will tell you a story while you eat your cake."

ORSERAH'S VERSION OF VAROKIAN HISTORY

Tandra, continued

Orram and I saw Orserah take a deep breath and steel herself against the jostling as Shawne and the young elll Da-oon climbed beside her into the big lounger.

"I love telling stories, but you must listen carefully and stretch your minds, Shawne and Da-oon, for I talk to children as though they know all words and understand all meanings—which they do, way down deep, beneath their elllonian plumes or human ears or varokian patches."

Steam rose in thin wisps from the crack between the hearth cover and the surrounding serving area.

"Varoks eat when they please, as you must know, Tandra—whenever there is a clean bowl available. Orram, see to your guests. I have important business here with my grandchildren."

Killah, Artellian and Jesse served themselves large bowls and crowded together on the warm hearthstones, leaving the couch facing Orserah for Orram and me.

With care not to overload her sensitivity to touch, the old varok placed an arm around each child. "I tell you this story, little ones, so you will know where you are, and when you are."

"We're here now," Shawne said, "on Varok."

"But what is Varok, and when is now? Only memories and lessons learned can tell us. Long ago this very same valley was very different. It lay in the shadow of Mount Ni as if it were asleep. It was a silent place. Only simple, repetitive voices and the quick movements of small creatures disturbed the silence. There were no varoks then. The survivors of the Mutilation had retreated to the hot acid plains far to the west, near the sea called Ahranhnye Allahn, the Ocean of Deadly Mists. There they found nothing but an occasional spreading mineral tree, and protection from radiation and the wastes of their predecessors. Over many ages of Varok their children and their children's children became a tough and adaptable species, survivors of the forebears' excesses."

"The varoks," Shawne guessed.

"That's right," Orserah said, "and varoks are glad to be alive. We are happy to be taller—but we are also sorry to have lost our marvelous wings. That's why we call it the Mutilation. I'm afraid we lost much more than just our wings. The planet's early tragedy is now written indelibly in our genes. The Mutilation bared the ends of the forebears' nerves, making physical contact difficult for us varoks. It also left our emotions raw and vulnerable. They are difficult for us to handle. I tell you this so you will understand why I have an attack of nerves every time you wiggle."

"Like Orram." Shawne smiled up at the kindly varok and moved away, just out of contact.

"Perfect," Orserah thanked her. "I will do better as time goes on. Now, for our story—it is only just beginning. The Mutilation carved away the wings of the forebears. As a result, the few survivors, the varoks, had an obsession so deeply rooted in their special experience that it has not diminished through all the ages. That obsession means we try to keep everything on this moon of Jupiter sustainable, so the populations and the level of consumption will never again grow beyond control. A dynamic readjustment to the steady state is our constant challenge, so that nothing will become scarce or poisoned again, ever.

"Long Jovian years in the past, a few varoks migrated to the silver-green valley beneath Mount Ni —a valley beautifully laced with red rocks from the Vahinorral."

"Here," Shawne noted, and the tad Da-oon grinned in agreement.

"Right," Orserah agreed. "Here the varoks built homes from the red rocks and mineral trees. They tilled the soil and planted fruiting trees, carefully mixing species to grow robust heterocultures, nurturing the balance of pest and predator to protect crops. In the deep dark-periods, the varoks gathered about their hearths to hear stories of the ancient winged ones, the extinct forebears, whose ruined resorts lay buried on the shore of Tahkallan just north of our nearby mountains, the Vahinorral, and beside the cliffs of Leahnyahorkah.

"Now, forty Jovian centuries since those ruins were

deserted—that's fifty millennia on Earth—many more varoks have come to live in our valley and in small locales with houses and farms scattered along the Ahlkahn.

"Here Orram grew up, and his father taught law to the ellls of the Forested Sea," Orserah continued. "You will attend the same school that they did, Shawne.

"Later, as a young man at the Concentrate, Orram became a biophysicist, as well as a distinguished amateur in philosophical history. Not long ago he was designated Master, one of the two thousand living varoks and twenty living ellls to be so honored. Shawne, your father is an important spiritual leader of Varokian society. Did you know that?"

"I thought so," Shawne said importantly.

"And he will continue to be, if he will listen to me."

Warning bells went off in my head, as Orram silently asked his mother to accept his decision, should he choose to decline the appointment.

She glanced at me with blue eyes adrift, then went on with her history. "Conn met your father at the Concentrate in Ahl Vior, and they became close friends. This house was busy with the laughing and splashing of ellls from the Forested Sea.

"Conn and Orram spent many pleasant hours comparing the ways of Varok and Ellason with the ways of Earth, which Conn was studying at the Concentrate.

"One day I asked Orram and his first mate, a landscape artist named Llor Non, to use one of their Replacement Survival Certificates to have a child. Llor Non agreed to use hers, and Orticon was born. But soon Llor Non became restless. She felt constrained by the deep ties this family generates. She left the family to pursue her life as a sculptor. Orram continued as before, submerged in his work as master of selective biophysical technology—until he accepted the job as director of scientific operations on the Elll-Varok Observation Base on your Earth's moon, Shawne."

"To complete the story," Conn interrupted as he came down the hearth stones shaking water from his plumes, "Orram discovered that we could do nothing more for Earth. Humans were not in a mood to listen to us, to put it mildly, so we abandoned the moon base and quit our fondest hopes for that planet. It was some consolation to Orram, however," he pontificated with a grin, "that during his last months at the base his own life did not come to an end—and, instead, came to fruition. He returned to Varok legally bound as family to an elll—"

"You!" Shawne shouted.

"What better choice of family could there be? Joined to me and to—"

"Me."

"—our dear Shawnoon, and to the microbiologist Tandra Grey—"

"Me," I echoed.

"And now it is time for your backstory, Tandra," Orserah said, meaning it kindly.

"Thank you, Orserah, but there are some stories best left untold."

"Oh surely, my dear—"

"One day. But not yet."

"I understand. There are deep probes that should never be done. They do no good."

"Exactly." Our bond sealed tight.

"Now, Tandra my dear," Conn said, taking my hand and leading me up the stone stairs, "will you kindly tuck me in?"

Orserah rose to her feet. "*Tuck me in*? What is this—*tuck me in*?"

"Someone has to see me to sleep," Conn said. "Tandra does a nice job covering me with mud."

"You will drown that poor woman. She has no gills, Conn."

Orram loved it. "I will revive her, Mother, if she doesn't return soon."

Orserah had to laugh. "You win, you three. I see that I have something to learn about this family of yours."

THE ORAN LOCALE

Tandra—next light

"Yesterday, we rested. Today, after a good breaking fast, we explore the Oran Locale," Orserah announced in a rare attempt at English. She went on in Varokian. "It was named for our family, Tandra, the Oran family. Our forebears came to this valley between the foothills of the Vahinorral and the Ahlkahn track in 1529 *ir*, just before the revolution for life-style choice."

"That's nearly 2700 Jovian years ago." I found the scope dizzying. "Tens of millennia on Earth."

"One of Orram's ancestors was on the team that discovered Earth in 1842.8 *ir*, about 28,000 Earth-years past. His descendent befriended one of the first ellls who came here some Jovian years later. Their friendship was a model of hope for the first ellls on Varok, who were stranded here when travel to Ellason came to be seen as unnecesary, hence rare. As a result, ellls are still a valuable part of Varokian society."

"I'm beginning to understand that Orram and Conn are linked by a very long history," I said.

She handed me a red stoneware plate and spooned onto it a cupful of golden food decorated with small pieces, a rainbow of vegetables.

"You would call this an omelet, I believe," she said. "But of course our egg-layers are not chickens. Please tell me if it is acceptable."

I tasted it, found it delicious, and asked for more.

"Only one more serving, Tandra. We can't have you overeating at my hearth. I could not bear the guilt of shortening your most precious life."

Orram overheard the last comment as he joined us at the hearth. "And will you allow my human partner a cup of web tea?"

"Of course, but be forewarned. It contains no caffeine. We varoks are too sensitive to that drug."

"I won't need the caffeine, thanks Orserah," I said. "The

withdrawal headaches are too unpleasant. Peculiar, isn't it—why both our species are cursed with too many nicotinic receptors when our genetic codes are so different."

"Chemistry is chemistry is biochemistry, I suppose," Orram said with a grin.

"You studied biochemistry as well as microbiology, Tandra?" Orserah asked.

"Only from necessity. I am a specialist in germs that cause infectious disease."

"So you will be working with Killah as well as Lanoll, the elll who helped me set up Orram's office." Orserah looked pointedly at Orram. "She supervises epidemiological studies for the Governor of Living Resources."

"My proud mother, I will go to Leyoon as soon as we have rested," Orram said. "We haven't yet regained all of the strength we lost on the trip out here from Earth's moon. It can't be helped. Our bone density is low, despite all the required exercising, centrifuge time, pressurized leggings, salt sodas—"

"And on and on, my poor suffering son. Seriously, Tandra, are you able to walk with me this morning?"

"I'll be fine, for a short distance," I said.

"I'll call daramonts. They can take us through the residential area and wait by the elll pond in the park while we visit the market."

"May I go with you?" Orram asked.

"Of course not. This is my trip with Tandra." Orserah smiled at her son but made no offer of a reassuring touch, as many humans would. It made me realize how much Orram had accommodated my need for touch, how much I needed to learn about getting along in varokian society. The next lesson came hard.

"This is your maintenance fee, Tandra, for the current cycle." Orserah opened a artfully woven basket she kept on the hearth and took from it several large coins. "The money may be spent only in this locale. You see embossed here Orram's grandfather. Spend it wisely and note when the next cycle will begin."

I should have known this was coming. "I can't take your money, Orserah."

"Of course you can. It is not mine. You are a certified resident of the locale. This is your maintenance fee. You will earn the money in due time, when you are well enough to help me in our obligations to the land."

"But that may be some time. When I am stronger, I would like to accompany Orram to visit the great-fish."

"And that is how you will earn your keep for now," Orram said.

"This is our way, Tandra," Orserah assured me. "Everyone on Varok receives their locale's maintenance fee and cares for the land, but you may take additional employment one day if you wish."

"I would not want to take another's job. I understand that only residents of the locale are hired by local businesses."

Orserah laughed. "I think you would find several people who would want to share hours with you, so they would have more time for their hobbies. I had better warn you—most people are hired for life. If the job changes, you change with it."

"And what would I do with so much money here?"

"It wouldn't be much more than the fee you earn tending the land," Orram said. "You may earn no more than fifteen percent above the minimum income before your tax rate will erupt."

"I'll be glad to earn my keep, here in your fields, Orserah, while I help Orram continue our work with Earth—and with Living Resources, if that is his choice. But I do not wish to take without giving."

"And of course you won't," Orserah said. "You have so much to offer, and such spirit! You'll find our local community, all our products and services, are of excellent quality, too. You may shop or trade with anyone in the locale, or accumulate money, if you wish—save it to support a creative hobby, or exchange it when you travel. Some use their savings to start local businesses; or you might buy a share in a business where you'd like to become a partner. However you use your income and your time, you will build value within the locale."

"I love it," I said. "So business profits are invested back into the local community?"

"Yes, but it's neither socialistic nor capitalistic," Orram added. "Those are both growth economies based on debt, designed to produce more gadgets than need dictates, and more paper money than material wealth. The focus here is on the quality of the things we make—and time well spent."

"Here! Here! Students of economics—no more profit *über alles*." Conn made his appearance, dripping water on the stairway. He gave Orram a spiral salute then wrapped his long dry tongue across my nose, soaked my new varokian tunic (a gift from Orserah) with his morning hug, and moved toward the elder varok.

"Stay away from me, you sloppy green mess," Orserah said, a smile in her eyes. "We are off to visit the locale. Take two bags and a large pail, Tandra. I keep them here in the entry. We will need to buy web flour from the mill and shop for calcium and protein to feed the emaciated bones and musculature of your fellow space travelers."

"Sounds appetizing," Conn grimaced. "I'll eat out tonight."

"*Eat out?* What do you mean *eat out*? Out where? There are plenty of fish in the locale freezer. *Go fish!*" Orserah laughed at Conn's surprised expression. "You see, I have been studying the games of Earth's children."

Orserah turned to me. "Pay no attention to that rude elll. Are you warm enough, Tandra? Take my jacket. I'll show you how to ask the daramonts for a ride. Conn, you are in charge of the tads' orientation to the locale. Here are some coins for them to spend. See that they select healthy treats, and tell them to mind the garden. They are not to go into the web field or visit neighbors without permission."

"Okay, Grandma," Conn said. "But I expect you to bring home more fish. Your freezer is nearly filled with other things. I think you need a larger one, now that I am home."

Orserah and Orram's father had acquired a freezer to hold the fresh fish brought to them as gifts by ellls who visited frequently from the Forested Sea. Now, that freezer served as storage for the six homes nearby.

"Our shared freezer will do, Conn. The local company assures me that it will last until Jupiter turns blue, and if it doesn't work perfectly, they will fix it. I will not pay the tax required to retire a perfectly good machine, and I am not obliged to fill you with more fish than you need, you big tad."

Orserah and I bid Conn and Orram a good morning and gathered our tins and bags of tough web stalk fiber. We walked through the garden under Varok's impressionistic sky, and waved to three daramonts grazing on old stalks in the web bushes. They looked up, and all three loped to within two meters of us. Their doe-eyes, as big as llamas' and just as beautiful, looked down at me from three meters or more.

"Spread open your arms like an elll," Orserah said.

As I did, they made a "hah" sound and circled me slowly. Some bowed low, offering their ears as handles.

"Good." Orserah sounded relieved. "They are all offering you a ride. They are very curious, but they know enough not to compete for your favor."

"But I have nothing to give them."

"They clean out old stalks and graze our web fields in exchange for transport. Show your hand to the daramont you choose, and he or she will make it possible for you to mount. Step on his 'knee,' the bent part of his haunch, and hang onto his mane."

I chose the smallest daramont, who inspected my webless fingers before he sat on his haunches like a huge dog.

When I stepped up on the massive knee, the daramont slowly rose so I was able to slide onto his neck. Meanwhile, Orserah had been scooped up onto a young mount sporting a white crest.

"Hang on," Orserah called, and we were off to the locale's center.

The daramonts followed the paths that joined the scattered houses and skirted the garden plots. Each plot had a distinctive look, for most were specialized for barter or local sale. Orserah supplied eggs to the locale's market and raised just enough vegetables and fruit to feed her extensive network of family and friends. Others farmed berry-like fruits or grew plants that required special care. I recognized the delicious hart we had eaten the day before, a brownish fruit shaped like a turnip. It hung on long slender branches inserted like straws into the black earth.

"First we unload used containers," Orserah said at our first stop. I helped her take a sack of bottles from the daramonts to a large container set behind one of the food stores.

We walked on, and the daramonts followed us to a garden of flowering vines decorating a cluster of sausage-shaped buildings. As we meandered through the shops, I was charmed by the variety of plants tucked away in odd corners, near displays of handmade clothes and web cloth, health-aides and grooming tools, decorative objects and art, books and hand-writing implements, and small electronic devices.

Orserah dug in her satchel and pulled out a collection of handwritten credits—IOU's and barter agreements. "I will trade these for new clothes for you and Shawne," she said. "The locale web cloth is closely woven. It will be warm and durable, not like the imported material that has been appearing on these shelves lately. Do you prefer skirts, slacks or wraps?"

"Slacks will be fine, Orserah," I said. "Thank you."

We entered a small shop displaying several plain materials in muted colors. Some cloth was especially soft, though woven so loosely it hardly seemed practical for sewing. Orserah asked for local cloth, but there was little choice. A light blue caught my eye. She didn't miss my preference. "We'll have enough for slacks in that color," she said.

"The new cloth is much cheaper, Orserah," said the shopkeeper.

"I would hope so. It wouldn't last three cycles." Orserah hesitated, then she pulled out more credits. "It's no matter," she said, "we'll take the local cloth."

"It's too much, Orserah," I said. "I'll just use the clothes I brought from Earth."

Orserah would not consider it. "Your leggings, 'jeans' you call them, are excellent for work in the fields. My daughter will have the blue for travel and dark periods at home."

So it was settled.

I wondered if some of the newer material could be from Mahntik, as Conn had suspected on the Ahlkahn. If so, she could use a lesson in quality control.

Orserah led me to the local children's exchange, where we picked out a sturdy pair of mud boots for Shawne. Then we made our way to the central park's open air food market. Orserah filled her basket with brown, red and yellow vegetables and fruits, roots, stems and leaves.

She named each plant as it went into her basket, but I knew the names would mean nothing to me until I watched her prepare or cook them. We toured the rest of the shops, including a bio-transport business that could have passed for a bicycle shop in North America. Then she introduced me to the locale's exchange center.

"Here you will pick up your maintence fee for the next cycle, Tandra. I believe you would call this place a bank, but it has a very limited function, compared to Orram's description of banks on Earth. You may keep your extra coin here, and the exchange center will provide checking and payment services on the money for a small fee. You may seek a loan by providing the rights to something of equal value."

"Whoo. One hundred percent collateral."

"Yes, naturally. But I forget, Earth banks create money when they make loans, don't they—and charge interest? We don't do interest on Varok, thank the forebears, so we don't need to grow the economy to pay it. As a result, our prices remain the same over the years."

"No inflation. No money-making-money schemes. With only local currencies, how do you buy things that can't be grown or made in the locale?"

"There are no restrictions on import or subsidies on export, just a heavy tax on long-distance transport."

"Which explains Conn's upset with seeing L'orkah web products sold so cheaply at Lake Seclusion."

"As well he should be. Sometimes we export our excess web products in payment for goods we don't manufacture here, but these things are usually limited. I'm afraid I love some of the fruits grown only at the Springs of Harinlegh—but that is a very expensive trade, with the cost of transport and spoilage. Ripe fruit doesn't travel well."

"Unless it is genetically engineered to survive shipping."

"Can you preserve the ripe flavor in that way? No one would buy the fruit otherwise."

"One could always hope so," I said, remembering the tasteless tomatoes available year-round in North America.

When we returned to our daramonts, we found them braced against a huge tree with a thick soft bark resembling velvet. They were sleeping soundly.

"Let's let them rest. We can wait in here," Orserah said, knocking on the unmarked door of the residence the soft tree embraced. She called out a name. An elderly varok opened a window overlooking the path and shouted a warm invitation to visit.

I could barely understand what he was saying, so I assumed it was old Varokian or a regional dialect. Since varoks depended heavily on mood scanning, using their patch organs to assess the needs of a relationship before a direct interaction took place, their language became secondary in some locales, and varied. Those varoks who lived near water and who often dealt with ells had a most tuneful slang full of "l" sounds, imitating the long-tongue accents of that aquatic species.

When I looked puzzled, Orserah translated.

"What are you about, Orserah?" The old man said. "Welcome home, and welcome to your human daughter."

"Good morning, sir," I said, using my best Varokian.

"How do you do with our changing lights?" He spoke more slowly now, enunciating in standard Varokian. "You must miss your brilliant sun. I often wondered how Earth beings could tolerate such a dangerously bright object in their sky."

"An interesting question, sir. We soon learn not to look directly at the sun, it is so hurtful. Perhaps it's a bit of genetically programmed learning in all Earth's species."

"Yes, it must go back to the evolution of your sight. And do call me Arnak. I would so enjoy a visit." He disappeared from the window, and moments later opened the doorway. "Please come in."

"I'll be back in just a moment," Orserah said. "I spotted a neighbor in the market."

She hurried off, and the old varok led me into his welcoming chamber. He ushered me to a seat by the hearth, which was designed like Orserah's for eating around a cooking cover. He had left the door open, and within minutes Orserah returned with varoks of all ages, who introduced themselves as neighbors.

They settled on the floor when the hearth seats were taken.

Most carried web cloth bags or backpacks laden with purchases. They took turns asking me questions about Earth, nodding slightly when I had answered in mind so another person could voice, for my convenience, a related question. In time, the conversation turned smoothly to the odd appearance of poor web cloth in the locale and stories they had heard about crowding at Lake Seclusion, where the cloth was woven.

"Orram and Tandra will be interested in Lake Seclusion," said Orserah. "Perhaps it resembles the problems they studied on Earth."

An elder didn't even try to suppress the anger that threatened to undo her. "What are we exporting to pay for this poor cloth we see in the stores? I don't approve, not at all."

"Nor do I ," said a younger varok. "How does the manufacturer meet the reponsibility for their products, through final disposition or recycling? So much of this cloth must be disposed of, every cycle. How do they pay the cost, with such low prices?"

"I have often wondered," Orserah said.

"It's as though the weavers wanted the cloth to wear out quickly—so we would buy more."

I felt the blood drain from my face. "You have just defined planned obsolescence, an old trick on Earth—one of the favorites when business ethics turned sour in the interest of profits."

"But where is the value in low quality products?" asked the youth.

"We call it 'the bottom line.' Businesses are required, even designed, to accumulate money for their major owners over all other considerations, so they lower costs and increase income in every way possible—with cheaper materials, deceptive packaging, lower pay, dumping wastes, even planned obsolescence—to accumulate profit. Everyone is trapped into that ethic; the savings required to support less affluent people's old age often depend on passive investments in large businesses."

"We are all part owners in local businesses here," Orserah explained, "but never passive. And our customers—our neighbors— would tell us straight away if any problem arises with quality or pollution. Why would anyone tolerate such things? The costs of production, including wear and tear on Varok itself, are included in our prices. Whoever creates costs to the environment pays those costs, which certainly improves efficiency, I can tell you."

"Efficiency?" The old anger that drove me from Earth flared too quickly. "We have forgotten what that means on Earth. It's as though it's a bad thing—some kind of heresy, along with the word *conservation*."

I took a breath, and tried to explain, more calmly. "One of the worst tragedies on Earth has been the huge waste of excess food that rots away while people go hungry. People can no longer afford access to land to grow their own food."

As I finished the last sentence, my voice cracked, and I felt the sympathy in the room engulf me. The varoks rose to surround me, afraid that I would go irrational with sorrow for the planet I had abandoned. They were growing in concern, not knowing what to do to ease the alien out of her dangerous grieving.

"I'm fine," I managed to stammer. "We humans can get quite emotional without endangering our reason." *Or can we?* I thought back to my last weeks on Earth, pursued as a dangerous radical by those who did not want to hear what my family and I had to say.

My Varokian was not good, but Oerserah's lovely friends could see that I had recovered. "That's why I am here—to learn from you, to learn what Earth must do to secure a future without suffering. Thank you for listening and understanding."

Was this how varoks lived? Constantly sitting on their emotions in order to maintain their reason? In that moment I understood more clearly what release meant to Orram and why the mind-link was of prime importance in varokian life. Our link made it possible for Orram to laugh and indulge his feelings.

Varok began to turn away from Jupiter's dark face, and the darkening glow of the colorful sky signaled the end of the light-period. Orserah rose from her seat at the hearth, and we said our farewells.

The daramonts were waiting near the door, perched awkwardly on the path so their haunches didn't smash anything growing.

"Our host supplied our mounts with a fine meal," Orserah said. "I hope that our visit didn't tire you too much, Tandra."

I was filled with appreciation for the warm welcome and the kind sympathy reflected in the varoks' questions. I felt very safe, at home. Orserah had her answer without words.

ORTICON'S VIEW

Tandra—moments later

As our daramonts tip-toed back through Orserah's garden, we spotted Shawne, Orram and Conn on the greatporch steps under the mineral tree, shredding web stalks for fodder.

"Thank you, my friends," Orserah said to the daramonts, handing them choice stalks from the pile. "You have had a long day for our convenience. Please select a ripe hoat from the garden before you retire to the web fields." Quickly she restrained my hand from giving them a condescending pat on the neck.

I respected the message and lifted Shawne onto my shoulder so she could see the great beasts disappear into the dusk with long, calculated leaps. She helped me carry our bags of fresh fruits from the locale's orchards into the entry hall, trying to name them. There we found Orticon coming down the hearth steps. He seemed preoccupied, so I sent Shawne to the food center with Artellian to find storage bins for our purchases.

"I thought you had work to do at the Concentrate," Orserah said to him, honestly puzzled.

"I have more important work to do."

He passed by and went to his father on the porch, his face taut with barely-repressed emotion. "I will go to the Free-minds, now."

"Not until you finish integrating the knowledge you have taken at the Concentrate," Orram declared, his expression equally intense. I had seen Orram so fiercely determined only once before—when he made the decision to rescue human astronauts stranded on Earth's moon, endangering Elll-Varok Science's hidden presence there.

"All that information is rattling around in your neurons with no place to go, Orticon," Conn drawled, trying to sound disinterested. "You don't want to let the information impression of your brain stand raw. It will rot or grow mold."

"Nothing will happen to my memory." Orticon said.

"That's precisely the problem," Orserah snapped. "All those light-periods on the impresser will be wasted, and you'll be left with many juvenile notions plucked at random from an enormous bank of useless information."

"I will not return to the Concentrate until I know that I have done all I can. Varok is in crisis. The Free-minds need me now."

"I would feel better about your going if I understood why," Orram said. "What crisis do the Free-minds see?"

"You. Your return is the crisis. You and the Earth ship that followed you."

All our eyes turned to Orram.

"We haven't confirmed there was a launch." Orram's voice was quiet now. "Our contacts have been silent, and we've had no word of a ship coming from Earth. Wait, Orticon. Return to the Concentrate until the situation is known."

"There isn't time. Varok is changing—in ways that you refuse to see, Father."

"I'll second that one," Conn agreed.

Orticon started, obviously surprised at Conn's support.

Orram looked to me for confirmation.

"I can't know how different Varok might be," I said, "but I see you struggling to deny the warning in Leyoon's message, Orram."

Orticon acknowledged me with a twist of his hand, then faced Orram. "Varok is changing for the good, Father. We are breaking away from worn-out patterns of limited local subsistence and suppressed technology. Soon we will see the beginning of monumental progress."

"Progress?" Orram said. "We've seen lots of progress on Varok, in just the few orbits we were gone—new perennial food crops;

more efficient electricity from waste plasma burning; advances both philosophical and physical; expressive art forms, new musical instruments—"

"Except when Mahntik walks in the door," said Conn. "Then you might as well set the clock back three millennia."

"I don't see why you criticize Mahntik, Conn. She has been a good mentor to the Free-minds . . . Yes. That's it, isn't it?" Orticon's tone was hard with accusation.

"I believe she manipulates more than Free-minds," Conn said, refusing to take Orticon's bait. "I think she could be ignoring global economic law or not paying her taxes. Her prices are too low. They can't include all her costs."

Orticon stiffened.

I was puzzled. "How could she do anything illegal? Anyone can know her business by reading her mind."

"True," Orram said. "Varoks don't have secrets, but the right to physical and mental privacy in personal affairs is protected by law. It takes time to discover a cheater."

"That's why she's doing business so fast," Conn said.

"I don't like your accusations, Conn," Orticon said. "Mahntik has done nothing but provide a better product at a very good price."

"Then hers must not be the weak cloth we saw today." Orserah looked to me for confirmation.

"It was beautiful," I said, "but clearly not made to last."

"She smells of extravagance," Conn muttered, "which is a synonym for waste."

"What's wrong with extravagance?" Orticon flared, hands frozen at his sides. "We could do with a little more. Grandmother, why shouldn't we have a laundry of our own? We are a large family now. Why should we have to carry dirty clothes to the common machine?"

"I would never have a machine around this house sitting idle for more than one light-period," Orserah said. "If the time becomes filled on the Serahn family launderer, then we will find another."

"You must look like an old fool to the humans," Orticon said. "Even the poorest people on Earth have their own laundry machines."

"Not on the Earth we just left," Conn said. "—and don't insult Orserah, Orticon. You'd better apologize."

"I'm sorry, Grandmother. Let me try to explain. It's not selective technology we're attacking. Free-minds don't think every technological development should be made into some kind of gadget, useful or not."

Orram laughed. "Well, that's a relief."

Conn warmed to the argument. "Selective technology challenges genius and keeps it honest at the same time. It demands efficiency, and proven technological progress."

"But the Free-minds believe we've been too selective."

"Nonsense." Conn's temper erupted. "We've got the most sophisticated society in this solar system. We've got the high-speed Ahlkahn. We have comprehensive, instantaneous information and communication systems. We have the best wind and tide generators, efficient transport devices, the most intricate nano-aides and medical tools in the sentient neighborhood. And do you know why? Because we've always insisted that new technology produce gadgets that are useful, real improvements, as long lasting and efficient as possible."

"Like my weed-eating robot," Shawne interjected as she skipped into the garden.

"You're letting our baby run that thing?" Orserah burst out, defusing Conn's temper.

I took a deep breath, not knowing whether to worry about Shawne or be glad Conn didn't go over the top and send Orticon into crisis.

"Shawne and I call it 'Ragweed Tummy.' It's perfectly safe, Grandma," Conn said. "I stay with her. In the last few light cycles we've made enough electricity to run the small plow."

"Give yourself a chance, Orticon," Orram said, stepping between his son and Conn. "You have not finished integration at the Concentrate. Give your brain time to wrap itself around what Varok has achieved. Nothing is dictated. All must vote. Resource quotas and standard of living are chosen by a two-thirds majority of all sentient life on Varok—no easy feat, I can tell you. Take time to understand how we've secured the future."

"Nothing is predictable, Father. All living systems are complex."

"You're right, Orticon," Orram said. "Economic systems are like complex ecologies, not simple machines driven by linear equations. So although Varok's future is secure, I agree it can't be predictable." He paused and let his frustration drain away. "Checks are in place to keep wild fluctuations to a minimum, most of the time, unless chaos takes over, or someone farts."

"Dad, please." Orticon shot me an embarassed look before doubling over. Was he laughing? Or crying? Probably both. I wanted to put my arm around his shoulders, but knew better. He took some time to recover. "The steady-state is no longer relevant, Father." His voice broke, but his tone was gentler now. "Varok has changed. She will soon realize her full potential. Even if you cannot accept this maturation, you must understand that the low depletion rates have made us vulnerable. We have no infrastructure that can protect against invasion. Now that Earth knows where we are, we could be in serous danger."

"That's ridiculous," Conn said. "Look at what's going on there. They don't have the resources to build a better mousetrap, much less an invasion fleet."

Orticon focused on Conn. "And if they don't come, think how we could live if we used even half of what we know. We could make Earth's most elegant cities look like backwater slums."

"Earth's most elegant cities are already morphing into backwater slums," I muttered, but my thoughts were with Orram. He was suffering from Orticon's cold welcome after years of separation. *What is my role? Surrogate mother? Alien hanger-on?*

Orticon stared at me. "It is time for us to live like the masters we are—before human beings descend on us and take the resources we have failed to appreciate."

He turned toward Orram. "Stay out of my mind, Father."

I felt the wound open deeper. The attack had found its mark, for Orram had been about to read his son's mood to better understand his concerns.

"Perhaps you can understand me, Tandra," Orticon said. "The steady-state concept is thought irrelevant on Earth, isn't it?"

"It is not taken seriously," I said. "Perhaps it's considered too difficult. Growth is considered essential there, to pay interest on debt and to provide jobs for more and more people. The Earth's economies are based on debt, not barter and pay-as-you-go. The steady-state works here on Varok because the size of the population is not overwhelming, and it doesn't change. On Earth that must happen first. Then a steady state would have to be approached gradually, with diminishing quotas and limits on debt."

"The steady state works," Orticon enunciated, "only because Varokians are browbeaten into a poor existence by their fear of the mind-scan."

"Any varoks not willing to share their thoughts with other varoks cannot have honorable intentions," Orserah said sharply. "Trying to suppress normal mood-reading patch contact is unnatural. It's impossible."

Conn's temper took off again. "Orticon, you've bought into pure nonsense. Besides something to eat and pride in what you do, a strong roof over the latrine, and a warm pool to make love in—besides these, there are no real needs, just invented desires."

Orticon's control snapped. "I mean what I say. Everything." His face contorted with his effort to regain rationality. "Your insults won't change my mind, Conn."

"I've heard enough, Orticon," Orram said. "Your fact impression is not yet integrated; it is clouding your mind. I won't listen to any more of this Free-mind talk until you have finished at the Concentrate."

"Then it is settled," Orticon said with complete calm. "I leave for L'orkah—now."

ORLAH AND MAHNTIK

Tandra—moments later

"Orticon's politics are all mixed up with his family emotions," Conn said. "He'll show up again when his curiosity about our new family has overcome his idealism."

Orram gave Conn a smile of thanks. "Enough for now. Tandra, why don't you go with the ellls up to the pond. I'll take a moment to see if anyone out at the kaehl house has laid any eggs."

He knew just what I needed, and my love spoke silent volumes to him.

Orserah opened a hand to Artellian as he stepped out to the porch. "You, dear old elll, you look like you are about to squirm out of your hip plumes. Why don't you take a good sleep in the pond? Conn will be happy to be your school, I'm sure. He also looks tired, but won't admit it. Wrestling with Orticon is not easy."

Grateful for Orserah's sensitive patches, Artellian smiled and threw her a thank-you with a spiraling fin. Jesse and Killah came to the hearth to talk with Orserah, while Conn and I climbed the hearth rocks with Artellian.

"First another short tour," Conn said.

He led us past the pond to the central waste collector near the algae garden, pushed open the insulating barrier, and climbed the last rocks leading onto the roof. A good supply of fresh water filled the collecting tank near the mist trap. He checked the light concentrators, then made sure that the pumps taking compost and used water to the garden were running smoothly.

We looked out over the garden to the moth colony and the small animal shelter for the egg-laying kaehl and semi-wild ilara. All was quiet except for the muted clicking sound of the egg-layers in their yard.

A narrow path wound through the outer web fields, then crossed a line of trees running between the distant fields and the foothills of the Vahinorral. At the crest of a hill, some distance from the house, moved two tall specks, probably varoks.

Conn and I followed Artellian to the pond, stripped off clothes and wet-sweaters and dove in. Once relaxed on the water's surface, Conn quickly fell asleep. I untangled myself from his long arms and watched him settle comfortably on the bottom with Artellian.

A few moments later, while I was drying my hair beside the hearth, a cold breeze crossed the room. It stirred Orserah's rock-climbing plants on the hearth steps and sent the old varok straight out of her chair.

A tall varokian woman stood in the open entryway with Orram. Her face, smooth and expressionless, rode in a frame of long dark hair streaked broadly with silver. It was sculpted in taut lines that matched the complex folding of her walking clothes. Too contrived for my taste. She was beautiful, I decided, but her look had a harsh quality. The smile of varoks was not in her eyes.

Orram ushered her to the hearth. "Tandra, Jesse, I present the geneticist, Mahnate Tikahn, called Mahntik, and," he added, as an older shadow of himself entered from the porch, "my brother, Orlah, Oran Lahr."

Orlah made a shocking contrast to Orram. His full height was lost somewhere in the slump of his shoulders. He looked nearly human, his visage wrinkled—hardly varokian at all. An easy fullness of silver hair around his ears hid his patch organs, and drooping folds of skin around his eyes and mouth exaggerated the nervous twists in his expression.

In earlier days, Orram had told me, Orlah had drifted from job to job, from mate to mate, restless for more communion than he could sustain. Because his relaxed good nature and generous ways had an elllonian quality, Conn had grown very close to him. Now Orram's older brother simply looked worn.

Mahntik, next to Orserah, was a study in varokian presence. She swept around the room and perched on the hearthstones as if to command our full attention.

Her eyes darted across Jesse and me, then she concentrated on Orram. "Welcome home, Orram. You look extraordinary. I will travel with you to Leyoon's presentation. You will want company."

"I'll have company, thank you, Mahntik. Tandra and Conn and I will go with Artellian to see Da-oon to his adoptive school in the

Forested Sea, then we will travel on to the Theater of Great-fish."

Orserah gave me a pleading look, and I moved away from the hearth into the common entry room to be with her and Orlah.

"I see that you will not be coming home this season," Orserah said quietly to Orlah.

I moved to block Mahntik's view, realizing Orserah did not want to be heard or read by her.

"Yes," Orlah said. He shook his head, as if to deny Orserah further access to his mind. "I will stay on L'orkah. I have taken work with Mahntik. She is a geneticist, you know."

"I see that she fills your mind, Orlah," Orserah whispered, "but I wish that I could read more happiness in your mood."

"I have not yet found consummation, but I feel I will soon attain it."

"With this Mahnate Tikahn?"

"Yes."

"I wish you the release and happiness of mental union, Orlah, with all the family's blessing—but I see no joy in your mind when you say that woman's name. Do not seek consummation with such determination that you lose sight of the barbs that are caught in your soul. Clear them away first."

Orserah tried a mind-scan, but Orlah nodded "no" and moved toward the hearth. Orserah and I followed quietly.

"I see that you are disturbed about your son," Mahntik was saying to Orram. "Perhaps I can help. Orticon gropes toward the Free-mind philosophy. You should stretch your mind to understand it, Orram. The Free-minds believe that Varokian life is stifled and smothered by all our stingy picking and choosing."

"I thought the Free-minds objected to the deep probe in legal proceedings," I said.

"They do, Tandra," Orram said. "Mahntik is confusing the Free-mind philosophy with unrelated economic views."

"You, yourself, are terrified by the very thought of change, Orram," Mahntik pressed, ignoring my comment. "The Free-minds realize we need to grow our potential, the infrastructure to enhance our lives, and our defenses against possible threats from Earth." She threw the barest glance in my direction.

"Be careful with those ideas, Mahntik," Orram said. "Nothing we do is inconsequential. Small changes we make every moment can make huge and unintended differences in time."

"Are you trying to frighten me, Orram?" Mahntik said.

"Of course he is, and I don't see why not," Orserah interrupted. "It is said that you are wasting energy and hurting local markets by transporting your new web cloth beyond your locale, at unsustainable prices."

"That is not my doing, Orserah."

Conn appeared on the hearth stairs, his eyes angry, though still at half-mast from sleep. "Who's doing it then, Mahntik?" He sat on the hearth stairs, watching water from his plumes drop to the stone floor and drain quietly toward her.

"Energy should not be wasted, of course," she said to Orram, getting up from the hearth and stepping away from the water, "but we are in danger of saving too much, especially if we don't allow the free use of energy for scientific exploration. If results are predictable, nothing is learned."

"Good point, Mahntik," Conn said. "Do tell us what it is you have learned recently."

"We have learned enough to protect Varok from the danger you have unleashed by revealing our existence to Earth," she snapped back at the elll.

"Human civilization peaked several Jovian years ago," Orram said. "Human beings of 2050 CE pose no threat to Varok. They are seriously divided; they couldn't agree to launch anything significant."

Mahntik shrugged. "Oh, but they already have, my dear. Aren't you in touch? The human situation has grown desperate. Who knows why they are risking everything to come here now? The Free-minds believe we should prepare to defend ourselves."

Conn laughed. "Earth couldn't raise a fleet of armed space ships any sooner than she could fly the Red Spot. Food and peace and potable water and sun-warmed shelves stocked with contraceptives are what Earth needs—not little moons of Jupiter."

"Humans live better than we do," Mahntik said.

"No longer," I said.

The emotion in my voice caught Mahntik's attention.

"Only a small percentage of humans live in comfort, Mahntik," Orram explained. "The rest suffer. Here, our lifestyles are stable. And with our locales self-sufficient and independent, no single attack can cripple us."

"We have no large industrial base," Mahntik insisted. "We couldn't possibly defend ourselves."

"We don't need to," Conn countered.

"You speak nonsense, my dear elll," Mahntik said. "Or have you become a traitor to Varok, a spy for Earth? I know that you and Orram are in constant communication with Earth. You know very well what preparations are being made there." Abruptly, she turned toward Orserah. "Now please excuse us. Orlah and I must return to L'orkah. I have viral cultures to tend."

"You always get bored when the arguments go over your head, Mahntik," Conn said. "We have no secrets from Earth. No secrets and no way to help them, except through example."

Placing a hand under her arm, Conn began to lead her toward the door. She jumped at the touch and pulled away from the elll. The rest of us could almost taste the hate boiling up between them.

"Don't apologize, Orserah." Mahntik's voice had a tin edge. "I'm quite used to Conn. Goodbye—for now, Orram." She locked her intense blue eyes into Orram's troubled gaze and probed his mind, so deeply and for so long, Orserah grew visibly annoyed.

Jesse Mendleton interrupted with an unusually poor imitation of Varokian speech. "Perhaps I may go back to L'orkah with you, Mahnate Tikahn? I would like to learn more about your island."

Conn laughed, and Orram retreated to the hearth, silently congratulating his human friend on the ploy.

"Of course not," Mahntik sneered. Caught unguarded, she revealed the full depth of her disdain. "Orlah was concerned for his family. That is the only reason we came here. We don't need human spies on L'orkah. Orram, I will see you at the Theater of Leyoon." Abruptly, she swept out the door. In silence Orlah followed her, looking back at Orserah, briefly twisting his hand with a feeble spiral of farewell.

Orserah felt the bristles of my mind stand in fury at Mahntik's arrogance. "So, Tandra, my poor varokoid," she said, "you suffer your human condition, feeling the need to repress your anger for our sakes? You will get your comfort from Orram. He is wedded to your thoughts, but I pray you don't ignore his varokian nature. He would mate with that woman in order to learn her strange mind, if he needed to."

III. TANGLED WEBS

Life knows life—no matter how primitive.
When it's not starving or angry,
most complex life recognizes honest respect,
insists on it and honors it in others.

—*Tandra, talking to Shawne*
about the egg-layers
in her care

THE RUINS

Mahntik—on the island of L'orkah, the next light-period

He would not have me, Mahntik raged to herself. *Yet.*

She glared at Orlah and shut off her conscious mind, daring him to try and read the mood that covered her thoughts. His gray-blue eyes bored irritating holes in Mahntik's awareness as he guessed she was feeling Orram's rejection.

"Stop staring at me."

How long could she tolerate his unquestioning, stupid devotion. Orlah stood too close, too ready to bend to her will. Those who knew him said the years had not hardened his eyes nor cooled his heart, as they should.

Orlah's loyalty will be unquestioning, Mahntik thought, *but why did I think he could give me entrance to Orram? Orram. How could that infuriating varok pretend to be in mental consummation with a witless human being?*

"I . . . I have not had a chance to tell you before." Orlah did not meet her eyes for more than a moment. "I am sorry that your new strain of web bush has not yet been accepted for wide distribution. Living Resources may be checking out the stalk quality, or maybe the potency of the berries? I thought your cloth was superior to the cloth made from the old webs. I can understand the council's argument, however. It would be very disruptive to local web growers, if you suddenly distributed your webs to all parts of Varok. Don't you agree?"

"Of course, Orlah. We will grow the web bush only here on L'orkah as a genetics experiment. That is quite within the law."

Orlah was desperate to read her mood, Mahntik noticed. She closed down her mind a little more and watched his frustration grow. It was delicious to exercise such control.

"Superior webs at a lower price—I don't see any harm in proving a worthy argument."

"Yes." She took a step toward him. "Are you ready for me, Orlah? When we met in Ahl Vior, I knew that I could take you as mate—if you were of the same mind." She held a forearm open to him.

"You know my mind, Mahntik, but I am concerned for Gitahl. Does he know that you intend to change mates?"

"Of course, Orlah." Mahntik checked to be sure that her mind was closed, then she rearranged herself on the circular hearth couch.

"Gitahl is no longer anything to me but a business partner and adviser," she said. "I have not mated for a long while. I asked you to come to L'orkah to work in web production because I saw this potential in you, perhaps even the potential for mental consummation."

Orlah sat beside her, and his eyes searched her face with a soft yearning look she could hardly bear. She braced herself for the intrusion of his thought. Oddly, it was not unpleasant; Orlah was Orram's brother.

Carefully, she expanded her mind, hoping to fool him into believing that he had access to all her thought, and she found that she liked having him review her carefully selected consciousness. How maddening. She did not respect him; he was a wandering fool, searching for an ideal consummation he could never realize. She had taken him to L'orkah on a whim, as a plaything—and a tool to get to Orram.

Enough. She halted the expansion of her mind. Orlah was tricky—luring her emotional response with real affection and empathy. She had better get on with the mating before he touched her too deeply.

Tentatively, they began the varokian ritual, touching forearms, touching minds. Though Orlah's body was slightly soft, it was well formed and attractive. Mahntik was quickly aroused, the arousal quickly satisfied. Then, while Orlah prolonged the contact beyond endurance, she distracted herself by planning how to see Orram alone at Leyoon's theater.

When at last Orlah was satisfied, Mahntik retreated to the food center. He had managed to incite in her a raging appetite for Orram. The younger brother's mentality would be a far greater challenge than Orlah's idiotic loyalty. Would she dare open her mind to Orram, just a little? The danger of such an experiment sent thrilling visions through her imagination.

"You will not easily seduce Orram." A rough-toned announcement intruded on her thoughts, and a chilling laugh echoed across the food center.

Mahntik's hand froze on the knife she held to a fresh stalk-loaf, while her patches sought the intruder's identity. Then she laughed coldly and turned to face Gitahl.

His stance was ripe with defiance. In a distasteful sort of way, Gitahl was more distinctly varokian than most varoks. His face was set like a plastic mask, its stark lines inscrutably rigid in front of the patch organs prominent on both sides of his head. His hairless skin was raw-looking and veined, not with blood, but with nerves. Small eyes, glaring and strange, lay bare of lashes on a tall forehead.

She turned back to the stalk-bread and cut several square pieces. "Actually, you came just in time, Gitahl. I was about to take Orlah out to see Sartak. We have business with the ahlork."

"It can wait. I have a message for you from the Free-minds."

"The Free-minds?" Mahntik placed the bread into a finely woven basket and added a handful of dried fruit. "What news?"

"Orram's son, Orticon, has joined them."

"I thought he would. Isn't that delicious?" Mahntik savored the irony. "The son of Varok's newly returned hero—the most conservative mind on Varok—a Free-mind. So? Why do they think I should care?"

"Orram will be Governor of Living Resources."

"He refused the position."

"Leyoon will convince him to take the job," Gitahl said. "He has decided you are a danger to Varokian society. The *ll-leyoolianl* are gathering evidence against you."

"Who says that? The Free-minds?" Mahntik pulled her mouth into an imitation of a smile. "There is no evidence to be gathered."

"Really?" Gitahl reflected Mahntik's non-smile. "Have you been paying all your fines for shipping webs and cloth beyond the legal limit?"

"I do no shipping."

"The ahlork make many trips across the Misted Ocean to Vior."

"Of course. You know I've been paying them in web berries." Mahntik laughed. "I should apply their hours to Global Varok's guarantee of employment."

Gitahl's eyes narrowed. "Beware of using the ahlork poorly, Mahntik. If their work in the ruins stops, it will be noticed. The quotas of rare minerals must be filled."

Gitahl turned his attention to a piece of stalk-bread. "Nice of the Free-minds to warn you about Leyoon. I can't imagine why, but they believe you represent a new spirit on Varok—an adventurous spirit, able to lead all lovers of privacy to a more honorable, closed-minded society."

"'To be free of the mind-probe is to be reborn with the integrity of one's potential,'" Mahntik quoted from the Free-minds' Petition For Independence of Mind. "Oh, that is so good." She allowed herself a full release of genuine mirth then quickly gained control.

"So, Leyoon accuses me. We'll see if his threat is real. The ahlork Nidok and Sartak will join us at the great-fish theater. They have another delivery of wild web seed to make near Ahl Vior. No one will prevent my redesigning the web fields of this planet."

Mahntik creased her face with a cold smile and closed off her recent memory. "Orlah is here. I want him to meet the ahlork called Sartak and direct the planting of new web fields here on L'orkah. Join us at the hearth. We'll see what he knows about Orram's son Orticon and the Free-minds."

They found Orlah sitting on the black stones of the hearth, waiting. Mahntik hated him for being exactly where she had left him.

"Orlah, you know Gitahl, I believe. He will take us to the ahlork, and I will show you what needs to be done." She set the basket of bread and fruit on the hearth. "Gitahl brings news. Your brother's son Orticon has joined the Free-minds. Now why would he join such a motley collection of confused egos? Surely, the Free-minds' objection to the mind-probe is based more on rebellion against authority than on reason."

"I think Orticon is quite sincere, Mahntik," Orlah said.

How perfect. She would openly sanction the Free-minds'

objection to the mind-probe. Then, having won their confidence, she would appeal to their fear of Earth and their tendency to favor a "free-mind economy." *Perhaps they could be convinced that rights to sell resources – like the minerals in Gitahl's ruins – should rest directly with those who take responsibility for land and property, not with society at large. If the economy were truly "free," land would be owned outright. There would be no depletion quota, no limit on the free distribution of goods or the free growth of new web strains. Varoks love the new cloth from L'orkah. They don't want to be limited to what they can get locally.*

"Do the Free-minds realize the importance of arming Varok?" she asked Gitahl, not caring about the answer. "Did you know that some of them are already toying with the idea? Even now some are studying nuclear engineering."

"Really?" Gitahl spoke dismissively. "I have heard nothing of a nuclear reactor. They are more concerned, obsessed really, with their dislike of the mind-scan."

"Then we had better be sure that they understand reality," Mahntik said. "Earth is becoming a serious threat. There are rumors that a space ship is heading here. Orram and his watchers on the moon base were deceived by those closed-mind Earthlings." She got up from the hearth, then took a cloak from its peg beneath the stairwell and opened the large doors to the foyer.

"Aren't you finished eating? Hurry Orlah. We go to Sartak. Bring that bread with you. Go for more food if you must. I will stop at the lab to see to my cultures. Quickly, please."

Orlah and Gitahl followed her outside and went off to the nearby locale to replenish her poor supply of food. Shops and homes perched on the hillside like embedded yurts, while efficient sailing vessels hugged the shoreline, moored to structures capturing energy from the tides and currents in the channel.

Mahntik continued down the graded pathway toward the genetics laboratory. For generations, varokian gene engineers, suppliers of new organisms approved for safety and advantage, had practiced their art on the isolated continent. It was still the only major industry on L'orkah, other than the ahlorks' reclamation and recycling work in the ruins.

When she reached the lab, she passed two varokian scientists who had been working late. They nodded with understanding when she complained that she needed to tend to delicate cultures.

In her office Mahntik reviewed her messages and approved the light-period's work schedule directing her lab techs to refresh all cultures with nutrients at their required intervals, inoculate new varieties, and clean the lab benches with disinfectant.

With that work done, Mahntik moved swiftly to the second floor. She entered the large containment lab where her most dangerous experiments in gene-splicing were conducted, and finished her work as quickly as she could. She checked and refreshed her new batch of viruses. Some required reinjection into fresh ilara eggs, others fed on a rich broth of insentient life. Most had been grown and regrown with various inventive combinations of nucleic acid codes.

"Routine work, a never-ending chore," she complained on her maser cell to Gitahl. "Germs mind their own schedule, not mine. I am ready now."

She met Gitahl and Orlah where the path crossed the outlet to the Misted Ocean. There they strode off the main road onto a narrow path that took them into the dry brush.

Five kilometers to the west, where the land rose in gentle undulations to meet the mountains, they came upon a hidden basin cradling a small lake. In the sky's golden light, it shone lush with clear water settled in the midst of rock plants and the ancient ruins of the forebears.

Like a sea of forgotten toys, the broken shells of the immense buildings covered the hills of L'orkah for tens of kilometers in all directions—from the lake to steep cliffs overlooking the Misted Ocean. More than four thousand Jovian years ago they had been the forebears' indestructable business complexes designed for mass production and sales, elaborate aerial suburbs once linked together by elegant, perdurable landing platforms—monuments to a luxurious technology that had covered and used up all of Varok ages ago.

Now they were desecrated by ahlork, Mahntik thought, *parasites feeding off a proud civilization they had never appreciated.* Even while she coveted the output of the ahlork who mined the ruins, Mahntik resented their presence there, for the now desolate, once noble forests of plasti-glass and steel had endured all the ages of Varok—through the building of the Ahlkahn, the wars between species, the Establishment of Balance, through the revolutions for growth, to the Rule of Stability and the coming of the ellls, the codification of Elll-Varok Law with the limits and quotas Mahntik hated.

Varoks should be living in such glorious structures, not mining them for rare minerals. Haven't I contracted for much of this land? Everything on it should be mine. Resource auctions are demeaning competitions.

Mahntik hated being responsible for the mess ahlork made with their mining. She would take what she needed to expand her business, paying the ahlork directly for their scavenging when she needed them. She would accumulate plenty of credits to buy all she wanted, for she had no intention of paying the rabble voters' taxes on excess profits.

As Mahntik and her companions worked through the low shrubs and lush foliage near the lake, she congratulated herself. How Gitahl would worry if he knew how much she had accumulated by pricing her web cloth so low. Already it competed with the tariffs designed to protect local web production in every locale of Vior. *Immobile capital, indeed. I'll provide credit and spread my own "capital" wherever I please. I've worked and saved for this all my life.*

Keeping her thoughts to herself, Mahntik led Orlah and Gitahl across the open meadow below the lake's basin and entered the northernmost ruins on a path worn deeply into the debris.

"Hurry, please," Mahntik shouted. Gitahl turned back for Orlah, who was not keeping pace. Mahntik did not wait for them. She strode up the slope to a large outcropping of rocks that hid the entrance to their destination—a large, square, featureless building set deep in the earth. Three ahlork sat on the berm over the entrance watching the varoks as they approached.

NIDOK

Nidok the ahlork—in L'orkah's ruins

Nidok's wing-plates tightened painfully as he and two other flock leaders followed Mahntik and two varoks into the building and sailed past them. He landed with his two companions on tall metal structures, and nervously pulled at the scar on his greater lip with his prehensile wing tips.

"Don't rattle." The ahlork Sartak caught Nidok's wing tip in his own. "Mahntik will suck out all thoughts before we have chance to speak."

"No she won't," Nidok insisted, watching the varoks walk toward them across the huge underground chamber. "Their code says no picking brains uninvited."

"Ha. You are fool to believe that." The third ahlork, a slow, lumbering beast called Susheen, stared at Nidok with disdain.

Nidok decided he did not belong at this meeting of skeptics and web berry addicts. He'd had enough of the berry's dizzy-making, the loss of control that came with the sweet juice. He would find out what plans Sartak and Susheen had made with the varokian woman, then he would keep his flock in the cliffs, away from Mahntik's new web berries. He wanted no more drunken encounters with ells on the ahlkahn.

As the varoks approached, Nidok recognized the Oran family scent on Orlah. Amazed, he also picked up the unmistakable scent of sexual contact between Orlah and Mahntik, and grew very curious.

"This is Orlah," Mahntik said in a poor, unconcerned imitation of ahlork sound. She waved a hand toward the varok in a deprecating way, implying that she would maintain full control. "Orlah will supervise the cultivation of the new fields. They extend from the ruins of Tahkin to the ilara spawning grounds in the west. New webs from the western hills of L'orkah will go immediately to my looms in the valley of Mount Ni. All the stalk feed will go to the silage towers in the Ruins of Va Varallah."

"Too far. We wear down our wings," Susheen objected.

"Nonsense. Carry nothing but seeds if you are so weak," Mahntik said. "Va Varallah is much closer to L'orkah than Mount Ni, you fool. In spite of your uselessness, you will have all the berries you want."

"All?" Sartak asked.

"All," Mahntik said.

"The web bushes lie too close to the ilara's foul spawning grounds. Stop them stealing unripe berries," Sartak demanded.

"Stop them yourselves," Mahntik said. "Their eggs are good food. Eat them. Carry seeds to my agents or scratch them into any fields you like, and you will have all the berries you want. Nidok, after you deliver web seed to the fields southwest of Mount Ni, I expect you to accompany Gitahl to the theater for Leyoon's presentation."

"Yes," Nidok agreed. "I fly to Gitahl at the theater."

"What?" Mahntik laughed, a sneer turning her lip. "You won't ride the Ahlkahn when you have the chance? I can get you passes, Nidok. Charge the ride to me. You will be a geneticist's courier, a rare honor for an ahlork."

"A rare dishonor, to be errand boy for varoks," Nidok mumbled, daring to voice the thought, guessing Mahntik was too absorbed in her schemes to pay him much attention. "I prefer to fly," he said.

"As you will, Nidok, but be at the theater in time. Gitahl will need you there."

Without ceremony, Mahntik turned away and marched from the building. Orlah and Gitahl followed.

Foolish of them not to seal the bargain, Nidok thought. *If the varoks had taken the scar from my wing-plate, we would be bound to them. As it is, Sartak will do as he pleases. He takes all the advantage he can, as I have.*

He looked up sharply when the varokian woman suddenly reappeared alone and strode quickly to Sartak, who stood apart with Susheen. Nidok enjoyed watching his fellow ahlorks' wing-plates tense then droop in submission as she approached.

"One more thing," she said, looking down at the ahlork. "I believe that the new fields of western L'orkah are rich in selenium.

The webs have taken up enough of that element to make warming cloth, like the cloth the forebears made ages ago. We will weave rhenium fibers into the selenium-enriched cloth. Susheen, you lead the ahlork who mine Gitahl's ruins. Find rhenium there and purify it. The cost of extraction is not important, for the warming cloth will save enormous heating costs and pay for itself. It will be quite legal. I will buy mining rights for the rhenium at the next council auction. Gitahl has promised me a fair trade for our quota."

"Is rhenium in Gitahl's ruins? I don't think that," Susheen said. "It is rare."

"If it is anywhere on Varok, it is there," Mahntik said. "The fields of L'orkah are rich in selenium. The forebears had warming cloaks made of selenium webs laced with rhenium fibers. We know that. The rhenium for the cloth must have been produced somewhere near here. Find where."

She turned abruptly and disappeared, leaving the doors to the large chamber swinging wildly behind her.

"Rhenium," Susheen sorted. "Why do I find rhenium for varoks? It is too difficult."

"Because rhenium buys our best berries," Sartak growled.

"Grow your own berries," Nidok muttered, not intending Sartak to hear.

In warning, Sartak's wing-plates opened to full cock. "Mind your foul lip, Nidok. We don't grow the berries. We don't poison ourselves with nasty chemical feed or pest-killing dust. Mahntik's varoks do that. We are not so stupid. We have something better now. Follow me."

I think you will do what Mahntik orders, Nidok mused.

Sartak led Susheen and Nidok deeper into the underground building. A narrow passage seemed to extend forever into the darkness. Every few meters they passed entrances to wide chambers or locked rooms.

"This hall leads to the new meeting ground of the Greater Flock." Sartak said. "Now I tell you why. We find Free-minds here."

"What is this long corridor?" Nidok interrupted, trying to break the spell. "It must be underground Ahlkahn."

"Ha." Sartak sneered, imitating the pout that Nidok's scar drew on his lip. "If this is railroad, where are tracks? Try not to be fool, Nidok. Look here."

The passage opened out into a large room filled with desks and panels decorated with switches, dials and remote viewing instruments.

"Not long ago I saw young varoks come into here." Sartak strutted proudly as he talked. "They came one by one, not seen. I circled far up until all were inside. Then I followed and listened." In the dim light of the control vault his voice was terrible with secrecy.

The ahlork moved on and came to the end of the control room. It was closed off with double doors. Carelessly, Sartak burst through what must have been intended as a sealed entrance. "The beam not alive yet," he declared importantly, and his two companions came up to stand beside him on a high balcony.

Far below the ahlork, on the lower floor of an enormous room, a number of small computer centers lurked behind thick, leaded walls lined with trucks, loaders and stacks of heavy equipment. Tall, portable manipulators stood about like giant robots guarding the complex.

The balcony on which they perched extended into the room and split into three long tunnels. Two ended within the great cavern, but one continued out of the room into another building visible through the narrow windows at the far end.

"The forebears' fast breeder reactor," Sartak exclaimed. "This is nuclear power station and experimental center. It is very old, but it will be now alive. Do you understand? The Free-minds rebuild the forebears' reactor. They soon will insert fuel rods. The Free-minds can give us power we need to mine rhenium for Mahntik."

"Impressive," Nidok said, "but nothing for my flock. My flock delivers Mahntik's seeds. We take her good berries. We don't like dangerous machines. We don't talk to Free-mind varoks. We don't go in closed buildings."

"All right. All right, Nidok. Go your way," Sartak said, his small black eyes riveted on Nidok's set expression. "You will deliver seeds, and we will find ways to capture Free-minds."

"Free-minds are varoks. Varoks will be difficult," Susheen said.

Nidok heard the threat in both their tones. "Of course varoks are difficult," he agreed, eyeing Susheen carefully. "My flock helps the Greater Flock with difficult varoks, Sartak. I help with Gitahl."

That was a close call, Nidok decided. Sartak had almost trapped him into a disloyalty. "We are no traitor. I forgot. You need Free-minds to make power."

"When we learn to make power, we have easy work mining rhenium. Free-minds are no longer use to us. We will have power more than varoks," Sartak laughed. "Call your flocks now. We go to Free-mind lair in ruins and tame varoks."

Nidok had no enthusiasm for the kidnapping of varoks. *And for what?* he asked himself. *What would ahlork do with an antique power station run by Free-minds? How would we keep them captive? As miners, we have our place in Varokian society. What place does this nuclear machine give us? A place as criminals and idiots, that's what place.*

Outside again, as his flock responded to the call for the Greater Flock put out by Susheen and Sartak, Nidok grew more disturbed by what they were doing: *We could not live better. In the ruins we have respectable work, recovering what the varoks want from the ancient structures. The ruins are endless—and they oversee all the best hunting on the shores of both Vior and Leahnyahorkah.*

Why do I do Mahntik's errands across the Misted Ocean? he asked himself. *For berries? Well, no longer. Mahntik would have me ride Gitahl's shoulder like a pet ilara. I will hear Leyoon, and we will see what is to be done for ahlork, not for varoks.*

Nidok almost missed the flock's descent into the ruins, so intense were his thoughts. As they landed, he was aware of the clicking of wing-plates all around him. Ninety ahlork had come for the attack on the Free-minds. Ahlork were perched on every open window and landing platform surrounding the ruin where the Free-minds had taken shelter.

Stark windowless walls and steel skeletons of tall buildings towered over him, dwarfing him and shutting him off from the sky. He cringed a little, for he was born to the open land and the free wind.

We have no use for cities.

Ahlork preferred to browse alone or in small groups, hunting small creatures on the edges of Varok's great forests or rummaging for varoks' wastes in the recycling centers of the urban areas. Only in the last few millennia had Nidok's people begun to range in large flocks, grumbling hoarsely about their lost heritage.

Long before the varokian forebears took rock in hand to fashion crude shelters, ages before the light-hoppers farmed mollusks in the red sands of the Forested Sea, eons before ellls and the *ll-leyooniantl* came to Varok from Ellason, the ahlork flew in straight lines, hunting Varok's small game at their convenience. No enemy pursued them, no creature challenged their hunting patterns, for they were the lords of the air. Varok was theirs.

During the ahlorks' dominance, the forebears of varoks and light-hoppers and daramonts were only just beginning to pass on accumulated knowledge to their young.

The ahlorks' loss of dominance—their lagging behind in Varok's evolutionary race to intelligence—was blamed by varoks on their lack of prehensile digits. They regressed to chasing simple prey on the hot acid plains. A kind of over-blown territorial imperative ran high between flocks. The quest for a larger hunting plain or a higher nesting cliff drove them to conduct frantic campaigns against each other.

The ahlork lost respect in the long, tangled pathways of the ellls' sense-directed logic and in the varoks' demanding integrity. The antagonism between the species never really ended, but the enmity found some relief in ill-tempered insults, enjoyed by ellls more than by varoks to the present day.

In attempting to take Free-minds prisoners, Sartak was driving the old rift between species deeper.

With a sensation of being swallowed, Nidok entered a huge room that had served as lobby and reception hall for an ancient hotel. Pillars of an enduring biphasic concrete stood in rows, half buried in ancient debris, reaching in silence toward high marble perches and a lattice of elegant beams made from Varok's finest preserved woods. *Rotting high limbs for wasted brains*, Nidok thought.

"Keep clacking those noisy plates, Nidok," Sartak croaked contemptuously. "We want to give the varoks good warning; it will improve the sport."

Nidok's eyes grew large with shame, and he went forward more cautiously. Suddenly three varoks jumped out at them from a hidden space behind a large pile of rubble.

"Take them," Sartak commanded, and the varoks, expecting a direct attack with extended wing-plates, were easily surrounded by three ahlorks' wings locked together.

The ahlork dragged the varoks out into an open area between buildings, and Sartak called for more ahlork to capture the next batch.

Nidok pitied these newly matured youth, three or four Jovian years at most, inexperienced varoks just out of the Concentrate. They knew nothing of danger, and they didn't seem to know enough about ahlork to insult their way out of this predicament.

Out of three openings in the broken walls of the ruins, a dozen or more varoks emerged and scattered in every direction onto dusty paths through piles of debris. With gleeful shouts, pairs of ahlork swooped down on the slower, crouching bipeds and trapped them in cages of sharp, chitinous wing-plates.

"Now," Sartak called to the flock, "we drag the varoks to their nuclear power toy. They show us how to play with it. These Free-minds now free our minds." He laughed into the face of one frightened young varok.

The youth looked vaguely familiar to Nidok. He moved closer to catch a scent. Oran family again. This must be Oran Ramahlak's famous prodigal, Orticon. Nidok sniffed once more, and Orticon jumped back in fright. *Yes. Oran family.*

"You—you're right," Orticon stammered, not knowing which ahlork to fear more, the angry leader or the sniffing scar-lip. "The reactor is just a toy—a machine to try our knowledge. That's all. If you need a good source of power, we can give you a tap into the ocean wind sources we control. Or we could get methane from the genetics lab waste digesters. We'll show you."

"Later," Sartak said. "We use bad gas only when we need more power than your nuclear plaything provides."

What a fool Sartak is, Nidok thought, *to give himself away to varoks like Orticon. If the boy were a true son of Orram, he would read every crevice of Sartak's mind. He would see that you don't need power for anything but your stupid ego — dominance, or getting back at Mahntik. Remember that, Nidok,* he told himself, *never let a varok think your mind is worth probing.*

ON DARAMONTS TO THE TOP OF VAROK

Tandra—the Oran locale

A glorious new orange light on the Vahinorral glowed with touches of blue lightning far above the high mists. Orram and Conn and I enjoyed the view from the exposed red root of the ironwood tree supporting the porch of Orserah's house. Nearby, Shawne played in the sandbox Conn had built for her. It felt delicious to relax for a moment. We knew it wouldn't last long. We were gaining strength rapidly, recovered enough from our long space trip to feel a bit restless.

"You're as eager as Da-oon to swim the deeps of the Forested Sea, Conn," I said. "Perhaps you should have gone over to Lake Seclusion with Killah and Jesse and the tad. You could have finished your recovery there. And you, Orram, need to quit inventing chores. Let's all go to Leyoon now. We're strong enough to travel."

"I can help Grandma Ors'rah, I can," Shawne said, running from the garden sandbox. "I can make the plow go with Ragweed Tummy, my robot. She pulled the rake from Conn's hands and started off for the egg-layers' yard to freshen their straw bedding.

"Doesn't Shawne want to go with us?" Orram asked.

Conn gave him a look. "Haven't you checked her mood lately? She would love to stay here and help Grandma Horse. Right, Tandra?"

"I think so. I'm a little apprehensive about leaving her, but traveling through Varok will mean more to her when she's older."

"So, let's go at next light," Orram said.

It was agreed. Shawne seemed delighted to stay with Orserah and take swimming lessons from Artellian. We slept through the last of deep dark, then loaded daramont packs, while reassuring Orserah that we could carry enough web stalks for them and good food for ourselves.

Daramonts loyal to Orserah took Conn and Orram and me across the web fields of the locale toward the foothills of the Vahinorral. Colorful mesh-plants lined the narrowing trail, replacing the cultivated edibles that graced the wide paths between lodges. After I exclaimed at their delicate beauty, my daramont, sensing my excitement, ran large loops into the meadows at every turn, finding new varieties of low bushes and tall blossoms to show me.

Too soon the wild tour ended. The mounts refused to carry us beyond the lower slopes onto the side of a sharply deepening canyon.

Conn's temper flared. "You can't leave us now," he said. "We haven't even reached the saddle-hold."

The daramonts made a quiet point by nosing Conn's walk-hardened feet, and before the elll could protest further they tossed our packs out of their saddle baskets with clever teeth. As they lurched away across the fields, Orram called thanks to them.

"Ding-blasted overgrown rabbits," Conn said, exercising his English. "Now what do we do?"

I laughed at the elll and tossed him a pack. "We honor the ancient traditions of Varok. We walk. The daramonts are quite right, you know. Your feet are so tough, you have no excuse to demand their service. Hove to."

Conn caught the pack and slung it on his back, but he didn't like it. "Before our assignment on Earth's moon, daramonts were everywhere, grazing along the paths to the sea, always looking out for an elll to carry, especially over the top up there." He waved a hand toward the crest of the Vahinorral. Its stark rocky peaks loomed high above us, dressed in a thick white mist I hoped would soon clear.

Before the light-period ended we had trudged up the steeper

reaches beneath the summit, gasping for Varok's wafting oxygen, stopping now and then to douse Conn's wet-sweater with water from bright streams running across the path into the canyon.

When Orram stopped to scan the high slopes and catch his breath, Conn collapsed heavily onto the snarl turf. "I don't see any relief. There are no daramonts to take us over the mountains," he grumbled. "Where are all those blamed beasts? They're as scarce as ilara around here."

I didn't realize we should be seeing more flocks of the bird-like creatures. Perhaps that was why web crawlers were so evident in some web bush fields. Ilara fed on the crawlers.

"Can we make it on foot in time?" I asked. "Leyoon's presentation is two light-periods from now."

"Leyoon will take two light-periods just to say hello—and four more to introduce his latest fleet of philosophers," Conn said.

"I'm truly sorry," Orram said. "I didn't expect to walk so far. I suppose I could have ordered a shuttlecar. In earlier times we would have been picked up by the daramonts long before now."

"Did you hear that? At last he agrees with me, Tandra."

"Where do we meet Jesse and Killah and Da-oon?" I was feeling just a little anxious in this wild land.

"They will meet us at the saddle-hold, just a few more turns up the canyon," Orram said. "The meadows spread wide there, before the steep climb begins."

"They'll meet us if they find mounts on their way here from Lake Seclusion," Conn said. "All the daramonts seem to have gone to better stalks. The fields we've passed are sick with web crawlers, and they haven't been pruned for six seasons." The elll rested his head on his arms and scanned the boiling mists above. Something far overhead caught his eye. "I'd swear there are ahlork up there. Can you see them, Orram?"

"No. You must be seeing them in your infrared range," he said. "I can't make them out on my own. Tandra?"

"Black specks. I think they're moving in straight lines."

"Take a look through my head, Orram," Conn said, shifting his eyes and blinking hard to clear the drying. "I'm sure those are ahlork, but they're too high."

"I'll try." Orram scanned the elll's visual reception with his patches and saw through Conn's eyes a shimmering movement high overhead. "They're not flying like ahlork. Too purposeful."

"Another thorn to prick through your blanket of complacency, my good varok," Conn said. "Ahlork on a mission. Now would you kindly tell us why you have been so . . . varokian on this trip. You haven't made me laugh since we left Orserah's lodge."

"By all that growls on Earth, I don't want that job as Governor of Living Resources, Conn. I want to stay home. I want to ease Orserah's last cycles. I want to live, to join minds with you and Tandra, to continue the coversation with Earth. I want to explore all we can be together. That takes time—and peace. Being Governor would leave us neither."

"We'll get there, Orram, old stick. We'll see what Leyoon has to say then go right home and stay there. Let's get it done."

We hurried up the cliffside path. Around the next bend we found the broad meadows of the saddle-hold. Conn collapsed onto a soft patch of thick leaves and rolled over, his back-fin tucked deep into the mossy hide beneath his wet-sweater. "I'm afraid our best chances for peace may lie in a little detective work for the great-fish. I don't like ahlork sneaking around up there so high, and I don't like the lack of daramonts here. Why hasn't Living Resources kept us informed? Maybe we should report it. And I don't like Mahntik's fancy new web cloth, and I especially don't like watching her dig her claws into Orlah—and don't look now, but I don't like being followed. There's an elll behind those rocks over there. I've seen her twice now."

"The elll we passed at the farm near Orserah's house?" I asked.

"I haven't seen any ellls." Orram retrieved his pack and pretended to adjust it as he looked around.

"You're not into noticing details lately," Conn remarked.

"There was an elll by the neighbor's barn watching us leave," I said.

"The same, Tan. She's a small round one, probably a loner."

"There they are!" Orram waved to a human and an elll as they came into view on daramonts, moving over a nearby rise. Killah was mounted on a bronze, and Jesse rode the largest, with Da-oon in his arms. They were followed by a six slim mountain daramonts.

When they stopped, I moved slowly toward the unmounted beasts with an offering of stalk bread. One or two lowered their powerful necks and turned dog-like faces to me, taking the bread eagerly with sensitive broad lips.

Conn got up and talked to the daramonts in Elllonian, negotiating for a ride over the summit of the Vahinorral. "We are worried about your stalk feed," he said. "Have you had enough?"

The daramont sporting a broad black mop for a tail shrugged and turned his lips into a figure eight.

"Better eat what we have, then." The elll dug into his pack and handed out the stalks.

While the mounts chomped with flat gum plates and swallowed the mashed stalks, Da-oon rolled between them, lightening our mood with his trust. The huge beasts delicately teased the elll tad with flexible four-toed hoofs.

When they had finished eating, Conn took my hand. "This biped is Tandra, a human being from Earth. She belongs to my dry school."

One daramont responded eagerly. He extended his neck until he stood four meters high, rocked slowly forward, and, camel-like, folded his forelegs on the ground, presenting me with a mountain of flesh to climb.

I clung uncertainly to the short mane that ran to the end of his tufted tail, and made my way onto the broad back. It was too wide to straddle, so I pulled forward until my legs found enough neck to grasp. The daramont shook gently to be sure I was secure, then he sprang into a loping gallop, stopped abruptly, and began to graze slowly back toward the others. I just managed to stay on.

"They cannot refuse ellls, by law," Killah told me when the mount brought me back, "but they will test you, and they won't be misused. You can see that they are wise enough to value their independence, but they are barely conversant enough to protect it. The Elll-Daramont Accord was written to protect them from commercial exploitation and experimentation."

"The human beings are inexperienced in crossing the mountains," Orram told the lead daramont. "Do you have cage saddles?"

Another mount answered by taking Orram a short distance to a rock shelter where the full-body saddles were stored for the trip over the mountains. The varok selected two and brought them back for Jesse and me. Da-oon sat securely in front of Killah. Two daramonts without riders wandered off, intent on grazing, but one lingered behind as if waiting for his rider. Conn exchanged a questioning look with Orram, and, with the slightest gesture, they agreed to keep a close watch for the elll that would probably follow us on that mount.

With great leaping strides the daramonts took us bipeds up the steeper hills. Soon the soft turf gave way to patches of snarl as tall as the mounts' knees. In the highest vales the loops wove a dark forest of thick trunks three meters high. Our mounts pushed on through the bushy growth. Just before the snarled trunks became impossibly thick, they suddenly ended, and the mountain rose above the strange twisted forest in a jumble of red granite.

Conn saw another flash of blue far below. "Wait," he called to the daramonts. The worry in his voice brought them together into a protective circle. "We're still being followed. It seems to be a blue elll."

"Blue ellls are usually harmless, unless they're scorned, like some human women I've heard of," Orram said with a nod at me, as though daring me to react to his teasing.

"Then why hasn't she signaled to us?"

"She has her own business, don't you think, Conn?" I said. "Perhaps she is doing some kind of survey for Living Resources."

"I don't like it. Let's get out of sight for a moment."

Immediately the daramonts moved off into the rocks. Nothing stirred but the uneasy mists. A repeating current of ammonia made me reach for the oxygen mask I carried as a precaution. Minutes passed.

"No one is coming," Orram said to Conn. "Let's go on. Maybe she'll come over the top on the daramont that waited for her." Conn nodded and led us around one last patch of snarl to the jumble of house-sized boulders spilling down the precipice on the far side.

"We have to ride down that?" I laughed, crying inwardly in protest, knowing the answer.

BLUE ELLL AND GREAT-FISH

Tandra—descending the Vahinorral

"Don't try to direct them like you would a horse, Tan. Daramonts do their own thing. They take you. They'll choose their own path. Concentrate on relaxing."

The daramonts moved around and over the massive red boulders, until they came to the outermost crest of the Vahinorral. High pinnacles towered above the mists in the west. To the east, as far as we could see, smaller rocks stood along the summit like sentinels on a fortress. Here and there stray loops of snarl threaded their way through the piles of colorful mineral that spilled into the gray waters of the Forested Sea far below.

Carefully at first, then with mounting assurance, the daramonts stepped from boulder to boulder along the crest. Conn sat like a green mountain king on a mythical beast, watching the restless mists, his confidence flowing in unspoken ways to the daramont beneath his legs—probably through the lack of tension in his muscles, unlike mine.

My mount surveyed the rocks with a steady, sweeping gaze, testing each direction from every rock, as if he knew that the way down was made more treacherous by the momentum he would gain. Briefly he stood fixed, poised and tense, ready for his first leap, his path chosen. Then he took off down the broken mountainside. I clung to the thick mane in desperation, sure that this living roller coaster must have gone off its track.

The first leap sent my stomach flying, as a dark swirl of mist flowed from the east across our path. My daramont checked himself, then plunged ahead as the mist cleared, leaping from boulder to boulder, pausing, changing course, hopping shortly where the large boulders failed to provide a clear path, bounding ever downward over the top of the treacherous jumble.

Just when I was beginning to enjoy it, the exhilarating ride ended on the shore of the Forested Sea. Orram and I asked our mounts to turn around so we could watch Killah, Da-oon and

Jesse finish their ride. Da-oon let loose with a joyous elll whistle as their mount came off the mountain and took the ellls across the beach right into the shallow waves teasing the shore.

Conn sat high on his daramont staring out over the sea, as though longing for the embrace of deep water. The waves shone like molten obsidian, their undulating black sheen meeting orange swirls of mist glowing in the auroral light. Behind him, a rock tumbled down the mountain. We froze. Minutes passed, but all was quiet on the steep slope of giant boulders.

Killah dismounted into the waves lapping at the red sand. "I'll send out a call for a school to take Da-oon, Jesse and myself out to sea. It won't take long." He disappeared into the water, leaving the rest of us to calm the excited Da-oon. He was eager to begin his elllonian schooling life after an infancy spent in the confines of the aquarium at the Earth moon base.

"Only a little more waiting, my dear tad," I told him. "How long, Orram—how will Killah make contact?"

"The ellls' sonar transmitter is on a large rock just to our left, only about thirty meters out," Orram explained.

"A transmitter way out here?" I asked.

"They're distributed widely across all Varok's seas, often near land crossings like this one. Killah's call will be heard and repeated by all schools within ten kilometers."

Killah emerged from the water a few moments later, shaking the water from his crown plumes. "We're in luck. There's a school of ellls only four kilometers out. They should make it to shore in a few moments."

We settled down to wait, sharing a farewell meal of dried moth cakes with Da-oon.

Orram pointed out the silent ruins of an ancient ocean resort that stood on the shoreline some two or three kilometers distant. "The red sand of the Vahinorral periodically buries the ruins, then blows on, leaving them uncovered—like raw wounds that won't heal. There are no varokian locales here. The closest one is at the Theater of Great-fish."

"Raw wounds," I echoed, feeling grief in him as old as the forebears, the kind of grief I felt for Earth.

"I don't like being followed—it reminds me of the raw days when I was treated as a traitor for promoting restraint on Earth. Who could it be, Conn?"

"I don't know. Someone who doesn't want Orram to be Governor of Living Resources? I've been watching, but no one has come down the rocks yet."

We were interrupted by the sudden, rowdy emergence of ellls from the shallows. They greeted us humans with curiosity and wet hugs and hearty elllonian good wishes, and soon Jesse and Da-oon and Killah were shouting their farewells from the shallows.

"Don't drown that human being," Conn hollered to the school, following them into deep water. "It's the big hairy one. They don't do well under water. You all right, Jesse?"

My fellow human looked a bit uncertain, but he nodded and waved.

Conn coasted back to the beach, and in the shallows shook vigorously, running his fingers back through his head plumes to smooth them—a futile gesture that made me smile. "I told Killah to keep a close watch, on everything," he said to Orram.

"I am not Governor of Living Resources yet."

"Who can refuse Leyoon?"

"I can. Believe me," Orram insisted. "Let's call the daramonts now. The Viorlegh Peninsula is at least ten kilometers away."

"You go ahead. I'll swim over later."

"When?"

"When I've caught the elll who's following us. I saw blue plumes coming down the eastern rocks as I was swimming in."

"Be careful, Conn." I laid a finger along the angle of his jaw.

Catching my finger and drawing it under his chin, he prolonged the touch. "You know me well, Brown Silk. Enjoy the great-fish. I won't be long."

Conn—on the shore of the Forested Sea

Conn lay quietly in a stand of tall reeds that grew in the shallows below scattered rocks of scree, watching the daramonts take Orram and Tandra into the ruins along the shoreline path. He almost missed seeing the blue elll. Her daramont disappeared down the shore path at a full leaping gallop.

Conn scrambled for deeper water. He thought he could make it to the ruins before her daramont picked his way across the rubble of collapsed piers that blocked her path. He'd been lurchng dolphin-fashion across the water's surface for three minutes before he realized just how weak his swimming musculature had become. He was falling far behind. He made a leap and let out a call for help, then struggled toward the shore. *No daramont could resist such a call.*

"Aeyull." He screamed as he made for the beach, heedlessly crashing through the sharp reeds.

That did it. The daramont dipped to a halt and came loping back to find him.

Luckily the reeds had not sliced deeply into Conn's moss tiles, but the wounds were enough to satisfy the beast.

"Here. And here," Conn said as the daramont's medicinal tongue lapped at the scratches. "Ouch. Yes. Thank you. I don't think I can swim further. May I share your back with this elll?"

The beast nodded its reply, and only then did Conn dare to look up. He saw a wonderful, smiling face. This was no runaway schooler. This was a well-adjusted loner, probably an educated professional, a seasoned elllonian female with pleasantly rounded proportions—a beautiful, blue-plumed woman.

"You win," she smiled, sliding off the daramont's neck and giving her torso a shake to settle her plumes.

"Good. Now tell me why you were following us."

"I wasn't following you, and you certainly weren't worth racing."

"Who are you working for? Mahntik?"

"Why Mahntik?" The huge eyes beneath the royal blue brows narrowed with alarm.

"You've got to be high on her fancy web berries to follow us across the mountains." Conn grabbed the elll's arm and pulled her close to check her breath.

It was sweet and fresh, and her body smelled of the wry dampness of ellls. He was soon lost in eyes as soft as the deep-sea luminescence of Ellason.

She touched Conn's neck with a lingering webbed finger, and he responded with the awakening of his elllonian maleness.

The touch was too much like Tandra's, he admitted to her later, and yet too different. It renewed old schooling memories, and the longing that went with them. Then the touch became very elllonian, very definitive, as her tongue caressed the hedonic glands beneath his chin. "You should know," he said. "I have taken a family ring with a varok and a human."

"You don't need to explain," she said. "I would honor any ring that does not tear at elllonian finger-webs."

She took Conn's hand and straightened the Oran-family ring over the tender folds of his interdigital webs. A swirl of polished moon-glass glowed warmly, housing a handsome sapphire and matching diamond, set off from a large emerald. It was identical to the ones Orram and Tandra wore.

"Orserah tells me this is your symbol of the three neighbors: Earth, Varok, and Ellason," she said, "soon to be solar brothers at last, if your family experiment works."

Conn stared at her, afraid to believe his good luck in finding an elll who could understand. "Who are you?" he asked.

"First things first," she said, dropping his hand. "Does the ring mean you can't take an elllonian mate?"

Conn laughed. "No, of course not." He thought again of Tandra and the jealousy he had felt for the human's mental union with Orram. Tandra was not a mate. *As intimate as one, perhaps, committed to me and to Orram as family, but not as mates. Humans don't mate with their pet dogs. No. Tandra and I have been through that one. I am not a pet elll for the human. Then what? Certainly the relationship is too intimate to take a mate without knowing how Tandra and Orram feel about it, or at least how they feel about my choice.*

He studied the beautiful elllonian face. He could not lie into the lights of Ellason. "I don't know yet," he said. "I would never insult you. The family is too complicated already."

"Well then, if we can't mate yet, we can school a bit as we follow Tandra and Orram. I will be working for Orram. I was tracking ahlork for the Department of Living Resources when you crossed my trail. I lost them then, and I didn't want to intrude on your party, but I decided to continue on to the great-fish theater and watch Leyoon's presentation."

Tandra—moments later

On the Viorlegh Peninsula, in the midst of a large field of volcanic rocks and geothermal formations, there lay hundreds of deep pools and miniature beaches caressed by wind and wave. Orram and I asked the daramonts to wait while we found the great-fish who lived in the undersea caves nearby.

Leaving clothes and capes on a dry boulder, we entered the warm geo-thermal pools and watched small plant-like creatures scurry out of our way.

Three massive shadows moved swiftly toward us as we entered one of the larger pools. I felt a shiver shake the roots of my being. These were the great-fish, the *ll-leyoolianl*, immigrants to Varok from the deeps of Ellason, ancient cousins to ellls, creatures who did not sense the world as ellls or varoks did. The most respected of Varok's intelligent species, they were the conceptual founders of the Concentrate and tutors to many of Varok's masters. They conceived wholeness in patterns of thought, sensed complex implications in unrelated activities, and read meanings in the movement of events.

How much direct mental contact they achieved was only suspected, not known, for they chose to communicate with varoks from an extensive vocabulary of signs and symbols sculpted in mud. My theory was that their brains, like ours, selected parameters and constructed geometric images that designed representatiave models to make predictions. My skeptical mind decided that our second-guessing them was about as precise as complexity theorists trying to predict avalanches in hills of sand.

Three dark forms the size of killer whales surrounded us in a tight embrace of welcome. I found the expression on each dolphin-like face quite pleasant, for the two sensors above their great mouths seemed to accent soft smiles.

With a flick of powerful, prehensile side fins, each great-fish rolled to touch my hand with an underfin. Then they glided swiftly on, the tapered fins trailing beneath elongated, pyramidal bodies that gradually narrowed into long tails ending in expressive, graceful forks.

"This is Leyoon." Orram told me, gesturing to the largest great-fish. "He was my teacher when my father came here as liaison from Ahl Vior to the Forested Sea. Follow me now. Watch the images in the sand. I will translate for you."

We swam behind Leyoon to a lemon-green expanse of tall fronds swaying in concert on the floor of a large tide pool, shallow enough for us to kneel in the sand. There the great-fish quickly built three sculptures in stone and mud, then moved them about, built more, destroyed some, moved them again. The ever-changing arrangement was a magnificent living collage, a complex design of meaningful symbols. Orram translated: "Do not trust the ahlork. Their ways are changing—disrupted by forces strange to them."

The message continued, and, as Orram translated the great-fish's swiftly changing symbols, I felt as if we were reading Leyoon's mind. When he finished with a request that Orram become Governor of Living Resources, Leyoon drifted away to wait for the varok's response.

We watched from the surface, then Orram reached to the bottom, where he fashioned in the mud two symbols: a figure of authority and a strong negative.

With a swipe of his great prehensile fins, Leyoon scattered Orram's symbols into silt.

"Why?" The great-fish was too agitated to create a finished question.

Orram modeled the symbol for home, working carefully with the cohesive mud, shaping it in his hands.

Leyoon stood poised half out of the water, watching, his expansive fins and long conical tail moving swiftly back and forth. Hurriedly he modeled his response to Orram's polite refusal.

"You will be Varok's Governor of Living Resources," Leyoon's symbols declared. "You alone, Orram, with your knowledge of Earth, are equipped to be governor at this time. Go to the Theater of Great-fish now, and I will show you Varok's peril."

With a strange turn of one side fin, Leyoon moved to my side and spoke to my mind. "You will soon meet Lanoll, Tandra. Orram will need her report from the Forested Sea."

Without Orram translating for me, I couldn't be sure that I was understanding correctly. "You are more like varoks than anyone could have guessed," I burbled into the water.

Leyoon circled around me, and for an instant lay the front tip of his underfin gently across my lips. "Orram will not reveal our secret. Nor should you. In the end I pray it will serve you well."

I nodded as if I understood, then Leyoon embraced me with a surge of water from the powerful stroke of one side fin, and he whacked his tail on the surface in farewell.

LEYOON'S MESSAGE

Tandra—moments later, en route to the Theater of Great-fish

"Leyoon always waxes a bit more eloquent than necessary. Don't let his demands worry you," Conn said. He had met us at the tip of the Viorlegh Peninsula, where three daramonts stood ready to offer their services. Now he rode beside me as we made our way through the locale supporting the Theater of Great-fish.

"At first I didn't like the effect Leyoon's demands had on Orram," I said. "He was shocked to be bullied like that, but he agreed to listen to Leyoon's presentation at the theater."

"You wouldn't mind if Orram became governor? Already professionals in Living Resources are pursuing him. Lanoll followed us here. She's the elll who helped Orserah set up Orram's office. She has reports from the Forested Sea. She's a loner. She has a . . . special interest in us."

Words were coming hard for Conn, so I encouraged him with a nod.

Conn looked puzzled. His eyes searched my expression, as they did when he mistrusted his good sense. He took my hand. "I've been worried—because I suddenly realized how dependent you are on Orram and me. You're alone now that Jesse is gone off with Killah."

"I don't need to school with humans, Conn. It's okay. Once I sorted out all the topsy-turvy lightning effects here and experienced the varoks' open awareness, I felt wonderful, truly welcome. At home." I focused carefully on the center of Conn's huge gaze. "Don't forget that I am linked to Orram's consciousness. Everything he has ever been on Varok is like a shared memory."

"Still—I would hate to leave you just yet. You haven't learned everything there is to know about Varok or varoks."

"Or ellls." I dropped his hand as our daramonts separated to step around a thick growth of conifer-like trees.

"Tan, I need to tell you—I don't want to lose you, like I did when we first met. I'm driven—maybe it's just hormones, but it's so strong—"

"I know you, *rialka*. You won't ever lose me. You are the free half of Orram and me. I see that you need to school, and I will always come to your water—whenever you want me—though you have been busy mating a whole school of Lanolls. I wish you'd tell me more about her. Where is she? Leyoon wants to see her."

My direct reference to Lanoll relaxed Conn's knotted face.

"You have always worried too much about jealousy, Conn. We lived through that once. I wish you could know what a woman's relationship with her brother is like. Then you'd understand."

"Okay," Conn smiled. "I can imagine enough to get your point. Lanoll went ahead to see Leyoon. You'll meet her soon."

The daramonts quickened their pace as the western shore of the Forested Sea turned on itself. Framed with sand dunes and pebble bars, a quiet estuary spread before us like a giant mirror of water, the shoreline dotted with the wharves and log cabins of varoks whose business were interwoven with the lives of great-fish.

"Over here," Orram called. Beyond the nearest sandbar, he stood beside his daramont where a spreading shoretree shaded a sizable outcropping of rock.

We sent the daramonts on their way with the customary thanks and what stalks we had left, and Conn and I followed Orram under the smooth white limbs of the shoretree. A narrow path dropped between moss-covered rocks into a cavern that ushered us steeply downward. Intermittent roaring and sucking sounds, amplified by the cavern's dense walls, accompanied the trickling of water flowing from unseen cracks. Lit by a collection of bioluminescent mosses imported from the deeps of Ellason, the cavern shimmered with a warm blue light.

Around a bend the path leveled off. I heard the musical chatter of ellls and the booming tones of hundreds of varoks. We emerged into what Conn called the outer lobby of the theater, and a respect-ful hush fell over the crowd. Several ellls sent their green-tiled bodies into a standing salute, and they shouted, "*Bayon* Orram. Welcome human Tandra. Good schooling, Conn."

We threw our hands upward in acknowledging spirals, work-ing our way through the welcoming crowd to the wide archway leading into the theater.

There a group of ahlork blocked our path.

"Ho, Nidok." Conn called to one. "Following us about Varok, are you? Or have you come to bug—"

"Not here, Conn," Orram cautioned. "Nidok enjoys a battle too well."

I thought I saw the hint of a smile turn the normal side of Nidok's scarred lip. Probably my imagination. However, a differ-ent look altogether came from a second ahlork who pushed for-ward and stood firmly in Conn's path. He was a massive beast, half as tall as Conn but much wider, with little capacity for humor evident in his broad lip and stiffly held wings. A distinctive white marking around his neck and breastplates camouflaged a small transmitter hanging about his thick neck. The stain of web berries colored his lips a sickly red.

"Ellls are always spoiling ahlorks' fun," said a varok standing behind the ahlork. "Keep your ell to leash, Oran Ramahlak."

"Name yourself, varok, and explain your rudeness," Conn snarled.

The larger ahlork's wings tensed threateningly, as if he were bodyguard to the varok.

"My name is no business of yours, elll." The varok moved away, motioning the ahlorks to follow.

When the larger ahlork had disappeared into the theater with the varok, Nidok stood in Conn's path, tracing the long scar on his lip with his prehensile wing tip, his black-pea eyes locked into Conn's.

"Why do your friends come to a public meeting eating berries?" Conn asked. "Is this a new fashion among ahlork?"

I thought I saw Nidok's face nod very slightly.

"I take no berries this trip, Conn," he said.

"Perhaps your flock flies truer circles than others," Conn suggested.

Again Nidok's head gave a barely perceptible nod. "I listen now to Leyoon. Great-fish don't display with no reason."

"They don't display at all," Conn said, "and they don't like their messages interpreted second-hand. Why does your friend carry a transmitter?"

Nidok startled and turned away.

"Conn, Nidok was trying to tell you something," I whispered. Orram agreed.

"Was that varok Gitahl, who mines the ruins on L'orkah?" Conn asked Orram. "He makes my hexlines burn."

Orram nodded. "I think so. Don't irritate him, Conn."

"I would watch that one." Conn's temper was still high. "He came to see Mahntik when she was at the Concentrate. I've never met such a competitive so-and-so—except for that big ahlork with the necklace. He's called Sortak or something—flies the flocks of L'orkah's eastern shore."

"You knew him at the Concentrate, too?" I asked.

"I met him when I was in flight training. He was one of the ahlork employed to help out with aerodynamic psychometrics. Tough character. He had a cruel streak in him, which made for some pretty messy sessions. We used to get sick, coming over the Red Spot on our own. He thought it was funny."

I took Conn's arm as we walked down the corridor, and his mood snapped back to normal. "Now we'll see how you do with weird sensations, human. This theater will blow your primate mind."

"Then I'll hang on to both of you."

The theater was a huge bowl, encasing the air-breathing audience within a glass bubble underneath the Forested Sea itself. Everything—water and sand and salt plants surrounding us—was magnified, reflected and distorted by the huge crystalline walls so that the vision pulled and twisted my mind.

Quickly Orram ushered me to a couch. To help me organize the watery vision swirling around me, he joined my mind, and soon a semblance of order came to the scene.

Scattered in groups about the floor, dry varokian couches filled the center of the crystal globe with quiet brown and silver figures, moving with measured rhythms as they spoke to one another. In separate circles stood fountain-lounges for ellls, thickly lined with moss and fitted with small tubes that put out a fine mist. Ellls busily adjusted the play of water about their seats or made their way into the main presentation tank to drape themselves over and around leathery sealettuce. So many long green arms and legs busily greeting and exchanging pleasantries was like a swarm of giant worms playing in the rain.

From the curved sides of the globe hung tiny fountain perches already crowded with delicate green creatures resembling winged glass frogs. "The light-hoppers," Orram explained. "Superstitious, passive mystics, they are the doomsayers—the conscience of Varok's shorelines."

Nidok and several other ahlork flew to the large perches that hung near the dome's center. They created an annoying distraction with the grinding-tooth sound of their chitin-plated wings.

I felt momentary disgust cut through Orram before it dissolved into near-amusement. "They are not the easiest of creatures to love," he admitted.

We turned then to the surrounding water, for the great-fish were slowly coming into view, emerging from the depths of the sea to glide over the surface of the theater's sea bed all around our bubble of air. I counted twelve of them. Sleek flat-bottom bodies trailed long back-fins and fork-tipped tails through the water, their images reflected by crystals and mirrors scatterd on the sea floor, giving the impression of gentle spirits in the fluid light that bathed them from the surface above and bioluminescent orgnisms near the sea bottom.

Orram relaxed with me as the perceptive beasts began to weave complex schemes of deep-weeds and rock with their prehensile fins. Their movements became measured and careful, choreographed into changing patterns, as they shaped clay and carved soft stone into a representation of Varok's mythical spirit, Gurahn.

Orram stayed with me in mind to explain what was happening. *The Gurahn represents Varokian history, the essence of the planet and its life.* In this presentation it was a starving one-eyed monster, highly intelligent but crippled, its features contorted. Flashes of light from every direction accented the great-fish dance, painting an ever-changing three-dimensional picture as the gigantic sculpture morphed in form and meaning. Slowly, it grew heavy on one side, as if it would soon collapse, grotesquely out of balance.

Orram grew tense. *We came home for a promised future,* he protested silently, *not distortion and trouble.*

"Leyoon will make an accusation of treason before this presentation is finished," Orram whispered so that Conn could hear.

Leyoon catapulted around the watery stage, knocking all of the other great-fish out of his way. Then he set to work frantically enlarging the already too-large left shoulder of the Gurahn, until the immense clay and weed sculpture tilted. It could no longer stand upright. The audience gasped, anticipating the collapse of the symbol. Leyoon's message was clear: someone was threatening the structure of Varokian society with an insidious attack on its ancient stability. Its collapse was imminent, the danger ignored.

The play brought vividly to my mind the memory of Earth's impossible dilemma, the spiraling trap of greater and greater need, both real and invented, and the ever-increasing debt that prevented any rational slowing of economic and biological growth. Was Leyoon saying that Varok had entered such an unmanageable growth spiral?

As the Gurahn leaned further and further over Leyoon, the

audience protested his threatened suicide. Suddenly the great sculpture slumped to one side, paused a moment, then rocked back in a well-planned act of counterbalancing, timed with the appearance of a varokian figurine made of stone.

As the water darkened, signaling time for intermission, many eyes in the audience focused on Orram. I marveled at how Conn's fears seemed to mesh with what the great-fish were saying about Varok.

CONN AND LANOLL

Conn—at the Theater of Great-fish

The stunned audience quickly resumed subdued conversation, and a volley of gifts for the great-fish rained into the communications chamber of the watery stage—carefully prepared shellfish appetizers, shore-weed tarts, moth delicacies stuffed with tiny fruits.

Conn rose to his feet and searched the theater perches. "I'm going out, Orram," he said.

"Don't start any contests with Nidok, please. We can talk to him later, after the performance is finished."

"Right, Governor," Conn smiled. "I'll ask Nidok to come out to Orserah's house. He's a good sort when he's sober."

"There he is," Tandra said. The ahlork flew erratic circles above the crowd then headed out. Conn could see that one wing tip held a small package of wrapped leaves.

Conn caught up to the ahlork in the entrance corridor. "Sorry to remind you of the berry incident, Nidok," he said in the ahlorks' language. "None of my business really, what you do on the Ahlkahn—or in the higher flyways."

As he settled onto the corridor floor, the ahlork stared up at the elll. His greater lip quivered slightly near the twisted scar that embossed his square face.

"Come to see us at Orserah's house on your next trip," Conn said, plucking a yellow-edged plume from the base of his right sonic melon. He kneeled to the ahlork's height and handed him the plume, hoping Nidok would appreciate the challenge the gift represented. "We've got the best fish culture under Mount Ni, Nidok. You won't go hungry."

"I eat penned fish after I am starved to death," Nidok sneered, taking the plume in his lip and chewing on it.

"Good," Conn countered. "We'll rot the fish for you, rub them in sand so you'll feel right at home."

"My flock does not eat sand," Nidok said, suddenly serious. "I eat too much already, so my flock won't."

"I thought so." Conn did not laugh. "A martyr." He looked carefully into the ahlork's ink-drop eyes. There was no way to tell when the jesting should stop.

"Yes," Nidok whispered savagely. "I be martyr."

As three ahlork landed nearby, Conn turned and walked away, then leaned on the wall, pretending to ignore them, hoping they would think he did not understand their toneless chirps. The largest ahlork grabbed at the package Nidok held in his wing tip, and Nidok pulled the package away. "This is mine to deliver," he growled.

"No longer," the aggressive ahlork said with a vicious slash of his wing plates.

Conn saw it was the ahlork with the distinctive white necklace marking his chitin. *What is his name? Sortak isn't quite right.*

"I am told to watch you closely," the ahlork said to Nidok in the coded, chunky sounds of their native language. "You are almost too late to deliver your present. It must be done now."

"I will do as I will, Sartak," Nidok said. "Gifts are best given after performance."

"The gift is given now," Sartak insisted, grabbing the package away from Nidok. "Mahntik is no fool. She watches everything." Sartak flew off toward the theater with two other ahlork, leaving

Nidok alone. Conn decided he looked perplexed and angry.

"They're not of your flock, obviously," Conn said, walking back toward Nidok. "What are they trying to do?"

Nidok caught Conn's eye and looked pointedly away. The ahlork's wing plates reacted with a nervous flick at what he saw. Conn followed his gaze. Mahntik stood in the corridor watching them. Nidok said nothing more, but took flight and followed the other ahlork back to the theater. Conn hurried into the theater to find Tandra and Orram.

"You look like you're about to pop your gills," Orram said. "What happened out there? Did you see the four ahlork who just flew back here?"

"One was our friend Nidok," Conn said. "What did they do in here?"

"One of them threw a refreshment to Leyoon." Orram searched the elll's mind for a clue to his excitement. "Where have you been?"

"In the corridor. The ahlork had a very strange squabble over that gift. We need to retrieve it before Leyoon takes it."

"Leyoon has already taken it, Conn. He has always been careful to honor the ahlork for civilized behavior."

"I don't like it, Orram." He looked up as an ahlork sped out into the corridor. "There goes Nidok. I'll catch up to him and apologize. The great-fish will begin the show soon. I'll be right back."

"Apologize? For what?" Orram asked, but the elll didn't stop to answer.

"Hey there, Nidok." Conn found the ahlork hurrying away from the lobby, on his way out of the cavern.

The ahlork shuddered at the sound of his name and hurried on, looking for the corridor to end so he could get airborne. He had not gone far in his awkward hurry when Mahntik appeared at the theater's outer entrance. Her glance took in Nidok's tilting square body and the slim figure of Conn hurrying after him.

The elll tore a piece of moss off the cavern wall and munched on it as he turned away and started back toward the theater. His mind was in turmoil. *Can Mahntik read my mind at that distance? I'm probably too far.* He couldn't be sure. Instinct told him to ignore her.

Mahntik ushered Nidok out of the theater and disappeared.

Slowly Conn followed them, stopping every few meters to listen. He could hear nothing but the distant echoes of the great-fish beginning their finale in the theater behind him. He moved on quickly. The entrance to the theater cavern was deserted. No sound came from the beach outside.

Conn decided to go into the Forested Sea. Mahntik would suspect nothing if he relaxed in the shallows. Before he emerged from the cavern, however, he picked the dimming lenses from his orbs and slipped them into the tiny case he wore tied in his hip plumes. He imagined that his mind was harder to read when the lenses were off. He could stare at a mind-probing varok like Mahntik and confuse her, at least for a moment, with quick shifts in focus between infrared and the shorter wavelengths visible to varoks.

As he crossed the wide moss shore enclosing the shallows, Mahntik stepped from behind a thicket of dense seashore bushes. Her eyes locked blankly into Conn's, and he concentrated hard on feeling guilty, guessing that she would ignore varokian courtesy and read his unwilling mind.

"Don't tell Orram where I am, Mahntik, or I'll owe you one less favor," he said. Swiftly he retreated out of her range and headed for the water. He decided it would be prudent to skip Leyoon's grim message and swim, as Mahntik expected he would.

"Conn." A whispered call in ultrasonic stopped him as he sought the deepest water.

"Yeah. What? Who's that?" Conn startled, until he saw the blue elll swimming toward him. "Lanoll?"

"I wasn't sure you'd remember." As she rose to swim beside him, the round blue elll flashed a grin that drove all thought of Mahntik from his mind.

"After sharing your daramont?" Conn brushed an open hand lightly over her back plumes. "I never forget an invitation to mate."

"Now?" Lanoll glanced toward the theater.

"Leyoon's doomsday sermons aren't exactly my favorite theater fare," he said. "Let's go fool around in the shallows."

"I am usually very serious, Conn. I am no fool."

"Yes. Pardon my English jargon. It doesn't translate well. I would guess you are more like a varok than a salmon."

"A salmon?" Lanoll laughed. "That Earth fish that spawns like the ilara? I should hope not. I am as much a loner as you are, but I am no varok and no salmon. Come on. I'll show you just what sort of elll I am."

She grabbed his hand, and they glided through the shallows, where quiet water tugged at the base of great rocks, and thick growths of moss danced beneath spreading shore-trees. The waves swallowed them with a soundless gulp and they swam to the deeps. Together they danced the three-dimensional dance of ellls—sometimes drifting, tumbling free, sometimes cutting smooth slashes of green through the water, easing ever downward to the floor of the sea, where the cool mud wrapped them in velvet.

For a long while they lay quietly in the mud and talked with pressure signals and sonics of their lives as loners. Like Conn, Lanoll had come to realize that the school was not enough. She didn't know if she could tie herself to a small group of individuals as Conn had. What she wanted was an elll for long-term mate, preferably a loner who understood her needs apart from the school.

As Lanoll finished talking, Conn's thoughts turned to Tandra again. Jealousy was a terrible emotion, a feeling worse than clogged gills. He felt it sometimes, when Tandra and Orram moved beyond his elllonian mind into mental consummation.

Would Tandra tolerate Lanoll if I chose the elll for long-term mate? Despite what she said, how could she not resent the time and intimacy Lanoll would require?

He said nothing about Tandra to the lovely blue, and soon their talk focused on her work for the Living Resources office. Lanoll was responsible for sampling the inland seas, looking for signs of ill health while counting species.

"Someone who understands what is happening around Lake Seclusion has got to take the governor's job," she declared. "Too many varoks are crowded around the shore lands beneath Mount Ni. It's none of my business, but soon it will be. The lake shore has dropped and some bays are lined with algae already, as if waste is not being absorbed. But it's not just Lake Seclusion. Hoards of ahlork have been seen flying over the Forrested Sea."

"Hoards?" Conn laughed.

"I'm serious," Lanoll insisted. "There are too many ahlork flying behind Mount Ni and across the sea. It's Nidok's flock, I think. As soon as a new governor is elected, I'm going to press for a co-ordinated effort between land and sea census-takers to find out what's happening in that whole southern region."

"Orram is good at putting puzzles together," Conn said. "I wish he would take the job."

The two ellls continued talking as they drifted along the bottom. Soon Conn lost himself in the softness of Lanoll's body, until, with all consciousness abandoned, they mated.

He wanted nothing more than to drift on out to sea with her, to quit the land and its problems, to quit the knowledge and fear of jealousy, to become a schooling elll again at least for a time. But when Lanoll received a call from her school and begged Conn to go with her to the ellls, he refused. He was pulled too strongly toward Orram and Tandra and the decisions facing them.

"Orram will want my opinion," Conn decided. "I'll be working closely with him if he takes the job. I'd better get back and catch Leyoon's conclusion."

Reluctantly the ellls parted. Lanoll headed for deep water, to her school of ellls, and Conn drifted in the shallows, until his head came to rest out of water on a large eruption of moss caught in the roots of a spreading shore-tree. "Lanoll, Lanoll, Lanoll," he sang to himself, savoring for another moment the memory of her understanding touch and kind intelligence. "I would much rather dream of you than go back to the theater to watch Leyoon's sour message."

SUDDEN DEATH AND CAPTURE

Tandra—at the Theater of Great-fish

In the theater, the refreshment period had ended. On his way to a perch, one ahlork swooped low and sat on the back of Orram's seat for a moment, then flew off.

"Strange. Peculiar behavior. Was that Nidok?" Orram sat down and stared blankly into the water. "We must make no mistake, Tandra," he said. "We must understand what Leyoon is trying to tell us."

"Surely you read something from him earlier, Orram," I suggested.

"I don't think it's possible to read him accurately. Patch contact with great-fish is difficult and confusing. Leyoon and I have tried to communicate directly many times. Our minds are not wired the same. This image-modeling is the only reliable communication we have."

I said nothing, and Orram did not read it in me. My capacity to understand Leyoon's mind had surprised me no less than the clarity of my mind-link with Orram. I wondered why Orram found great-fish thought so difficult.

During the second half of Leyoon's presentation, Orram's alarm grew as the great-fish wove a tangle of weeds about a crude representation of L'orkah. The message soon took form with such precision that it could not be misread: new values were destroying the old; alien mentalities were infecting the ahlork; the Varokian steady state was broken by a deliberate, treasonous attack.

Orram looked for Conn. Would he agree with the interpretation? I scanned the darkened theater, but neither of us could find him.

The performance moved quickly toward a climax. I wondered vaguely why Conn hadn't returned to his seat, and I grew fascinated, then concerned, with Leyoon's increasingly odd twisting and turning, then the rhythmic twitching that traveled through his body.

For a moment he paused in his dance and looked in Orram's direction. His elegant glide back to the Gurahn stopped, and the great-fish drifted downward, flailing helplessly.

When he regained control he worked more feverishly than ever. The speed of the dance accelerated. The model of a remote island took shape quickly.

"The message will soon be complete," Orram told me. "Leyoon is suggesting nothing less than the demise of Varok's second civilization—not through ignorance or greed, but through some corrupt influence, some cancer that will eat at the heart and threaten the soul of Varokian society. If one can get outside of the details, grasp the general drift, the total effect, the message will be obvious."

We waited. *Where was the conclusion, the accusation?* Leyoon's dance had become labored and slow.

Suddenly the great-fish stopped. His long triangular body fought for relief from some indefinable agony, then his fins went limp, and he drifted toward the bottom, dying.

Orram ran to the crystal barrier. The audience rose to their feet or sailed off their perches, watching helplessly as Leyoon settled onto the ocean floor. One of his dimming light-sensors fixed on Orram's face, and I saw my varok startle as he understood some clear message.

The insistent mental whisper that alerted Orram also flooded my mind: "Give voice," it said, and I had an intense sense of Leyoon's focus on Mahntik. "Treason in all of Varok." Leyoon's look was agonized, demanding, pleading—then it grew pale and went blank.

Varoks stood tall and silent, struggling within to contain the denial they wanted to shout. Ellls gave voice with howls of protest, and ahlork circled the globe in confusion, demanding explanations with loud clacking sounds.

Orram clutched at his patches, fighting for control. I managed to hold him to rationality with assurances that we understood Leyoon's accusation, that we would act on it, that I felt the grief for him and could bear it, that we would find answers to Varok's new disease. Together we stared through the crystal into the barren waters as great-fish gathered around Leyoon's body and carried it into the depths of the sea.

The audience slowly left the theater. No great-fish came to us. Reluctantly we walked from the crystal globe, making our way through the deserted perches and moss water-seats and into the cavern entrance, where we expected to find Conn waiting for us.

Conn—at the same time, outside the theater

Conn he lay in the moss beneath the shore-tree, dreaming of Lanoll and soaking up the stillness of the shallow water. Memories of his peculiar exchange with Nidok kept intruding on his thoughts. *What had made him so nervous and Sartak so demanding?* The ahlorks' conversation had something to do with the food gift Nidok held, tightly wrapped in a prehensile wing-tip. *Mahntik's name was mentioned. Strange. But then ahlork are always strange in public, just like ells.* Conn laughed to himself. Leyoon would be furious with him for missing the performance.

From somewhere high in the shore-tree's thick branches, an ilara's song eased into Conn's awareness. It had a calming, mesmerizing effect. Pure and tuneless, the dancing notes of the insectlike bird chased the bothersome questions of his encounter with Nidok into oblivion.

Too bad ahlork don't sing like ilara, Conn mused. *Too bad they aren't as tiny as ilara. Nidok would be a likable fellow if he were six sizes smaller. He's not as paranoid as most ahlork. He doesn't show the disdain for the laws of Varok that lead most ahlork into trouble with the rest of Varokian society.*

With a frenzied beating of tiny wings, the ilara suddenly took flight, leaving its song unfinished.

Conn startled and sat up, and found himself looking into Mahntik's waxen face. "You out hunting ilara, Mahntik?" he growled.

She stiffened with the insult. "I'm sorry I disturbed its song, Conn," she answered with a taut, quick voice. "It may be some time before you hear it again."

Conn felt the explosive intrusion of a paralyzing substance enter the hexagonal meshwork of nerves on his left shoulder.

"Mahntik doesn't think. Conn will be missed," an ahlork whispered close to Conn's hearing. "Go and tell varok Orram, Conn is called to the Forested Sea. An old friend died."

"No, no, you fools." It was Sartak's voice. "Ellls don't pay attention to death. Tell Orram, Conn goes to his old school."

"Come along quickly. Bring the elll." Mahntik's voice.

For a moment Conn struggled against the tough wings of two ahlork, and then his lithe body turned to lead, refusing to obey his desperate commands.

A TRAP LEFT OPEN

Tandra—a moment later, exiting the Great-fish Theater

Gentle elllonian hands led Orram and me through the crowd into the great-fish caverns in the underground theater complex. Conn was nowhere to be seen. As we passed through the lobby we saw a robed figure hurry toward the entrance tunnel.

"Wasn't that Mahntik?" I asked.

"I don't think so." Orram was struggling to contain his grief.

"Get away. You be unlawful," an ahlork croaked at a varokian official standing nearby. "We separated from flock. You violate Pact Between Species."

"Leyoon's life has been taken," the official explained passively. "Your flock should not have flown off. Everyone present in the theater is subject to the investigation of Leyoon's murder."

"Murder?" Orram exclaimed. "Are you sure?" Instinctively he leaned into my mind for support. *There can be no murder, not Leyoon. No one would murder such genius. Such wide vision—*

"You have seen Leyoon die, Orram. We must contain the grief. He would rely on your trust in him. Stay with me." I found his eyes beneath the knitted folds of his brow, and they focused clearly.

"The great-fish are selecting a jury of three varoks to scan the audience," the security official explained. "During intermission Leyoon was given a gift of web berries laced with beryllium."

"Beryllium?" Orram reacted as if he'd been struck, but he stayed in control. "I understand. He was poisoned." His wide hands smoothed back the short silvered hair covering his patches.

"Do you know the elll named Conn?" I asked security. "He should be here somewhere, but we haven't seen him."

"After the performance no one left the cavern but three ahlork," the official said. "Are you all right, sir?" he asked Orram. "Those who have gone irrational with grief are in the varoks' conference room, trying to talk with each other so they can regain control."

"I am rational now, thank you," Orram said. "We must find Conn. Will you put out a call for him? Leyoon was a friend of our family."

"Certainly." The official nodded and left to make the call.

"Conn must have gone somewhere with Nidok and Gitahl," I said.

"Oran Ramahlak, come with me please." Relief was noticeable in the face of the elll who appeared. "I was sent to find you, and your consummate partner. You, Rallan Tahn, and Talorian Omak are chosen to conduct a mind-scan of the audience."

Orram nodded, and we followed the elll to a small conference room designed to facilitate communication between varoks and great-fish at the edge of the sea.

Three great-fish emerged from the deeps into the room's broadly stepped pond furnished with boxes of dark clay. For a moment they swam up and down and along the steps—graceful, furious arcs of smooth muscle and angry light sensors. Then, in haste, they carved symbols from clay to tell Orram that Leyoon's agony had followed a pattern unique to beryllium poisoning. Murder by ahlork was the most likely possibility. Since they mined the ruins, they were the only species with ready access to the element. Leyoon had planned the climax of his performance to accuse Mahnate Tikahn of treason. Leyoon had expected her to attend the performance. She may have anticipated part of his message.

"I did not see her in the audience," Orram signed.

"Sure?" one great-fish asked. "Leyoon planned a surprise accusation. We intended to have her scanned immediately, to reveal her treason."

"How can Mahntik be guilty of treason," Orram argued in great-fish symbols, "so large a breach of law, yet unknown to others?"

"Son Orticon will understand, Orram," the great-fish wrote in symbols. "Contact Free-minds."

"Orticon is on L'orkah for a conference of some kind."

"Find him. Find Conn. They are not here at Leyoon's death."

"Several ahlork and the varok Gitahl are also missing," Orram said. "We have put out an alert for them. One ahlork was called Nidok, an ahlork with a scarred lip. Another had breastplates marked with a necklace of white. He was called Sortak, according to Conn. Most likely they left with Conn just after intermission. They are probably having a verbal wrestling match somewhere on the beaches."

"You will honor Leyoon's wish."

"Yes. I can do nothing else now." Orram reluctantly formed the symbols and moved them into place. "I will be Governor of Living Resources, if the appointment is confirmed."

The great-fish tried to reassure him. "You have seen the imbalances of Earth. You understand what is needed. You will find the errors that have endangered Varok."

Inwardly, Orram groaned, but I saw him accept the challenge and face the facts. Varok's cancer had metastasized.

The dark-period deepened and retreated in the wake of a brilliant auroral display before the two senior varoks and Orram and I rested. Scanning the audience was grueling, unpleasant work that left us longing for sleep.

Most varoks were steeled to lay their minds bare, memories public and private put before the committee, so as to return to their homes as soon as possible, lest their fears overtake their senses. Ellls resented the depth of our intrusion, but they gave us no real trouble. Their minds were a confusion of exotic-hued vision and three-dimensioned echoes, but they gave no hints of foul-play.

The ahlork were just plain difficult, and defensive.

"None of the ahlork we scanned have been involved in a murder scheme," Orram mused, "yet they all suspect that a food gift was responsible for Leyoon's death."

Rallan Tahn agreed. "I found in their minds an association between the murder package and Nidok. Has he been found?"

"No," Talorian Omak answered.

"And where is Conn?" Orram asked.

"He would not leave without telling us," I said.

"The only person we found on the beach was the varok, Mahnate Tikahn," said an elll who stood guard nearby. "She was waiting for friends outside the theater. She did not see the entire performance."

"We had better scan her next."

"I'll get her for you, sir."

"It's too bad the performance stopped," T. Omak said. "Why didn't the other great-fish accuse Mahntik?"

"Because Leyoon did accuse Mahntik of treason," Orram said. "When Tandra and I came to the crystal barrier, Leyoon appeared to be dead, but when I touched the glass near him one fin uncovered two name-syllables that had been prepared for the finale. They were the name-syllables for Mahntik. Tandra heard the name echoed in his dying thoughts. Before we could think what to do, the other great-fish came to Leyoon. They deliberately destroyed the symbols before anyone else could see them."

"But why destroy the symbols? Wouldn't it be important to make the accusation?" Rallan Tahn asked.

"I thought so at first, but now I'm convinced that what the great-fish told us is correct. Leyoon planned his accusation so it would catch Mahntik unaware. The puzzle I must solve is in Leyoon's reasoning. Why did he think that timing was so important? What would be gained by a surprise confrontation?"

Someone is coming, I warned silently.

The door slid open and Mahntik entered, her mind flashing a probe into Orram's. "So Leyoon accuses me of—what, Orram? Of his own murder? Ridiculous." She gathered the rich lengths of her robe about her and moved toward Orram, her pale eyes softening.

"You are grieving for Leyoon, Orram. How is that possible? Most varoks would not be able to carry such a burden and function rationally at the same time."

"You know very well. Tandra is my link between emotion and reason," Orram said.

"A human link? That's impossible." She turned a cold gaze in my direction. "Nonetheless, I object to an alien being present during this mind-scan. You will have to manage on your own."

"I'm sorry, Mahntik. Tandra has full authority to remain. We are one mind."

"Are you indeed? You and this descendant of *animals*?" She used the varokian word for non-verbal species.

"I'll take that as a compliment," I said.

"The great-fish believe that Leyoon was murdered," said Rallan Tahn.

Mahntik ignored the other two varoks and focused on Orram. "I am very sorry you had to lose such a friend, Oran Ramahlak. But I believe that the great-fish are wrong. They are over-dramatizing his death. They over-dramatized the performance. I couldn't stand to sit through so much nonsense, so I took a walk on the beach."

"Did you see Conn out there?" I asked.

"No, I didn't." Mahntik answered with a glimmer of a smile that set me on edge.

"You believe Leyoon could not have died by poisoning?" Orram asked. "The symptoms were specific."

"You see my conviction," Mahntik said, visibly annoyed, but quite rational. "Beryllium takes several days to act. It was not poison that killed Leyoon. Now, if you don't mind, the authorities have kept me long enough. I must return to L'orkah soon. Genes and their host cultures wait for no one. Proceed quickly. Do what you must."

Mahntik stood before Orram, smiling seductively, edging closer than the scan required. "Enjoy your read."

Orram concentrated on her thought and together we found few memories of Leyoon, then nothing but visions of the empty beaches above the theater. *A changing sky, echoing waves.*

"Tell us what business you do with ahlork," I said.

Mahntik whirled to face me, a hateful expression flashing across her thin countenance.

She fears me. Why? We could all see Mahntik's mind was free of guilt. Then her fear subsided. *Echoing waves. My own puzzled expression, then Orram's intent gaze.*

"I know nothing of ahlork," she said cooly, "but I know when I am being subjected to trickery. This alien is distorting the mind-scan. I had hoped for something better for us, Orram, something better than quarreling. The human is not qualified to participate in an official mind-scan. I protest her presence."

"As you like," Orram conceded.

"That is a very beautiful robe you are wearing," I said.

Again the illogical jump took Mahntik by surprise. Orram's immediate scan of her mind revealed little. *A trick? My robe? Yes, chosen to flatter my complexion. Has it wrinkled?*

She looked at me again with disdain, then a strange lilt came into her voice. "It is a very old robe, Tandra. I do very little weaving these days. Please. I would like you to have it, later, of course." Mahntik's smile was obviously forced. "You will all come to L'orkah soon, I hope."

"You are very generous, Mahntik," I said. "I would love to have such a gown and to visit L'orkah."

You are pretending to be a fool.

Orram and I saw the thought as it washed through Mahntik's mind, then her annoyance seemed to fade, and her stony face took on a peculiar, hard set.

Like the slicing of cold steel, I felt the invasion of Mahntik's probe into my thought. I fought to keep my mind blank, but her attention leapt from image to image like an electric shock, dredging up related thoughts and flashes of memory as it went along, quickly giving Mahntik a clearer vision of our suspicions.

Back off, I demanded in thought. She did. Then she pressed deeper, beyond my natural shields. She tore at the core of my emotions, until it took great effort to protect sensitive roots. Gradually, one by one, my poorly developed human defenses fell—the anger at being badly treated on Earth, the frustration that no one would listen, then the guilt at leaving Earth's crises behind for a better life. And Orram. Fear of being too dependent on him. All was raw and exposed.

"Enough," Orram demanded.

"But it is such fun, Orram. There is so much trivia to learn from a human."

With that, my mind flew open, and Mahntik fell headlong into the deep well of my suspicion. The reflection struck too true. She backed off, alarmed and shaken.

Orram saw what had happened. Mahntik feared exposure, but exposure of what?

"Everyone on Vior is concerned with ahlork drunkenness these days." Orram spoke quickly, hoping to catch her unaware, as Leyoon had planned. The two other varoks stood silently, probing Mahntik. "What do you know of the source of the ahlorks' potent web berries and unauthorized crops?"

"I have no knowledge of ahlork," Mahntik said, exhibiting a peculiar relief that didn't escape me. "They must have stolen experimental strains from the genetics lab."

"Why weren't those thefts reported?" Orram asked, probing quickly for signs of evasion.

"But they were reported," Mahntik said with assurance, and her mind turned to paperwork, filed with care. "You will learn that, if you become governor, Orram."

"Tell me then, why you have sent ahlork to every corner of Vior to plant your new strains of web plants." It was a wild guess. Orram saw a quick flash of fear in Mahntik's mind. Then, oddly, the fear dissipated, as if it had been snuffed out.

Had he really seen it? A quick check of the other varoks and my awareness told him we had missed Mahntik's reaction. He searched the corridors of Mahntik's mind again but could find no trace of fear. If it had been a genuine reaction, the fear would still be there somewhere, even though carefully repressed. She couldn't have simply turned it off.

Mahntik read his puzzlement.

"For a moment I was afraid," she explained, "that the ahlork had done something to show contempt for my experimental plots on Vior. They have been approved, Orram. All is in order. The ahlork are testing new strains for the genetics laboratory."

Six young varoks burst into the room. "Do not subject yourself to more of this, Mahnate Tikahn." The speaker's eyes were bright with outrage. "We object to this interrogation, Oran Ramahlak. You have abused the mind-scan. Release this person."

"State the abuse." Orram's face was a mask of quiet dignity. "I have seen no one abused or insulted but this human, Tandra of the Oran-elConn-Grey family."

The six youths moved into the conference room and encircled us. "You have probed from two, sometimes from four directions on two levels. We have heard you make slanderous accusations to evoke emotional breakdown," one youth said. "You have scanned Mahntik's mind under invented pretenses," said another.

"Those who have nothing to hide do not fear the legal mind-probe, nor any variation improvised to evoke accurate memory," Orram said.

Talorian Omak spoke calmly. "In any case, I believe you are now free to go, Mahnate Tikahn."

Mahntik moved toward the entrance. "I will go with these young people and help them understand their mistaken assumptions," she said. "They are confusing privacy with progress." Something about the idea obviously amused her. "I was known as a rebel in my day, Orram, but no traitor. I understand these Free-minds—your son among them—far better than you." She swept from the room, tossing her hair as in triumph. "Come to me when you are ready to study youthful rebellion, Orram."

"You have our full confidence, Orram," the elder varok T. Omak assured us as he and Rallan Tahn left the room. "We will file our supportive account of your interrogation immediately. Something is not right with the way that woman thinks."

When the sound of their retreat faded, Orram sank onto the rock bench of the conference room, exhausted, his mind torn with grief, split with concern for his son and confused impressions of Mahntik, and distracted with worry for Conn.

Tandra—on the Alkahn south

"You know we needn't worry about Conn," I said. "He must have gone into the sea and lost track of time. He'll find us. He'll expect us to go to Ahl Vior to arrange for your office as Governor of Living Resources."

"He knew I would not refuse the great-fish." Orram's fatigue showed in the slouch of his shoulders as we rode past the Vahinorral.

"And surely Orticon will see where the Free-minds are too extreme."

"I'm not sure of that, Tandra."

"They must see that consensus is much easier in a society of open minds. That could be a key reason why the steady-state is possible here, and so difficult on Earth."

"But the Free-minds' philosophy begins by denying their very nature as varoks. Officially, they object to nothing but the deep mind-probe, but unofficially they call mood reading a sin—even while they can hardly restrain their natural impulse to join the minds around them."

"Irrational thinking like that requires an obvious cause to sustain it," I said. "Where there is no room for tolerance or questioning, there is usually a blind spot and some political will furthering some other agenda."

"But what is to be gained? Who stands to profit?"

"I'll bet not many ahlork are involved. They seem too independent—argumentative and wild—to side with varokian rebels."

"So who is responsible for the abundance of new web berries? Who is responsible for the disruption that Leyoon saw? And for his death? Mahntik's mind harbors no guilt. I am so sorry, Tandra. I have brought you from one chaotic planet to another."

"So Varok is less than perfect, Orram. Life everywhere, anywhere, is an unpredictable rat's nest of risk."

"I did not expect these risks, Tandra, not deliberate sabotage. I promised you security here, stability for Shawne's life. You expected some hazard from the ammonia storms, not drunken ahlork and murder. If only Conn—where is he, Tandra? He said he would be right back."

Focus, Orram. "Conn will be home before we get there, but no doubt he will follow his instincts first." I meant it. Conn was ready for a little independence and a lot more water.

"I hope you're right." All the light had left Orram's face. "I don't like it, Tan. He wouldn't leave us, not without telling us."

IV. ABUSIVE MOMENTS

Criticality—
Our lives are vulnerable
to one surge too many, one tide too high,
when we are caught in nested whirlpools.

One abusive moment can drown the belief
that we are okay, after all.

—Conn, on being held captive

THE PRISONER

Conn—the previous light-period

Consciousness seeped through the long deductive channels of Conn's mind like an icy stream, awakening him little by little to pain and dryness. He tried to move his legs, but they were held fast by something hard and cutting. When he discovered that his arms were lashed to his sides, he lurched violently against his bonds, his huge eyes flying open, then narrowing in anger.

An ahlork jumped back, giving a gruff cry of surprise.

"Go and fetch Mahntik, you clatter-plated bird," Conn growled through his drug-induced fog.

He heard the ahlork gurgle with laughter as another injection entered the elll's hip. Cursing and struggling vainly against the intrusion of darkness, Conn forced his eyes to stay open long enough to see that he was in a seacraft similar to those that crossed the Misted Ocean.

As the drugs again wore thin in Conn's brain, he struggled out of nightmare, resenting the loss of life's moments. Like an art movie in slow motion, the blackness filled with Jupiter's orange and brown-yellow stripes. Frantically, he dodged and swerved Tandra's long dark hair, his only guidance system. He must navigate past the magnetosphere, Io's torus, the ion storms of the Red Spot. It was no good. He could not get through to the safety of orbit around Varok.

The vision faded when he remembered Mahntik's voice and the hard touch of ahlork wings lifting him. Surely Mahntik knew that he would soon be missed at Orserah's house.

Conn opened his eyes, realized his arms and legs were free, and flipped onto his stomach in the instinctive escape position of elll. The surface beneath him was hard and smooth. It smelled of old dust.

Slowly the elll rose to his feet. He sensed hollowness beneath them. He walked gingerly, disoriented by the smooth planes, uneasy at the thought of being at an unnatural height in the ruins.

Dryness seared his lungs and made his collapsed gills itch.

On one side of the room a door beckoned. It was unlocked. Cautiously he opened it and stepped onto a forebear's landing platform and into the welcome embrace of a cool, moist wind.

A new light-period. The horizon was growing tall and bright with Jupiter's reflected light and the increasing tempo of long sheets of lightning. Far in the distance Conn could see the long line of Varok's largest inhabited land, Vior, holding steady in an ocean of seething mists. Far below, sharp rocks stood, poised lethally around the base of steep cliffs. He guessed he was standing on an ancient landing platform of the extinct winged forebears of varoks, high in the ruins of Ahlhork on the island continent of Leahnyahorkah.

Quickly he backed off the crumbling platform into the dusty chamber and crossed to the inner door. Its latch refused to yield.

He had not expected the door to be locked. Ahlork were known to play cruel jokes, but not this cruel. There was no water in this room. Ahlork would not leave an elll alone, imprisoned without water.

His temper began to rise but was cut short by the double thud of ahlork footsteps approaching from behind the inner door. He crouched and heard the ultrasonic whine of an antique lock releasing its grip.

When the door slid open, Conn jumped at the ahlork who entered, pinning its tough wings to its sides and forcing it to the floor. With a scream of rage the ahlork tore free, beating its wings and cocking its chitinous plates at a deadly angle. Conn ducked the thrashing edges and dove for the open door, but a second ahlork in the hallway knocked him down. A figure cloaked in dark green stepped into the room.

The door slid shut. Mahntik stood over Conn, scanning his mind. One ahlork hunkered behind her. When she was satisfied with the elll's mood, her eyes took on a more concentrated look and she began a deeper probe into his memory.

"Get out of my mind, Mahntik," Conn said, standing up and irritably brushing the dust from his legs. "I'll tell you anything you want to know in my own words. Your patch reading will put the bits and pieces of my memory into the wrong order. That could be very embarrassing, you know."

"I doubt that I could embarrass you, Conn, and I see that you are too angry and too—"

"drugged—"

"to be of much help right now." Her tone was neither friendly nor hateful, and her beauty had a raw edge to it. Carved of hard stone, crowned with swirls of obsidian and silver, her face was set with eyes like the coldest of pale amethysts.

Conn sank back onto the floor and leaned against the wall. The exertion of attacking the ahlork had made him dizzy. How many light-periods had passed since he was kidnapped from the beach near the Theater of Great-fish? Already his tiles were feeling the ache of dryness.

"Go and get the elll some water," Mahntik said.

The wide-faced carnivore nodded with a flap of his wings, strode out to the landing platform, dove into the turbulent ocean air, and clattered noisily down to the shore.

"I can't take that ammoniated water, you foul lackey," Conn called after him.

"Surely you don't expect him to go all the way back to the genetics labs, Conn. We are busy people here on L'orkah. We don't have time to chase your every whim."

"What is this, Mahntik? An experiment in torturing ellls?"

Mahntik took a few cautionary steps away from the elll as he rose to his feet. "Since you are too angry to be useful," she said, "perhaps you will satisfy my curiosity—for a bowl of fresh water. Have you really left the school to become family with a varok and two human beings? What is Orram to you? I don't understand this mixed family of yours. It must be some kind of bestial perversion."

"Clean up your mind, Mahntik. Love is never a perversion— unless it becomes a demand." Conn saw there was no avoiding her curiosity. "Orram is all those things to me."

"And the human female?"

"Shawne is my daughter, my sponsored egg, the tad I nurture, the joy of my life. When Tandra comes to my water," he said, pressing the advantage of emotion as far as he could, " I am in the deepest of Ellason's deeps. Her warmth is the heart of life itself, and I am aware of awareness when I am near her." While he spoke, he walked up to the varok and cupped her chin in his broad hand, knowing she hated the touch. "Have you ever written any poetry, Mahntik? It's good for the soul."

Mahntik backed away from his hand. "And what can this human creature give to Orram?" she asked. "Surely Orram is not in mental consummation with this human being, as she pretends."

Conn decided that she might as well have it all from him, since she had no scruples. She would take it from him eventually, anyway. "Human beings have no patch organs, but Tandra reads moods easily," he said. "She touches Orram's mind in a way that lets him feel emotion and operate rationally at the same time. The rumors are correct. They are in mental consummation, and I suspect they enjoy their physical union as no two varoks can."

The shocked reaction in Mahntik's eyes made Conn laugh triumphantly at his success in baiting her with a bit of exaggeration. "I am a loner, Mahntik. I know the emotion you're repressing. It's jealousy. You're using me to get to Orram."

"Of course not, you fool."

The disdain in her voice was unmistakable. Conn decided he had made a good guess. "All right, Mahntik, now it's time for you to tell me the real reason I'm here."

Mahntik's pale blue eyes gleamed. "It is not time to tell you anything."

On the platform outside, the ahlork landed, then entered the room with a bowl of water. It reeked of ammonia.

"Thank you," Mahntik said to the ahlork. "Just stir the water, Conn. The ammonia will soon dissipate." She turned to the door and disappeared into the hallway.

"Why are you keeping me here, Mahntik dear?" he shouted after her. The ahlork waiting outside shoved Conn back into the room and locked the door. "Mahntik? Mahntik!"

Conn went out onto the platform and looked at the waves pounding the rocks below. He was exhausted from focusing his mind on Orram so Mahntik wouldn't read his suspicions. "How much does she think I know?" he thought. "I may win some time baiting her with Orram, but it won't last long. I've got to get out of here."

MAHNTIK AND NIDOK

Mahntik—in the Ruins of Ahlork

Mahntik ignored Conn's shouts and hurried to the renovated freight elevator of the tall apartment ruin. "Get in here, you stupid beasts." She spit the command at the two ahlork who lumbered after her.

It startled them, as she intended, and they followed her into the hated enclosure. When the door closed, their salty musk flooded her nostrils. She knew they were watching her for the expected reaction to their scent—a turned upper lip, held breath, perhaps a gasp—so Mahntik smiled at them and breathed deeply. Then she stopped the elevator midway between floors.

The ahlork began to pant with claustrophobia. Their eyes stared at the floor as they tried to control their panic.

"I can probably fix this abominable machine," Mahntik said, looking pointedly at her hand resting on the controls, "but first you must tell me why so many ahlork have been gathering on L'orkah in the northern ruins west of the inland lake, Lo'nahrl."

The ahlork instinctively flexed their wings.

"You can't threaten me in this small space," Mahntik laughed, pulling a knife from the lining of her cloak. "I could slit both your throats while your wings are stuck in half-cock. Certainly you don't mind telling me why your flocks go to the ruins by the lake. We are partners. Have you found rhenium for the warming cloth? The webs have taken up selenium, just as I planned. I need the rhenium. Now."

"Yes. That is it," one ahlork croaked, "Susheen finds rhenium."

"You are lying," Mahntik said coldly, laying the knife at his throat.

"We know nothing," the other ahlork stammered. "You shame us. We don't know. We are not allowed to know. We fly alone and work for you."

Mahntik moved the blade to the ahlork's breast, prying up one of the delicate plates that covered his skin. "Do you mean Sartak has sent me outcasts as guards?"

The two ahlork were frantic. They would be useless in panic. She nudged the elevator control toward descent.

Feeling the sudden movement, the ahlork relaxed, and Mahntik probed their minds deeply for information about the gatherings in the north. To her surprise, she found memory of many young varoks in an underground building.

"What young varoks gather in the northern ruins?" she demanded.

Free-minds. Free-minds are held by ahlork. The proud thought jumped involuntarily into both the ahlorks' minds, along with a vision of the nuclear reactor.

"Thank you very much." A nasty smile spread across Mahntik's face. "Now I can learn the rest first-hand."

The elevator bumped to a stop and the doors opened. As the ahlork rushed out, Mahntik sliced both their necks with one vicious stroke of her knife.

Nidok—in the Ruins of Ahlork

Perched on a broken rail overlooking the sand-heaped lobby of the ruin, Nidok startled as his slaughtered fellows collapsed.

Mahntik looked up, motioned to Nidok, kicked the dying ahlork out of her way, and shouted, "Never again let Sartak send outcasts to me, Nidok. He is mad, if he is trying to keep Free-minds as prisoners."

She beckoned to him, and he flew to her reluctantly. As he followed Mahntik through the ruins, Nidok could barely keep his wing-plates from fluttering.

"You, of course, have more sense than Sartak's outcasts, Nidok," Mahntik said, interrupting his thoughts. "Tell me exactly which ahlork are keeping the Free-minds. Is it Sartak or Susheen's flock? And where are the Free-minds kept?"

"Varoks are held in nuc—," Nidok answered, "in strange place, a ruin under rocks, by the Greater Flock."

What could he do but answer? Acting stupid might help. Nidok was confused. He did not happily ally himself or his flock with this savage varok, yet the flocks could not be split. He hated what Sartak and Susheen were doing with Free-minds and ancient power stations, but the Greater Flock was one; he had to follow its flight. Perhaps Mahntik did not understand ahlork.

Don't think of it, he told himself. *Think first of the ruin we just left. What has Mahntik stored up there? Don't think of foolish experiments with ancient nuclear breeder reactors. Mahntik has not asked the right questions. She will believe that Sartak is keeping free-minds for pure mischief.*

"Why has no rhenium been found yet?" Mahntik asked.

"We survey all ruins of L'orkah," Nidok said. "There is none there. Perhaps Free-minds know of rare minerals mined by forebears."

"Possibly," Mahntik said. She said no more as they trudged on through the ruins, crossing with difficulty the sand dunes filling an ancient corridor between tall buildings.

Nidok longed to fly out of the ruins, but he suspected it would enrage Mahntik to be left behind. He was in no mood to anger her. He decided to lead her to the ancient reactor ruins where the Free-minds were housed, then retreat to his own kin on the cliffs beneath the Ruins of Ahlork.

As they climbed higher, the far-off cries of spawning ilara reached them. The ammonia-tinged flavor of the misted shore air was replaced by fresh breezes off the midland hills. Nidok rolled from foot to foot in a rhythm that mimicked the beating of wings. His forked feet were tough, and his squat body tilted easily from side to side. He felt slow but durable. With some relish, he noticed the exertion of climbing in Mahntik's breathing.

"The ilara feed on web berries before they are ripe," Nidok

complained, feeling bolder.

"Our new strain of berry is so potent you shouldn't need much to make you feel good."

"We don't like to lose our crop."

"Then do something about it," Mahntik commanded.

"Sartak already helps get rid of ilara. He eats eggs."

"Insolent ahlork. Is that why I tolerate you? You are your own beast, Nidok, and my best ally. I may have an interesting job for you. But first, how much farther do we have to go?"

"One kilometer. No more."

"Then stop, will you? I have something very important to tell you."

Landing platforms of all sizes and shapes stuck out from the hollow-eyed ruins like grotesque chipped eyelids. Nidok hated the tall narrow buildings, so he flew to a nearby landing platform to be higher, on a level with the varok.

"I have decided that you will be Conn's jailer," Mahntik said.

So Conn was the captive. Nidok was horrified at the thought. He panicked. *Is Mahntik close enough to read me?*

"Sartak sent me outcasts to guard Conn," Mahntik said. "I will no longer trust him. You understand very well, murderer, why Conn must be held—at least until Leyoon's death is explained and forgotten. We will tell Orram it was an accident, an ahlork contamination problem—Leyoon's death—a mix-up between those flocks that mine minerals and those who harvest web leaves for packaging. Do you understand me? The so-called mistake will be discovered shortly, when Orram arrives."

"Orram?"

"Don't worry, my square-faced friend. As Governor of Living Resources he will come fussing about web bushes. The announcement has been made. Until he is gone, we must keep Conn quiet and imprisoned and wet, but not too wet. And be careful. The elll is very clever. You will find him near the top of the tallest ruin on the southern shore. Here is the key. Swallow it, or whatever you like."

Mahntik laughed, and lost control of her reason for so long, Nidok grew impatient.

"Is it murder to put a complaining old great-fish out of his misery?" Mahntik asked, still not quite rational. "Is it murder to kill foolish outcasts—defrocked ahlork? Of course not. I would remember that, if I were you, Nidok. Lead on now. We will see if Sartak and the Free-minds are of any real use to me, with their nuclear antique."

Nidok rolled on until the ruins opened out and disappeared into the northern hills. He took to the air and landed on the mound concealing the underground structure where the Free-minds were held. On its reinforced tunnel entrance perched Sartak, waiting.

Mahntik called to him, disdainful laughter coloring her voice. "You can't keep secrets from me, Sartak. You can't have the Free-minds all to yourself."

"All to the Greater Flock, varok."

"The Free-minds have called me Savior of Varok. Don't you agree?"

Sartak flexed his wings.

Mahntik laughed. "Together we make a good alliance, Sartak. You needn't be satisfied with web berries and drunken orgies. Now we can be full partners."

"Partners? Flocks don't have partners, except those we choose by capture," Sartak said. "Trade of web products is enough for ahlork, if ilara don't cheat us from berries."

"I will help you with the ilara," Mahntik said. "That is no problem. You can't ally with the Free-minds without my help. They will use you as miners, then they will use the materials you mine to build the defenses of Varok. You will be left with nothing. You know that the Free-minds fear an invasion from Earth, don't you?"

"They be fools."

"Perhaps. But educated fools. They watch Earth and know what might happen there."

Mahntik is good at reminding ahlork of their ignorance, Nidok noted.

"Defenses or no, we will build what we will, you and I. This will happen much faster if we work together. You will see what I mean when I talk to the Free-minds."

Sartak flew off the roof and swept alarmingly close to Mahntik before landing. She stood unflinching as he passed.

"The Free-minds are here, eating." He led Mahntik down the entrance tunnel into a large hall noisy with varoks. The young tinkerers had improvised seats from blocks of rubble and old planks of synthetic material that had not rotted. The smell of raw piscoids and sea-flowers filled the room. Sartak perched on a high landing and pretended to be unconcerned with what Mahntik might say to the Free-minds.

"Welcome to our joint project, Mahntik. Well timed." The young varoks saw at once their chance for a srong ally, and several vied for her attention. "You know our fears are realized, and we are preparing for the worst. Earth is coming alive. The richest humans have banded together to make a space launch. Deep dark will come only two more times before they arrive on Varok and attack."

Nidok had trouble grasping the concept. *Attack? What for? Ilara eggs?*

Already, the excited young varoks were telling Mahntik about the reactor and how it would power their defense. *Proud fools.* Nidok settled himself on a collapsed balcony, where he could hear everything. Mahntik was laughing, promising the Free-minds that she would do all she could for their cause.

Nidok tried to make a logical connection between what he had heard Mahntik tell ahlork and what she was now telling the Free-minds. There was no similarity. He wondered if his memory was faulty. He had never heard a varok say different truths to different persons.

She was telling the Free-minds that Earth was threatening to raid Varok for raw materials, for precious metals, and for their advanced technology. Varok needed to build its defenses. The only way to do this was to build an energy base. Heavy industrial facilities would come next, with unlimited mining and development rights thrown open to competitive bids. The expanded market would no longer be restricted to the locale where products originated. Varok must grow its defenses quickly.

All nonsense, Nidok thought. *What do ahlork have to do with all that? What do we care for mining rights and threats from aliens who are land-locked bipeds?*

"You need to take more information from the Concentrate, my friend." A young varokian voice whispered at Nidok's ear bone.

Nidok had not seen the varok come up behind him, but the scent told him it was the Oran youth, Orticon.

"If you studied Earth you would know what excellent hunters humans are," Orticon said. "Ahlork would give them great sport, I fear. The challenge of hunting a vicious and intelligent aerial beast like you would be irresistible to them. You won't want humans to visit Varok. They are very hungry these days, Nidok. I suggest you continue to help us build Varok's defense."

Orticon gave Nidok a queer feeling. Wasn't he Conn's family? It was all too confusing. "My flock are not traitors," he croaked in Varokian. Then he dove off the balcony and rushed out of the stifling enclosure into the air, terrified that the boy would see guilt in the back of his mind.

THE PUZZLE AT MOUNT NI

Tandra—returning home to the Oran Locale

Reflections of red painted the crest of the Vahinorral and wrapped the valley beneath Mount Ni in a warm glow as we traveled on the Ahlkahn east from Ahl Vior. The quiet hum of the old levi-train lulled us into blessed sleep after our encounter with Mahntik and the Free-minds at the Great-fish Theater.

Shadowed by our concern for Conn, Orram and I awoke from restless sleep, set our lounge sleepers upright, dutifully ate the Ahlkahn's breakfast of ilara eggs and seasoned hoats, and settled into sharing thoughts and impressions of Leyoon's message. Grief for his death covered us like a deadening mist. Our fellow passengers, elllonian students and varokian teachers, were courteous and warm, sympathetic about the demise of the great-fish, but more interested in satisfying their curiosity about Earth.

"We hear the next ship will arrive from Earth before the third deep dark," a young varok said. "Who are these humans? We assume they are friends of EV Science."

Orram was tempted to scan their minds, but they did not invite that familiarity.

"You have not heard the news?"

"Tell us, or may we read you?"

"You're welcome to, sir. Since you communicate with Earth, we thought you would know."

"We have been at the Theater of Great-fish, and sadly occupied with Leyoon's death. We have had no news of Earth in several light-periods."

"A space ship has been launched from the North American continent. A brief announcement was made on some news channels. The ship is coming to Varok." The varoks surrounding us were carefully controlling their anxiety.

"Was there a reason given?"

"The humans sponsoring the trip are sending specialists, people who want to study how we do things here, they say."

"We have not been told of such a trip. I'm sure there has been some misunderstanding." Orram smiled to reassure the crowd. "Earth is dealing with some difficult issues, so surely, humans would not expend a huge amount just to come here. We are already having good conversations by maser about the adjustments they face."

The varoks didn't understand what that meant, so Orram and I spent the rest of the trip explaining the human dependence on debt and growth in paper money, how their prices failed to reflect all of the real costs of production.

Orram and I left the Ahlkahn amidst a surprisingly busy crowd at the Oran Locale station. As we watched the old train pull away, we were caught up in a swirl of activity. A number of daramonts circled the platform confused by the many ells and varoks looking for rides.

Orram was troubled. *What has happened to the quiet, slow, graceful quality of the valley? It now seems more like Ahl Vior.*

As we started the long walk to Orserah's house, Orram contacted Lillan's office for an update. He listened for what seemed a long time then asked her about any notice from Earth about a space launch. Lillan said our contacts there knew only what had been reported in the news—a joint venture by some wealthy people interested in our reports from Varok.

"We'll have to assume they will soon contact us," Orram said. "We may have some examples of steady state failure to show them, I'm afraid."

I was thankful for the open air and wide fields blanketed with earth-clinging plants in every shade of pastel, and skies draped with ever-changing light. The smell of rich earth and new blossoms helped to ease our worry.

"The statistics don't lie, Tan," Orram said, using Varokian to focus his thinking. "Web production is increasing over the entire Mount Ni area. Lillan's data have shown a sudden jump in all populations, even daramonts. If it doesn't stop, Lake Seclusion will be at risk of eutrophication. The only mystery, she says, is the daramonts' eagerness for promises of feeding. Strong stalks or no, the new web fields must not be good at providing fodder. And Leyoon. Why should anyone murder the great-fish for pointing out the obvious, that too much is growing out of control here?"

I saw a hollow sense of dread tear at the center of his being. It wasn't just Leyoon or the lake. The lake would recover when the influx was measured and the population dispersed, or it would gradually fill in and become another meadow. It wasn't just the crowds on the platforms of the Ahlkahn. It wasn't just the growth at Mount Ni. Complex systems, like the society of ells and varoks on Varok, were never static. Unpredictable amplifications of one aspect or another were always erupting, sometimes even going critical and chaotic before re-organizing into new patterns.

"You look haunted, Orram," I said. "Perhaps you should find words for the disquiet you feel."

"The usual checks and balances have failed, Tandra, and I don't understand why. It's the new attitudes that bother me—holding web berries and new cloth more precious—"

More precious than what?

"Ahlork are cultivating web bushes near Mount Ni." As he talked, I could see he couldn't quite believe what he was saying. "Ahlork are hunters, Tan, creatures of the inland seas, scavengers who live in caves, restless spirits ferociously jealous of their free flight. Why would they take up web cultivation? For the berries? Surely, Nidok's drunkenness on the Ahlkahn was just his silly experiment. Normally ahlork eat berries only during their mating festival. The Celebration of Web Fruiting is a highly ritualized period in flock life, dependent on flock-wide hormonal changes. Surely ahlork wouldn't eat a lot of berries out of season—"

"—unless they were addictive." I finished the thought to spare him the grief.

Orram nodded. "I'll ask Lillan to take careful count of the acreage planted by ahlork. We need to see how many flocks are involved without getting them into a flit. Jesse and Killah are at Lake Seclusion, so we will have good information from there. My first priority as Governor of Living Resources must be Leyoon's death. That investigation may have to be undertaken with the kind of subterfuge that is all too common on Earth. Only a varok joined with a human could act like James Bond." He tried a smile as he looked down at me, but his wide shoulders sagged over his long legs. "I hope this isn't as bad as it looks. We may have a long road ahead."

"Then let's watch the sky and the fields as we walk. Tell me about the small plants that grow by the path. They are so beautiful. Let's not miss them. I can hear daramonts thumping and far-off ilara singing. And the mountains are as red as the Sangre de Cristo range above Santa Fe on Earth."

"Conn must be tired of waiting for us." Orram took my hand in his, and we followed the path to Orserah's house, enjoying the moments together.

"Come here, Shawne," we heard Orserah call, "and you will see a surprise coming. Look out over the garden."

Shawne raced to meet us, and I scooped her up and set her into Orram's open arms. "Where's Conn? Where's Conn?" Shawne demanded as we entered the house. "Artellian taught me to swim."

"Conn's not here?" The pallor in Orram's tone matched the chill that ran through me.

"Maybe he found out something about the ahlork flights," I suggested.

Orram agreed. Any less frivolous excuse made no sense.

"Conn is no stranger to Varok," Artellian reminded us, coming down from the pond, "but he has been a stranger to the seas for many years. He will come home when he can, or when he chooses, if he chooses."

I panicked at the thought.

"It could happen, you know," Orram said, cushioning my mind with his own awareness. "Conn is a loner, but his schooling instincts may come unmasked when he swims again in the Forested Sea. It's been a long time."

Too late Orram realized that I had repressed all thought of such a possibility. I loved Conn far too much to let him go.

"You're being ridiculous, Orram," Orserah said. "Conn belongs here. He is gone for some good reason. Now come and eat. You're letting your empty stomachs rule your heads."

When Orserah's garden stew had warmed and regenerated us, we tried to settle down but found ourselves still anxious for Conn's return. The light-period turned to dark as Varok turned away from Jupiter.

Orram could not rest. He and Artellian stationed themselves at the communications desk and began to search, using every device at hand. By maser radio, electronic net and microwave transmission, they quizzed Conn's friends in the Forested Sea and at Ahl Vior, contacted the justice department, alerted the search team at the crisis center, and sent descriptions of him to all three oceans on Varok. No one had seen him since Lanoll left him at the Forested Sea.

At new light, when Shawne went out to the egg-layers' yard to gather their offerings, she spotted two daramonts traveling at high speed across the web fields. "Orram! Ramram! Here comes Conn. Mom, the dar'monts are really leaping!"

Orram cut off the information integrator, and we ran outside.

"That's not Conn. That's Killah and Jesse." I held Shawne close.

She liked the elllonian biologist and the human who had been Conn's first friend on Earth, but her disappointment brought tears.

The elll and the human quickly dismounted and strode into the house.

"I didn't expect you back so soon, Jesse," Orram said, easing the human's pack off his back.

"We thought we had better report here before we moved on," Jesse said. "Killah didn't like what he saw in the Mount Ni area."

"And did you like it?"

"The area around Lake Seclusion is heavily populated—for Varok, I suppose," Jesse said, "like a suburb on the outskirts of an Earth city like Philadelphia."

"There were no web fields on the eastern slopes of Mount Ni," Killah added. "None, Orram. All the old fields there have been abandoned. Many are infested with web suckers. That's why there are fewer daramonts in this valley. Many have migrated southwest of Mount Ni, where the new webs are grown by ahlork."

"The Ahlkahn is still crowded with Mt. Ni traffic," Orram said.

"They say that web products from the shores of Ranarallahn are shipped over Mount Ni to Ahl Vior by a new business involved in all aspects of web production," Jesse continued. "They have plenty of fodder for daramonts and webs for cloth. The web growers say they are within their rights to ship the webs across Ranarnahrl and east over the hills to Lake Seclusion because they are employing ahlork, thereby using less than two hundred transit-energy units in their allotted time period."

"Technically, they may be right," Orram said, "but it is unusual for varoks to rely on ahlork for new cultivation or transport."

"I'm not sure I would," I said.

Orram agreed, and we both thought of Mahntik, the appearance of her cloth throughout the region and her obvious connection to the ahlork. "Is there enough web bush acreage planted to feed the population of daramonts you've described?" Orram asked.

The elll shook his head and settled deep into the wet-seat by the hearth. "We didn't see enough fields there to supply berries to the drunken ahlork roaming the beaches. They must be shipping everything in from farther away."

"How can so many rational varoks and ellls lean so heavily on some obscure ahlork enterprise," I said, "and watch their suppliers go wild on potent fruit?"

Orram took a bowl of food from Orserah, who busied herself serving everyone, like the gracious hostess and mother-of-us-all she was.

"We pointed out the need for a contract," Killah said. "If the ahlork quit, it would be illegal for varoks to transport web products to Lake Seclusion. The energy cost by land or airshuttle is too high. The entire lake community would have to disperse, if the local ahlork culture of the new seed fails."

"Do the lake people understand that?" I asked.

"They don't want to worry about anything, seems to me," Jesse said. "They are ignoring the light-hoppers, whose claim is confirmed. The shores are overgrown with algae and moss. Their shore-lilies are suffering."

"The varoks like these new berries," Killah said. "That's the tail-end of it all. They like the fancy new cloth, too, and they like living by the lake."

"If this kind of thinking continues," I said, "couldn't the people at Lake Seclusion convene a general election to raise the entire population of Varok?"

"They could," Orram said.

Killah rose from the wet-seat and shook his plumes, cooling me with a fine spray of water. "The total population level hasn't been raised in generations. The Lake Seclusion horde could never convene such a vote, much less win it."

"It's within their right to try. What is not their right," said Orram, "is to increase population concentration in their area alone, even if they don't exceed the carrying capacity of the land. That could be happening already, since the consumption per person has gone up so much. The law is clear enough. Before going over to the Mt. Ni area, though, I must go to L'orkah and discover for myself why Leyoon was so intent on accusing Mahntik of treason."

"And Conn?" I asked, looking for confirmation.

"Of course," he said, "the trip will be a chance for me to do some searching of my own."

LOSING TOUCH

Conn—soon after Mahntik appoints Nidok his caretaker

From the landing platform of his apartment prison, Conn stood looking out, his eyes moving listlessly in a face that could no longer smile without pain. The Varokian sky shimmered and blinked with cascades of lightning. Continuous sheets of auroral blues and greens fell from an indefinable height, sending ribbons of light over the shadowed sea below.

Suddenly a flock of ilara rose from the cliffs. Conn found it difficult to focus on them. The channels of his mind felt dull and worn, plugged with the debris of too much time alone, too much time without water.

He imagined his taut skin and cracking muscles wringing out every drop of water to supply his brain with its vital moisture. Only occasionally now did a moment of clarity relieve his growing confusion.

Desperately he hung onto each flash of sanity, no matter how dim. The landing platform was too close; it would be too easy to end life-moments already damaged by desiccation and loneliness. He didn't hear the whine of the elevator nor realize that two ahlork and a varok had entered his small prison, a hated space between dank, rotting walls.

"Talking to yourself, Conn? That's a bad sign." The strange voice startled Conn out of his fantasy.

He whirled away from the landing platform. "You're damn right it's a bad sign. If I don't get into water soon, you'll have a crusty green corpse on your hands."

"Revolting thought."

"Who are you?"

"Gihn Tahlor. Don't you recognize me?"

"I thought so. Gitahl. So you are Mahntik's henchman. Why the hell is Mahntik holding me here?"

"Is Mahntik holding you? Why do you assume that? Perhaps she just wants to satisfy her curiosity." The peculiar vein-like nerves on Gitahl's forehead throbbed with tension.

"You lie easily to someone who can't read your mind. Mahntik is holding me. Her ahlorks turned a key in the door of my favorite apartment hideout here. Maybe she thinks she can bribe Orram—get a favorable deal for some get-rich-quick scheme. Is that it? That would be a new first for Varok. Surely she wouldn't go to all this bother just to find out what ahlork and I have in common."

"I doubt that she would bother with you at all, unless she needed you here. You over-dramatize your importance."

"Someone over-dramatizes it, that's for sure."

"But we have brought you some water. Nidok should be coming soon."

The two ahlork with Gitahl shuffled noisily over to one corner of the room and set out food and water for Conn before they sailed off the landing platform. Conn wondered what they were thinking, taking questionable orders from Gitahl. The varok stood watching them, rudely straining his patches for a glimpse of Conn's deeper thoughts.

Conn fixed Gitahl with a hard black stare and concentrated on his last encounter with Mahntik. "What's Mahntik up to these days, Gitahl," he asked, "besides covering the face of Vior with her new cloth? Why does she insist on looking for loopholes in Varok's excellent laws? She'd do well on Earth." He realized Gitahl was near the brink of anger. He must actually be involved in some grand scheme.

"Before we know it," he pressed further, "she'll be setting up a bank and creating money-making loans, charging interest."

"Why not?" Gitahl asked. "Your nephew—or is he your so-called 'son'—the varok Orticon, believes that varoks will soon pool enough capital to defend themselves against the human invasion and then live as they should, at least as well as humans on Earth."

"At least. Where is Orticon, you eefl egg? Take me to him." Frustration shook Conn's thin frame. He lunged at Gitahl in a fury, but stumbled and slumped back down to the floor as the varok stepped aside.

"You won't find any loopholes, you know," Conn said, hoping to goad the varok into revealing something. "Varokian laws are too old. The loopholes have been tried and sewn tight during a millennium of trial and error. Mahntik isn't that clever."

"The laws work. Do you see why, Shawne?" He reached for the child he saw standing beside him. "One, seven, four, zero, three, one, two. Who will be on Varok for you, little human, when I'm gone? Who will give you comfort?" The elll looked around, confused. Gitahl had disappeared. Another varok had entered the room. "Where did Shawne go? Oh, it's you, Mahntik."

"Take this, you fool." Mahntik threw water on him.

Conn grabbed her wrists. "What is that stuff you're calling water?"

"It's well water. You'd better have some. You're mind's wandering."

Conn's hands encircled her neck. "They'll call this self defense, you know. You can't imprison an elll and expect to keep him alive."

From behind Conn, Gitahl pulled the elll's huge, green, webbed hands off Mahntik.

"You will stay here as long as I need you," Mahntik said, blocking his way as he eased toward the door.

"Why do you need me? Can't you get Orram to bed on your own?"

A slow smile hardened her expression. "A nice idea, Conn," she purred. "I think you've hit on something. Orram needs to learn more respect.

"Oran Ramahlak, Governor of Living Resources," Mahntik continued in a tone syrup-coated and laced with sand. "What do you call him when he's in your water, Conn? He can be so wonderful one moment and so cruel the next. He won't allow me to distribute my new strain of warming cloth to the continent of Vior."

"Not unless you pay your taxes and transportation costs and locale tariffs, my dear," Conn snapped. He was determined to stay on his feet.

"I would make nothing after paying such taxes." Mahntik said.

"Of course. What the hell do you think the taxes are for? You can't spread your cloth all over the planet, even if your ahlork drunks are carrying it. Are you adding up all the real costs of your fine new web?"

Conn's eyes glazed over and he sat down hard on the floor. "It's not a dictated system, Shawne," he said. "Global Varok defines goals and provides incentives and services, expertise and tools, or defines problems, but the locales have to find solutions and make them happen without harming anything. Orram will count things, but he doesn't set the quotas for auction. The depletion rates are subject to revision by popular vote. At any time we could raise the amount of mineral ore we mine, if most people thought we needed more mineral."

Mahntik grabbed a handful of Conn's neck plumes. "Stop preaching, you slimy fool. What exactly did you see and hear at the Theater of Great-fish?"

"Beautiful seas." Conn shook his head. "Clean water to cheer an elll."

"Nonsense." Mahntik smiled. "You talked to Nidok, and you saw me there."

"I saw you there, all right, alone. Orram didn't want to be seen with you; it would compromise his chance to be governor." Conn laughed, in spite of the pain it caused him.

"Fool," Mahntik screamed. "You will live to choke on those words. I hate your foul satire. I know Orram had no intention of being governor before he was forced to it—"

"—by whatever ahlork stench you have anointed yourself with," Conn agreed. He kept his mind on web cloth, berries and ahlork. *But where had Shawnoon gone?*

Mahntik's slim figure flowed back and forth like a piece of wild seaweed; then it crystallized, and a broad silver streak in her sculpted black hair caught like a barbed thorn in Conn's eyes. He rubbed his outer orbs, trying to get the out of his mind. "Tandra's fingers play a melody on my back that is as soothing as a whispered pressure-song at thirty fathoms. Where are you, Sweetwater?"

Mahntik turned away—too abruptly. *Angry? Good. Lose it, baby.* Conn giggled to himself, enjoying the thoughts that came to him in English.

The iron varokian lady was pretending to talk to an ahlork. At the same time, Conn felt her mind-probe mash his brains as it poked around. "You double-minded witch. Where's your common courtesy? Quit reading my mind behind my back. I won't hide anything from you. Pull my brains out by the roots if you like. Just let me out of here. I'm too dry, Mahntik. Where is that water the ahlork left?" He pulled the bowl closer and began wetting the hex-tiles on his torso.

"All right, Conn," Mahntik said, "forget Leyoon." There was a vicious edge to her tone. "Tell me about your dry school, your family. It must be like the nearness of ellls in a school, in a psychological sense. Tell me all about Orram and his human being. Would she really know . . . everything about him?"

"You're nuts. You're obsessed with Orram. Still . . . I like your questions. It would be good to talk about Tandra and Orram." It was the next best thing to being home. "Sure, Mahntik. You should know all about Orram. It might do you some good. His mind is wedded to the sweetest person in this solar system, my soul sister, my comfort when the mud dries in my finger webs, his foundation in thought, my—"

The door slammed shut, and Conn enjoyed a good laugh, until his throat burned.

MAHNTIK'S HOUR

Mahntik—three light-periods later

From the upper story of her stone lodge on L'orkah, Mahntik watched Orram striding swiftly up the winding path from the genetics lab. She knew he had been interrogating the genetics lab staff and production personnel. He had had the decency to warn her—and how nice that he had come alone. Before the last sheets of lightning had left the sky she would have him tied to her in touch, perhaps in mind.

She dusted off the window seat with one of Orlah's shirts, picked up a sticky glass and a plate encrusted with forgotten food, and hurried back to the eating center. She threw out the dishes and looked for something to offer Orram.

No, she decided, nothing to eat. Just web berry juice. Orram should know what wonderful new things were happening to the living resources of Varok.

She hurried to the entry and opened the door before he reached the head of the path. "Welcome to L'orkah, Governor," she called.

"It's interesting . . . to see you so relaxed, Mahntik," Orram said, as he stepped into the atrium. "You know I am not here on pleasant business."

"Yes, of course. Leyoon's murder." Mahntik turned quickly from Orram's gaze and led him back to the hearth room, where she offered him a seat on the low pads surrounding the stone rim of the fireplace.

"We are still looking for Nidok and two other ahlork," Orram said, easing his long frame onto the stones.

"Can it be true that beryllium poisoning was responsible for Leyoon's death?" Mahntik asked. "It must act more quickly in great-fish than in varoks. It makes me wonder if the ahlork who mine beryllium and the web harvesters of L'orkah are squabbling again."

"Perhaps," Orram said shortly. "I have security looking into it. No possibility will be ignored. We are also looking for the varok Gihn Tahlor."

Mahntik's mind-block eased forward. Would Orram recognize the block for what it was? *Impossible. He would never suspect that such a talent existed.*

She let a few old memories of Gitahl sift through, so Orram would have something to read in her mind. *Gitahl had been a good mate. Now he is far too busy with his ahlork, directing the mining of allocated materials from the ruins.* The thought of loneliness spread over her mind, and, behind the block, she enjoyed Orram's hormonal response.

"No, I haven't seen Gitahl," Mahntik said, "and I'm not sure I know this ahlork, Nadok."

"Nidok."

Good. Orram did not see the lie.

"Let's sweeten our unpleasant business with something to carry us through the dark-period, Orram," Mahntik said, throwing off her outer robe as she got up from the hearth.

Underneath the crimson robe of new web cloth, she wore a wrap of finely woven threads in shades of peach and gold. The effect against her dark golden throat and silvered black hair was intended to be stunning. It was not lost on Orram, she noted.

"I have excellent web juice from the new strains here on L'orkah. And I should tell you, Orram, we have discovered a good strain for the selenium-rich fields of the forebears. We will soon have warming cloth here on L'orkah, if I win the bid to mine rhenium from the ruins, and if the ahlork find its source. The quota for rhenium is not sold. Did you know that?"

"I'm not surprised," Orram said. "It is a rare element—once used in metal alloys. The warming cloth was a luxury, even for the forebears. Are you sure you can justify the expense of production? The depletion quota may be no problem, but the energy required to extract the rhenium may exceed your allotment."

"We can expand our photonic processes here at the Genetics Locale to extract the rhenium," Mahntik said as she moved toward the food center. "You realize, of course, that the rhenium warming cloth will save energy that is now used to heat entire buildings."

She returned a moment later, reading Orram's mood. He was all business.

"Of course, the balance of power consumption is the business of the officers of Industrial Energy Allocations." Orram took a bowl of web juice from her tray as Mahntik sat down beside him on the hearth. "I will have to watch the waste output here carefully, however, if you build another photolysis facility. So far the ahlork have kept their mining wastes to a minimum. Your businesses harvesting webs and making cloth—how are you allocating the environmental costs within such low pricing? Transport costs?"

"There are none," she turned her open mind to the numbers in her official ledgers.

"I see. I understand that the valleys of L'orkah are planted with new web in extended plots. Have you had any problem with the web suckers?"

"None at all," Mahntik lied, sipping at her juice. "But then I have little to do with the growing of web bushes."

Orram scanned Mahntik's mind, and she smiled when he nodded, finding no memory of transport or added agricultural management beyond her experimental plots on the island.

"One last question or two, Mahntik," Orram said. "This web juice you're serving me, is it fermented?"

"Aged to perfection. It's quite old. Is it to your taste?"

"It's delicious. It has just enough zing to be pleasant."

"Zing?"

"A human expression, which reminds me. Our contacts on Earth have told us that a group of wealthy businessmen have sent interested students of no-growth economics here to study. Their ship should be arriving in less than three deep darks."

"That is alarming, indeed. I thought that Earth no longer had space travel capability."

"Our contacts were late in learning the details. The project was announced publicly with irritating, uninformative news releases."

"Even more alarming. Perhaps we should consider how to defend ourselves."

"I doubt that will be necessary, Mahntik. We have spoken with the ship and confirmed by telemetry. They are students sent here to study our economy and carry no notable weaponry." Orram changed the subject, his patches alert. "You really shouldn't build new photogenic facilities, but perhaps you can show that your overall investment rate equals the depreciation rate of your capital stock."

"It will all balance beautifully, Orram." Mahntik leaned closer, testing his approach limit. "You may scan my mind more deeply now. I know why you have come here. You want to see for yourself why Leyoon distrusted me. Perhaps you would like to tour L'orkah with me."

His mind is already a little frayed at the edges, Mahntik noted with delight.

"Aren't you a little warm, Orram?" she asked, placing a hand close to his cheek. "I certainly am. That robe was too much. Come with me. I will make you more comfortable." She stood up and slung the crimson robe over her shoulder. "We will start our tour with my house and find a lighter tunic for you along the way."

She led Orram up the broad staircase to the second story hallway, talking brightly all the way, moving her hands over her gown as she gestured. She was already in the sexual mode, ready for touch, and disturbed that he was not. Perhaps the drink had dulled his tactile sense.

I must not be impatient, Mahntik told herself. *He is infatuated with the human being, after all. His sexual mode is linked very strongly to her, if to anyone. I must find the varokian needs she cannot fulfill.*

"This is the best view of the Misted Ocean," she said, swinging into the small room where Orlah kept his few personal belongings. She pulled aside the insulating cover on a tall window overlooking gentle slopes running to the center of L'orkah. "Let's finish our drinks here. Orlah left this tunic for you when he went off to the fields just now. Take your comfort. You can scan my mind here."

Mahntik stretched out on a low couch and pushed three cushions to one end so Orram could sit comfortably beside her. She liked the way the gauze of her dress clung to her body as she moved, painting her figure with changing shades of pale yellow and orange in the darkening auroral light.

Orram was watching her with blurred interest. *The berries' potent work is beginning*, Mahntik laughed to herself behind her mind-block. *Orram is so drunk he doesn't realize that he put the tunic on backwards.* She could keep him in this state for as long as she wanted. She would time the juice carefully—give him more before he realized how much it had affected him.

Orram stood over her, hesitating, openly enjoying the varokian coolness of her seduction.

He sat on the couch and ran a sensitive hand over the length of Mahntik's body, openly enjoying her response. "So, you are quite ready for touch," he murmured. "Yours is a strange, clean mind, Mahntik. Uncluttered. I see you are ready. Gratifying. You are a work of exquisite sensual beauty. I must call Tandra. She will enjoy learning your varokian female ways. It will only take a minute."

As he activated the telecommunicator he wore on his belt, Mahntik got up quickly from the bed-pad. "I forgot to put away the moth cakes, Orram," she called as she ran from the room.

She hurried to the far end of the hall, to Gitahl's full-spectrum receiving and transmitting station, and activated the jamming signal. *Good.* She would have no bestial intrusion into her long-awaited moment with Orram. *Consummation indeed.*

He finished talking and waited for a reply. When none came, he got up slowly and put the communicator back on his belt. "Another time, perhaps," he said.

Mahntik could see the human impressions in Orram's memory. They were hateful to her, and they were now giving him doubts, in spite of his varokian assumptions of open consent.

"Let me get you more to drink, Orram," she said. "Your glass is empty. Then you may scan my mind as long as you please."

In the food center downstairs, Mahntik substituted red hoat wine for her own bowl of web juice, so she wouldn't lose too much control. When she returned with refilled glasses, she found Orram quite relaxed.

"You know that I find you very attractive," Mahntik said, pausing to catch his eye. "Now scan my mind, if you dare."

Their forearms met as Orram swam into Mahntik's strange, clear mind. *He can find no flicker of guilt,* she noted. *Search, Orram, look deeply. There are no memories of Leyoon or web bushes, no memories of business with web producers in every corner of Vior and L'orkah. Only a few innocent memories of the new web strains I have developed, and my patience with Orlah.* She let thoughts of the last two leak through.

Good. Her mind-block was secure. Passion rose within Mahntik and took control. The berry had apparently erased all reservations in Orram. He was as she had always dreamed he could be—thrilling as he towered over her, his eyes kindled with passion in a magnificent, smiling face carved from steel—the ideal of released virility.

"Since you have neglected to read me, I should tell you," he whispered, holding her at arms length, "along with my order to account for your illegal long-distance web cloth and berry distribution, Mahntik, I have directed my offices to evaluate your new strain of web bush for the silage quality of its stems and the potency of its berry. The economists will be checking on your energy use."

Mahntik reared back, furious with the success of his distraction. Orram's smile widened as she searched his mind. "Orram, such games you play! I should throw you out for doubting my mind." She let loose a volley of uncontrolled laughter, admiring his cleverness, but loving even more her own genius with the mind block. The sudden unveiling of his suspicions had not revealed one single damning thought.

NIDOK'S AWAKENING

Nidok—at the reactor, one light-period later

At first Nidok doubted what the Greater Flock might do with a nuclear reactor. Now, with ahlork keeping Free-minds as "prisoners," he was doubly unsure. Ahlork were less than partners with the young varoks. They were at best onlookers. The Free-minds had done most of the work to locate some ancient fuel rods and clean up the turbines, whatever they were. Ahlork knew nothing of such things.

Nidok lumbered after Gitahl through the electrical annex and into the control room bustling with young varoks. Here the walls were covered with long banks of dials, row upon row of electronic switches, screens and keyboards—computerized controls. As much as Sartak and Susheen liked to strut here, flexing their wings, they could never learn to run this place alone.

Ahlork are not technological beings. We took a different turn in evolution aeons ago. We flew high along the hunter's route, while the forebears learned to build their destructive tools.

Nidok stood in one corner of the control room, watching and listening. Orticon was dividing his attention between two data screens, dictating directions by intercom to Free-minds stationed in the mechanical annex. Nearby, Gitahl was arguing with someone. Nidok hung back, listening, waiting for his chance to speak.

"Count it up, Tahlan," Gitahl said to the younger varok who stood stiffly before him. "The mineral resources of this entire planet are well known. If we extract materials to seal those wastes in new canisters, we'll be discovered at the next audit. We are in a state of emergency. Orram's office has confirmed that a space ship is headed our way from Earth. This reactor may be our only hope for defending Varok.

"I'm willing to oversee the mining of a little extra uranium for this plaything of yours, but we'll have no exotic plans to seal up your radioactive trash. The defective fuel rods can go into the Misted Ocean. The fuel pellets are contained in good steel rods that would take another age to rot. In any case, no one would ever notice the contamination if the pellets did spill. The Misted Ocean is too deep and too rotten with ammonia. No one will be taking a swim there, eh?"

"I guess not," the young varok agreed, confusing the Misted Ocean near L'orkah with the Ocean of Deadly Mists to the south.

Suddenly Gitahl turned on Nidok. "Why don't you give yourself up, Nidok? The authorities are after you for killing Leyoon."

"I killed no one," Nidok said.

"Oh?" Gitahl laughed. "I saw you flying around with a package for Leyoon. I know my ahlork."

"I fly away with such packages."

"You would accuse another flock leader of murder?"

"I am no traitor to ahlork."

Gitahl laughed again. It was a mirthless, cruel sound.

"Now," he said, turning back to the young varok, "get rid of those fuel rods before we all bake in their gamma rays."

"Yes *aenahl*," the varok said. He turned quickly and stumbled over Nidok.

"Watch out," the boy cried angrily as he regained his footing. "Tahnor," he called to another Free-mind. "Keep these blasted ahlork out of the control room."

Nidok watched him disappear into the maze of computers and reactor controls. He was not surprised by the boy's tone; he had nearly gone over his cliff. Gitahl had added panic to the boy's irritation. The ahlork were being tolerated for Mahntik's sake. The Free-mind varoks chose to be here. They were not prisoners at all. And now they feared Earth coming here? At least ahlork needn't worry about those land-locked bipeds.

The whole reactor situation was a farce, a rotten ilara egg with no hatchling inside. *The Greater Flock is being used and shamed in the poor usage. Had it been Mahntik's idea to stage the kidnapping of varoks by the Greater Flock?* Ahlork were neither farmers nor reactor technicians, certainly not captors capable of holding varoks hostage. *For what?* Sartak and Susheen had led the flocks of L'orkah into an unnatural alliance with Mahntik. It would bring nothing but grief to his kind.

"What do you need, Nidok?" Gitahl's tone was honest, not condescending.

"Wells are too dry too often," the ahlork said carefully. "We do not water new web fields often enough. Plant food burns plants. We need more water."

Nidok recoiled as Gitahl read his mind. The ahlork hated it. He felt degraded.

"All right," Gitahl said. "I see we have a real problem here. We have taken too much water for this reactor project. I'll talk to Mahntik. We can drill a few more wells. Yes, that's what we'd better do. Orram will be watching water levels here very closely, now that he has seen Mahntik's new fields. He is a dangerous person, Nidok. Remember that."

Nidok nodded and backed quickly out of the control room.

"How is your prisoner?" Gitahl called after him. "Mahntik tells me you'd better keep him good and wet, unless you want another murder to your credit." His laughing made a horrible echo.

Nidok had tottered far down the long underground corridor before he realized a varok was overtaking him. He backed against the wall, expecting to be passed. Instead, he found himself pinned to the wall by the Oran family varok, Orticon.

"Who is your prisoner, Nidok?" the varok asked. "Should I know? Who is your prisoner?"

"Gitahl makes jokes to shame ahlork."

"Not this time. There is a call out for the elll, Conn. Who is your prisoner, Nidok?"

Nidok became suspicious. Wasn't this the rebellious son of Orram—the defiler of his sire's nest, a Free-mind?

"I have no prisoner you care about," the ahlork said. He hoped the boy would honor the Free-mind code and not scan his mind. Quickly, before his chitinous plates began to rattle uncontrollably, he galloped from the building and took to the air.

V. Renewals

Our minds are the most complex objects in the universe,
with far more connections than anything else known.

So why are they so hard to change?

You'd think they would self-organize whenever
they came across some new information.

—Oran Ramahlak (Orram)

ELLL AND AHLORK

Nidok—at the Ruins of Ahlork

Several light-periods passed, and no one came near the elll but Nidok. He did not like the way Conn looked. "Your eyes are ugly green smudges. Your dark half-moons in center have no sharp edges. Can you see my tile hairs? I bring you the best water I find. I think it is never enough."

"You got that right, Nidok. Now take a closer look at your boss, Mahntik. Why do you let her use you? Has she got something on you? Talk to me, Clatter-plates."

Nidok did not understand Mahntik. Why did she talk to Free-minds about Earth? Earth means nothing to Varok. Obviously, Conn had been kidnapped to keep him quiet about Mahntik's part in Leyoon's murder. Why would she say Conn would lead Orram to Sartak's reactor? *Is it Sartak's reactor? Not really. It is run by Free-minds.*

The ahlork was certain of many other things. He hated Mahntik, her treatment of Conn, the killing she had ordered, and the killing she had done. Considering the future, if she did betray the ahlork at the nuclear reactor, it wouldn't hurt the Greater Flock. They would fly away, too ignorant to be held accountable. Only the Free-minds would be caught there, producing illegal power for what? For defending against Earth? Or for making Mahntik's fancy rhenium web cloth?

Conn—another light-period later

Conn had moved to the coolest corner of his apartment prison. The fine moss of his skin was dry and cracked. Some had flaked off.

One light-period, the elll watched a flock of ilara head out across the ocean toward the web fields of Vior, lightning flashing off their reflecting feathers.

"Look at that sparkling sapphire necklace, Shawne." The elll drew the child's form close in his arms. "It must be a new constellation. The sky twinkles with one hundred billion stars, in patterns the ellls call Letters of Great-fish. I wish you could see them. There are too many stars, too far in the deep infrared for your eyes.

"There is too much we can't share, Shawnoon. You can't know the sonar signals of ellls. You have no pressure sensitivity. You'll never hear my ultrasonic shouts that paint a map of the warm deeps of Ellason. You'll never know the all-enclosing pressure of those deeps. I wish you could see the brilliant flashes of life in the blackness of Ellason's waters. Hundreds of light-decorated species dodge each other, back and forth, all over, here and gone.You'll never feel the gentle tapping over the plates of my body that tells me who is near—like Lanoll—or Tandra." He wept dry tears.

Nidok—soon after

Too many light-periods passed before Gitahl and Mahntik finally met Nidok on the wind-swept patio by the tall ruin where Conn was held prisoner, as per his request.

Were the varoks afraid to probe too deeply? Usually they read Nidok's thoughts as their first business with him. Now, they avoided seeing his memory, seeing that the elll could be very ill from being out of water so long.

They complained half-heartedly that Sartak and the Free-minds were demanding all of their time at the reactor. *Excuses! To an ahlork.* Nidok enjoyed his moment, but quickly snuffed it out.

The elevator whined and closed in on them, then finally released them. All three were relieved to find Conn standing on the landing platform. Though the moss of his skin-tiles was a sickly gray and his eyes bulged horribly, he was apparently surviving.

"We will finish our business quickly now, Conn," Mahntik said.

He turned and stared at them through the open archway.

"Just answer a few questions for me."

Conn said nothing. Many heartbeats later he began to speak.

"Come to me, Shawne. Let me tell you a story of how it all began. I'll tell you the Song of Time and Beginnings."

He began to quote the varoks' creation story:

Suddenly—
As if the thought were too powerful
Or the yearning for beauty too great—
There was Existence:
A violent, seething mass of all that would create
Time, becoming.
Existence emerged from—

"Stop it, Conn." Mahntik was not buying his madness. "Wake up. We're here to help you."

More lies, Nidok noted. *How can she do that?*

Conn's voice cracked with each phrase, but he didn't pause:

—from nothing,
The force of Being undaunted.

The violence of that becoming
Threw All-that-was into vast clouds of hydrogen,
Mushrooming silently into the void,
Swirling and spinning—

"Stop it, I say." Mahntik turned to Gitahl and talked too quietly for Nidok to hear.

Conn went on and on:

—and tossing up eddies a million years across.
Protons fused, whirling, shaping matter's embryo,
Then flew alone to fuse again far into space—
Pulling in and growing hotter,
Until gravity was at last denied by forces greater.

Thus came Sol out of Existence,
A small star riding on the rim of a far-seen pattern,
People of Earth would one day call Milky Way—
One of one hundred twenty billion galaxies—but
much more.

"I made up that last verse for you, Shawne," Conn interjected, "and there is more—but I can't remember . . ."

"Snap out of it, Conn." Mahntik controlled her rage with great effort.

"You have kept him too long, I say," Gitahl whispered. "He is dangerously ill from desiccation."

"Nonsense," Mahntik declared. "Ellls are clever at winning sympathy. Nidok will kill him with stupidity soon enough—then he won't worry any of us, including ahlork who throw packages to great-fish. Isn't that correct, Nidok?"

Terrified, he gave a shiver that rattled his plates.

"We had better take Conn to the lake, Mahntik," Gitahl said. "He is only half sane. He must be in water very soon, or he will die." The varok moved toward Conn as if to help him, but the elll turned away. His eyes glazed over again.

"You know, Shawne, this . . . woman, Mahntik, is a good example of why important decisions on Varok are left to individuals and local communities. Can you imagine what a dictator she would make?"

His huge eyes wandered around in his tattered green head like something lost, searching for water. Then he crumpled onto the floor.

Nidok waited while Mahntik urged a protesting Gitahl through the open door and the two disappeared into the elevator. He was barely able to quiet his quivering trunk plates. Quickly, he locked the door to Conn's apartment from the inside and stared with anxious eyes at the elll, still curled up on the floor, asleep or unconscious. Then he took off from the landing platform with a frantic beating of his plated wings.

Conn—moments later

Conn crouched in the coolest corner of his apartment prison, no longer waiting for water or longing for home. He could not lie down to rest, for the pressure sent waves of agony through his tiles. He waited for the next dream to begin, wanting nothing but freedom from his waking nightmare.

Finally his mind found relief. He was in the Forested Sea. His legs moved easily up and down in the cool, rich water, sending his broad, webbed feet into a relaxed thrash. With the short leathery fin along his back fully extended, he pulled his arms to his sides and shot through the water like a slim green porpoise, building up speed as he dove. Then he angled sharply upward and broke the surface, leaping over a large patch of weeds that shimmered in the last light of Varok's short day.

On the beach, Shawne screamed and began to call: "Conn. Conn. Connconnconn!"

An ahlork rose into the air and yelped with glee when he saw Conn coming to the rescue. "Munch, crunch, good lunch you've packed your fleshy human baby."

Shawne met Conn in the warm shallows, and they sat in the mud together, watching the ahlork fly off. "If anyone could make friends with an ahlork, it would be you, Shawnoon," Conn said.

"He was nice to me at first, Conn," Shawne said. Her words triggered her tears, and she cried heartily in Conn's arms.

He sent an ultrasonic greeting into the water. Calling the school reawakened his yearning for Lanoll. Or not Lanoll. No. It was Tandra he missed. She had awakened his need to be loved for himself. He must get home soon, to tell her that.

"Can you find your Conn, New Life?" Some ellls called to Shawne.

"Of course I know my Conn," she answered breathlessly. "He is the only loner here besides Lanoll, and he has red and yellow picture plumes on his head."

"You know ellls well indeed," someone exclaimed. "Your tad is thoroughly wet through, Conn."

"Not with this water, she isn't. It's too blamed dry!" Conn shouted.

Nidok burst into the room from the landing platform. "Quiet! Quiet! Quiet your green tongue, elll." he rasped.

"I'm dead already, Nidok," Conn murmured, as he grasped at a fading image of Lanoll swimming by.

"Hush. Does water quiet ellls? You have water—soon! Only quiet. Quiet. Now eat these. I tell you a joke to help you live. More humans will be coming to Varok. Soon."

"That's pure kaehl pucky, Nidok. Shawne, where are you? Shawne, Earth couldn't sail a solar balloon to the moon, the way things are going there."

"Nice poem, elll-brain. Now quiet. Eat these."

He placed six leathery ilara eggs beside Conn.

"What are these? More ilara eggs?"

"Eat them," Nidok demanded. "We have too many. Ilara destroy berry crops."

"Berry crops?" Conn hooted. "You won't have web bushes very long if you eat up all their berries."

"Quiet! Quiet! I get mad with anger, like Mahntik. I get you more water now."

The ahlork hurried away into the air, and Conn eased slowly outside, onto the platform. He moved as close to the edge as he dared and stared at the rocks far below. He could see Nidok gathering foul water. Further down the shore someone was walking among the rocks. There. Something moved between two huge boulders. Conn strained his eyes, cursing the fact that they were not designed for long distances in air. Flashes of blue (a cool shade to his infrared vision) then a brief shimmer of green (elll color) when a brilliant sheet of lightning lit the lower shore. Ellls, with varoks, working in the Misted Ocean. Perhaps they were looking for him.

How much time had passed? Certainly he was missed at home. Why was he waiting here so long? Maybe he was late, and Orram and Tandra were looking for him. He couldn't remember why he was up so high, waiting for an ahlork.

He groaned aloud with the torture of full awareness. His family must be suffering. Orserah would miss him, and Orram needed him, needed to know something about Mahntik. Tandra—he must get back to her and engage her in his mating with Lanoll.

Ignoring the pain, Conn tore a handful of plumes from his head and selected the two he prized most. Both were a delicate green color, uniquely decorated with patterns in red and yellow. He pulled a long frond from his left hip and tied the plumes together with a human-style bow. Tandra would recognize the plumes, and the bow would tell her that he was still alive. He threw the plumes out into the misted ocean air and watched them sink to the rocks far below.

"What now?" Nidok landed heavily. He urged Conn back into the room with a taloned foot, then dabbed water over him with cupped wing tips. Whenever they brushed him, Conn winced. Realizing that the ahlork was trying very hard to be careful, he sat down and relaxed under Nidok's clumsy touch.

"You know," Conn said after a time, "you don't have to go along with Mahntik's wild ideas. I wouldn't trust her." Conn caught the neutral black beads of Nidok's eyes holding steadily on his own.

The ahlork said nothing.

"You ahlork mine the ruins without disrupting anything. Your flocks know what's useful and what's trash. Mahntik is a throwback to the over-blown days of the forebears; she's an anachronism."

Nidok stopped his work hydrating the elll to listen.

"What do you think Leyoon's performance was all about?" He struggled to hold on to the lucid moment. "If you ahlork side with Mahntik and go for the big market, you'll lose your mining contracts and your prestige. You'll lose, just like the forebears lost. Already you're eating ilara eggs to save your berries. Don't you realize that the ilara flocks are what keep the web suckers under control?" Conn's throat was on fire with pushing so much dry air past his water-starved tissues.

Nidok poured the last of the water over Conn's head. The elll moved to speak again, hoping to get through to the ahlork before the visions returned. Just then Sartak landed on the platform outside. The necklace-trimmed ahlork grunted and clacked as he moved quickly over to look at Conn, then he turned around and headed out again.

Before Sartak could fly, Nidok called after him, "Ignore me and I break your wings."

"He's no use," Sartak said, nodding toward Conn. "You waste time. I need help at genetics lab. We sort cultures and fly past Mahntik."

"What cultures?" Nidok asked.

"Germs are best to tell varokians an ahlork story."

"You are talking riddles," Nidok said. "Where is the insult?"

"No insult. No word games," Sartak said. He laughed with a mean rattle in his throat. "Nuclear keeps young varoks busy. Germs are much easier, much better. We threaten, and we use germs to threaten more. We begin the new age of ahlork."

"Good God." Conn groaned. "Threaten what? Why?"

"Soon the Greater Flock will cover all Varok with new web berries."

"You're crazy," Conn croaked painfully. "Berries and germs?"

"You are dead, elll, I see that," Sartak sneered. "No worry here for you. Give him no more water, Nidok. I order you. Gather your flock, harvest the webs of Mount Ni, replace with selenium webs. Warming cloth is soon woven beneath Mount Ni, by our varoks, not Mahntik's."

"Mahntik has textile factories at Mount Ni?" Conn snapped fully alert. "And you will take them over by threatening her employees with germs? You'll all die of wing tip crust before you get any cultures out of the genetics lab." Conn managed the sentence before he was overcome with a painful fit of coughing.

"Be quiet, elll," Sartak said. "Your mouth spits nonsense. Eyes are unclear. Gills shrivel from lack of sleep in water. Why don't you end your life-moments? They be no longer worth living."

"I'll decide that," Conn whispered hoarsely.

"He is better after water," Nidok said.

"Water is wasted now," Sartak cried, kicking over the empty bowl. "Go, Nidok, or I call you traitor. Plant selenium webs for Mount Ni looms. You have no time for ellls."

"We can't do germs. Berries are enough. Leave lab to Mahntik."

"I leave nothing to Mahntik. Not when Varok belongs to ahlork by breaking vials of germs." Sartak sneered at Nidok with a turned lip. "We took varoks and held them. Soon we make them make electricity."

"Ahlork don't need electricity," Nidok grumbled.

"This is new age for ahlork," Sartak stormed. "Do not argue. Deliver your new webs seed. Forget this elll. Mahntik uses you too well. Show your face near this elll again and you are traitor to the Greater Flock." With that, Sartak dove off the landing platform.

With a great effort, Conn reached out to Nidok. "You've got to stop Sartak. Mahntik could have some pretty diseases in her lab—ahlork diseases. Sartak could ruin every life on Var-ok-k—" The elll choked as his throat caved in on itself. Fire and ice cut off his lungs. He could take in no more air. He felt his nostrils flare as his gills opened and closed, stretching desperately for water. He grasped his throat, trying to force away the terrible rawness.

Nidok retreated in terror, unable to decide what to do.

"You're not stupid, Nidok," Conn gasped. "Help me, you clatter-plated bird. Help me!"

ORTICON RECONSIDERS

Orticon—the same light-period, on L'orkah

Orticon felt ridiculously young in Mahntik's presence. She exuded a sexual challenge wherever she went, even here in the reactor control room, dressed for work, supposedly, in a fitted jump suit.

He sat across from her, sharing a quick meal, when suddenly she leaned over their improvised table in the reactor control room as if to confide something.

"As long as the ahlork think they are full partners, they will cooperate," she said in a tone hinting urgency. "Our economic base must be established before we put them back in their place. Meanwhile, the photonic hydrogen reserves we are producing will help us mine the rhenium and keep the web fields healthy. We will soon convert to chemical fertilizers and pesticides to ensure better crops and more frequent harvests. The new web strain has been approved for universal distribution."

"It has?" Orticon was amazed. He had thought the problems in the new strain outweighed any benefit.

"Our profits from the warming cloth should provide enough working capital to build up a respectable militia in time to meet Earth's ship. Isn't that what you Free-minds propose?"

Orticon put down the dried ilara meat he was eating. "Earth should see what we can accomplish, if we are to meet their challenges."

"The only way we can expect to draw all of Varok to the cause is to demonstrate how a truly free society defends itself."

"How can we be sure Earth is a threat? Orram thinks they are too weakened by their geopolitical problems."

"That's why Earth is attacking now," Mahntik said. "I have seen the evidence at the Concentrate. Humans hate us for leaving them without aide. They are likely to do anything, now that their water wars have started up again. Didn't Orram tell you?"

"My father has said that any talk about danger from Earth is nonsense," Orticon said. "They no longer have the wherewithal to mine their own moon."

"Orram is joined in mind with a human now; he no longer cares for Varok. We must build our energy base very quickly. The Earth ship will be here when Varok has been in Jupiter's shadow only two more times—two deep darks, Oriton. That is barely enough time for an ilara chick to lay its first egg. After this threat from Earth is gone and the steady-state has blossomed into rapid growth for all Varok, heavy industrial development will follow. Mining free from quota limits will be thrown open to competitive bids. We will rebuild the ruins and enjoy the rights that come with owning our own land—doing with it as we choose, as we need. The defense of Varok will then come more easily."

Orticon studied the strange light blue of Mahntik's eyes. *How can she contradict herself so easily? There would never be enough capital to build a defense base after rebuilding the ruins. Did she just call Orram a traitor? What does Orlah think of all this?*

"Don't worry about your uncle, Orticon." Mahntik was reading him. "Orlah does as I wish. He is my dependent, I am sorry to say. He does the Oran family no honor. I will care for him, but he does need your help."

She smiled so strangely that Orticon instinctively looked into her mind. There he found a vivid memory of his father, Orram, an intimate memory, that chilled his mood. Then it was gone.

Startled by the memory's disappearance, he probed deeper.

Mahntik laughed. It was a cold sound. Then she got up from the table. "Free-mind indeed," she chided.

CLOSE ENCOUNTERS

Tandra—at the Oran Locale, the next light-period

"It has been too long," Orram told me as we woke to a new light-period. "The security teams have been searching for Conn for too many light-periods. There is no sign of him, not even in the Forested Sea."

We had just risen and settled into the worn ironwood root benches that framed the front porch when Orserah appeared with a young varok. He looked like a human boy of twelve, so was probably just over one Jovian year. Both he and Orserah were carrying sacks of fruit.

"Forgive me, Arlahn," said Orserah, "I need to tend to my family. Take your fair share of eggs from the pen. Remember that I've changed my order. Charge me with twice my normal supply of fruit and hoats."

The boy looked uneasy. "I'm sorry we can no longer barter for your webs, Oran Mother," he said, trying and failing not to look at me with curiosity. "The new cloth is softer; all the new fashions use it. And the berries are quite valuable."

"Just be careful of those new berries, Arlahn," Orserah said. "I suspect some unconscionable monster has engineered them to be addictive. Harrahn's old web genes have served us well for generations. They will continue to do very well for us. Now run off home before I go irrational."

The boy ran to the edge of the garden, where he jumped on a single wheeler and rode off.

"He forgot his eggs," Orserah snorted. "Now I'll have to deliver them. I just hope the layers can supply enough. None for breakfast, Orram. I'm so sorry, Tandra. We may be forced to convert our fields to the web seed the ahlork have been peddling."

Orram was not amused. "Mother, you know we will not convert to the unapproved web. The new strain needs more work or a hybrid alternative. In any case, Living Resources can't allow locale economies to be disrupted by cloth transported from far away."

"You will have your work to do, Orram, my dear son. Leyoon died for these web problems, and now Conn is lost. Please be careful. You should not have gone to this Mahntik person." Orserah was breaking down, going irrational with frustration. Orram took the bag of fruit from her and guided her to an ironwood bench, where he found her mind and brought her back from the fragile cliff edge of her emotion.

She recovered quickly. "Now," she said, "Concerning Conn. We can't let our fears destroy us. There is nothing to do but wait for news from the security forces. Many ellls, varoks and ahlork are searching in the deepest natural weed traps of the inland seas. When they think to look in the shallows of the more comfortable beaches, where the females play in thick tasty moss, he will be found. Meanwhile, you must concentrate on your work."

"You ask the impossible," Orram said, but he retreated to his desk to call Killah and Jesse at Lake Seclusion. "While you search for Conn, you had better survey all registered web crops near Mount Ni and L'orkah. Mahntik and I may both be victims of some ahlork chicanery."

"We'll be off then," Killah agreed. "I'll feel much better looking for Conn myself, while we do the field work."

No sooner had Orram signed off when Orserah came in from the garden to announce the arrival of a visitor.

A blue-plumed elll rode directly to the porch where I stood waiting.

"I am Lanoll," she said.

My hand spiraled up in greeting, but a hard knot formed in my stomach. The elll's smooth green face was very beautiful. The wide mouth and delicately gill-slatted nose of her face were framed with tiny blue plumes. She smiled, but her great black eyes swam with agony and the fringe of plumes on her forehead was knotted with tension.

"Conn has not been found." Her voice quavered.

Orram left his office to join us.

"I don't understand why Conn didn't go to the Forested Sea," Lanoll told the varok.

"Do you know why he was expected there?" Orram asked.

"A message came from an ahlork with a large scar on his greater lip. The varoks at the theater remember him well."

"Nidok," I said. "The same ahlork that bothered us on the Ahlkahn."

"Yes. Nidok. And he was very angry or upset; it is hard to tell which. That is why I came here. When I heard about the ahlork with the scarred lip, I felt we could find Conn. I believe he has kidnapped him, Orram."

Orserah joined us with the elll Artellian close beside her. "But Conn is respected by ahlork. He has a rare skill for trading insults with them."

"Are you sure he's not in the Forested Sea?" I asked.

Lanoll tucked in her backfin and sat beside Orserah on the porch steps. "As a double check, we sent a tracer signal over the ultrasonic network and asked the schools to check all the beaches, the deepest natural weed traps, and the more treacherous ruins—but I am sure Conn would have come directly to me, if he were anywhere in the Forested Sea."

"You are a loner, aren't you, Lanoll?" Artellian asked. "Do you need time for adjustment to Conn's absence?"

"No." Lanoll took a moment to be sure. "I couldn't adjust now, not until we know—I feel sure that he is still alive. He must be. We were so well bonded, sure that our lives together would be all the school we would ever need."

The certainty in Lanoll's voice drove at the knot in my stomach.

Not jealousy, Tandra. Orram spoke to me in thought, knowing my mind. *Lanoll is Conn's mate. You are his family. He can encompass both of you.*

I struggled to focus the sadness I felt. *Help me, Orram. I could lose him.* Orram held firm. *Conn would never allow such a loss, and neither would you. Neither would I, though it took all our lives to work it out. If you will accept Lanoll, you will be absorbing a part of Conn that was denied you before this.*

The thought helped. I felt the knot begin to loosen its grip as I relaxed more into Orram's awareness, releasing the deeper fear I had avoided.

"You feel Conn is in serious danger?" I asked. "I hear it in your voice, Lanoll."

"Yes. The great-fish have told us not to trust the ahlork. They are in transition—bedeviled by some new awareness. Perhaps Conn trusted them too much."

"We are watching all new patterns of behavior in the ahlork," Orram assured her.

"It may be getting more complicated, Orram," Lanoll said. "The Office of Mineral Resources reports that Mahntik has bid on all the remaining rhenium depletion quotas for warming cloth."

Orram nodded. "We'll ask her to sell back any excess mining rights. She won't need them all. Her fields on L'orkah are not large."

"Another thing. Ahlork have been seen throwing waste into the Misted Ocean."

"Any details?"

"The ahlork wore coverings, and they were handling broken containers with tools, as if they were hot."

"Peculiar. The ahlork don't wear cloth, and they rarely use tools."

"Some ahlork at Va Ahlean have taken to wearing capes lately, but the report said these ahlork were wearing protective clothing."

"It makes one think they were handling something contaminated or poisonous," Artellian offered. "Leyoon warned us. The ahlork are involved in some real mischief this time, Orram."

I grew more alarmed. "If Conn discovered it, they might have killed him."

"I think not." Orram's certainty was some comfort. "The ahlork are only roughly civilized, but they don't do real violence."

"They might hold Conn, though," Lanoll argued, "if he knew anything that would shame the flock."

"Or if he knew anything about Leyoon's murder." My human experience suggested the worst.

"There is nothing more we can do for now," Orram said. "The ahlork caves and ruins are being searched, not only for Conn, but for the ahlork Sartak and Nidok as well."

"One last thing." Lanoll grew calmer as she concentrated on business. "A peculiar brightness has been noted in the bioluminescent mosses of the Unbounded Sea. The labs have found it is due to high concentrations of strontium. Do you have any specific directions, Orram?"

"Only to trace the strontium, of course, and do let us know when you hear anything about Conn."

Lanoll—one light-period later, on the southern shore of L'orkah

Beneath the ruins, Lanoll joined the twenty varoks and ellls trying to retrieve radioactive wastes thrown by ahlork into the Misted Ocean. Studies with acoustic holography showed the ocean precipice to be strewn with long metal containers, some irregular or broken. Lanoll considered it likely that they were partly filled with tablets of uranium dioxide and crude plutonium oxide. When she reported to Orram from L'orkah, Artellian joined the discussion.

"Where could ahlork have found that nuclear fuel, Artellian?" Lanoll asked. "Was there an ancient nuclear power plant on L'orkah?"

"Yes, I believe so."

"At least the ahlork had sense enough to realize they were getting into something risky."

"Officially, the supervision of ahlork mining on L'orkah is done by Gihn Tahlor," Orram said, "but Gitahl is not answering his calls."

"I haven't heard anything of him, Orram," Lanoll said. "I'll continue to help here, and to look for signs of Conn." She signed off, feeling less hopeful.

She moistened her wet-sweater with seawater, donned a mask, hood and protective clothing, and joined the varoks working on land, stacking fuel rods brought up by diving ells.

Lanoll found the retrieval work grueling, tiresome and diffi-cult. Time and time again the recovery crews, swinging from hov-ering airshuttles, descended into the deadly mist, struggling with grappling hooks and electronic detectors in cumbersome suits. Now, just as Lanoll took her turn in the air, ahlork appeared.

Lanoll saw them swirling around the airshuttles as if they were mad. They had little chance of damaging a shuttle, but they were distracting the crews and endangering the workers suspended in the mists.

In full fury, Lanoll screamed at the ahlork and came at them with a grappling hook. A storm of crackling wing-plates closed in on her, forcing her to the ground. A sharp tug pulled her over and an ahlork flew off with her helmet and hook.

"Come back, you devil," she hollered, scrambling after them. Two varoks joined her in the chase. They followed the ahlork along the shore until the rocks barred their way. There the ahlork soared over the ruins crowning the sheer upper slopes and let Lanoll's gear fall to the lower shore.

With a cry of outrage Lanoll began her climb down the steep cliff, followed closely by the varoks. Her feet shouted a painful protest through her padded wet-boots. She watched the varoks re-trieve her helmet and hook, then sat down on the crumbled shore and tried to think. Time was unbearable while Conn was missing. What else should she be doing to find him? She could not search every room in all the vast spread of the forebears' ruins, but, be-fore she gave up, she would try.

With a sigh and a glance at the shells of tall buildings tow-ering above, she started back up through the rocks. She had not gone far when a spot of warmth, a bright color, caught her eyes. She clambered over a stack of boulders to reach the treasure. It blew away from her and hung from a jagged point of rock like a triumphant flag.

It was the plume of an elll. Lanoll reached up and caught it in her webbed fingers—a long head-plume, decorated with yellow and tipped with a unique red spot. Lanoll cried out with joy. Conn. It had grown at an odd angle near his right ear-plaque. Quickly, thoroughly, Lanoll searched a wide area for more plumes. She found only one more, also distinctively marked with red and yellow. She did not find the bow Conn had tied around the plumes. It was lost to one ilara's curiosity, and now lined a spawning bowl in the nesting grounds beyond the ruins.

Slowly the full implications of what she had found dawned on Lanoll. Conn would never willingly part with those plumes. He had been injured on the rocks. Lanoll clutched the plumes and burst out in wild protest at his suffering, shaking the ruins with a wail of anguish.

Conn

Thirty stories up, Conn heard the wail, and, in his delirium, enjoyed it immensely. He had never heard such a fine expression of elllonian grief at losing life-joy. He agreed entirely.

Nidok

In the air above, Nidok heard the wail. Convinced it was Conn's dying protest, he flew in a panic to the elll's prison.

Lanoll

Lanoll saw an ahlork land on a platform high over her head. Cursing it, she set off down the path to get help. She would make a thorough search of every rock on L'orkah's shore. She believed Conn had been pushed off of the tall cliff ruins onto the rocks below. She had to know. Ellls handled decisive tragedies well. They did not grieve for what could not be undone. Uncertainty, however, and pain, were difficult to bear. They stole life-joy.

Nidok

Nidok found Conn still alive, his graying face pressed pitifully into his small bowl of water.

The ahlork was thoroughly unnerved by the wail he had heard. *Such agony must not be. Not at the hands of ahlork. Let Mahntik slaughter her own prisoners. Ahlork will no longer do such torture.* He would hide Conn below the ruins, in the ahlork caves carved into the steep cliffs above the Misted Ocean. There the elll could be closer to water. No varok would find him there, not even Mahntik.

It would be a dangerous move. Official varoks and ellls were working just below to the east, retrieving the Free-minds' nasty fuel rods. Soon they would find the reactor. Soon they would find Sartak and the Free-minds.

With a flash of insight, Nidok determined he would no longer defer to Mahntik in any scheme. He would no longer persuade his weary flock to haul web seed back and forth across the Misted Ocean, nor destroy ilara nests and choke on the acrid dust of fertilizers and pesticides. He was tired of nursing old friends who had gone mad with too many new berries, tired of being hunted for a murder he had not committed.

Mahntik had killed two ahlork. He would not join her in another murder. Ahlork were the first of Varok's intelligent species, the first masters of Varok, the noblest of all those who spoke. They caused no one to wail in such a way. Ahlork would not stoop to the cruelty of varoks. Sartak was the traitor to the Greater Flock, not Nidok.

When it grew dark, Nidok chose four powerful ahlork from his flock to carry Conn to the family's large cave facing the Misted Ocean. There a deep depression in the floor of the cave would serve as an improvised pool for the elll.

The ahlork managed the elll's transport with some difficulty. Conn complained with annoying elll hoots every time a wing plate crossed his tile-lines, but he was too weak to fight off his porters. With clumsy efforts of wing tips designed more for picking at sea food than supporting the weight of ellls, four ahlork balanced his lanky body between them and descend with a mad flapping of wing plates off the prison's landing platform and down toward

Nidok's cave in the cliff face. They overshot their mark and were forced to clamber back up the rocks with their load, but at last it was done. The limp elll was slid into the rocky bowl on giant sea cabbage leaves in the back of the cave.

Throughout the next light-period and into the dark, Nidok and his family worked at filling the pool with water. Each time the water grew murky or low, the memory of the elll's wail tore through Nidok's mind, and he sent everyone scurrying after more water and containers to carry it. "Steal something from Mahntik," Nidok ordered.

Conn lay in the blessed sea bath, unconscious, exhausted or dead, they couldn't tell which.

NEW TIES, MORE SURPRISES

Orram—the next light-period

"Lanoll." At the sight of the beautiful blue elll coming into his office at Orserah's house, grief for Conn threatened to choke off Orram's reason.

The elll startled.

Orram solved her dilemma by gesturing to her with open arms.

"Tandra keeps me rational," he explained. "She carries both our fears." He offered the elll a chair in the corner of his office, and his static face took on a new light. "It is very good of you to come to us, Lanoll. You will be a healing balm to us all."

"Even to Tandra?"

"Especially to her."

Orram could see the doubt cross the elll's open mind, but he said nothing more. Tandra would provide her own assurance soon enough. "Tell me now," he said, "tell me exactly how the search for Conn was conducted after you found the plumes. You took a terrible chance, antagonizing the ahlork by searching near their nests in the ruins. The ahlork are not themselves lately. We must be cautious."

"I didn't forget the great-fish warnings," Lanoll said, "but I was desperate to find Conn. We searched every rock on the shore, then every ruin along the coast within two kilometers of where I found the plumes. We then sent airshuttles to search the cliffs. There were no remains. Nothing. Just these two plumes." She kept them secured in her case for dimming lenses, as if they tied her to some remote hope.

"Was there anything unusual about the ahlork rooms you searched?"

"In a few rooms the dust had been disturbed, but there were ahlork signs in all of them. It was impossible to guess where an elll might have been held captive."

"I see that you are no longer grieving for Conn's loss of life-joy, Lanoll. You believe he is dead, but please understand that to be sure myself, I must go to L'orkah and continue the search."

"Orram, Conn would never have torn those plumes from his head while he was still alive. He must have been destroyed. Not knowing, believing he is in pain somewhere, is more grief than I can bear. I truly believe that he is gone. Now I can continue to be of use to the living."

"Forgive me, Lanoll. I can't let him go, not yet, though I understand why you must."

"You know the minds of ellls very well."

"You understand me then? I must hope that he still lives. If he is alive, I will do him the most good by staying rational. Did you trace the strontium to the fuel containers found beneath the cliffs?"

"Yes. The nuclear wastes were from an archaic nuclear power station. Some were corroded and broken. Some ceramic beads of uranium dioxide were lost in the Misted Ocean."

"Your report has gone to the Energy Resources Council. They will investigate and find the source of radiation, but any fuel would be depleted. It would never make an efficient pop, much less useable energy.

"I hope Orticon isn't involved with this nuclear reactor venture, but it smacks of something the Free-minds might try. They have not integrated their history impressions. The knowledge and expertise of such reactors were lost ages ago, along with the planet-wide infrastructure."

Orram glanced at her mood. He saw yearning and loneliness, so he asked a gentle question. "When will you return to the Forested Sea? The great-fish continue Leyoon's work."

"I will do whatever you ask." Lanoll paused so that the varok could see how her memory of Conn filled her mind, then she went on. "I will never return to the sea as part of a school, Orram. I was Conn's mate for just a moment, but we were loners together, knowing we wanted that for a lifetime. The school is not enough for me now."

"Then you must join with us as family, Lanoll. Go to Tandra in the garden. She will confirm it." Lanoll met Orram's eyes with a relieved and hopeful smile, then moved away on quiet webbed feet, around the heat-absorbing stone wall of Orram's office and into the light-drenched garden outside. Orram could see the red sheen on Tandra's dark hair flash in the glow of mid-light as she rose from her knees to greet the elll. For a moment the question that hung between them was almost palpable, then the elll and the human came together in an improvised but unrestrained embrace.

Tandra—moments later

As we came into the house, I introduced Lanoll to Artellian and encouraged them to go to the algal pond to begin Lanoll's adjustment to the family. "I will get Orserah, Orram and Shawne," I said.

Soon we were all in the pond, swimming a primitive water ballet—the varoks hanging quietly on the surface as Lanoll and Artellian and I coasted around and between them, careful not to brush aganst them.

I tried to follow Lanoll, tried to understand her mood. *Why has she accepted Conn's death with so little evidence? Because it gave her relief from the grief she felt, believing he might be suffering? How can anyone be so pragmatic about such a powerful emotion?*

She came to me underwater and pushed me to the surface then circled around me, her face contorted with some kind of pain, as if we had lost our connection. I tried to reassure her, capturing her face in my hands, and it seemed to help. Then, in one concluding burst of speed, Lanoll raced around all of us. She had defined our signature in water. The adjustment was made.

"Rest here for a moment," Orram said to the others, "we will all gather at the hearth at first dark.

As I climbed out of the pond and dried off, Orram urged me to join him in the office. "There are more dimensions to your grief for Conn, Tandra. What is it?" Gently he lifted a tear from my eye.

We walked down the stones and sank into the long couch beneath a window that looked out over the distant mountains of the Vahinorral.

"We have come so far, Orram. We have passed so close in this universe. Why must we miss? I am grateful that Lanoll has come to us, but I find her failure to grieve now that she believes Conn is dead—I find that hard to bear, and I find your delayed grief even worse. I miss Conn with an ache so terrible, and it means nothing to anyone but Shawne."

Orram sat back, stunned. He searched desperately to understand my mind. Had he misread me? "We have learned from our differences, Tandra," he said feebly. "The ells don't grieve death—you know they grieve only suffering—but in that, they remind us that love for the living must continue."

"I need to grieve for Conn, yet if I do—"

"I will be all right, but try to indulge it alone, Tandra. I couldn't stay rational, riding through such pain with you."

"Orram, I am not varokian. I don't indulge or not indulge my grief. It is there. It exists. Now. Always. I will grieve for Conn for the rest of my life. Though you and I look the same, you are descended from an aerial being more like Earth's ancient pterodactyls than her mammals. Our differences are a narrow chasm only atoms wide, but that chasm is infinitely deep."

"Our minds are one, yours and mine," Orram insisted. "Our biological origins are mechanical details of no real consequence."

"I agree. Our minds have brought us very close." Ignoring my body language, Orram's mind drew in to the wellspring of my emotion, and our talk continued beyond the forming of words.

We three will be together again soon. I can't believe that he's dead. Orram's thought reflected back on itself from my fears. He watched my mind as I scanned the faint lights of silver in the softness of his dark auburn hair. When he turned up to me, his brow betrayed a faint shadow of doubt.

"What more can we do?" I whispered as if to myself. *We must find him, Orram. I need him even more than I expected to. I am not enough for you.*

Orram sat up, startled to see that the thought had taken such firm roots in my mind.

"How could you expect to be varokian as well as human?" he asked aloud. "You have never expected to be everything to Conn. Can you be more to me than myself? We are one mind, a hybrid, a unified mentality enhanced." *Together as human and varok we are capable of far more than either alone.*

I know that—

Orram traced my cheekbones with a sensitive finger, pouring all the concentration of his love into his touch. *Yet you want to be everything to me. I feel the longing you feel. You want to fill every corner of my desire, and you feel you have failed because I have an appetite for someone varokian.*

I know it is nothing but jealousy, Orram—

"Look deeper," Orram said, catching my face in his palms. *You are responding to the monogamous thread in your human genes. That thread runs very deep. I have no such heritage for sexual conduct.*

I couldn't hold back a feeling of loss. *I know how Mahntik excited you. The mood you felt colors your memories. But there's something else.*

I was drawn into the dark crystal of Orram's gaze and spoke softly in varokian. "Your memories of your visit to Mahntik are not like the other memories we've shared. They are blurred, somehow out of focus, shallow. I'm afraid to come too close to them. I don't trust those memories. They will be a barrier between us if we don't clarify them."

"Yes," he said. His conscious memory was mine to explore:

upstairs in Orlah's room, Mahntik near the window, the second glass of
web berry juice emptied into a nearby plant when she left the room. The
memories began to blur, fading in and out.

"You were getting drunk on that one glass of juice."

"Of course." Orram agreed. "That one bowl was enough to
fog my mind. Tandra, do you remember when Conn wrestled
the ahlork in the Ahlkahn? He thought they were drunk, and he
proved it by taking berries from one ahlork's pouch. I'm sure now.
Renegade ahlork have found the potent variety in Mahntik's new
strain. That would explain their eagerness for the berries before
the Celebration of Web Fruiting."

"Their spawning festival?"

"Yes. The old web berries ripen only in season. The ahlork use
the occasion for spawning rites."

"No wonder the ahlork are changing."

"That's all we need—ahlork with addiction problems."

"And Mahntik openly serving the potent juice. I don't need this
right now, Tan, I really don't. The astronomers have spotted Earth's
space ship. We will soon be in direct communication with them."

ORRAM AND ORLAH

Mahntik—late the next light-period

Mahntik did not usually spend much time beside her hearth.
When she ate, she ate systematically, with annoyance at the time it
took. She rarely prepared anything that required heat.

Now, with some difficulty, she produced an even bed of ironwood coals to roast small bits of egg-layer meat for Orlah. Then
she retreated to her clothes room and wrapped herself in a luxuriant blue length of warming cloth. She checked her image in a

large reflective crystal. *Good. Soft. Casual. Not blatantly seductive, but inviting, enough to be distracting.*

Orlah arrived promptly at the waning of light. At the door, he stood before her, his deep blue eyes straying along the drape of the cloth she wore. He entered the hearth room timidly, overwhelmed by the gift of the meal. It was the kind of hope-ridden devotion Mahntik detested and found difficult not to scorn.

When they had finished eating, she stood at one corner of the hearth sipping web juice. She had fastened her deepest probe into his mind, and saw that he was unhappy with his task as overseer of the ahlork who worked the new selenium web bushes on L'orkah, but he could not admit it.

When Mahntik spoke, she managed to hide her disdain at his failure to sense her probe. "Do the fields have enough water now, Orlah? Is Nidok satisfied?"

"The new webs are growing well. Yes," Orlah answered.

Mahntik indulged in watching her own beauty reflected in Orlah's admiration. Then, for a moment, she felt his faith in her overcome his fear. *The fool. He believes in me completely. He truly believes in my brilliance, that I can overcome . . . what? My anger? He truly loves . . .* Quickly she withdrew the probe from his mind.

"I have tried everything—" Orlah paused for a long time before he went on, fear gripping his tongue. "I can't make the selenium web stalks ferment properly. The silage spoils before it is ready. I have no more feed for the daramonts at Mount Ni. Are you sure that this web strain is approved, Mahntik—not another? It seems deficient. The berries come at all times, whenever they please, and they are potent—too potent, I'm afraid."

Mahntik smoothed her blue cloth to hide her tension, as Orlah nervously hurried on with his admonishment. "I don't think warming cloth is worth the price these bushes extract. They seem to require heavy feeding with extra-soil nitrogen."

"That is no matter, Orlah. Of course the strain provides superior webs and cloth, or it would not have been approved."

"Has Orram found it superior?" Orlah asked. "I understand he has ordered a re-evaluation."

"Orlah," Mahntik said softly. "My new web cloth passed all

the tests that a new product should. It is not merely useful, it will soon be a necessity in this society. We will warm varoks instead of buildings. It is a great saving. Also, the webs are clotted into cloth with much less expenditure of energy."

"That was not true of the strain I saw at Mount Ni. The webs are thin there and prone to breakage. A lot goes to waste."

"Oh? Then we will not use them for cloth. I have calculated that the webs grown on L'orkah have a lasting quality that outweighs the extra expenditure in energy to transport it to our markets at Mt. Ni."

"Increases in the use of energy are only rarely granted," Orlah said.

Mahntik's mouth drew in. "My hydrogen allotment has been increased for this project." She hated to compound easy lies with a riskier one; energy allotments were too easily checked on the public boards.

"I didn't know that." Orlah was shocked. "What industry is doing with less to balance your increased use?" he asked.

Mahntik's eyes grew soft again. "I forget. It need not concern us."

"But I am still confused. The ahlork say that Orram ordered a ban on further distribution of seeds from the new web bush. Did they mean the selenium bush or the new plain web?"

"I'm so sorry, Orlah. I forgot to tell you. The ban on inferior strains came through while you were out in the fields." Mahntik's mental block was firmly in place. "No wonder you are questioning me. The new selenium strains have been approved. The ahlork are always getting things backwards."

Orlah looked more confused than relieved.

How horrible to be so blatantly open. Orlah was too easy to read, too yielding, too vulnerable. She was about to say something encouraging, when she heard the hearty call of a visitor outside. Her face grew brilliant with anticipation at the sound.

"Orram," she called, moving quickly to the atrium. "Enter. The hearth is still warm with food."

Orram came in through the large carved doors, stamping the dust from his feet. When he saw Orlah, he smiled and strode forward, facing his brother with an open mind. "You look well, Orlah," he said. "I have missed you. Come. Join my mind. Mahntik will excuse us if we catch up on our lives for a moment."

The brothers clasped arms. Their eyes were deep with searching that unnerved Mahntik. Then Orlah's work with the farming ahlork began to raise questions in both their minds, and the specter of Conn's likely death rose between them like a devastating nightmare.

Inwardly, Mahntik celebrated one less problem.

When the knuckles of the brothers' hands turned white against the smooth brown of their arms, Mahntik interrupted with an offer of food.

"You must keep your ahlork in order, Orlah," Orram said, accepting a slice of stalk bread. "That is one reason I have come."

Abruptly he turned to Mahntik. "Your new strain has been denied. The webs are too weak for existing cloth-pressing equipment—"

"I agree. We should update the equipment for the finer cloth."

"That is an impossible expenditure of energy and materials, Mahntik. The old equipment was built to last as long as web bushes grow. Also, the new berries are addictive."

"Addictive?" Mahntik glared angrily as Orram turned back to Orlah.

Watch me closely, Orram, her mind demanded. *How can my eyes show anger and my mind be so blank and free of emotion? Oran Ramahlak, how do you like that puzzle?*

He turned to face her, trying to read her mood. She relaxed her glare, deciding it was too dangerous a game. *Orram is not stupid, and his experience watching Earth could have opened his mind to unthinkable possibilities.* She took little notice of Orlah, who looked on with a strained expression.

"Go to Nidok now, Orlah," she ordered, "and see that he replants all but the experimental plots."

"Wait." Orram took Orlah's arm again. "There is more between us, evidence that Conn may have met his death here on L'orkah."

"Two lost plumes cannot mean Conn is dead." Orlah's disbelief saved him from grief.

"Nothing is confirmed," Orram said. "But there is little hope."

"I feel sorrow for your uncertainty and your pain," Mahntik said.

"Yes, thank you," Orlah said, stepping away to discourage a deeper probe from Orram. "Now, please, I must go." He glanced at Mahntik, and she nodded sharply.

Orlah hurried from the room.

Orram turned to Mahntik and asked silent permission to probe her mind. She agreed, and he scanned quickly but deeply. He found nothing—not the slightest grain of real information about web bushes or berries, no idea who Leyoon's murderers might be, no knowledge of Conn and no residual guilt. He noted a clear memory of finding the ahlorks' source of reactor rod debris in an old ruin to the west of the shuttle station.

"Leyoon was wrong about you, Mahntik," he said. "Once again I am satisfied that you are innocent of treason—other than the crime of drugging an official of Varok to satisfy your own personal desires." A hint of mirth lightened his face, and Mahntik allowed herself a genuine smile.

"You are very varokian, Mahntik," he said, "and as beautiful as Varok itself." His eyes took in the full impact of her draped figure.

"You don't bother to conceal your admiration, Oran Ramahlak."

"Should I?" he asked. "Orlah is not part of your consciousness."

"Orlah is a dreamer, and I have tried to ease him toward the truth, that we could never join—but I will always care for him. I hope that your first encounter with me did not disturb your consummation with the human being. They are monogamous, technically, I believe."

"Human beings are very adaptable. My appreciation for your beauty has brought Tandra closer to my varokian nature. Tandra and I are one mind, Mahntik. I am half human in consciousness."

"Interesting," she said.

"Your beauty makes me long for Tandra. My mind is completed in the human, and my body is one with my mind. I need no varokian mate."

Mahntik found it difficult to conceal the effects of his rejection. When her outrage was firmly planted behind her mind-block, she

lowered her head, inviting patch contact. "Of course, Orram," she
said, congratulating herself on her control. "One touch is all I ask.
You have held me in suspicion, insisted on scanning my mind,
even trying all sorts of odd human tricks. I need some token of
your new faith in me. I have dangerous work to do here on L'orkah,
if the ahlork are stealing web strains from the genetics lab and
misleading Orlah."

She watched Orram's mind for his reaction. *Good.* His curiosity about Orlah's guilt was now satisfied, and his attention was
diverted back to the ahlork.

Orram suddenly changed the subject. "The Energy Resources
Council has sent a security force here with me to decontaminate
and close the nuclear reactor the Free-minds were trying to reactivate. Did you know of this, Mahntik?"

She didn't expect the question or the probe that accompanied
it, but her mind was still safely blocked, a constant habit that had
begun to weary her. "So that's why they have been so strange lately." She sounded surprised, then thoughtful, repressing her anger
at being suspected again. "A nuclear reactor? It must be the one in
the north, by the Lake of the Passage."

"We will know where it is soon, I expect," Orram said. "Oddly
enough, it seems the ahlork are involved. The Energy Resources
Council will investigate. Aside from improper disposal of the
radioactive wastes and fuel containers, we have no evidence that
they have violated energy efficiency requirements."

"You won't have evidence until they actually use more power
than they are allotted, I suppose."

"Or until an illegal source of uranium is found. The resource
surveyors are looking at the quotas sold, and looking for Gitahl
for questioning. They have joined with the security forces that
seek him for information about Leyoon's murder. In any case, we
must be cautious not to alarm the ahlork and drive their activities
further underground."

Mahntik let herself enjoy the pun, behind her block. "So, how
can I help you?" she said. "Will you continue the search for Nidok
and Gitahl while you are here? Perhaps you should stay for the
ahlorks' Web Fruiting Celebration. They usually overindulge

then. You should see what the new berry does to them."

"Surprising as it may seem, the ahlork are motivated by some grander scheme than berries. We should learn what it is, before we move in on them. Leyoon warned us that they act as if they are under some influence alien to their nature."

"I wouldn't put much faith in great-fish prophecies." Mahntik rose from the hearth with a flourish and paced around it. "The last great-fish performance was obviously over-dramatized. Leyoon took himself too seriously. I suspect he was senile."

"The counterbalancing of the Gurahn was carefully planned. Leyoon was no fool."

"But he was arrogant," Mahntik said. "His success in influencing varokian thought had set his organs. His play was a clever reinterpretation of history, but nothing noteworthy for current times."

"So you think the performance was a reenactment of Varokian history?"

"Of course. You do not?" As Mahntik laughed behind her mind-block, she surveyed Orram's thoughts. She saw that Orram was puzzled.

Where is her mood? She is not easy to read.

"Leyoon was not portraying history," Orram said.

Mahntik rose from the hearth and moved close to him. "I want you to stay on L'orkah for several more light-periods." She made her longing visible in her mind. "Will you stay here? We can work on the ahlork problem together. Make this your home while you are on L'orkah. Help me to help Orlah. I see we can never be one, but he believes in mental consummation with me."

Mahntik noted with surprise her own muted sorrow at thinking of Orlah, of his wasted potential. She let the feeling filter through her block, drawing Orram in. She was about to scan him when he turned away, and she saw that he was still nearly overcome with grief for Conn.

"I must go to Orlah," he said. "Neither of us should be alone now."

He strode to the door and was gone before Mahntik could protest.

Moments after Orram left, a wild banging of chitinous plates shook the outer door of Mahntik's house. She threw the door open to two ahlork.

"Varoks are everywhere in the ruins," one reported. "They will find power station. Nidok is gone. He delivers nothing to Mount Ni. He and Conn are gone from the ruins. We hear news of Earth invaders coming."

"How dare you intrude with your problems into my home!" With a surge of rage, Mahntik drove the beasts back across the entry pavement.

VARIATION ON A CELEBRATION

Conn—the same dark-period

High in Nidok's cave above the Misted Ocean, Conn gradually awakened to time and place, and realized with a start that Nidok was ignoring the mating ceremonies.

The ahlork's Celebration of Web Fruiting dated back a hundred millennia. It was their custom—or the result of their genetic programming—to come to the island continent L'orkah when the web berries ripened to a deep golden red. They came across the sea from their hunting grounds along the shores of the inland seas of Vior. Those ahlork too weak to complete the flight across the Misted Ocean dropped into the seething, cold water and were considered well lost, the species cleansed of weakness. The survivors arrived on L'orkah exhilarated by their success, ready to mate and celebrate their mating by gorging on web berries.

Now, since Mahntik's potent berries could be found over most of Varok, the celebration had lost its historical meaning. Some ahlork chose to stay on the continent of Vior, for the berries were just as plentiful there.

"I could be helping myself, you know." Conn grinned at Nidok as his face floated to the surface of the shallow pool in the back of the cave. "You could go on to the celebration."

"To celebrate ahlork shame? I wash my shame away in this elll's water." Nidok continued scooping water from a bag made of animal skin and dribbling it on Conn's raw hex-tiles.

"You sure do know how to give an elll a bath," Conn lied. "I didn't know you could cup water in your wing tips like that. Ouch. Watch the wing-plates, old buddy."

"No one knows enough ahlork," Nidok grumbled. "Everyone thinks we do nothing but chase wounded cliff-flyers and mine dung heaps for varoks."

"I've yet to see a varokian dung heap."

"I show you Mahntik's web fields, if I fly there again."

He threw the last of the freshly gathered water over Conn and gave the collecting skin to the youngest of his brood of six. "Go and fill this," he ordered. "The elll must be kept wet with fresh water."

"It would save your family a lot of trouble if you'd just help me get to the nearest lake, Nidok." Conn watched the mists swallow the youngster as he dived out of the cave.

"You are not ready for that trip," Nidok said.

"What you really mean is there are varoks swarming over the ruins looking for something, and you don't want to get caught with me on your hands, right? What are they looking for, Nidok?"

"Something Mahntik has taken."

"Me?"

"What else?"

Conn could tell Nidok was lying. His eyes took on a strained pear-shape. The elll rose unsteadily onto his feet. "I wonder what you're going to do about Mahntik. She won't be happy to find me gone."

"She is never happy," Nidok said, settling with a decisive clatter onto a sharp-edged rock near the mouth of the cave. "She is told you fell from landing platform and splattered shore rocks with green."

"She must have collapsed with grief." Conn laughed, hobbling slowly around the cave to test his legs. "Ahlork are not as stupid

as Mahntik likes to think." His huge eyes centered on Nidok, trying to fathom his mood. Nidok had been preoccupied and restless since Conn first came to the cave. No doubt the elll posed a
nasty problem for the ahlork. Nidok knew something of Mahntik's
schemes, and he didn't like them. He knew that he couldn't avoid
her for long. Soon he must either surrender Conn or use him to his
own advantage. It made Conn feel like a helpless puppet.

"I see that Nidok, an ahlork among many, is a fool like the rest."
Conn used the beast's name with a tone that conveyed honor.

Nidok stared across the long sweep of naked cliffs that rose
from the Misted Ocean. Here many ahlork still lived as their ancestors had lived, hiding their broods away in deep caves, choosing not to nest in the ruins like rootless scavengers. "Yes," he said,
"Nidok is fool. But no part of greater fools' Greater Flock."

Conn had never heard an ahlork speak so seriously. For a moment he felt ashamed of his insult, then he realized that the beast
had not been insulted. He had simply agreed. "You do not like the
alliance of the Greater Flock with Mahntik?" Conn asked.

Nidok's square face came around and his great lip stretched
into a queer sort of grin. "The True Flock forms no alliances. It is in
this cave, pampering ellls." The ahlork's wings scraped the ground
as he jumped down from his perch and stood before Conn. "It is
Sartak flies with a sour name. Call *him* fool, Conn. He forgets the
True Flock."

Nidok rummaged along the shelves etched into the rock and
presented the elll with a wing-plate piled with potent berries.
"Eat," he insisted. "Your insult is not wasted on me. Re-dominion
of ahlork is begun. Here. Now."

Conn watched Nidok with anxious eyes, knowing that the
beast had come to some decision. His plans were far too important
to be entrusted to an elll, one who might yet fall into the wrong
hands. *So what the hell*, Conn laughed to himself. *Might as well put
on a good berry-stupor with the clatter-plated chap.*

He scooped up a pile of berries from Nidok's wing-plate and
stuffed them into his mouth. "Down the hatch, Cave Buddy. Here's
to ahlork. May their nests ring forever with praise for the courage
of Nidok."

"May their wing-plates crackle with the name of Sartak, enemy of the True Flock," Nidok bellowed in muscular tones, and his greater lip wrapped around a substantial heap of berries.

"The True Flock flies forever," Conn sang out. "May its droppings find Mahntik's long hair."

"May Susheen fly up her fine robes." Nidok laughed heartily—a deep gargling sound—and lumbered off to fill a large skin with berries. He settled on the edge of the pool while Conn relaxed into the water, and as the light-period waned, the berries disappeared at a great rate.

The elll and the ahlork continued making toasts as their mouths grew thick with the berries' acrid taste and their minds grew loose and careless with its drug. The dark-period turned the cave black, and occasional flashes from far-off sheets of misted lightning lit their faces as they wallowed in exaggerated emotions, verbosely grateful to each other for saving lives and flock.

"I don't know how to pet an ahlork," Conn said drunkenly, looking for a soft spot to vent his inflated affection on Nidok. "If I were a human and you were a dog, I would pat your head. If you were a varok, I'd give you a spiral salute. If you were a human, I'd kiss your fat broken lip. You're the most unlovable piece of walking crockery in this solar system, Nidok. Frustrating. How can I thank you for saving my life?"

"You do this," Nidok said, leaning so close to Conn that his greater lip stirred the elll's head plumes as he spoke. "You tell everyone Nidok holds ancient honor of ahlork on his wing tips. All varok must know. Restoration of ahlork to councils of Varok begins with Nidok of Leahnyahorkah and none else. The True Flock flies with Nidok."

In spite of his drunkenness, Conn sat back, flabbergasted at Nidok's pronouncement. "All right," he murmured, "all right." He could think of nothing else to say, so he curled up in the cave's pond and soon drifted into a blessed, healing sleep.

When he awoke, a new light-period had begun. Nidok sat next to him, still munching berries and dribbling water over parts of Conn's body that were sticking out of the water.

"Thank you, dear friend," Conn said cheerily, sitting up. "You are the most gracious of Varok's beasts—to bring me water when the Celebration of Web Fruiting is in full swing. The berries are a little potent this year though, don't you think?"

"Never too potent. No, not at all," the ahlork slurred. "How are your tiles now they are dipped in berry juice? Do you grow back more fuzz? Are you cured, elll-friend? Tell all Varok. The ahlork Nidok saves Conn the elll from great agony. Do you tell that?"

"Of course I will, Nidok. I will tell Varok of your countless trips to the Lake of the Passage with skins of fresh water to cure Conn the captive. It will make a beautiful tale to tell the grandchildren of Orram. You have sealed the alliance of ellls with ahlork, Nidok."

"And varoks and humans. Alliance of ahlork and all Varok is made." Nidok teetered past the shelves, now nearly empty of berries. "But I forget myself. I eat all berries from our celebration. I go now and get some more. No one sees me coming, and no one sees me leave. Remember that. All are on other side of island. I fly now and bring you more berries. You are all alone for a long, long, long time now."

Nidok laughed his strange hoarse gargle and headed for the outlook rock to take his accustomed leap into the air. From there he looked back at Conn. "I forget. I made for you present." He tittered through pursed, leathery lips and dove straight down into a nasty mist gathering at the foot of the cliff. Soon he reappeared, dragging a long braid of ammonia weed. He thrust the end of the weed into Conn's hands. "Goodbye, Conn. Thank me now. It be a long walk to celebration and back."

For a moment Nidok shuffled on his perch, reeling from the distorted vision and dizziness that came with an overdose of the berries. Then he flew high, carrying with him the other end of the woven seaweed. His drunken noises echoed from the cliffs for several moments, then they gradually faded away.

Conn looked around the cave for the last time and tested his voice. "I hope Nidok has sense enough to make a run for Vior. If Mahntik learns that I'm still alive, his goofy life won't be worth a seashell." Making vocal sounds hurt his throat, but the Varokian words didn't crack, a good sign of improving health.

He pulled at Nidok's seaweed rope. It was braided loosely of strong fibers and seemed to be stuck fast at the top of the cliff. He would have to trust it. *How am I going to get up this stinking rope?* He groaned. The rest of the dark-period would not be enough time to get to the shuttle station—not the way he felt, with his tiles still half-eaten away and his muscles flaccid and unused and his whole aquatic structure still creaking from the severe dehydration he had suffered.

He tested the rope once more, grasping its slippery circumference with his large hands. Tentatively he inserted a toe into the loose braid and found that his whole foot would fit into the weave. When he tried his weight on it, the rope gave a few centimeters, but it held. He laced his fingers into the braid over his head and inserted a second foot as high as it would reach. The rope began to sway dizzily over the mouth of the cave, but slowly he inched his way up. *My poor toe-webs.*

At last his tired fingers found a firm grasp at the top of the cliff. He scrambled up the last few steps and threw himself onto the lip of the rock, then lay still while the ache in his feet and hands subsided.

There was no sound but the rush of mist through broken walls. Conn was in the center of an ancient patio, which still sported the half-nude stone figure of a stout forebear. Around the remains of the statue's wings Nidok had tied the seaweed rope.

Conn looked up and was startled to see an ahlork directly overhead. It circled slowly, then tipped its wings, spun once in the air, and headed off across the Misted Ocean toward Vior. Nidok. Greatly relieved, Conn felt waves of emotion ripple freely down his thin face. To think that an ahlork could care like that. "God help him, I hope the berries take him safely across the ocean," he thought.

Conn set off directly north, toward the Lake of the Passage. He thought he must be near the middle of the ruins. He couldn't be far from the tall ruin where Mahntik had kept him imprisoned.

It was not easy going, for the sand beneath his feet soon quit, and coarse stones laced the soil that had invaded the ruins. He hunted for something to make a shoe, and tied two pieces of synthetic insulation onto his feet with lengths of tough grass.

He made good progress then, but he was still in the ruins when Varok 's face turned toward Jupiter and the dark-period lightning sputtered and went out in the flood of warm light. He turned east and worked his way to the edge of the standing structures, where he could look out over the folded hills marching straight into the taller peaks of L'orkah. Less than a hundred meters away, a huge outcropping of rock stood separated from the ruins, shielding the remains of an underground shelter half-buried in an island of nitro-bush and sand.

Just as Conn moved into the open, an ahlork croaked sharply. It spiraled down directly over him, then broke into flight, flapping noisily toward the coast. He had been seen.

Conn ran toward the underground shelter, moving cautiously through the surrounding outcrop, keeping under cover. His cushioned feet made little sound. As he came upon the shelter's massive wall, set into the rock, a wide doorway suddenly came to life and opened with a low grinding of its mechanism. A single varokian figure emerged from the crack in the doorway. It waited while the door closed, then moved toward the rocks where Conn was watching.

VI. PERILOUS ENCOUNTERS

A butterfly has little effect
on a tornado
in a complex system.

A new tornado must grow
out of fresh winds.

—Orram, in a message to Orticon

TREASON

Mahntik—the same dark period

While Conn was climbing Nidok's rope, Mahntik and Gitahl surveyed the ahlork celebration, watching the berries' drug take effect. Thousands of dark square forms jostled chaotically in a wide valley shadowed by the mountain Horkorral. Sharp wing plates clacked as the lumbering beasts competed for space on tall rocks or ran for fresh servings of berries. Their rioting boiled dangerously into the air without warning.

Suddenly Mahntik turned away, letting her warming cloak whip against Gitahl's legs. He startled with the contact and glared after her. "I have seen enough," she said. "Intoxicated ahlork have been known to attack varoks."

"I'll go with you."

Mahntik didn't look back as she strode down the rocky path to where her rover was concealed.

"Since you released the new strain, we are continually plagued by ahlork. You were a fool to grow this strong berry in such quantities," Gitahl said, with a careless show of anger.

Anger is an improvement, Mahntik thought at the edge of her mind, so he would be sure to read her insult.

"I have destroyed the pestilence," she said. "The crops are safe."

Gitahl hurried after her. "I don't care whether your crops are crawling with web suckers or not. I'm asking you to use your good sense. Your new web bush is a nitrogen glut. Orram will soon wonder where you get the energy to produce so much chemical fertilizer."

"Orram will know nothing, unless you tell him. He didn't have the sense to search the other side of the ruins while he was here. I kept him too busy." She let the vision of their last encounter creep to the front of her mind where Gitahl couldn't miss reading it.

"Orram will learn all about your nitrates from the ahlork."

"The ahlork would not dare breathe on Orram without my consent."

"You have tamed the wild ahlork," Gitahl said. "And taught them to seal their minds. Congratulations."

"They are more tied to me than you can imagine."

"Well then." Gitahl pulled her to a stop and smiled grotesquely, reading Mahntik's inner mind as far as he could. "Perhaps you can put a quick end to their complaining. They say that water from the wells of L'orkah is no longer fit to drink. You had better check for nitrates. I suspect you have replaced too little natural fiber in the soil. You are doing nothing but running water past your fields and washing your expensive nitrogen into the Misted Ocean."

"And you have been listening to too much ahlork complaining." Mahntik quickened her pace. The conversation bored her. Gitahl was beginning to sound like Orlah.

"I will take water samples immediately," Gitahl said, climbing into the small rover behind her.

"You will not." Mahntik's eyes flashed. A harsh wind blew the hood from her face. "What is not known cannot be whispered to Orram or to that elll, Lanoll, he just took into his family. She sniffs about every puddle on Vior like a dung-fish."

In spite of himself, Gitahl enjoyed Mahntik's pugnacity. "I urge caution. You are dangerously over-extended, growing too much, too fast. The land will not support it, and shipping selenium webs to Mount Ni is insane. You could grow fuel crops without so much risk and expense."

"Fuel crops waste my time. Selenium webs sell very well—now that I am accepting advance orders for rhenium fibers to weave with them." Mahntik laughed. "There will soon be a thriving metropolis beneath Mount Ni—tens of thousands of varoks dependent on my webs and warming cloth. Orram wouldn't dare put down my new selenium strain once it dominates the fields on the banks of Lake Seclusion."

"You are talking treason upon treason," Gitahl hissed. "Don't give Orram an excuse to stay on L'orkah—and watch Orlah. He is too open. You should confine his so-called experiments to L'orkah. Orram will be watching him closely."

"For that reason," Mahntik said, as she started her methane-driven vehicle, "I told Sartak to spread the new selenium web plants over the face of Vior. Orram has blind spots. He can't argue against a web bush that has already seeded wild. He had no quarrel with my other strain until the berries proved too strong. And he will have no further quarrel when he sees Varok cannot do without my strains. My webs, the berries, soon the warming cloth, even the commercial stock digesters—all have monopolized the market very successfully."

"You are forgetting how normal varoks function, Mahntik. Orram will read everything Orlah knows. But tell me no more. I have heard too much. I will not be involved in these mad excesses."

"You are already involved, Gitahl." She let the motor idle. "You managed the ahlork who murdered Leyoon for me, didn't you? You know what lies within the ruins. Where do you think my pesticides for the web bushes come from? Fool. They come from the fossil organics my Free-minds take from Varok's 'forbidden' reserves in the ruins *you* manage. Quotas indeed. No one will tell me how to run my business. Resources are there to be used, by those strong enough to take them." Mahntik feigned a laugh. "Now you are a *most* fruitful subject for mind-scans—you know far more than just one secret. You might as well give me your help and enjoy your share of the profits."

"Your ambition is losing its charm, Mahntik. You are playing the game too close to the edge, stealing mineral reserves. And you've sent Orlah, of all varoks, to oversee illegal web fields on Vior? That fool will get caught. Orram will make the law of local usage hold, though he violates its principles every time he turns you on a bed-pad."

Mahntik smiled at Gitahl's assumption. It was a transparent attempt to drive her into anger. She reached behind her, took his arm and pulled it around her waist, sending a violent shock through his nerves. "Orlah reports that the new web bushes are all delivered—as far away as the Yat Ahlean—and very few questions have been asked." She inched closer. "Unfortunately you're right. He is as much an idealistic fool as his nephew Orticon and his Free-mind friends. They think that we're messing with the reactor to build weapons for defense against an invasion from Earth. Imagine it."

"You're insane." Gitahl laughed, enjoying Mahntik again, now that she had jarred his nerves into the sexual mode. "Don't you realize what kind of anger those overzealous Free-minds will unleash, when they realize they've been played like idiots?"

"You have no faith in my plan, Gitahl—but you soon will. I will bring all of Varok to my feet, begging for my wisdom and loving me for rebuilding the glory that once lined the shores of Varok. Orram has found me guiltless, twice, of any crime in these ventures. My mind is as pure as the Springs of Harinlegh." With that, Mahntik threw off Gitahl's arm and drove the rover recklessly over the rocks and through the ancient streets to her lodge.

Students—moments later

A noisy crowd of varoks was gathered on the street near Mahntik's house—young professionals, obviously high on web berries, returning from nearby outbursts of the ahlork celebration. Mahntik and Gitahl ignored them.

At her own outer door, Mahntik turned to Gitahl, blocking his entrance.

"My compliments, Mahntik, to your genius," he said, "if not your patience. You may indeed have all varok dependent on your webs and stolen minerals before the damage is realized. But beware how you taunt me. When you are through using these others, your body and your mind's secrets I claim as my own."

As he turned from her door, he bumped into two students.

"Oo—nono. Wrong house," they slurred, and quickly retreated.

Approaching a bakery twenty meters down the narrow path, the students, staggering and laughing, watched Gitahl walk away toward the genetics laboratory. Then they entered the bakery and reported what they had heard to Oran Ramahlak, Governor of Living Resources.

FRIENDLY ENCOUNTER

Conn—the same dark-period

"Orlah." Conn whispered as loud as he dared. "Orlah."

The varok startled and froze in the open entrance to the reactor.

"Orlah, unlax, you poor excuse for a varok. It's me, Conn."

"By the breath of Harrahn. Conn?" Orlah took a step toward the rocks where the elll was hidden. "Orram thinks you're dead."

"Sorry about that. It's your old buddy, Conn—still alive and burning his gills out with air, as usual, if you'd care to believe it."

Orlah moved into the rocks and found the elll sitting cross-legged on top of a large boulder. "By all that is dear to varoks, is this you?" The look in Orlah's eyes said too much. "What has happened to you?" He was near to breaking with some emotion between horror and sorrow. "You are nothing but fins and plumes. Your tiles look as if they've been scraped raw."

Conn slipped down into the shadows of the rocks. "Am I that bad? I've been feeling much better lately. Nidok's conversation is not as dry as Mahntik's."

"Mahntik?"

"A very captivating woman. I still haven't figured out why she locked me up, unless she murdered Leyoon."

Orlah looked away from Conn toward the sea, his shoulders shaking, his body bent and thin, as if he had aged years.

"Why are you here, Orlah? Orlah? What's in that building?" He knew the varok was badly shaken, close to an emotional break. "Why are you here on L'orkah? Still hanging onto Mahntik? Or were you looking for me?"

"Yes. Yes, Conn. No," Orlah stammered. "Quiet. There are ahlork coming."

They hid in the rocks as two ahlork clattered to a landing alongside the buried building and disappeared inside. Soon they re-emerged, talking excitedly. "I tell you I saw elll. He is not dead. Nidok has lied to Greater Flock."

"It be some other elll," the second ahlork croaked. "Nidok is no traitor. I say berries now and less worrying about ellls."

The ahlork flew off to the west, laughing noisily and cuffing each other with cocked wing-plates, trying to knock each other out of the dark mists.

"You've got to help me," Conn whispered to Orlah, "I've got to have water. There must be some in here."

"What? In there? No—I don't know, Conn."

"Well, let's take a look. Is it safe, or is it full of ahlork?"

"Yes—er, no. Everyone is at the celebration."

"Let's go in and take a look."

Conn moved swiftly toward the door, but Orlah urged him into the rocks on the north side, through a smaller entrance.

"There should be water in this room over here," Orlah said, trying to divert Conn's attention. The elll followed him silently, sensing his nervousness. They walked past banks of switches and dials and remote viewing screens and entered a large area sealed with double doors. It was lined with multi-directional showers and shielded disposal carts.

Once inside, Conn did not need much light to understand what the building housed. "Orlah, this is an old reactor."

There was no mistaking the decontamination apparatus and the huge hemisphere housing the reactor, partially visible through a viewing window—familiar to Conn from his studies. This was a nuclear power station, ancient but coming alive. It must have served the forebears ages ago before it was suddenly abandoned. Now it had been partially rebuilt.

Conn found a working decontamination dock and stood under its warm shower for a long time, until Orlah grew visibly nervous.

"Interesting place. Glad they got the showers working," Conn said, shaking the water from his head plumes. "What do the ahlork do here? Play pick-up sticks with old fuel rods? Why re-build the place?"

Orlah said nothing.

"Are they licensed to use anything here? The fission products of the uranium in these ancient contraptions would have decayed hundreds of Jovian years ago. There's no longer a nuclear materials industry large enough to support a startup, is there?"

"I really don't know, Conn. I really don't. I have been curious about this place. Only just now did I learn what was here, during the celebration when the ahlork were drunk. It will soon be taken over by the Energy Resources Council, I suppose. I should lead the security forces here."

"I wouldn't bother. Any reaction someone might get going would be too inefficient to make enough steam to run a light bulb. This is crazy. Where are the moderators? Graphite or heavy water would be long gone."

Orlah relaxed a little. "I learned about this just now, Conn. I don't know anything about it."

"I'll bet ten berries Mahntik knows about it," Conn said.

"I doubt it. I haven't seen anything about it in her mind."

"Apparently quite a bit goes on here. Who would dream of re-activating one of these old power stations?"

"I work in the fields. I oversee ahlork growing experimental new web strains. I haven't had much chance to learn what goes on in the more remote areas of L'orkah. We shouldn't be found here, Conn. I suspect it may not be ahlork alone working here. It must be Free-minds who have rebuilt this reactor. They have recently come to L'orkah—a goodly number of them—and they talk of strength-ening Varok's defense. An attack from Earth is coming soon."

"Ridiculous. You can't trust anything Mahntik says about Earth. And the Free-minds? They're too young, too naïve." Conn was terrified of the harm they might do to themselves. "They don't realize how this industry functioned. It takes long experience in the tricky business of uranium and plutonium bench chemis-try. The Free-minds would have no idea what they're doing. I sure hope you're wrong."

"In any case, they are fanatic about their opposition to the mind-scan and the need to defend Varok from Earth. They mustn't find us here. I will lead you to the Lake of the Passage. You will be safe there until the security forces come. Then you can travel home with them."

"I would much rather you found a rover for me, or a dara-mont, so I can get to the shuttle station and home to Vior as soon as possible."

"It's too far. We would be seen. We mustn't be seen."

Conn sensed that Orlah was nearly irrational.

"Quickly now," Orlah continued. "Through here and we're out."

Once they were making their way away from the reactor into the ruins, Orlah took control of his panic. "The ahlork had you penned up in the ruins on the coast?" he asked.

"I was Mahntik's prisoner. The ahlork are her lackeys."

"You must be mistaken," Orlah said. "She and I . . . She could not have hidden that from me. From Orram. You must have had dehydration hallucinations."

"I tell you I was Mahntik's prisoner."

"Please. We must be quiet, Conn. It doesn't matter—ahlork or Free-minds—but the ahlork will be looking for you. You say you've been seen, alive and escaping? You can't try to get to the shuttle station yet, in your state. I'll plant evidence that you died trying to escape through the rocks, while you recover in the lake. That will be your best hope for getting off L'orkah and back to Vior safely."

"All right," Conn agreed. "I'll assume you'll have the evidence planted and my second death established among the ahlork in— say four light-periods. Be sure Mahntik is told. It will make her so happy. Meanwhile, stay clear of anyone who might see me in your thoughts. I'll get a good rest in the lake and try to grow back some muscle and fuzz."

"Can you hurry any faster, Conn? It is nearly light. We mustn't be seen—by anyone."

They hurried out of the underground complex and moved into the brush, failing to notice the slim varokian figure that followed.

HUNTERS AND HUNTED

Conn—the lake at Lo'nahrl

Conn spent four light-periods at the bottom of the Lake of the Passage before his gills and his overworked lungs began to recover. When he felt strong enough to go back out on dry land, he tied lake moss around his feet with shore reeds, stood up successfully, stumbled ten meters up a nearby hill, and collapsed. He needed more time to regain tile and hexline integrity. As he inched on his belly and rolled back toward the lake, he found a cache of hoat meal, a food Orserah added to many dishes, believing it to be good for healing. Orlah must have left it for him.

Dry-shock nearly felled him again before he regained the lake. Once there he had trouble controlling his impatience, as his body slowly drew strength from the water. Though desperate to get back to Orram and Tandra, his mind focused on Lanoll. When would he see her?

Nidok—while Conn is in the lake, recovering

As he headed over the Misted Ocean toward Vior with a small flock, Nidok's wings beat more and more slowly, until they left almost no trail of swirls and eddies in the thick orange fog. He was enormously tired, for he had no time to hunt the warm thermals that usually carried his flock to safety on the continent.

When at last they reached the Springs of Harinlegh, Nidok's followers met several flocks gathered on the lush, sweeping cliffs overlooking the shore. Many of the ahlork had carried heavy loads both ways across the Misted Ocean. They were replacing the webs of Mount Ni with the selenium webs raised on L'orkah—the job Nidok had refused for his flock. All were tired and rebellious, and eager to hear Nidok's talk of independence.

"I fly to the courts of Ahl Vior," he shouted to all who would hear. "I accuse Mahntik of murdering two ahlork."

Emboldened by the flocks' raucous cheers, he urged, "Ahlork

are not slaves to web berries and nuclear machines and violent varoks. No longer do ahlork haul Mahntik's poison to Mount Ni. The Greater Flock is divided." He waited for angry objections to fade into shocked silence.

"Sartak is wanting to steal diseases from genetics lab. He is degraded. He is not True Flock. Susheen is mad for web berries. Both must be stopped. The True Flock is born. Wait for me here. I return to lead you against Sartak's violence and Mahntik's slavery."

Nidok and a small contingent chosen from his flock took boldly to the sky for Ahl Vior, on a rising current of raucous, gravelly cheers.

Nidok—in Ahl Vior

Surrounded by varokian parks and buildings, Nidok lost confidence. He did not know what to do, where to go, or what to ask. He left his lieutenants in a small stand of trees near a large plaza, and wandered the halls of three massive buildings near the Concentrate, unable to read or to understand the rows of controls governing the elevators and message centers. In the end, he left the fourth building at the urgent request of a nervous young varok wielding an ominous cleaning machine.

He wandered along a clay roadway edged with moss, pretending to be one of its normal foot travelers. A few curious ellls on daramonts asked if his flight were impaired. One varok rode by in a shuttlecar, apparently intent on some emergency. Nidok could not bring himself to stop the varok. He kept walking, trying to waddle a straight line while deciding what to do. He had no idea how to accuse someone of murder.

He followed the roadway across a broad meadow and through a deeply shadowed park of spreading trees, until he came to a broad pool of clear, deep-emerald water. He bounced onto the soft moss that framed the pool, and flew onto a huge overhanging branch, hoping that an unsuspecting elll would emerge from the water.

At last an elll tad floated belly-first to the surface and blew a stream of water and bubbles at Nidok.

"I do worse than that," Nidok said.

"You are the only ahlork I've seen in eighty million light-pe-riods who hasn't been drunk on web berries," the child shouted, crawling out onto the moss bank. "What are you doing here? This is an elll's hiding place."

"What will ellls hide from these days?" Nidok taunted.

"Ahlork." The tad giggled. "What else?"

Nidok's sense of the game got lost in reality. "And no wonder. Ahlork are tainted with murder," he said.

His serious tone so shocked the tad, he dove for the bottom, where his school was napping. Immediately an elder surfaced.

"Can we help you?"

Nidok appreciated the elll's concern. "A varok kills two ahlork and the great-fish Leyoon," he said. "I do not find where to go to tell this."

"You know who murdered Leyoon?" The elll gasped. "You must go to Orram, the varok Oran Ramahlak, immediately. He lives near Mount Ni, but is often at Lake Seclusion. There is some trouble there."

With nothing more than a formal nod to the elll, Nidok flew from the garden and out over the Concentrate, calling his com-panions to fly beyond the entrapping buildings of Ahl Vior. As they beat through the mists toward Mount Ni, Nidok wondered if ahlork would ever outlive the shame of being involved in Leyoon's murder.

To all ahlork he passed, he called the distress signal of his species. When they responded, he told them of the degradation of Sartak and Mahntik's exploitation. His reputation and strong tone convinced many. Before he was within sight of Mount Ni, hundreds of ahlork had abandoned their errands for Mahntik to join the True Flock at the Springs of Harinlegh.

Others, however, completed their deliveries and quietly sailed off across the Misted Ocean, intending to warn Sartak that a great flock of fools was coming against the Greater Flock.

Nidok's group and three young hangers-on arrived at Mount Ni buoyed by new support and expectations of redemption, ready to begin the ahlork's historic walk into the legal life of Varok.

Nidok was no longer cowed by the masses of buildings and unfamiliar devices of Varok's literate society. His mission was a holy one; the emergence of a new ahlork civilization had begun. The True Flock was gathering faster than he dreamed possible. Mahntik and her web berries had lost their deadening hold.

He asked directions of many varoks before he found one who knew where Orram kept his office.

"What do you want with Orram?" It was an elder varok, up to his waist in water, fishing in Lake Seclusion. He spoke in the ahlork's own tongue. "He is Governor of Living Resources. He is too busy to worry about your flock just now." There was just enough taunting in his rough imitation of ahlork-sound to please Nidok. To be answered in one's own tongue was a fair compliment. Few varoks bothered to learn the aerial beasts' language.

"I come to accuse Leyoon's murderer," Nidok said proudly in Varokian, returning the compliment.

The elder's eyes narrowed suspiciously. "Orram's office is in the third lodge west of the outer rocks on the lake's southern shore."

Nidok offered his thanks with a grunt. He noticed that the old varok had quit his fishing and was running along a path toward the nearest sand cabin, but he gave it no thought.

The ahlork flew quickly along the shore of Lake Seclusion, intent on finding Orram. The lodges near the eastern end of the lake crowded closer and closer to each other as they approached the shore. Nidok shuddered and stretched his wings as he led his fellows out over the lake for a clear view.

The third house west of the outer rocks was easy to spot. Several varoks stood on the beach, apparently deep in discussion. Nidok recognized the unusual varok with the small, distinguished head and well-hidden patch-organs. *That must be Orram.*

He landed with an extra clatter of wing-plates to impress the circle of bipeds. Then he strutted over to confront them from the ground. "You are Oran Ramahlak, I believe," he said in his best Varokian to the varok with hidden patch-organs.

The biped backed away, obviously alarmed. "No," he said. "I'm Jesse Mendleton. I am no varok."

"That's him, all right," another varok said, peering at Nidok.

"He's got a long scar on his greater lip."

"Nidok, ahlork, you are to come with us," a third varok said.

The three varoks and an elll Nidok hadn't noticed before came forward all at once, their linked arms forming a canopy over Nidok's head. Nidok's flock mates stood back warily.

"Of course, of course we come with you," Nidok said, laughing at their precautions. "We have come to tell Orram about murder of Leyoon. We won't leave you so soon. We come very far."

"This way then," the stiffest of the varoks intoned.

While his companions waited on the beach, Nidok followed the varoks and the elll to a small sand-brick cabin set near a larger building marked with letters. Nidok took pride at recognizing the first symbols as "Office of," though he did not understand the rest. A large shuttlecar waited between the two buildings. Its engine sent a quiet whistling vibration through the fresh lake air.

"In here please," the stiff varok demanded, opening the rear entrance of the shuttlecar.

Nidok had no intention of riding in a closed vehicle. "I talk to no one but Oran Ramahlak," he said. "Tell me where he is, and I fly there."

"Get him in," someone shouted, and Nidok felt his extended wings grasped, their sharp covering of chitinous plates held closed. He was lifted and pushed into the airshuttle, and the door was slammed shut.

The ahlork watching from the water's edge rose into the air and sliced down on the varoks, exploding with furious insults, their wings at full cock.

"Lay back your plates," Nidok screamed. "They make a mistake. A flat wing will do."

Without breaking their dive, the ahlork closed their wing-plates like so many Venetian blinds and knocked the bipeds to the ground with the sides of their fully extended wings. Three fell senseless, and the fourth, the human, rolled with the blow and scrambled off for help.

"Hurry. The latch is here," Nidok screamed, as the airshuttle rose and headed for open water.

The ahlork easily overtook the slowly accelerating airshuttle but were shaken loose again and again as the vehicle maneuvered back and forth. Finally they gained a firm hold on the rear safety lights and worked the rear door open. Nidok leapt into the air and led his angry companions directly east, away from Mount Ni. *Ahlork will have nothing more to do with such varoks*, he decided. *We fly to find Conn.*

DEADLY ENCOUNTER

Conn—at the Lake of the Passage

Five more light-periods passed. Early on the sixth, when the auroral haze had streaked the hills in a pleasant blue-green light, Conn rose to the surface of the lake. All was still. His tiles pulsed with the signals of living creatures sending waves of compression, bioluminescence and electro-magnetism through the water. He glided on his back and scanned the shore. Broken walls gave the beach a disheveled appearance. Tumbled stones outlined the merest hints of wide courtyard paths leading into the ruins. Web bushes spilled over jumbled slabs of carved rock.

Conn swam toward the web bushes. They seemed out of place in these dry hills. As he rose to the surface, his ear plaques picked up the rustle and clatter of ahlork busy on the shore.

Alarmed, he dove and swam a hundred meters to a patch of blue water-weed growing into the ruins. He worked his way cautiously through the weeds and the sunken foundation of an old boathouse until he had a clear view. A stretch of brilliant sand, made of the fractured ceramics that had once graced the ancient resort, separated him from a cultivated field of web bushes. More than a dozen ahlork were scraping berries from the long branches. Some moved slowly through the bushes dragging heavy bags. Others chopped at the earth with the sharp edges of their plated wings.

I never thought I'd see an ahlork work like that, Conn told himself. *What is going on with Mahntik and Orlah and the ahlork?*

On top of all the input of his many senses, the intense longing for Lanoll clogged his chains of reason. Or was it the need to be home, deep in Orram's caring intellect? Or Tandra's life-loving wonder? Or Shawne's open-ended acceptance? He longed to tend the water gardens at Orserah's house, start another strain of box-walkers or steak-fish, and bring Lanoll home to the family. It would complete his school. Yes. Tandra would love her.

He must get home, must tell them all about what Mahntik was doing here. The attempt at restoring the nuclear power station was a disaster in the making. Mahntik would invent any story to turn young varoks or ahlork minds to her purpose. *What is her purpose? What does she have to gain from sabotaging Varok's stability?*

To prepare for a reconnoitering hike across L'orkah, Conn found a tough moss in the shallows on the northern edge of the lake. There he fashioned a crude wet-sweater by lacing four-foot lengths of the moss together with tough weed stalks. Then he went hunting. He dove to the bottom of the lake and swam in wide circles until his tiles picked up the pressure pattern of large, barbed petals scanning the water for passing fish. Slowly, he zeroed in on the voracious plant. It looked like a giant rose in full bloom, but its outer petals beckoned dangerously, ready to snap closed sensitive edges and hold fast anything that ventured too near.

For bait, Conn caught a fish hiding in the mud. He dispatched it with a bite, then, holding it by the tail, swam just out of reach of the carnivore, brushing the fish over its petals. When the petals snapped closed on the fish, Conn threw himself under the great rose and uprooted it. Too late its petals felt their new danger and reached backward to entrap the elll. A few barbs struck at the back of his arms, but he quickly found the stem of its food bladder and pulled the organ from the dying plant intact.

He cleaned the tough sack with the shell of a sand slug and fashioned its stem into a shoulder strap. Then he filled it with fresh lake water, and laced it shut with reeds. One of the largest petals of the plant made a workable pack, which he filled with edible weeds and fish.

Ready at last, he rose to the surface of the lake wearing his newly woven wet-sweater. The burden of food and water he slung over his shoulders. Nothing stirred on the western edge of the lake. He let himself drift slowly along the bottom until he reached the shore. Then he stood quickly and ran for the nearest clump of nitro-bush.

"Ae-yulll." He stifled a cry of pain as his third toe-web came down on a small rock. *How could I be so stupid?*

He walked back to the lake, much more carefully this time, and scrambled among the shore weeds. Within minutes he resurfaced, shod with tough moss sandals.

Like something hunted, he slipped through the brush to the southern hills overlooking the ruins. Some were denuded, their brushy cover blackened in wide areas. They had been burned, cleared for the new web bushes just emerging from the poor soil. He moved cautiously down the open slopes until he was on the far side of the rocky outcropping that camouflaged the reactor. No ahlork were in sight. Only the distant mewling of ilara could be heard. He moved in closer, crawled under a nitro-bush, and settled down comfortably in his wet-sweater to wait.

Before long, two ahlork flew directly over him and perched on a large rock guarding the entrance to the reactor. Their wings drooped with fatigue, and their greater lips danced like partially cooked el eggs. One was marked with a necklace of white plates— Sartak. They both reeked of web berries.

"Mahntik betrays us, Susheen," Sartak said angrily. "We get germs from her genetics place."

Conn tried to remember what Orlah had said about reactor rods the ahlork were dumping. Were Free-minds involved? He couldn't remember. He worried that Orlah was right—perhaps he had suffered some brain damage.

"I spit on your germs," Susheen growled. "Mahntik makes more germs for ahlork, if she likes."

Sartak rocked on his large talons and spread his wings, careless of Susheen's nearby lips. "The Greater Flock will control

Free-minds and reactors and germs."

"I argue for the Greater Flock," Susheen screamed. "The Greater Flock will not take germs. How do we clean up germs once we will let them go?"

"We don't. The germs will clean up varoks." Sartak's laugh sent a chill through Conn's hexlines. The ahlork was mad. "Come, Susheen," he commanded, "or I call you traitor to Greater Flock."

The two ahlork hopped from the rocks with a scraping and clacking of wings, and soon disappeared into the dark shadows of the western shore.

Conn followed them. As the waning light-period sent a dull glow over the ruins, he walked the cliffs over the Misted Ocean, where he found a tumbled field of rock and sand pocked with small pools of water, the ilara's spawning ground.

Most of the ilara females had chosen pools and deposited their eggs. They were now waiting for the squabbling males to settle down and fertilize them.

Conn moved into the spawning ground, trying to stay hidden in the rushes, and settled into a thick cluster of them to rest in a shallow pool. Dreamless hours later he awoke to the sudden rush and clatter of chitinous wings speeding past him. He dodged, and stumbled across a nesting pool, smashing it to mush and mud.

The disengaged ilara flew to a nearby rock, shouting her protest. One egg lay broken beside the pool, and Conn felt keenly the ilara's distress. He lifted the broken egg by its ruptured shell. Most of the contents were still intact, but the shell was strange, soft and rubbery. Conn downed the egg, counting it a good breakfast, and then decided he had better make a quick nest count. Something was not right. He decided it was not only the rubbery shell, but also the small number of the ilara's spawn. Other nests were empty, and most of the existing eggs had soft shells.

He left the ilara grounds and worked his way toward the web fields near the western cliffs. Another ahlork sped past him in the dark. He ran into the leafless bushiness of web plants, a huge field of the stuff with ahlork farming it, as they had near the lake.

Three ahlork took to the air as Jupiter's light began to fill the eastern sky. A torrent of lightning spilled into the ocean. Ahlork moved back and forth on the edges of the large field, searching for something. Conn rolled under a large shrub. Matted threads of the leafless plant caught in his plumes, and larger twigs rubbed on his pressure plates. The ahlork circled around him, flew over the sea, then came directly back. Conn huddled closer to the plant; he was sure that he had been found.

The ahlork swooped over him and flew directly on. Then a moist, acrid spray hit his moth-eaten skin. He shuddered with the sting as something toxic grazed the hexagonal lines between the tiles on his upper back. Tumbling out of the bushes, he ran for the nearest water in the ilara grounds. The ahlork were flying back and forth over the field, preoccupied with spraying the plants.

"I'll be damned," he muttered, remembering the crop dusters he had seen on Earth.

He found a large boulder, moved slowly into its shadow, and relaxed. When the ahlork finished spraying, he moved back into the field and tucked a few web twigs into his pack for Lanoll to analyze.

Just then a rover came into view at the far end of the field, swerved toward Conn and and banked to a quick stop.

"I see that the lake has done you some good, Conn," Mahntik called over her rover's engine. "Are you on your way home? Climb in. I'll take you to the shuttle station."

"Very cute, Mahntik. Nice rig you have there. Your new reactor couldn't make enough electricity to power that energy hog you're riding. Do you lay hydride eggs?"

"So you have been to the reactor." Without hesitation, Mahntik ran the rover at Conn. As he dodged into the web bushes, she stopped and turned back, laughing. "Come along, Conn. I'm sure you want to get home now. The ahlork have mistreated you long enough. Let me give you a ride to the shuttle station."

"You wouldn't dare drive this contraption to the shuttle station. You'd be fined for wasting fuel."

"This is a medical emergency. You need help getting home to Vior. Your tiles look as if ahlork have been scratching at them, looking for rare minerals. You clearly have some desiccation damage."

"I was taught not to take rides from people who shut you up in skyscrapers to dry out. I've decided you've got a flawed character, Mahntik, and terrible manners."

The varok's face was strangely distorted by a cold laugh. "Ellls have such poor memories, Conn. Don't you know why you are here on L'orkah? You are supposed to make a count of the ilara eggs and report the average spawning-pool number to Orram. I have the estimate of the total flock number for you, and some shocking statistics about the escalating numbers of eggs the ahlork have been taking. We also need to keep watch on the food sources for the light-hoppers. Their mosses are not growing as lush as they once did." She shrugged and shook her head. "You don't remember that I promised to get this information for you? You are ill with desiccation damage, aren't you, Conn? Perhaps you had better come back to the genetics lab with me before you leave for Vior. The airshuttle you want will leave in less than a light-period. We had better hurry."

Conn couldn't help but admire Mahntik's story. "Where did you learn to tell lies, Mahntik?"

"I don't understand your human word, Conn. You are not well."

"Stay away from me, Mahntik," Conn shouted, moving deeper into the web field. "You're mad."

Mahntik's rover lurched straight at him. He plunged to the side. The rover crashed through the web bushes as he scrambled to his feet and ran toward the thickest growth. Behind him, the terrifying hiss of the methane drive drowned all his senses. He stumbled on, his feet screaming against the abuse. He dove behind a cluster of thick branches just as Mahntik's rover reached his position.

The vehicle lurched violently to one side, nearly throwing Mahntik free, and then it stopped dead, caught in the bushes like a fly in a spider's trap. Mahntik hung in mid-air, screaming out her mindless rage, as Conn escaped across the field and into the wilderness of rocks below the western cliffs.

Six ahlork—at the fields above the Ruins of Ahlork

The six ahlork who eventually came to investigate Mahntik's screams found her unhurt. They gathered around to enjoy the curious sight of a varok in an insensible rage trapped in a small rover hanging at a ridiculous tilt from a web bush. Their rough laughter attracted other ahlork, and soon twelve of the chortling square-headed beasts were gathered around Mahntik's wreck.

After conferring among themselves, three young ahlork decided that the varok was hollering about the elll they had reported in the fields earlier. They took off and flew over the rocks to look for him, but in a short time they tired of searching and returned to the more amusing scene in the web field.

ORLAH'S PARADOX

Conn—moments after the crash

Long straight rows of web bushes gave Conn cover as he escaped from the curious ahlork circling Mahntik's disabled shuttle-car. He moved toward the Misted Ocean, up the slopes that met the ruins below the steep southern cliffs.

He took no chances, keeping to the ruins, moving steadily during the next dark-period.

At first light he found a dank cellar and curled into his wet-sweater intending to sleep, but sleep would not come. The reality of Mahntik's insane attack was more than he could forget. It was as surreal as the reactor and ahlork spraying web bushes. Were they all mad, all hooked on addictive web berries? He could see no other logical connection.

Finally the light began to fade again. He climbed out of his cool retreat and let the last of his water drip onto his wet-sweater. Then he took his bearings. Here the ruins were filled with sand. They covered the cliffs that reached their full height on the southern-most point of Leahnyahorkah.

Conn needed more water, and started toward a path leading down the rocks in a zig-zagg along the cliffside and down to the sea. Suddenly, with an ear-shattering clap, a dark shadow hit the sand nearby.

Conn scrambled blindly for the nearest path, but a phalanx of sharp edges threw him to the ground.

"Watch him, varok, if you want life," an ahlork voice demand-ed of an unseen person. "Move from here and you will be feed for my nest. We will decide what we do with this elll."

"Come back here, you raw-toothed heap of shingles," Conn shouted at the ahlork, as some of them clattered off through the rocks. "All right, Mahntik, where are you?"

"It is not Mahntik." A withered voice sounded from the rocky path that led down the cliff, and Orlah stumbled into view.

"Orlah, thank God, Harrahn or not," Conn shouted. "I thought Mahntik had sent her clatter-plated bully-boys to finish me off. I guess these ahlork are not going to fall for her nonsense after all. And you have found a way in with them?"

"All that—when in reality I have been told to hold you until Mahntik can summon medical help. You vastly underestimate Mahntik, Conn, and you overestimate both myself and the ahlork."

"Which ahlork, Orlah? Nidok saved my life."

"And Sartak would take it. His flock sits above on the rocks to learn all they can from us."

"So tell me a story I can believe, Orlah."

"Yes. Perhaps you can help me make some sense of it." Orlah looked at Conn with heavy eyes, then sat down on an irregular rock, oblivious to balance or comfort. "I am near consummation with Mahntik."

Conn looked up at the ahlork. "That should interest you foul birds."

They shifted restlessly on the rocks but said nothing.

Orlah's eyes sought Conn's, hopelessly yearning for approval. "We work at it constantly."

"I'll bet you work at it," Conn fumed. *Such a consummation would be nothing but parody. Consummation is a spontaneous process—two varoks fall into each other's minds as inevitably as water seeking its level.*

"Yes, routinely," Orlah admitted. "We spend one-quarter of every other light-period since Orram—"

"That fiend! She's driven you over the brink." Conn paced furiously around Orlah, his sparse crown plumes trembling. "Can't you see that she's using you, the way she's using the ahlork?"

The elll raised his voice so the ahlork would not miss anything he said. "She's leading Sartak and Susheen into a trap. She's pretending to be their friend, then she will sic the varoks on them when it suits her purposes, when she needs someone to blame. Is that the kind of mind you want to call your own, Orlah?"

The ahlork moved down the rocks, listening.

Conn stopped his pacing and let his fury drain away. He risked placing his hands on Orlah's shoulders and looked deep into the varok's eyes—the way he had looked into them when they were very young, when Orlah was experimenting with his maturing ability to scan minds.

"You don't have one unkind bone in your body," Conn said. The soft melody of his voice nearly sent Orlah into despair. "You'll never consummate with Mahntik, and she knows it."

"She wants this consummation as much as I do," Orlah argued. "She knows she can never have it with—" He stiffened with the unfinished thought.

"All right. Let's put that aside, Orlah. But you've got to tell me all you can about her schemes. You can't be part of her treason."

"I know nothing about any treason," Orlah said.

"Surely you have seen it in her mind—something, anything, about my capture, about web berries."

"I see . . . nothing in her mind."

"You can't mean 'nothing.'"

Orlah stared silently at the ground.

"Surely you can't expect to find consummation with this mind, this 'nothing.'"

Orlah made no reply. His eyes swam in confusion from the rocks at his feet to the shoreline below.

"I'm sorry," Conn said. *He is so overwhelmed and blinded by Mahntik, Orlah can know neither her mind nor his own.*

"You haven't seen the web fields all over this island?" Conn asked. "Surely you know of the fields near the Lake of the Passage. You took me there to recover. Apparently Mahntik is shipping products and seeds from those webs all over Varok."

"I spend my time in the web fields. That is all."

"Orram would never allow shipping such long distances, if he knew about it."

"True. There are probably more than he knows—"

"And he wouldn't allow poisons let lose into the soil and water. Did you know the ahlork are spraying everything with poison to control the web suckers?"

"I know nothing of ahlork spreading chemicals. Mahntik is growing new strains of web," Orlah said. "One produces better cloth. The other takes selenium from the soil here. She adds rhenium filaments to the webs during weaving to make warming cloth. It could save much energy. That is all."

Conn needed no patches to sense that Orlah believed what he was saying. "Let me tell you more," the elll said. "The ahlork are cultivating large mono-cultures of web berries for Mahntik. That's why the web suckers grew out of control, and they're burning good natural forage to do it. And what is more crazy than Mahntik's scorched earth farming is the fact that she's toying with ahlork at an old reactor."

"These schemes of ahlork are not Mahntik's doing."

"Ahlork don't run nuclear reactors." He looked again at the nearby eavesdroppers. "They're carnivores, fishers, shoreline scavengers." The elll's temper flew wild again, then quieted suddenly, in his usual manner. "Can't you see it, Orlah? Can't you give me some idea?"

"No. No. I know nothing of these things, and they are not in Mahntik's mind." Orlah sat hunched over on the rock, silent in his effort to regain control.

"They must be," Conn said. "When I get home I'll have to press charges against you for suppressing information about the reactor."

"I didn't know. I didn't realize what the ahlork were doing, what the Free-minds were doing."

"Mahntik manipulates the Free-minds, too?"

"These things are not in Mahntik's mind, I tell you." Orlah struggled for calm. "Conn, you are not yourself."

"How could she lie to you? Did you see no clues in her mind that she took me from the Theater of Great-fish and imprisoned me in these damnable ruins and nearly dried me out of existence?"

"You have been seriously dehydrated, Conn. You have always hated Mahntik. You are imagining too much."

Conn quickly checked his temper. He would learn nothing more if Orlah went irrational.

An intense sorrow doused his senses, as he remembered joyful daramont rides with Orlah through the red rocks of the Vahinorral. *How many times had we drunk sweet red algae beside Orserah's warm hearth, while Orram and his young son listened to the tales of our wanderings? How have we come to this, shouting at each other while ahlork preen their plates on the rocks above, pretending not to listen?*

"Think carefully, Orlah," Conn whispered. "You must have seen some hint of my imprisonment in Mahntik's memory, some vision of ahlork spraying the web fields, some of her guilt in sending you off to help with illegal web distribution. Surely you couldn't have repressed all that."

"No," Orlah said, calmer now. "I'm sure I have repressed nothing, Conn. I drink of Mahntik's mind as deeply as I can. I savor every drop, I remember every current, I taste every subtle flavor I can. I don't repress the memory of anything I see in Mahntik's mind."

"Then you are nowhere near consummation," Conn exclaimed, his elllonian dislike for paradox driving him wild.

The ahlork shuffled back and forth nervously.

"I'm not sure about the web fields, but somewhere—everywhere—in Mahntik's mind there must be some residue of my imprisonment."

For a moment Orlah was silent. Then his voice moved tonelessly over his words, and his body sank deeper into its posture of hopelessness. "I realized some time ago that the new web bushes were replacing the old strains on Vior. They had grown far beyond the limits of the experimental plots Mahntik described to me. I don't understand how she could have missed that."

"But you found nothing in her mind when you deliberately probed her on that subject?"

"I had the same clear impression I always have. Please, Conn, you are intruding again where common decency forbids it."

"A clear impression?" Conn persisted. "When you were in her mind, deeply joined there, you had a clear impression?"

"Stop it, Conn. You go too far."

"And you have not gone far enough, Orlah!" Conn grabbed the collar of Orlah's tunic and pulled him up from the rock. "Mahntik tried to kill me. Twice. When she saw me near the reactor she tried to run me down with a rover. Now tell me—for all our sanity— what is clear about being in Mahntik's mind? *Clear* doesn't make sense. Consummation involves a melding of all thought, all feeling, all memory—everything. It's not a simple mind-scan. Nothing should be clear."

The volatile elll took a calming breath. "Have a look in my head, Orlah," he said. "Try to probe, as deep as you can. I will call up the nasty memories. You will understand the paradox that's bursting my logic channels wide open."

Orlah

Into the maze of Conn's mind . . . that is Mahntik leaning over the elll, mocking him, asking him personal questions about Orram . . . coming at him with her rover. It couldn't be. These impressions bear no resemblance to the fragments of old confrontations in Mahntik's memory.

Fighting his way to some rationale, Orlah knew that the elll also felt the frustration of blind alleys of explanations that didn't work. Together they accessed the emotion, the anger and frustration, that flowed around that tangle of blind alleys. Orlah had never been so deep within the thoughts of an elll. Like a tiny insect, he struggled as if trapped in the tender web of Conn's logic.

"Compared to your convoluted elll mind, Mahntik's consciousness is a small, neatly kept room," Orlah murmured. *There, the flow of thoughts is shallow and cool,* he continued in thought. *Here a million*

*channels open in every direction, and thought flows wide and deep. How
are you ellls able to think at all?*

Orlah touched the dark, repressed horrors far behind Conn's
consciousness. The narrow passages were twisted and burned.
Aeeyull! Nothing but pain there. To Conn those channels of memory felt black and shrunken, charred with knowledge too terrible
to retain.

Orlah retreated, and remembered. *"How can my eyes show anger
and my mind be so blank and free of emotion? Oran Ramahlak, how do
you like that puzzle?"* Mahntik's thoughts had grown added dimensions, run along new channels, as she challenged Orram at the
lodge. There one moment, then gone.

"No, no! Mahntik!" Orlah's face crumpled with dismay.

"You had better leave that memory to itself," Conn said, bring-
ing Orlah back to the moment with a bell-like voice, smooth and
calming. "You are too unsettled by my memory of Mahntik's hos-
pitality, and so am I."

Orlah looked up, shocked by Conn's awareness. "How did you
know where I was?" For a moment a wave of hope washed over the
varok. "What have you seen in my mind?"

"I could feel your footprints, walking through my memories
as I dragged them up—and you were talking all the time. It was
good to have you there, Orlah, like riding through the Vahinorral
together again."

"Then you didn't hear Mahntik challenge Orram?" Orlah
sagged toward the ground. "I have remembered too much, Conn.
Help me . . . a shifting vapor, unreal . . . I have seen Mahntik's
mind . . . fade. Or was it mine?"

Conn

Conn bent over Orlah, not with a comforting touch, but simple
closeness that might help the varok regain his reason. "Tell me
again. What have you seen? It's okay. Never mind, I got it. Come
back to me, Orlah, there will be time enough for dealing with other worries." He spoke as calmly as he could manage.

"Walk through my mind to your heart's content, Orlah. It

ought to be better than wallowing in the cold sewage of Mahntik's mental septic tank."

"Translate! Translate!" an ahlork's voice screamed. "Translate Earth words. Translate." Sartak and three other ahlork appeared from behind the rocks, followed by four, five, then seven and eight more. They crowded above and around Conn and Orlah, making guesses at what the elll had meant.

"Go fly, Sartak," Conn said, glancing pointedly at the berry-stained patches around his neck. "You heard about Mahntik trying to run me down in the web fields. She doesn't love ahlork either, you know."

"Of course, elll. Mahntik uses ahlork, too," Sartak said. "Only Gitahl is our friend. We don't trust this brother of Orram who wallows in Mahntik's 'zaptik tonk.' Translate that. Translate or I smash your throat, elll."

Sartak lunged at Conn with his wing edges cocked, while two ahlork jumped the elll from behind and held his long green arms in a painful grip.

"Septic tank, not 'zaptic tonk,'" Conn enunciated into Sartak's square face. "Let me go, and I'll tell you. A septic tank is a closed underground tank and runoff system used on Earth to collect human waste and allow it to rot with the help of anaerobic bacteria."

"Ridiculous." Sartak screamed with delight. "You will call Mahntik's mind such a thing? You will call Mahntik's mind a closed runoff of human waste?"

All the ahlork exploded with croaking laughter.

In spite of himself a chuckle escaped from Conn's throat. Then, suddenly, the paradox in his mind realized the solution—Mahntik's mind was a closed runoff.

"Orlah." The varok looked up at him, with eyes a dead pale blue. Conn took the varok by the shoulders, trying to shock him from his depression. "When we were tads on Ellason, we were told legends, stories of varoks who would do evil things because they could elude a normal mind-scan."

"Yes," Orlah said. "Those legends are often retold on the hearths of Varok."

"Old stories sometimes grow from fact," Conn said. "A

mind-block would explain why Mahntik could lie to you."

"Mahntik will lie to you, also?" a dark-plated ahlork asked Orlah. "You will tell us this. We will not harm the victims of Mahntik." His fine plates clicked sharply as he walked defiantly up to Sartak. "The Greater Flock will release these two."

Sartak's wing-plates flexed to full cock. "I will be Sartak, and I hold this elll, Conn, and Orlah, hostages for the Greater Flock, until ahlork have no blame for nuclear reactors and murder."

"I will be Susheen," said the dark ahlork, matching Sartak's stance. "I will say ahlork who feed Leyoon poison are no ahlork. They disgrace the True Flock." As if on cue, his flock closed in around him.

"Is murder to feed web berries to great-fish?" Sartak countered. Six of his flock moved forward in his support.

"What do my ear plaques hear you saying?" Conn demanded angrily. "Is Leyoon dead? Did some of you platter-faced birds kill Leyoon?" He whirled to face Orlah. "Did you have any hint of this from Mahntik's mind, Orlah? Did Mahntik plan Leyoon's murder?"

Orlah doubled over, burying his head in his arms as if wishing away consciousness.

"Forgive me," Conn cried, profoundly moved by Orlah's collapse. "I shouldn't have pushed you that way."

"We will have enough of varoks and ellls," Sartak shouted. "Susheen, bring your flock, follow me to the genetics labs. Now."

"Agreed. Enough for Mahntik," a young ahlork shouted. "Ahlork of Sartak's flock will be slaves no longer."

"The young grow foolish on web berries," Susheen said. "Sartak's ahlork would roost where radiation and foul genetic mutants will tear our bloodroots. You lead us to death, Sartak."

Enraged, Sartak flew at Sushseen with shearing wing tips. "Son of a fouled nest," he shouted, as he slashed the elder down. "Ahlork will be just beginning! We will rule Varok again!"

No ahlork dared to help the elder. Conn bent over him. Susheen was dead of a broken neck. Orlah stared, immobilized with horror, then grew incoherent as despair drowned his reason. "I want to go home. We must get home," he cried, and Conn caught him as his body crumpled to the ground.

"To the genetics labs!" Sartak cried. "We will throw germs into varokian water holes."

"No. You will not do this." Orram's son Orticon emerged from the ruins, armed with a long piece of twisted steel. "I will alert Mahntik to your treason. She will destroy your flocks if you attack the genetics lab."

Orticon

"You, Sartak, have broken your agreement to aid Mahntik and the Free-minds in the strengthening of Varok," Orticon stated. "Do not go near the genetics lab."

Orticon's crude iron weapon waved menacingly across the ahlork's frightened, square faces, until, one by one, they rose into the air and disappeared over the Misted Ocean.

"Orticon, you poor excuse for a delinquent, you need to help us," Conn said. "Orlah has gone lulu."

Orticon ran to the elll and eased Orlah from his arms. "Conn. Great Harrahn. What's happened to you? I thought you were recovering in the lake. You still look terrible."

"Still? You knew I was in the lake?" Conn slumped to the ground. "Too much has happened to me, thank you. Guess I left the lake too soon."

"I have watched too much since I saw you leaving the reactor complex with Orlah. And just now I have heard too much of Mahntik and her treachery—pesticides, burning and clearing good forest for webs, these things I suspected. But kidnapping, murder, and now a mind block? If that is true, she will be very difficult to prosecute, Conn."

"Orlah can probably tell us more tales, later. But what do we do for him now? I've got to get him home—and first get a message to Orram and Tandra. They don't even know I'm alive."

"Then by all means—I suppose they might be missing you, just a little," Orticon said with a somber smile. "Better talk to Orlah while I call in your less than tragic fate." Orticon activated his personal maser cell, left a message on Orram's office phone, then contacted security at L'orkah's shuttle station. "I am Orticon of the Oran family. We need medical help for the elll Conn of the same family. He's been severely dehydrated. Send an airshuttle to the cliffs below the northwest Ruins of Ahlork. Please contact the home office of Living Resources. Tell them Conn is alive and being treated for prolonged dehydration. Please try to contact my father, Oran Ramahlak. He has been looking for this elll—Conn of the Oran-elConn-Grey Family."

Tandra—earlier that morning

"Killah, this is Tandra calling for Orram."

"He's not here, Tandra. Lanoll has come and gone, back to L'orkah, I believe."

"Then perhaps Orram is still there. Can you tell me how things are going in the Lake Seclusion area?"

"The situation on the Mount Ni foothills has begun to snowball," Killah said. "We found the ahlork are using pesticides and chemical fertilizer on their web crops there. There's already too much fertilizer washing into Lake Seclusion. El eggs there are not able to hatch in the altered chemistry. The light-hoppers are struggling; the lichen they eat has been crowded out by algae. Meanwhile, pesticides have been found at all levels of the food chain. It's causing great-fish dyscrasias. There's no predicting what will happen next." He took a tired breath, and went on. "Jesse and Artellian have gone to Mount Ni. We think the ahlork, and probably some varoks, have set up a black market there—with goods coming from L'orkah, probably from Mahntik. Her prices can't be including all her transportation and environmental costs; they're just too low. Local web businesses are failing around Lake Seclusion in spite of the population boom there."

"All this, and so quickly," I said. "We're seeing similar changes in the web fields here, but not as sweeping. I've logged your report in case Orram comes here before you reach him. Please call if you learn where he is, or Lanoll. No one seems to know where they are." I set down the receiver.

Why hadn't we heard from them? Had Mahntik taken Orram in, as she had Orlah? Or had she done him in?

SARTAK AND MAHNTIK

Mahntik—later the same light-period

Mahntik threw open the door of her house and emerged into the dim flashing of a blue-green light-period.

What does Gitahl think he is doing? Has he lost his senses, calling me back to the genetics labs now. If he were recognized, he would be scanned for information about Leyoon's murder, and his knowledge of the reactor would surely be discovered.

She was not worried about the few varoks stationed around the genetics lab. Here she reigned as Director of Genetics Research; she would not be questioned—especially about her work. Who would suspect that she diverted much of her effort from unraveling the genetic fabric of infectious viruses to weaving microscopic disease organisms? Who would endanger her research cultures by poking around in the lab's collection of pathogens?

Ingenious pathogens, she congratulated herself. *Prions that combine the most vicious invasive properties of viruses with the best biochemical devices of infectious bacteria.*

When she reached the lab, she hurried past the guards, explaining that she needed to tend to delicate cultures. They did not doubt her.

She moved swiftly past each of many locked doors to the lift. The halls of the second floor were as strangely quiet as the first. All the labs were deserted. When she came to the large containment lab, where her most dangerous experiments in gene-splicing were conducted, she found the double sealed doors standing wide open.

She hesitated, stunned by the unmistakable sound of ahlork, then she stormed ahead and came upon Sartak, standing in the middle of the lab, filling it with outstretched wings.

"Get out!" she screamed.

The ahlork were busy emptying the incubators and refrigerators of culture tubes. With a gargle and a shrug in her direction, they went back to work.

Sartak wound a prehensile wing-tip around Mahntik's wrist,

pulling her down to face him. "This varok kills more ahlork than ellls," he shouted. "Lock her in."

Two ahlork started toward Mahntik, but she smiled at Sartak, taunting him. "You wouldn't dare turn on me. Gitahl. Gitahl!"

"Gitahl is gone," Sartak sneered. "So sorry."

"Your ahlork are handling cultures that could kill them." Mahntik's fear began to darken her tone. Why had Gitahl lured her here? Had he betrayed her, after all?

"You are no longer master of ahlork," Sartak said, taking a basket of culture tubes from the wing-tip of another ahlork and holding it over her head. "The Greater Flock will now take all Varok. Ahlork don't rebuild ruins with nuclear power. Where do ahlork do mining, where do ahlork nest, if varoks live in ruins?"

"You ahlork are not immune to the pneumonic plague in that basket," Mahntik said, struggling to remain calm.

For a moment, she saw that Sartak was disarmed. He knew very little about germs, but he had heard of the pneumonic plague.

"You are mad, Sartak. How do you know which cultures to release? Some will infect the ahlork and destroy the entire Greater Flock, as well as varoks."

"I am not mad, Mahntik. You will teach us microbes." He opened his wings to their full span, releasing Mahntik and knocking over bottles and a drop analyzer. Two ahlork seized Mahntik. The sharp edges of their plates discouraged her.

"You will tell us all of it." Sartak said. "We serve you no longer. You serve us. Never again you use ahlork to feed rotten ellls."

"I did not release Conn," Mahntik screamed, her mind closing over with terror. "I found him in the web fields. I thought you had released him—to betray me. I tried to kill him, but he escaped. The ahlork in the fields wouldn't help me—wouldn't bring him back."

Sartak's black eyes pierced her, and she could see that he enjoyed his control, but feared her irrational state. "Just mark the plague cultures," he said, "and we let you go, for now."

Mahntik pulled away from the ahlork and marked three racks of cultures with a wax pencil. "Watch what you do with these."

The ahlork flew from the broken windows and soared away over the ruins with their lethal cargo.

Mahntik wasted no time reporting the theft to the guards, then she made her way back to her house and called for Gitahl. He was waiting for her. Mahntik stood before him in her bedroom, more aware of her own heightened senses than his dangerous mood.

"Why don't you lose yourself to your anger, Gitahl? I would like to see you incoherent with emotion just once. What are you trying to repress? Anger? That Sartak let me go? I suppose. Yes. That's it, isn't it?

"Too bad, Gitahl. You have allied yourself with a flock of imbeciles. Why would you turn on me? Am I mad? Perhaps. But not nearly as mad as Sartak. He left me with too many cultures. He didn't have sense enough to take them all. The ahlork will learn just how dangerous it is to play with such things, and we will have the beasts back under control."

"You would release disease into the ahlork's waters? That is mad. I am done with you, Mahntik. Those cultures would be traced immediately back to your labs, just as your stupid marketing schemes with webs and berries and silage will soon be traced back to you. Orram is no fool."

"No more than you, Gitahl," Mahntik murmured, touching his forearms with provocative fingers. "Don't think evil of your true mate."

"True mate? With a mind too shallow to wet one's knees?"

"You dare insult me?" Mahntik struck out at him with a vicious kick.

Gitahl caught her leg and threw her to the bed-pad. "You trapped me into being accused of murder, Mahntik—and I was ready to excuse the mistake. But it was no mistake, was it? You meant for me to be seen at the Theater of Great-fish with the ahlork. That would put me safely out of the way, forced into hiding. But now you have gone too far. My time is up. L'orkah is swarming with Free-minds and Energy Council officials. Fool! Fool to tell Orram about that reactor. I can never stay hidden now."

"No one calls me fool," Mahntik said slowly, from where Gitahl had thrown her. Her eyes flashed and her breast heaved with the passion generated by his dangerous anger.

Gitahl moved toward her.

"You are of no more use to me, Gitahl," Mahntik said, backing away. "Orram will find you too soon now." Mahntik hated Gitahl, and feared him—yet she was drawing him on, firing his rage with her sensual challenge, hoping he would go irrational.

Suddenly it was too late. Gitahl turned and left the room, leaving Mahntik with her warped desire, clawing at emptiness.

VII. Impossible Choices

There are bifurcation points,
forks in every road,
at every level of our lives.

Most irreducibly random as a coin toss,
and many subject to the possibility of amplification—
hence nothing we do,
nothing we choose, is inconsequential.

Some call this built-in meaning.

—Tandra's diary

A DIFFICULT HOMECOMING

Conn—on the shuttle home

Orlah seemed to be asleep on the hovershuttle's bench, still irrational. When they were far over the Misted Ocean, Conn reached out to Orticon.

"Surely you can talk to me now," he said. "I won't argue with you. I know you hate normal everyday patch contact, but I think you're nuts. I'd give two toe-fins to be able to read moods."

To Conn's delight, Orticon laughed. "You've said that before, but it was your left sonic melon you would give. You don't need patch organs; you do an excellent job with empathy."

"Empathy is an inexact talent. Varokian patch contact gives you more information. But since I don't have my patches on today, how about telling me what's happening? Were the Free-minds involved with the ahlork in some crazy scheme to reactivate that old nuclear reactor?"

Orticon stared ahead. The shuttle passed beneath a sheet of light falling from the auroral horizon into the acrid mists below. "Maybe it wasn't so crazy, Conn. A human space ship will soon land on Varok. Many believe it represents a new danger, one with no end."

Conn failed to keep the annoyance out of his voice. "Has Mahntik got you wrapped in her fancy silk, too? Like Orlah? She has the talents of a spider."

"Don't insult her, Conn. She may be right about the danger from Earth."

"She's not right about anything, Orticon, especially not about Earth." He leaned back and decided not to push the youth too far. He seemed to have learned something on his recent travels. It was much more pleasant to think of Lanoll—and Shawne. How had she adjusted to Varok? How many questions had he missed? He daydreamed of her chubby arms around his neck and the sharp jab he would feel as she stole a plume from his hip.

"I have questions for you, Conn."

"That's good news. Shoot."

"I am not as certain . . . about things, as I once was. Please answer seriously."

Conn's hoped his tone and the intensity behind his eyes would give Orticon what he needed. "I promise."

"I don't see why Mahntik wanted to distribute a new web strain outside her locale. There is no profit in producing more than is needed—"

"Unless you extend credit and rake in the interest. Credit means people can buy more, so you convince them they actually need more—say, by making sure things wear out fast."

"Credit? What would people be willing to put up as collateral just for extra cloth?"

"Nothing. Mahntik's success depends on unsecured credit, unreported income and unpaid taxes, or my name isn't The Green Scab."

Orticon seemed to be considering, so Conn went on.

"Mahntik has forgotten that you can't grow forever. You can't make something out of nothing and you can't get perpetually more efficient.Bottom line—you can't grow the economy and think technology will solve the disruption it causes to Varok. We're already seeing the price for Mahntik's web schemes. The population around Mt. Ni is exploding."

"Our populations have always been stable."

"They'd better be. Our resource quotas and the whole steady-state economy work only because our populations don't grow—well, that, and because total recycling is enforced, and the system is based on real goods and resources—not on debt and balance sheets. Mahntik would like to change all of that."

"Okay, so we keep resource depletion near zero," Orticon said. "That's fine for securing some unknown future, but the result is that Varok is totally undefended—we could lose everything. We should thank Mahntik for awakening us all to the danger."

"Mahntik *is* the danger. Think about it," Conn said. "Varok's best defense is in the fact that every locale is self-sufficient. You've studied Earth; it's a web of dependence on huge electrical grids and single points of mass production and long-range distribution—even essentials like food and water are targets for attack. How is someone going to cripple Varok, when the essentials of life here are spread out so evenly across the map?"

Orticon paused before answering. "Growing up on Varok, I assumed everything we needed came from local production, if we didn't grow it as a family. Each home has its own waste disposal and recycling. Every locale its own wind or tide generator, its own unique solutions—"

"Solutions that a centralized body like Global Varok couldn't possibly solve as well, from a distance, since they can't be familiar with each local situation or individual problem—like building house ponds for loner ellls."

"But that's just it, the locales are limited in scale." Orticon gave Conn a look that said *gotcha*. "Varoks need to collaborate in order to advance technology. It takes teamwork and more infrastructure than a locale can build alone to learn new science, create high-tech devices—"

"And health services. Low energy wheels, mass transport, electronics and communication, our space program . . ." Conn was relieved they could agree. "We need the regional centers so we can work together on the big projects."

"Like defense."

They continued in silence until they came to Nihrahn, the boundless cliffs of Vior. Rising straight out of the Misted Ocean for a thousand meters, they sent a sharp thrill through Conn. He let himself believe he would soon be home. At the shuttle station, Orticon signed out an emergency medical shuttle to get Orlah and Conn home without delay.

Just as Orticon cleared takeoff, he stiffened at the controls and focused the airshuttle's scanners. "There are ahlork following us."

"Never mind. I'll lose them." Grimly, Conn took the helm from the youth. He eased the airshuttle to high speed and left the common travel lanes to fly straight over the Springs of Harinlegh, where he was startled to find large numbers of ahlork gathering. He turned and sped south at reckless speed through the Ruins of Harin, and followed the Ahlkahn past Ahl Vior into the valley beneath the Vahinorral.

At last, no ahlork in sight, they reached home. Orserah's house appeared across the fields, a promised re-awakening to rock and living trees.

Tandra—moments later at Orserah's lodge

When I heard the powerful, breathy sound of an airshuttle, I left my work with Orram's maps and data sheets and hurried onto the porch. I expected Orram and Lanoll, home in a rush from their work at L'orkah, having received the dire news from Lake Seclusion. Instead I saw Orticon, looking as dour as ever. Orlah sat in the shuttle, still and silent, his eyes staring and blank.

Beside the vehicle stood a tall, thin elll. His silhouette was drooping and frazzled. Some plumes on his head were gone, leaving bare spots on his green scalp. He looked starved, worn down to the essentials of his swimming frame. Moth-eaten tiles hung limp from his leg and arm joints. A huge wet-sweater of ragged moss hung from his shoulders in strips and pieces held together with a rag of stained, lichen-encrusted synthetic.

He turned to look at me from a scrawny face overflowing with huge black eyes.

"Conn?" I glanced at Orticon, and he answered with a nod. Hope began to rise in my throat, but it did not taste sweet. If this were Conn, he was a ragged green remnant of the once wiry sea giant.

I ran to him with a sob, and we clung together as if existence itself would slip from our grasp. "Thank God you're alive." I backed off and shook my head, crying and laughing like a varok out of control. "Let me take that wonderful wet-sweater away from you and help you get cleaned up. Your tiles are matted. It will take me six light-periods to pick you clean." I fumbled with the moss hanging on his slumped shoulders.

"Be careful when you take it off," he smiled broadly with a cracked, dry mouth. "It's holding me together."

I guided him toward the house, while I spoke to the still silent Orticon. "Please take Orlah to his room. I can see that he has left the moment."

Orticon helped his mind-crippled uncle from the airshuttle and disappeared into the house as Conn sat down on the porch to rest.

"Conn, what has happened to you and Orlah?"

"Long story, that one, Tandra. Maybe it's enough to say we both saw Mahntik's true mind."

Orticon reappeared, and I felt his eyes on mine, as though to read my mood. I no longer repulsed him.

"Orlah is already asleep, Tandra. I had better fix us all something to eat."

"Thank you, Orticon. But first, Orserah is in the far fields. Please go to her. She will be glad to see you, and will want to help Orlah."

Conn leaned against the hearth stones, dozing between bites of food, barely acknowledging my questions. "Where have you been? What happened, Conn? No, keep eating. Thank goodness, we'll have time to talk."

"Conn, go to the pond so you can sleep," Orserah said, coming cautiously in the door. She smiled, but her eyes misted over as she took in his worn tiles.

"Orserah! I've missed you—almost as much as I've missed your stew. Beautiful mother-of-ellls, you know I will welcome sleep," he agreed, shaking his eyes open. "Come tuck me in, Tan."

Orticon's disdain for the elll-human relationship resurfaced all too clearly in a shake of his head as we began to climb the stones.

"You are assuming an unnatural physical intimacy between Tandra and Conn that may not exist," we heard Orserah whisper. She was outraged. "Conn's instincts are clearly centered on the elll Lanoll—which would be clear to you if you used your patches as they were meant to be used!"

I helped Conn up the stones to the algae pond, and we drifted together in the warm water. We said very little, sensing each other with all our beings. When our excited shaking finally quieted to an occasional shiver, I went to work on his tiles, and Conn began to talk in condensed phrases as he struggled to include me in his past.

"Mahntik had the ahlork shut me up, dry, in the ruins."

"Mahntik? Conn, but she—"

"Nidok—the scar-lip that attacked me on the Ahlkahn—he couldn't stand it; he saved me. Orlah helped me hide in a small lake, then Orticon came along. Where the hell is Orram? Nidok couldn't have killed Leyoon. Mahntik may be behind that, too. Sartak has gone mad. He killed Susheen. He's threatening to take disease cultures from the genetics labs as weapons."

"Diseases—I don't understand. Why?"

Conn paused to drench his gills before continuing. "Mobs of ahlork are on their way here to sell berries—to expand the black market. Mahntik's been growing more webs, telling the ahlork to spread new strains all over Varok. She's madder than a dry elll. She and the Free-minds had some scheme going with an old nuclear reactor. There's no telling what she's planning to do. And we've got to get help to Nidok. And there's Lanoll—the elll—"

"I know," I said, trying to smile.

"You've seen her?" Conn's eyes brightened with hope and worry.

"Lanoll came to the family when she thought you had been killed. She is adjusted with us, Conn. We are her school."

"Lanoll's been here? Adjusted to you?" The green moss of Conn's face seemed to fade. "I only mated with her once—"

"It meant so much to her, to love you, Conn, a loner like herself . . . She was drawn here, no longer able to school, grieving because she was afraid you were suffering, then believing you were gone. She has taken the ring."

"From you and Orram, not from me; I am an elll for humans—for you and Shawne. I can't have her pushing you from my water."

I laughed. "This is all backward. She won't push me from your water, Conn." I took his face in my hands and whispered into his head plumes. "Nothing will ever push us apart, not even ourselves. Lanoll can learn to cope with us. It shouldn't be difficult. She's used to sharing her mates with a whole school of ellls."

"But you are human," Conn insisted, pressing my lips to the tender spot beneath his chin. "I know what you're going through. I've experienced jealousy. It's torture."

I bit my lip. "Yes. I can see you know all about torture." I could say no more. His arms gathered me in and we drifted together in silence for a long time. I was oblivious to everything but the ripe-olive smell of his elllonian skin, the stillness of his chest as his gills took over his breathing, the lazy rippling of half-recovered muscles as his legs and back-fin slowly stirred the water, keeping me above the surface.

"I'm tired, Tan," he said. "I've been dry for too many light-periods. If you still want a pet elll, you got one."

"You know you're safe from that," I said, remembering our first go-around on that issue. "I will never try to possess anyone ever again."

Conn gave me a questioning look. "Except Orram. At least he is an absolute for you, Tan. Half Orram's neurons are yours."

Yes, half, I thought. *How can I tell him about Mahntik and Orram when I don't fully understand it? Leyoon accused her of treason. But kidnapping Conn? Killing Leyoon? Orram could not join with such a mate—Varokian hormones cannot be that blind. So where is he?*

"Perhaps I don't need an absolute, Conn."

"What are you saying?" His tired eyes opened, nearly filling his face.

"It's just that I am learning to run the homestead without Orram," I stammered. "His work as governor often takes him away from home, and Orserah is no longer young." *He has been gone too long.*

I held Conn as he drifted off, and watched him sleep for some time, the deep sleep of one kept too long from safety and rest. Then I retired to a bench near the pool to reflect.

Tandra—the next morning

At first light we were all awakened by an excited cry from Shawne. It came from the garden. "Mom! Gramgram!" She plunged through the massive double doors to the hearth room and pulled Orticon outside with her. "I found these ugly bugs all over the web bushes. I've never seen one before." She held up her hand. "It's gross. Dirty white."

As I descended the steps to the hearth, I saw Orserah join

them. "The white web suckers are common only near the Springs of Harinlegh," Orserah told the child. "It is very unusual for them to appear so far south."

They watched the wriggling insect as it crept along Shawne's palm, looking for forage.

When Shawne offered it a handful of web-stalks, it set on one with hungry pincers, attaching itself securely to its favorite meal. Shawne took it out to the egg-layers yard.

"Tasty bug?" she asked the shaggy creatures in Elllonian, offering the stalk.

The little beasts showed no interest, but continued scratching in the dirt.

"Sadly, egg layers don't eat web suckers, Shawne." Orserah looked out over the fields. "But the ilara do. I wonder what has become of them. I've seen so few lately."

"We'll kill the bugs, Grandmother. All of them! Don't worry." Shawne smashed the web sucker under her boot.

"That could be quite a lot of stomping, to keep up with those pests. The ilara are much better at it. Tandra, we'll see what Conn thinks of this later, after he is rested." We followed Shawne toward the lodge.

"Grandmother," Orticon spoke quietly. "Conn was in bad shape on L'orkah. He has not been entirely himself."

"What can you mean, Orticon?" Orserah said.

"He has made some strong accusations against Mahntik, which cannot be true. How could she hide knowledge of his imprisonment?"

"Tandra, is this true? Conn accuses Mahntik of holding him captive? Did he say anything when you were with him last night?"

"He said that Mahntik sent ahlork to kidnap and hold him." I spoke carefully. "She may have been involved in Leyoon's death. Leyoon himself accused her of treason against Varok."

"But not kidnapping and murder," Orticon said. "Leyoon may have disapproved of Mahntik's plans for Varok, but she couldn't have done murder without revealing some hint of guilt."

"Glad to hear you admitting you've got patch organs, Orticon old buddy." Conn regarded Orticon from the top of the hearth stones. "But you have a lot to learn about Mahntik."

"Conn. You're really back!" Shawne ran to the steps and threw herself into his arms. "You look awful," she said, poking the smooth spots worn into his tiles. "How come you lost so much fuzz? How come you're not dead?"

"Because Mahntik kept me closed up without water, and because Nidok saved me."

"Are you accusing Mahntik of kidnapping—still?" Orticon demanded.

"Take a look, Orticon, Orserah, the vivid memories are all there in my head."

"You know I will not scan you." Orticon was defiant. "You know I am a Free-mind."

Conn looked pleadingly to Orserah. "You've got to see it. Someone must know."

"I'll try, Conn," Orserah hesitated, "but you know it is very difficult. Your brains are—"

"Like tangled webs," Conn tried to encourage her. "I know, our minds are loaded with heaps of sensual data—difficult to read. We can sort them into tangles of deductive reasoning, but now mine are tangled with emotions I'd rather not explain in words."

Orserah leaned toward Conn and looked intently into his eyes for several minutes. "It's not good, Conn. I can that, but you have always disliked Mahntik."

"I've never accused her of kidnapping before, have I? Now I'll add murder to the list. She murdered two ahlork by Nidok's witness—and probably Leyoon. Read deeper, Orserah. It's all there."

"Some of your memory of L'orkah seems badly distorted, Conn."

"I didn't have hallucinations until my moss started flaking."

"I must believe you, Conn, of course," Orserah said, "or believe your belief—but you must realize that Orram has scanned Mahntik very carefully, more than once. Before he died, Leyoon accused her of treason. The great-fish must have been wrong, or Orram would have seen her guilt."

"She is able to block her mind," Conn stated, again inviting Orserah's reading.

"Of course that's impossible," Orserah spoke gently. "Mind-blocks exist only in children's stories."

"Or in rare mutants that supply the basis for such stories," Conn said. "If we can fill Orlah with enough of your excellent food, he and I may be able to put together evidence to prove that the block exists. He, too, found a paradox between my memory and his knowledge of Mahntik's mind. He may have seen the block. That's why his mind's gone on vacation for a while. He's grieving for a dream turned too ugly and sour."

Orticon looked at me and Orserah, and I knew we shared a doubt about the condition of Conn's mind.

Conn looked to each of us in growing desperation. "Orticon, don't you understand how Mahntik's lying relates to what is happening at Mount Ni? Mahntik's attempts to control the web markets are blatant disruptions that will undermine the local basis of the Varokian economy. The point is, damn it, no one can see her guilt."

"Varok suffers because the economic basis is too localized." Orticon returned with visible relief to the familiar Free-mind argument. "Mahntik understands the need to protect Varok. "The humans are coming, Conn, with official intent. There's no doubt now. The invasion is authorized by Earth's World Federation."

"Our human visitors may have official sanction for their trip now," I said, "but they're mostly students, funded by a few concerned oligarchs wealthy enough to send them. They're armed with nothing but their complexity economics textbooks."

"You know about the Earth ship?" Orticon looked at me with reawakened suspicion.

"Since Orram has been gone, I have continued the discussion with Earth. I got news of the ship as soon as the Word Federation sanctioned it—well after they launched. There was disagreement over it on Earth, but a few economists and business people ignored the rest and launched a voyage here to study the steady state. They can't believe it's possible without an overbearing government. Yet they say that they understand very well that time is not your enemy when enough is saved and reused. They know Earth is in danger from overpopulation stress. They realize vital resources are scarce, and they hate what the overburden of waste is doing to fresh water and the oceans."

I felt as if I had made some impression. Orticon seemed to be listening. "If Leyoon was right, then Mahntik is ignoring the most basic principles . . ."

"They'll hold, Orticon," Conn said. "Mahntik has underestimated the commitment of varoks to the steady-state. Don't invest in her causes. She serves no one but herself."

"Conn, Mahntik may be selfish, but there is only so much she could do before her guilt would be obvious to other varoks," Orticon insisted.

"Orram has been watching her closely, Conn." I hated to raise the point.

"She's fooled Orram into thinking her mind is free of guilt, because she's learned to block her mind." Conn looked from me to Orticon. "Perhaps only an intensive deep probe could get past—"

"So our argument comes full circle," Orticon said. "I abhor the fact that Varokian law is based on the deep-probe; it is a demeaning invasion of privacy. I will never condone it."

"This society is based on common values, " Conn said, "not mind-scanning. It's dedication to future stability that makes Varok tick, not coersion. And not unecessary nuclear gimmicks. Why are Mahntik and the Free-minds messing around with old reactors?"

"I've said it before, Conn. The Free-minds believe Varok is vulnerable because of its tight rationing of resources," Orticon said. "We need to expand our energy infrastructure and use more resources to build up our defenses."

Conn's eyes narrowed with frustration. "Right! Some Earthlings would be eager to agree—an arms race is great for business."

Orticon scowled. "And what's wrong with growing businesses, making a better life?"

Conn went ballistic. "Don't even think it! Don't you realize the deep pit Earth has dug for itself, going that route? How are human beings ever going to get off their dependence on cars? Start converting highways to railways? How will they shovel their way out of their dependence on war and the debt mess? Require more collateral or convince everyone to pay-as-you-go, as they did before

World War I? Or maybe they'll put a stop to the rich man's game of casino economics. Maybe they'll limit income differences to 10%. You think they'll do that tomorrow? For Harrahn's sake, don't buy into Mahntik's schemes. Technology can't solve these kind of problems. Don't take Varok down that road."

Rings and Scars

Tandra—that evening at the pond

"We've put it off long enough, Tan. Tell me what's wrong."

The elll knew me too well. I could no longer hide the fears that plagued me. *Orram is so much more than I had guessed—a Master on Varok—the perfected society. With my lack of supportive family as a child, my escape into work, never thought I could marry. That's why I adopted Shawne. How could I sustain the complex relationships this Varokian family demands?*

The tips of Conn's sensitive fingers explored my hands and found each new callous. Field work in Orserah's webs had strengthened my body and my hands. I had realized quickly how important and time consuming was our obligation to the land.

Conn held me at arm's length and studied my dark eyes as I treaded water. "You're not happy, are you, Tan?" His huge orbs drank me in as he reached out and set me on the bench Orram had built into the pool. "Let's start with something easy. Why are the web fields in such bad shape?"

"They are infested with web-suckers; there aren't enough ilara to keep them in check."

"It figures," Conn said. "The ilara are in bad shape on L'orkah. There won't be a decent migration for some time, if ahlork keep dumping pesticide on the web fields above the spawning grounds."

"Ahlork?" I was incredulous. "Farming, using chemicals?"

"They are not working alone," Conn said carefully. "Our good friend, Mahntik is behind the ahlorks' web-farming. She's paying them in addictive berries, Tan. She has no conscience. None."

Mahntik. Does she have Orram on L'orkah? Willing or no?

"Tandra, you must tell me. I can't read your mind. I am not Orram."

"You've got to trust me." I felt more than a little desperate. "I'm learning to be something more than human. I've already come part way—with you and Orram. I can go further. I must."

I couldn't keep back the tears then. *I have failed Orram. I can understand his attraction, but I can't accept it. I'm too human.* The thought had taken a firm hold on my mind.

"We'll send Lanoll away," Conn said. "It's too much to ask. You can't deny what you are, Tan. We'll tell Lanoll it can't work—"

"Oh no." I held him away and looked into the searching blackness of his eyes. "No, no. It's not Lanoll. Don't blame yourself, Conn. It's Orram."

"What about Orram?"

How can I tell him that Mahntik might already be Orram's varokian mate? That she fills the gap my own humanness leaves in his life? It shouldn't matter. Orram and I are of one mind.

"He needs a varokian mate, as much as you need an elllonian one. I can accept that. It's not easy, but I've seen his need. He is very attracted to Mahntik."

"So? I was very attracted to you when you first came to work for EV Science."

"Please, Conn, you must listen. Mahntik is clearly ambitious, but she simply could not be involved with the ahlork's cruelty," I tried to speak convincingly, hating myself for the fake tone. "Orram knows her very well. He would never . . ."

Conn glided to the edge of the pond and slid up onto the deck near me. "Orram would never what, Tan? What?" He grasped my shoulders in the iron grip of his broad hands. "Out with it—all of it."

I bit my lip hard and took a deep breath. "I am a human being, Conn," I said, hoping to buy time for him to calm down. "You know that better than I do. You and I had our problems at first. My possessiveness crimped your loner style more than any school could. My assumption of dominance drove you wild, but so did my sensuality . . . because your sensuality was too much for me. We humans and ellls evolved, with all other species on our planets, with a hearty dose of reproductive hormones. Varokians did not. The mind link is everything to Orram; it should be enough for me. Yet I am human, nothing more nor less. I couldn't possibly fill all of Orram's needs, any more than yours. The problem is simple. I can't accept Mahntik as Orram might need me to."

"Funny. I have that same trouble." Conn laughed bitterly. Then he realized I was serious. "Orlah, maybe, but not Orram?"

I tried to explain, as his face filled with confusion. "You see—it isn't possible. Mahntik couldn't have kidnapped you. Orram has . . . traveled through her mind—more than once. There is no guilt there. And he has searched deeply. Surely he would unearth some hint of such a memory, even if she were very skilled at evasion."

"He could sludge through her mind forever and never see any guilt."

"But there is no varok in history with the ability to control what mind-reading patches can read. Only tales to frighten children."

"When Orlah is able, we will talk through it all. Tan, why can't you believe me?"

"I want to, and I am with you, no matter what. But you've got to help me. Stay calm, show me you are yourself. You were too dry, too long."

"Mommy. Connconn." Shawne ran up the hearth stones and jumped into the water.

"Not in your muddy jeans, baby." I hollered too late. "Shawne, won't you please go put those with the laundry? We'll have a good swim together before bedtime."

"Hey there, my muddy tad." Conn lifted Shawne up over his shoulders and swam wide circles, sending her into gleeful giggles with quick turns. He set her gently on the deck, and sadly watched her disappear down the stones. "So my memory and reason are impaired."

"Not that I can see," I said.

"Arguing with me as usual." He faked a sigh and tried to smile. "And me hardly fresh from the grave."

I caught him by the shoulder. "Now I know you're really home. You sound like your old self, as if you were never dead at all."

"I've been worse than dead, and someday I'll tell you about it—but then I'll also tell you what flowers bloom in the strange hearts of ahlork—and that will be your cure, too."

"I don't understand."

"Ahlork may be as belligerent as hobbled daramonts—but I owe my friend Nidok more than my life. He knows the truth in all this, and he is out there somewhere right now, trying to stop his species from destroying themselves working for Mahntik."

"It's always Mahntik, Conn. Ever since we approached Varok."

"Even then she was angling to get her claws into Orram."

"It's all right, Conn. I have seen his attraction to her, like any varokian consummate mind-partner would. Whatever else, she is a remarkable woman. I could never give Orram the varokian sexual experience she does."

"You give him much more. The mind link is everything to varoks. They're not hung up on sex like us Ellasonians and Earthlings."

"Perhaps." I smiled. "I realize evolution took a different turn here, but I have to be realistic."

"No wonder Orlah was so strange," he said. For a moment Conn stared into the pool. "Damn Mahntik. Damn her! Tandra, Orram would never mate with her, knowing she had kidnapped me." He pulled me to my feet. "I will take that woman's brains, Tan, and tear them out root by root, until I have proven that she blocks her mind from reading."

A violent shiver raced down my spine as I searched the rage in Conn's expression.

"Are you going to believe me, Tandra? Or are you going to stand there and tell me I'm crazy? Orram couldn't be wrong. Conn's mind has dried out—is that it? The poor elll has come home deranged from desiccation. That's it, isn't it? I've suffered brain damage."

"Conn, I don't know—"

That's all it took. Those three words destroyed him.

In a rage, Conn tore the floating cultures of the pond to shreds before he was spent. "Mahnate Tikahn," he said through clenched teeth, "Orram has mated with Mahntik. The author of Varok's cancer—Leyoon's murderer—my torturer. That's what you're trying to tell me, isn't it?"

The hurt was terrible to see. His orbs passed wildly back and forth across my face. "I won't tolerate Mahntik's name in this family." Conn pulled the precious symbol of our family from his finger and threw it from the pond, taking a painful price in web-tissue with it.

"Conn, no."

"If Orram wants Mahntik to have a ring," he said, his voice flat, deathly calm, "tell him to give her mine." He dove to the bottom of the pond and refused all my attempts to raise him.

Conn—several light-periods later

Light and dim hours passed over the pond many times, while Conn clung to the bottom, raging against a dilemma he could not solve. *Am I mad? How much was real? How much dreamed?*

Now, staring at Tandra near the bottom of the algae pond's murky water and wondering how long she would hold her breath, Conn decided he must be mad, after all—or she was. She wasn't bluffing. She was hanging onto him with all the will power she could muster. *She must be terrified. If she gulps water before she passes out she will drown. Do something!*

"Damn fool!" he cried, yanking her to the surface and throwing her out of the water.

Doubling up on the deck, she gasped and choked, then reached out for him again. "Don't shut me out like that again—ever."

He leapt onto the deck and knelt beside her, pulling her head into his lap and pounding her on the back. "You all right, Lunkhead? You all right?"

"I'll be all right when you agree to talk to me," Tandra said, coughing away the water she had taken in.

"Why talk? If I'm mad, I won't make sense." He took her long, dark hair in his hands, gathering it together and wringing it out.

"Tandra," Orserah's voice called from below, "I have tried to contact both Orram and Lanoll, again without luck. I have left another set of messages for them."

Conn turned Tandra's face toward his and glared his question at her.

"We called them, of course." Her voice shook and her eyes poured with tears. "What would you expect us to do? How could I tell them you'd come home all right, but you'd pouted yourself to death before they could get here? You haven't eaten for two light-periods. That's a good way to prove you really are brain-damaged."

"I didn't mean to scare you, Tan." Conn grieved at the thought of giving her so much pain. "I really didn't. I just couldn't face the thought—God, Tandra! To come home after all that and not be believed!"

"I know. But you've got to realize, Conn, Mahntik passed every test Orram threw at her. Her mind was clear. He tried to surprise her, several times, with sudden mind-probes. Orticon would really be upset if he knew. Orram felt some obligation, after the first time, then real guilt at probing so deeply, so often, uninvited. Then he became fascinated . . ."

"Hormones dissolve family rings. I thought you had it all, you two."

"We may look alike, Conn, but our genes come from the opposite ends of evolution; they don't even share the same sugars."

"Do all our lives boil down to chemistry in the end? Is that why you can stand all this? Tan, you've got the damnedest philosophy—"

"If I wanted to just mate with anything that came along, I would have stayed on Earth. I went off with two aliens because we had become family—entwined souls whose lives would be incomplete without the others. Don't let Orram see you without your ring, Conn. It will break his heart."

"Sorry, Tan. The school is out of adjustment, until we all know where Mahntik swims."

They started down the stones to the hearth, but Conn heard something below that brought him to a dead stop.

"Of this I am sure," Orticon was saying in hushed tones, "Conn has suffered brain damage. He is convinced that his desiccation hallucinations are true. He believes that Mahntik imprisoned him, then tried to run him down with a shuttlecar. Orserah, that can't be true. Mahntik works for the strengthening of Varok. Her mistake has been to trust too many ahlork. She is no murderer. My father must know that. Otherwise he would never have taken her as mate."

"We don't know that he did," Orserah said.

"I do. I . . . It was instinct. Mahntik startled me with her words, and I glimpsed into her mind . . . but only for a moment. She was with him. In sexual mode. There was no mistaking it, though I left her to her privacy very quickly."

"I see." There was no recrimination in Orserah's voice. "I will agree only that Conn has suffered a great deal. He is not well."

"He is full of hate. Have you ever seen him like this before? Normal ellls shake off their emotions very quickly. They never sustain such dedication to—"

"Dedication to what?"

"Dedication to seeing Mahntik strung from the nearest tree," Conn answered from the hearth steps.

"Can it be possible, Conn?" Orserah asked, going to him and taking his hands in hers. "How could Orram's observations be so wrong about her?"

Conn loved Orserah for her directness. Such open confrontation was exactly what he needed. He could already feel the defenses of his mind recede.

"Of course, it's possible. I could have suffered some permanent damage," he admitted, sitting with Orserah at the hearth. "I could be stuck with some hallucination or other—but I don't think so. Not about Mahntik's role in my hilarious adventures on L'orkah."

The elll sank onto the stones and took the wet-sweater Tandra found for him. "I'll tell you why I think I'm quite sane, Orserah." In as few words as he could, he recited everything he remembered about his encounter with Orlah and the ahlork, including their joke about Mahntik's "zaptik tonk."

"Read me, Orserah. It's all there, perfectly good memories. The distortions are earlier, only during my captivity."

"My dear, I do wish I could see more clearly. I have never been schooled in reading ellls. You know that. I have tried. It's very obscure. All I know is that Mahntik has invaded your memory with something that makes you feel terror."

Shawne appeared in the archway to the great porch, her eyes wide with excitement. "There are lots of those flying square-heads coming closer to the garden, lots of those ahlork things."

"Get your father's hunting spear, Orserah," Conn said. "No ahlork can take an elll armed with one of those things. Orticon, better close all the entrances to the house. If it's Sartak and his mob, we may be in for trouble."

Orticon quickly made the rounds of the house, shutting all openings as though for a storm, and Tandra sent Shawne to Orlah's room at the back of the house, deep underground.

Spear in hand, Orserah watched from the upper hearth stairs, where the skylight gave her a good view of the fields.

"How many?" Conn called to her from his station at the front entry. "Are they closing in?"

"Twelve. Fifteen. More coming in to the far fields." Orserah gasped. "One is coming toward the house, Conn. He's landing in the garden. There. Now, can you see him? He's an ugly one."

"Nidok!" Before Orserah could cry out, Conn was out the door and tossing the ahlork into the air. She ran down the stairs and joined Tandra and Orticon on the porch, looking on cautiously while the two friends finished their raucous reunion.

"Come in, come in. Welcome to Orserah's house, you lob-lipped heap of porcelain."

"Ahlork know Vior too well these days, Conn," Nidok answered, rather sadly. "We chase up and down all Vior to find you."

"Have you eaten?" Orserah asked politely. "What of your flock? Can we get them something?"

"Grandmother." Orticon was close to panic. He backed inside, blocking access to Shawne, but she dodged around him to watch.

"If you excuse us . . . allow us," Nidok said, trying hard to maintain varokian courtesy, "we feed in your fields and garden. We have long flight back to L'orkah. We can do nothing more here."

"The fields are yours, of course, friend of Conn," Orserah said, trying to remember the proper ahlork phraseology.

"What are you doing here, really?" Conn asked, leading Nidok to the hearth.

"We try to accuse Mahntik of two ahlork murders, and your kidnapping, and Leyoon's murder. It is not easy for ahlorks who are also accused. I could not see Orram at Mount Ni. They do not believe ahlork at Lake Seclusion. They trap them."

"But not for long, I see," Conn laughed. "Damn their hides. This is the True Flock then." He watched the nearest of them as they began browsing in the garden. "You've done it, Nidok, you water-hawk. Do you know your rights?"

"The rights of ahlork no longer exist. We abused our legal position on councils of Varok for many ages. Now we don't know how to earn our way back."

"You've earned it already. You will soon have a fair hearing. When Orram gets back, I will go with him to Ahl Vior and make the accusations about Mahntik. Stay, and go there with us."

"No, no." Nidok backed away. "We will be gone in this light. Orram's flock does not listen to ahlork accused of murder. I found you, Conn. I know you are safe in your chosen nest. That is enough."

"My father would see that you got a fair hearing," Orticon interjected.

"I am too guilty. Mahntik paid me to take this elll, Conn, to the ruins of Tahkin. I kept him locked there until he got too dry. My flock is put in danger by doing what Mahntik says."

Tandra came to life at that, and reached out with the traditional ahlork sign of submission, touching Nidok's greater lip. "We must understand each other, Nidok. You said that Mahntik the varok employed you to kidnap Conn?"

"We took Conn from the shallows at the Theater of Great-fish. Mahntik was working with the Greater Flock, but my flock grew weak with her berries. No more heavy errands for her. No more jailer for Conn. Ahlork tease and argue and steal, but no good ahlork causes pain or death."

Nidok wrapped the tip of his wing around Tandra's wrist. His beady eyes glowed with determination. "Justice is not traps and trickery. Ahlork do not write words and laws and join councils of Varok. We are hunters and scavengers, not thinkers and manipulators. Conn will see justice for me. He shared my nest."

Nidok loosed his grip on Tandra's wrist and gently touched her lower lip. "I go hunting now, for ahlork gone mad. I go to L'orkah and stop Sartak before he poisons the waters of Varok. He is not True Flock."

"You talk with words of failure for all ahlork," Conn said, "a detachment from the rest of Varokian society. Everything we accomplished in the cave, all the trust you stiched into a rope of seaweed will be lost if you don't know my loyalty to ahlork. Do your worst. Seal our fates together."

Conn then spoke in Nidok's tongue, remembering an old ahlork ritual. "Don't go until you finish the nesting we began on L'orkah. My wings have only begun to harden."

Nidok slowly turned to face the elll.

Conn walked to the ahlork, kneeled to his height, and presented to him an open wrist. "I pledge you my faith, my legal support, along with whatever you want or need from me. Give me your scar, Nidok, so all Varok may know we are brothers."

"Orram will know you are mad," Nidok growled. "Don't be fooling."

"Give me your scar, you ridiculous berry-sucker. I don't babble things I don't mean."

"Your arm shakes so much I will cut ten arteries if I give you the scar." Nidok began to circle around the elll, his square body tilting back and forth as he shifted from one foot to the other.

"Are you going to throw me out of your nest, Nidok?" Conn wasn't sure if it was frustration or fear that made him tremble. Why did the infuriating beast have to act like an ahlork—now, of all times?

"Scars do not fade. Once made, you share shame of ahlork forever."

"Cut me now or go soak in berry juice, you clatter-plated bird."

"Call me *bird* again and I cut your throat—next!"

Nidok lunged at Conn, and swiped the mossy end plates of the elll's wrist with a flexed wing-tip.

Conn winced.

Tandra gasped and came toward him.

"Stay back," he warned.

Nidok recovered from dealing his dangerous stroke and whirled back, lashing out with his prehensile wing-tip to catch the bleeding wrist. He pulled Conn's wound to his greater lip and regurgitated an acrid-smelling intestinal juice onto the wound. It would heal slowly, with a raised scar. Minutes passed before he released Conn and fixed his unreadable glare once again on the center of the elll's black orbs.

"Our nest is one," Conn said, fighting against a wave of nausea.

"And our shame."

"That's a helluva word to use on the True Flock. We have no shame. Godspeed and destroy what shame you must."

Nidok laughed his gargly laugh, and without a sign of farewell, took off from the porch.

Conn and Tandra watched him rise into the air. The ahlorks' noise, like the sound of cracking glass, spread over the fields as the flock rose from the house and disappeared into the dark mists gathering in the valley.

Tandra took Conn's arm to check the damage.

"It will be all right. Nidok knew exactly what he was doing."

"He is a renegade," Orticon said, when they returned to the house. "Nidok has broken the Greater Flock."

"He or Sartak, for chrissake?"

"Perhaps Sartak. Yes." Orticon's brow furrowed very slightly. "I saw Sartak murder Susheen—but Nidok's story does not hang together. Mahntik was not seen at Leyoon's performance, only shortly afterward. Gitahl was seen in the audience, not Mahntik."

"For the sake of Harrahn's bloody nose, Orticon. I saw her in the cavern right after intermission. I saw her bend over me and sneer when the ahlork shot me full of dope. I saw her laugh at my dryness and drill into my brains while I dried up in her prison cell in the ruins. I saw her run a shuttlecar at me. Ellls have lousy imaginations, Orticon."

ORLAH AND CONN

Tandra—two light-periods later

Finally, Orlah showed the first signs of a return to his rational mind.

Orserah had kept vigil, trying to reach him with words, then with patch contact, with mood-sharing and deeper thought-sensing. Nothing could shake him free of the emotion that held him prisoner.

Being underground, Orlah's room was very quiet. The surrounding rocks encased it in muted insulation. Orlah lay on a sleeping mat under a skylight that drenched the room with a pale auroral glow. I entered one light-period when Orserah had just finished spooning warm soup into his mouth.

"He's taking very little now, Tandra," Orserah said. "What else can I do? I have tried patch contact. I have tried physical contact. Nothing seems to move his mind. There is only one vision there: one of rage and betrayal and lost hope. I cannot get past that image with my probes."

All through the next dark-period Conn joined Orserah in working with Orlah, but they could not move beyond the hateful image in his mind. Orserah was close to despair when she finally retreated to her room, exhausted from another day of failed attempts to reach her son.

I took her place and gave Conn some support.

Orlah sat on his bed-pad, his eyes fixed on the changing light spilling down in sheets from the skylight above him. Even with professional help, we could find no handle to pull him out from under Mahntik's betrayal.

Conn decided, since he had found a way to the varok's mind once before, perhaps he could make it work again. I suggested jealousy of Gitahl or Orram as a path in, before realizing it didn't make sense. Varoks were accustomed to consulting one mate before taking another, but furious jealousy was not in their store of emotions. It would not throw Orlah into a prolonged irrational state. The key must lie elsewhere.

As the elll stood thinking, he became aware of Orlah's presence in the corridors of his logic. Conn tried to lead, but Orlah would not follow any thought that led away from his anger toward himself or Mahntik.

Conn went back, felt the presence again, and tried to lead Orlah's disappointment in another direction. He reviewed Mahntik's character. *Consider her concern for self and real fear of humans, her ambition, her excuses for treason. Had she masterminded the ahlork revolt?* Orlah either didn't know or didn't care; he failed to follow Conn into that speculation.

Did she really mean to rebuild the ruins? The reactor? Would she disregard Varok's careful selection of technology, the counting of resources, to create a world of her own design? How would she use the wealth she had accumulated? Would she resort to nuclear blackmail, build an explosive device, in order to force her way with Varok?

Probably, the presence confirmed—but something else held the focus of Orlah's rage.

"The overflow. You saw the block." Conn spoke the words aloud. Orlah stirred.

She almost led you into a false consummation, with only a small part of her mind. Then you saw her true mind, when you were with Orram. I feel a blankness. Orlah, call up the memory. You saw the full extent of her mind when she challenged Orram, and you exploded with wrath at her betrayal. You saw that she was capable of anything. Varoks don't lie; they can't. Trust is inherent—and she broke that basic trust, denied that genetic honesty.

"Yes," Orlah spoke for the first time. "Yes, enough!" His hands flew to his patches. *I hear you, I see the world again—but the vision is still there, Conn. It's a thin film before everything I see. I cannot live with that always before me.* He began to retreat from Conn's mind.

"Oh, no you don't," Conn said. "Stay with me." His eyes were black strands of pure logic. "Stay in my mind forever if you have to, but don't go crawling back into rage," Conn demanded. "Orserah needs you at home. We're going to need you to stay put, and take care of Orserah and Shawne. Tandra and I will soon have to make a brief trip; we have a septic tank to pump out."

Orserah joined us as I helped Conn bring Orlah to the hearth. She made gentle contact with him and immediately called for Orticon. "For the sake of your Free-mind friends, you've got to hear Orlah's story," she said. "He has seen Mahntik block her mind. She can let a varok see into her mind only to the extent she chooses— and fool him into thinking some real depth has been read."

After watching Conn and me work with Orlah, and hearing the few words he would speak, Orticon could no longer deny the idea. "Have you told my father all this?"

"There was no time." Orlah watched the floor as he spoke. "I realized too late what I had seen."

"We must warn Orram. We've been calling for him and Lanoll daily. We can't reach either of them, Orlah. I can't imagine why." Orserah's worry was beginning to show.

Orticon said nothing, but at next light, he left the house with a pack of food and sleeping gear, planning to be gone some time, "to find himself," Orserah explained, "and about time. He could use some fresh air between his plaques."

"If you're feeling okay, Orlah, I'll be off, too," Conn said, "to Mount Ni. Lanoll and Orram must be working out of that office. Surely he's not still on L'orkah."

Conn—several light-periods later

"So! Made it, did you?" The elll Killah snorted as Conn burst into the Living Resources office on the lake shore. "About time, I'd say."

"Well . . . the swim across Lake Seclusion was very therapeutic," Conn replied.

Killah's dark green face opened into a joyful grin, and he playfully cuffed his fellow with the flat of a befinned hand. Then he stood back and surveyed Conn more closely. "You look like an eefl in spring moult. Are you sure you're all right?"

"I'm growing back a few plumes. Nothing Orserah's stew can't fix."

"How is it out there?" Jesse Mendleton's respect for Conn echoed in his tone.

"Worst storm I've ever seen on Varok." Conn shook the condensed mist from his plumes. "Is Orram back yet?"

"No."

"What about Lanoll?"

"Nothing from her, which is unusual. Her reports are usually regular."

Conn pulled a fresh wet-sweater from his water pack and slipped it over his head.

"You'd better fill me in on what's been going on here, Killah. It might give us a clue where to start looking for them." Conn cut himself a large slice of stalk bread.

"It's a long story," said Jesse. "First some water—and a good strong drink to warm your gizzard."

"If it's the new berry juice, forget it," Conn said. "After watching the ahlork fight that devil-fruit, I'll take none—except with Nidok."

"Nidok? Leyoon's killer?" Jesse had no love for ahlork. "We almost had him once. Came in here looking for Orram."

"He didn't kill Leyoon." Conn headed for the deep water-tub set up for Killah in one corner of the cabin. "You tell me your story, then I'll tell you mine, and we'll see how they fit together."

"I don't like the sound of that," Jesse said.

The elll climbed into the tub and sank contentedly to the bottom.

"Our story started when Lanoll noticed unusual numbers of high-flying ahlork over the Unbounded Sea," Killah began, eyeing Conn worriedly as he surfaced. "She checked them out, even had some followed. They came from L'orkah, from Nidok's flock—"

"Until recently," Jesse interrupted. "Now an ahlork called Sartak leads the pack. He flies to L'orkah infrequently, but his flock has been seen all over Vior.

"Lanoll discovered that Nidok's flock was carrying Mahntik's new web seeds to the Mount Ni area, then the berries appeared as if from nowhere." Killah rummaged in a portable cold chest and laid out a plate of dried moss and egg-layer meat for Conn. "This ahlork called Sartak seems more interested in the berry market than anything else."

"I suppose it's all black market now," Conn said, munching

thoughtfully as he sat chest deep in water.

"And hard to trace. Move over, Conn. I'm not going to dry out while you soak. "The potent berries get mixed in with the legal trade. There's grumbling about local prices being too high. Orram has ordered the reversion to growing the old strain, but the new berries are very popular."

"Damned if those berries aren't addicting," Jesse said. "When that was discovered, the market went underground in a hurry. It's brought the dregs of Varokian society into this area."

"The berry was bad enough, but the soft quality of the new web's cloth also attracted a healthy black market," Killah said. "At first varoks would pay ridiculous prices for it. Then, quite suddenly, the new cloth became very easy to get, the prices went way down. Regular webs can't compete. Meanwhile, more and more varoks are moving into the area to enjoy the lake and fill the jobs more population makes. It's a snowball effect."

"This used to be a beautiful spot," Conn said. "I'm not surprised a population bubble erupted here, but I didn't like getting my hexlines into that algae crud the lake is starting to grow."

"The Council on Living Resources has been overwhelmed, chasing down plantings of the banned strains and trying to find the ahlork responsible." Killah submerged and took on a good gill-full of water before he came up and switched to lungs. "Then things began to pop. The light-hoppers were having a fit because the shore of the Unbounded Sea was choked with algae. The ilara flocks began to shrink—"

"Very few eggs per nest on L'orkah, and some are soft-shelled," Conn interrupted, then sank again to refresh his gills.

"Also, pesticides have moved up the food chain, " said Killah, "and we have seen ahlork spraying the new web fields around Mt. Ni." He finished, then lowered himself up to his eyes in the water of the *uuyvanoon*.

"In any case—" Jesse addressed Killah's eyes and the tops of Conn's sonic melons. "Would you two please come up where I can at least see your faces? That's better. In any case, we think they're using chemical fertilizers too. We've found nitrates in the local well water. We've got a crew out there constantly policing, but it's impossible to stop it all."

"Just when we began to get a handle on things," Killah said, "warming cloth appeared on the market—a real, honest-to-fore-bears warming cloth. But there aren't any approved web strains that can take up that much selenium. Descendants of the fore-bears' selenium webs are notoriously hard to grow, and their stalks are worthless."

"Did you check with the genetics lab?"

"Mahntik was questioned about it. She said the selenium webs were grown only on L'orkah's experimental plots. Maybe Nidok, or this new one, Sartak, has been stealing selenium web seeds from Mahntik's experimental plots, and carrying to the Mount Ni fields from L'orkah. Now we suspect they are carrying selenium itself, to add to the soil here."

"There are other possibilities."

Killah looked sharply at Conn, but Conn didn't elaborate, so he went on. "Meanwhile, the daramonts in this area began to drift away to the western shore of the Unbounded Sea, because silage was short here. Our labs have tested the new stalks now; they are rich in selenium. That silage sours very quickly, and daramonts won't touch it. The old webs are disappearing."

"Short of introducing Earth-style subsidies to grow the old webs—" Jesse put up a hand to stave off objections. "I know, noth-ing on Varok is subsidized, of course, we can't fix one market dis-tortion by creating another—but short of that, there's not much we can do until we get the illegal webs under control."

"The ahlork seem to thrive on the quantity of their sales, not their quality," Killah said.

"The ahlork, yes." Conn climbed out of the tub. "Clever beasts, ahlork. Do they pay taxes on all their contraband?"

"You're kidding," Jesse said, not laughing. "No, they don't, any more than they own any quota to mine rhenium."

"But we may have them there," Killah said. "We gathered re-cords from the local merchants. They show that more warming cloth has been sold than the rhenium quota would allow. The ahlork must be mining rhenium on the side, too, illegally."

"Clever, clever beasts." Conn preened his plumes and gave

Killah a wry smile.

"By Harrahn, you smug thorn," Killah erupted. "Would you kindly tell us what's so funny?"

"It's not funny at all," Conn said. He could feel his mood darkening. "I'm trying to suggest that varoks—and not just Mahntik—may be involved in all of these activities."

"Oh, they are. They are." Killah leapt out of the tub and paced the small cabin. "That's what makes this so difficult. They're sneaky as hell. If they get caught, they know they're in for a mind-probe, so they don't take any chances. None."

"And why haven't the normal checks on local growth worked here?" Conn asked. "Crowding shouldn't be allowed to exceed the carrying capacity of the land, which is dependent on the average consumption of each person, which is way out of bounds here. Right? Are they ignoring the living standard voted in last round? Why haven't prices risen with the demand? Why haven't availability and quality suffered from the danger and expense of transporting so much, so far? Don't you suppose there's a central plan, some determined mind driving all this?"

"Gitahl," Killah said. "Orram decided he was behind the ahlork, coordinating their movements. He can't be found. But you've got to realize, Conn, Varok's problems are bigger than one person can cause. You've got the beginning of positive feedback loops—population growth, non-selective technological change, now economic growth—"

"Growth, and I expect we'll soon see the income inequality that goes with it, " Jesse said. "It's all too familiar. Things may be spiraling beyond any one person's control, but at its core, I'm convinced Varok's new consumerism is fueled by the same kind of oligarchy we just left on Earth. We're dealing with the type who'll buy power at any cost to others. Market sabotage, resource depletion, pollution, . . . Just be glad Varok isn't trapped into an arms race, too."

"Don't be so sure."

Killah stopped pacing and fixed his gaze on Conn. "Okay, your turn. We've heard some crazy rumors. What's been going on with you?"

"Oh no you don't. You've got to fill in the holes you've left in your story."

Killah climbed back in the water, still staring stubbornly at Conn. "You ask questions, if you see so many holes," he snapped. "I've told all I know."

"All right. Who decided that Nidok was Leyoon's murderer? Why was Leyoon's accusation of treason dropped so fast? Why is Gitahl still loose?"

"We haven't been able to find Gitahl to bring him in for the mind-scan, and the direct evidence against him is limited anyway. He was seen in the company of the ahlork who dropped the package to Leyoon—that is all. On the other hand, Nidok was seen carrying the package of poison just before Leyoon died."

"Who reported that? Mahntik? My beautiful hostess?" Conn held out his wrist. Nidok's scar was still a nasty red against his green tiles.

"Ugly wound, Conn. Dangerous." Jesse's face curled at the sight.

"You've taken an ahlork's scar?" Killah wasn't sympathetic. "By Harrahn, Conn, you are mad."

"I don't think so. Let me tell my story now. Mahntik will kill me, first chance she gets. If you give a damn for my hide, at least believe that. Orticon may believe I'm brain-damaged. It's true I had dry hallucinations. But Orlah has evidence that Mahntik can block her mind from reading."

Jesse and Killah exchanged a look.

"That's why she can drive all this web business," Conn pressed on, "but come through a mind-scan looking clean as Ellason's deepest waters. Orram has tried to surprise her, but I'll guess he has seen in her memory only what she has chosen to show him."

Conn gave the others a moment to consider, then he went on. "I saw Mahntik at the Theater of Great-fish. She kidnapped me, dried me to a green frazzle, then tried to kill me with her own private rover, after Nidok had helped me escape. He's gathering a large flock to turn Sartak's flock around. That's why I took his scar. He needs all the help we can give him."

"That's a lot for us to swallow," Jesse objected.

"Believe it. Nidok can lead the ahlork back from the brink,"

Conn said. "Orlah can confirm I'm in my right mind. So can Orticon, though they've both had a few shocks lately. Mahntik nearly destroyed Orlah with the paradoxes her deceit created. Most likely she is working with Gitahl to control the ahlork's farming ventures. Orlah is home resting. Orticon is traveling around Vior, trying to wrap his head around all this—and the fact that an Earth ship is on its way here. Mahntik has the Free-minds scared out of their common sense, preaching imminent danger from vicious attacks by ecology students from Earth."

"That's a wild tale," Jesse said.

"And it gets wilder," Conn continued. "Mahntik is urging the Free-minds to prepare for an alien invasion."

"Ridiculous," Jesse said. "I mean about Earth, not you, Conn. Five youngsters in one old research vehicle does not a space invasion make. I'll be sure to meet them when they land, to help prevent any trouble."

The sound of a shuttlecar stopping beside the cabin sent them all to the door, where they met the golden-fringed elll, Artellian.

"Conn!" Artellian clasped him with shaking arms.

"Never say die, I always say," he laughed.

"You sure you're all right?" Artellian looked him over.

"Well enough to miss my new mate. Where's Lanoll? Doesn't she work with you?"

"Migod, Harrahn. Where can I begin?" Artellian said. "The ahlork have gone mad—fighting on L'orkah and the northwest coast of Vior. We saw Sartak—got his records—he'll finally learn to pay taxes. All was fine there. Then this mad ahlork—I think it must have been Nidok—a huge flock came in from L'orkah and began attacking Sartak's flock. Horrible. And varoks, lots of them, got in the middle of it. We thought we saw Orram, but then he and Lanoll disappeared. We were on the beach of the Unbounded Sea, Harallahn, when Nidok's flock came over. We ran to the shuttle for cover. We thought Lanoll was right behind us. When we started the shuttlecar, she was nowhere. We searched for a full light-period. We couldn't find her."

Panic turned Conn's stomach. He moved to the tub and put his head under water to clear it. "Wait now," he said, emerging. "You said Nidok's flock came over?"

"His flock met Sartak's over the web fields," Artellian said.

"Nidok's flock would know her. They would never harm her." Conn grabbed his water-pack and filled it with one quick dunking. "Who's going north with me and Tandra?" he asked, heading out the door.

LANOLL AND THE AHLORK

Lanoll—the previous light-period, near Harallahn

Lanoll was not prepared for what she saw. Obediently, she followed Sartak through the battleground where Nidok had made his first attack. The western beach of the Unbounded Sea was a nightmare. Slain ahlork lay with injured varoks, their bodies scattered about the lower walls where they had fallen.

As she came to a stop behind Sartak, she found herself surrounded by six ahlork with wings cocked for the death thrust. No one spoke. She was taken to an open ruin where a hundred ahlork perched on low, crumbling walls, eyeing the elll with darting glances.

"Wait here," Sartak demanded. Lanoll was left standing beside a lone mineral tree, surrounded by square faces and clicking wing plates. On the horizon, the continuous lightning sputtered out, leaving a pale aurora as background to its infrequent, restless dart throwing. A harsh wind started off the sea.

She leaned against a low-slung branch to relieve the pressure on her aching toe-fins. "Conn once told me ahlork could find their manners," she complained loudly to any ahlork who would meet her eye. The jibe got no response.

"Why don't you clean up the mess here?" she ventured again.

"Susheen says you fight to vindicate the shame of ahlork. So clean up your dead, and bury the varoks who have died on your behalf. I speak for Conn. I am Lanoll, his mate in life, now a member of the Oran-Grey-ElConn family. It is not too late to quit this violence; it shames all ahlork."

Her challenge brought no response. She had never seen ahlork act this way, silent and dour in the face of well-intentioned insults.

Trying a new tack, Lanoll spoke traditional ahlork sounds. "May your nests be free of thorns and your waters rich. Your race is a noble one, but you fly with wrong leaders. You can take your place as the most ancient conscience on Varok. Nidok will restore your nests to the highest cliffs. All of Varok stands behind you, if you respect the lives of others. I speak for Orram."

"Not if you speak of Nidok with same breath," an ahlork gargled. "Orram tries to capture ahlork. Show us Conn's ring, if you want us to hear your words."

Lanoll held out her left hand, where she wore the ring that Orram had fashioned for her as a member of the family: a swirl of glass from Earth's moon set with a sapphire representing Earth, a diamond for Varok, and a large emerald representing Ellason.

Several ahlork flew closer and crowded around Lanoll to view the ring. "There is no ahlork in your family; it is incomplete," one shouted.

"Nidok will walk far to see the Greater Flock restored to real honor, honor unstained by berries and blood."

The rasp of a varokian voice interrupted, close to Lanoll's ear plate. "Stop your prattle, elll. I'll kill you, if you persist in stirring up these insects."

She spun around to face Gitahl. The increasing winds blew his hair into a strange tangle. The dark had grown intense, making the unseen wind more terrifying. Above it, the clatter of ahlork in flight could be heard.

"Look to the wind," an ahlork shouted above the restless clacking of the flock. "Fly into the storm. Nidok's flock is coming!" The cry threw the ahlork into a desperate struggle to gain the air. They bruised and cut each other, heedless of their wings in an effort to escape attack.

Before she could run, Lanoll found herself wrapped in Gitahl's arms, towed against the tide of ahlork, and thrown into an airshuttle.

Tandra—at Orserah's house

"It doesn't make sense, Conn." I held his family ring in my open palm, but he refused to put it back on for the trip north.

"Orram tore that ring from my finger," Conn insisted. "Only he can put it back."

I looked at Orserah across the hearth and encouraged her to say what was on her mind. The beautiful old varok loved Conn dearly, and she was miserable, holding on to reason with great difficulty. "Orram's emotional health is in danger, being disconnected from Tandra—and now he sees your empty finger, Conn? Impulsive, emotional behavior is one elllonian trait you should have given up when you joined this family."

"It's much more than that, Orserah. Orram's attraction to Mahntik is more than I can tolerate. I can't be family with Orram, if his mind is full of that traitor."

"We don't know that they even mated, Conn," I said. "I was just afraid they had. I'm being too human. Please don't indulge that in me."

"I'm sorry, Tan, Orticon was pretty clear about what he saw. You have to accept there's something between them, but you have every reason not to welcome that viper into this family, Love."

"We have become more than we can be alone. I won't let you destroy that."

"You wouldn't want to do it again though—would you?"

I flashed him a look of real anger.

"All right, nothing funny now, I promise." He moved closer to the hearth so he could touch my face and study my eyes as he talked. "If Orram leaves her, once he knows what she is, we have little to resolve. But if he believes I am brain damaged and Mahntik is worth a snip, the school has lost adjustment. The pressure patterns no longer mesh. As long as he defends Mahntik, I am Orram's enemy."

"Impossible elll noise," Orserah said. "Now leave me, both of you. Find Orram. Shawne and I will manage with Orlah and our neighbors. Now I must know what I should tell Orram, Tandra? If he is able, he will call, and he will want to talk to you."

"Tell him we are nesting with Nidok." Conn was serious.

"Tell him Conn is as stubborn as ever, but I have chosen to gamble on him—again. He will understand."

Shawne—the next light-period

Shawne pushed her sharpened stick under the marble weed and watched its thorny fruits dance on wiry stems as she felt about the center of the root. A sudden thrust with the stick, the delicious sensation of bursting something evil, and she moved on to destroy the next weed. She pretended she was murdering web-suckers—or better yet—ahlork eggs. All but Nidok's flock. Conn wouldn't want Nidok's eggs punctured.

She could hear Orlah inside the house, still trying to use the house transmitter. *Too bad the radio is broken. Orlah couldn't even talk to Artellian or Killah at Lake Seclusion. Poor Orlah, he could barely keep his temper under control.*

The child dropped her stick and ran through the garden to the egg layers' pen. She wished Orlah would read to her more, or take her to some of the wonderful places he had told her about, *the places where daramonts hide and light-hoppers swim upside down.*

The sky was growing very dark with high mists. Shawne picked up a short rake that stood against the egg layers' pen and opened the gate to sweep their debris out into the garden. There was barely enough lightning to see by.

Suddenly a daramont leapt into view from behind the house. The beast deposited Orticon with a shake of its enormous neck, and raced off without taking a drink at Orserah's trough.

"Orticon is home," Shawne shouted as she threw down her rake and crashed into him, throwing her arms around his knees. He winced with the intense sensation, but his carved walnut face cracked with a smile.

Orticon

Reacting to the child's exuberance, Orticon whirled her around in a circle, as Conn often did, before setting her down gently.

"Now look what you've done." He peered down at the little human. "You have dropped your rake in the egg layers' yard and left their gate open. They are all over Orserah's garden, eating the best vegetables."

Together they ran back and forth along the rows of roots and broad leaf plants, shooing the rotund, shaggy little beasts back toward their enclosure.

By the time the last of the egg layers was home safe, Orticon had abandoned himself to his youth. He playfully ran with Shawne among the fruit trees, shouting and waving his arms in mock distress at being chased. As he turned the chase around, Shawne ran for the garden, tripped on rough ground in a plot of edible roots, fell sharply, and bounced up crying to the sting of a painfully skinned knee.

"Here, let me look at that, Shawne." Orticon knelt beside her to examine the shallow dirt-streaked scrape. *How many times have I fallen, running through this same garden? How many times have my knees taken up the soil in just this way? How similar the stinging pain must be.*

Without further thought, Orticon brought his mouth down to Shawne's knee, and he cleansed the wound as he would his own, spitting out the dirt and blood until the scrape looked ready to heal.

"That feels much better," Shawne said, getting up with a limp. "Thank you."

"And I thank you for being a brother to my grandchild," Orserah said, smiling at them from the edge of the garden, her forearm extended to Orticon. Her calm face, framed with dampness from hours of frustrating work at the communication panel, reflected a love that neutralized Orticon's feeling of failure.

"It's no good," Orticon said, lowering his forehead to Orserah. "I've been to all the communication centers on this side of the valley. The storm is spreading north from the Unbounded Sea. No one can make contact with Lake Seclusion. There is an ammonia alert out for the entire valley northwest of Mount Ni, and high winds are reported over the Springs of Harinlegh. The storm center seems to be spreading toward L'orkah. It's blocking all signals between us and there now. We can only hope that Conn and Tandra got through before the travel lanes were shut down."

Orserah nodded, grateful for his mind contact. She found new warm clothes for Orticon and refreshed the hearth pot with web-berries.

"The old variety of berry," she announced proudly. "I won't have my family tainted with those foul pills Mahntik engineered. You should hear the tales—"

"I have heard far too many, Grandmother. I have seen fear and guilt in many minds. Many varoks settle at Lake Seclusion on land that is others' responsibility. They refuse to honor the locale's limits. They barter for the new berries and bring in excess web cloth for sale. The berries are like a new religion, a new experience not to be missed: to get drunk and share hallucinations. When the berry is taken in large servings, all the natural varokian barriers to touch disappear. Varoks speak like ahlork, and touch in public hearths like egg layers—"

"—or ellls," Orserah interrupted. She was watching Orticon closely.

The youth met her challenge. "Yes, like ellls. How could this happen on Varok? We've always assumed the possibility of danger in new substances, like these berries, until safety is proved. Even people on Earth—I think it's Europe—have been doing that for decades. They call it the precautionary principle."

"So Earth has done something right?"

"I found much to admire about humans during my studies at the Concentrate."

"What about Tandra and your father? You were fast to criticize this family."

"I feared that a human could not understand Varok's traditions. And now I have seen varoks do much worse. Conn and Orram and Tandra have accomplished a miracle, relating so closely, but they have a ways to go, don't you think?"

"They have many ways they could go."

"I mean . . . Tandra's human expressiveness and jealousies are alien to this world. She did not take it well when Father declared himself varokian, sexually. I think Conn no longer knows if he is elll or varok or some human hybrid. He treats Tandra like an elll with patch organs."

"You may be right, Orticon." Orserah smiled at his insight. "But there is more, isn't there?" Her eyes opened with surprise when he again inclined his forehead to her in invitation. "Are you truly reconciled to the mind-scan?"

"I look willingly into your mind and see faith." His boyish eyes danced with discovery. "Our natural patch contact is not like the invasion of the deep probe. I will take what is freely given, as varoks always have."

He neglected the cooling bowl of food in his lap. "I can't believe what I have seen in the valley. Some kind of trust has been broken. People neglect their locale's craftsmen and buy Mahntik's inferior products from half way across Varok because they're cheap. Something more has been lost—the built-in ethic that says enough is enough. It's as if enhanced experience overrides all other values. Varoks talk of new clothing styles, as if that mattered enough to disregard durability.

"At Lake Seclusion, the land, the lake, the light-hoppers are paying the cost of the new web farms. It's as if varoks think they can assert their superiority over all the other life on Varok—just to serve a love of berries and new cloth."

Orserah's sad smile reflected pride in her grandson. "To contain five intelligent, communicative species—each with conflicting demands—has always been Varok's problem."

Orticon nodded. "I was sure that adding another—especially human—would destroy the peace of this world, or at least this hearth. But perhaps our family is a model for closer relationships between the species of Varok.

"Conn, Tandra and Father discovered that they were made of the same substance, spiritually I mean. Then again, we are literally made of the same elements. Carbon chemistry is the handiest for fashioning large molecules that synapse and catalyze and allow us to think. Why shouldn't our thinking have common elements? Then I realized, it's not just Earth and Varok. In this galaxy alone there are a half a billion suns with planets that could support life—and at least 200 billion galaxies in this universe. All told, the chance of other intelligent life—life that we can relate to—is very large."

"Oh, how I know! And then to live it, Orticon. To actually live it, knowing every minute that you share life with a universe full of conscious beings." Orserah reached out to him, and their hands spiraled upwards. "So this trip of yours has brought you home, Orticon. Your mind is free. You lay it open with no reservations."

"It's worse than I thought it ever could be out there, Grandmother. They call my father and his ancient rules outdated. Leyoon was right. Varok is at risk of catching Earth's addictions. Mahntik's belief in growth—rebuilding the ruins to their former glory—I understand why the great-fish called it treason. I just hope my aversion to the mind-probe was not so misdirected."

"So, dear Orticon, I see that you will no longer be blinded by your convictions. Faith that cannot question either its assumptions or its implications is not worthy of an honest mind."

"Of course," Orlah said, joining them in the garden. "Your questioning has had its good results, nephew. You and the Free-minds may yet awaken the councils of Varok to the need for more respectful limits in the use of the deep probe. They will listen to mature arguments."

"Thank you for saying that, Orlah." Orticon allowed himself more and more enthusiasm as he spoke. "In my trip around the foothills, I saw berry addicts groping for help—and getting it, because the varokian mind is open."

"You talk as if the berry were used . . . overused everywhere."

"It is. It's a terrible addiction, Grandmother. Killah and the human Jesse Mendleton suspect Mahntik is behind most of it. And if Mahntik can block her mind, she can devise any kind of scheme and appear free of guilt."

"That may be true," Orlah said, "but if my suspicions have any basis in reality, you had better find Gitahl. He may be the only mind capable of proving that Mahntik is guilty of treason."

"But you have seen the block," Orserah objected.

"And it has left me . . . hurt. A good defense lawyer could argue that Conn and I are not reliable sources of memory or mental image. Our evidence for Mahntik's mind-block would never hold up in court. Can you find Gitahl?"

"Perhaps. I still have contacts." Orticon hated the idea of betraying his Free-mind friends. "We'll find him. I'll go to L'orkah; I should be able to go around the storm from the west."

CHANGING VIEWS

Mahntik—that same light-period

Mahntik made her entrance down the stairs to her hearth room swathed in yards of luxuriant warming cloth. She smiled at the delegation of Free-minds scattered about her hearth, secure in her sense of control. *Fighting amongst themselves, the ahlork are no longer a threat. Orram is away, looking for the disease cultures Sartak had stolen.*

"We have good news, " she announced. "The Lake Seclusion Locale has voted to increase their population density. Our business is growing rapidly there, and we have a growing inflow of capital to rebuild the defenses of Varok—we will show our visitors from Earth that we cannot be taken, in any sense of the word."

She stepped from the stairs onto the hearth stones, so she could look over the crowd of youth as she spoke.

"It is not important that we have been overruled in the matter of the nuclear reactor," she announced. "It was inevitable once the ahlork became involved. We are winning, my friends, winning the hearts of New Varoks—those who will defend our right to live to our best potential, our right to repel invaders from Earth!

"However, high purpose alone does not build industry. The long-term defense of Varok still rests with you. Defense against future human invasions must begin with a significant economic base. Such a base is being established beneath Mount Ni."

"Don't the taxes take most of your excess income?" one Free-mind dared to ask. "How have you alone saved enough to begin to build the industry needed for weapons design and manufacture?"

"Taxes are graduated in order to assure equity," Mahntik tried to reassure him. "But there is no restriction on savings. And Globak Varok has granted me a special exemption for our work."

The youngster was not deterred. "But how could you accumulate so much? In every locale, the money supply is held constant to discourage production beyond need."

"I have redefined our needs," Mahntik snapped. *How shocked these naive enthusiasts would be to know what fraction of my earnings are reported, how many of the credits in every locale are owed to me now.*

"When we shift production to defense items, which other things will go out of production?" another youth asked. "Which will give up their resource quotas, and in which locales?"

"Ah—there is a mistake in your thinking, dear boy," Mahntik said, adding just enough edge to her voice to emphasize patience with his ignorance. "There is no longer a limited supply of anything—for us. Our purpose is more sacred than resource limits, more important than depletion quotas! Who among you would disagree? To be strong, Varok must grow. It is time we utilize our natural potential. It is foolish to save our resources for the unknown generations of some unknowable future—or for invaders from Earth!

"We needn't walk, when we could ride," Mahntik declared. "We needn't wear handmade rags. We needn't deny ourselves imported delicacies and simple conveniences. The materials are available. Think about it. There is nothing wrong with building more shuttle transport, more labor-saving devices. Why do we live like simple farmers when we have the knowledge to live better than the forebears?"

She paused to let the idea sink in, watching with relish the Free-minds' shocked reactions to her blasphemy. As she expected, many of the youths nodded, agreeing heartily.

"The stability that varoks worship is a false god whose creed is denial and control, whose commandment is enslavement by the mind-scan," she continued, relishing her performance. "Our descendants will thrive on what we leave. They will have their own moment of dominance, using the technological base we create to advance toward unknowable heights! We are presumptuous to try holding evolution to our level. What we call waste or desolation now may be called necessity or beauty by future generations, by the species that replace us.

"It is this future we defend. The human invaders land in the next deep dark. We have a significant number of varoks who will confront them on their arrival in Ahl Vior, but we need more. We must overwhelm them immediately, before Global Varok sequesters them. We will take the humans captive before they enter the rehabilitation center. We will show them, and through them, all of Earth, that Varok is strong, and Varok is for varoks!"

"Varok is strong!" many Free-minds cheered. Several raised fists. "Varok is for varoks!"

"Our preparations for defense cannot proceed, however, until the ahlork Sartak is brought down. He has taken some dangerous cultures from the genetics lab. He is threatening to contaminate all the waters of Vior. He thinks varoks will bow to his blackmail. You must find him and destroy those cultures with fire, before he releases them."

"What kind of cultures?" a stern young female asked.

"Pneumonic plague, among others," Mahntik answered. "Need I describe them all? Go immediately. Sartak's flock was just seen in the ruins near the lab. Arm yourselves with lasers. Now go!"

The youth streamed out of the house, leaving her satisfied with her success. The Free-minds were hers. Soon she would dictate her terms to all of Varok.

Smiling to herself behind the mind-block, she thought of Orram. He would like her blue warming cloth. Shimmering with rhenium conducting fibers, the cloth responded beautifully to light—and wore out fast, losing its warming quality. The demand for more would continue.

When we rebuild the ruins, Orram will enjoy my apartment high over the hills of L'orkah—a penthouse carpeted with self-warming fibers, freshened every cycle. A wide expanse of windows will look out over the beautiful shores of the Misted Ocean.

Orram will not approve at first—a wasteful extravagance, he will say. Rhenium is too rare, too expensive to mine. Then I will lay him down in the warm softness of the rug, and he will understand that life is too short to live without maximizing all experience.

Mahntik wondered how much Orram had seen in the web fields of Vior and L'orkah, what Conn had told him. No matter. She would explain it away. The elll was mad, and the ahlork were providing the perfect vessels for blame. Lying was a new and exciting art. The possibilities had no limit. She could invent anything to tell Orram, shape it in her mind with the right sampling of real memory, and he would believe it.

In high spirits, she went to the food center to eat. As she walked into the large pantry, two varoks, strangers, entered the room. There was the smell of stale berries about them, and Mahntik saw the drug's effects in their eyes. She probed them. They were nothing but opportunistic thugs, minds badly distorted.

"Don't bother to read us," said the taller and uglier of the two. "We'll tell you what we're about. Berries is our business, just like yours." He grinned, mocking a real smile, and showed a row of red-stained teeth. The silver streaks in his brown hair were dull with neglect, and his tunic and rough leggings had been worn many times since they had been cleaned.

"Business? I'm not interested."

"Oh, you'll be interested, all right, won't she, Hartan," the tall one said.

The smaller varok dug into the deep pockets of his ill-fitting tunic and came up with a handful of full-value credits made out to Mahntik—in distinctive ahlork scrawl.

"Where did you get those?" Mahntik raged, grabbing the notes from his grimy hand.

"It says 'Sartak' right there, see?" Hartan said. Pulling Mahntik roughly to him, he forced her hands, still grasping the notes, back into her face. "That's enough for my business."

"The ahlork Sartak pays you more than we realized, Mahntik," he said. "You are not paying the taxes due on all your earnings—that's what I think—that's why there's so little money coming back to Vior. There are lots of new varoks and ellls at Lake Seclusion. They love your new berries, they need your warming cloth. But now the working hours are getting too short. Even those already employed are complaining about too little wages. It's not nice to take all your earnings from Sartak's ahlork. We can't raise the maintenance wage and spread the working hours. How will we encourage more new arrivals? Who will buy our webs?"

He swung around and grabbed Mahntik's neck in his large hands. "We've taken over Sartak's operation. Is that clear? We now have that market. It can keep growing—but only if you pay a reasonable tax to the authorities so we don't attract attention. Understand?"

Mahntik nodded. His hands were shutting down her oxygen. She was losing consciousness.

"We've got to begin shipping more food into this area, from Vior. Trade, you see?" Hartan's eyes were cold with fury. "I want a fleet of shuttles to replace the ahlork—they're nothing but a drunken nuisance now. We can transport berries and daramont forage across the Unbounded Sea much faster with shuttles. Varoks on Lake Seclusion want more daramonts on their side. That will take more feed. Your damn new web-stalk doesn't make good silage. We need to re-seed some of the old fields. Now write those credits over to me, and tell Sartak to do the same from now on."

"All right," Mahntik gasped. "I see you have more sense than ahlork."

He let her go, and she fell to the ground, coughing.

Orticon—a few moments earlier at the shuttle station on L'orkah

"I can barely hear you through the static. The storm center will arrive on L'orkah in another light-period. Now, quickly, Grandmother, while the reception is good."

"Something must be done, Orticon, do you hear me? Orram still has made no contact. Tandra and Conn found no sign of him or Lanoll at Harallahn. They must be on L'orkah. You must warn the authorities about Mahntik. I haven't been able to get through."

"Everyone is on full alert here. The ahlork—Orserah?" He heard nothing but a faint hiss. Minutes passed. Nothing.

He delivered his request for a search team at the communications desk, but, as he expected, little could be done during the storm. "Security has been all over this island looking for Gihn Tahlor. You're welcome to try, too, but . . ." The stationmaster let his voice trail off with a shrug.

"My father, Oran Rahmalak, has not responded to calls in some time. Mahntate Tikahn is involved, as well as Gitahl. She is suspected of the kidnapping of the elll Conn, and the murder of two ahlork. We have reason to believe she is not a normal varok, that she should not be trusted."

The stationmaster regarded Orticon doubtfully, but agreed to let him check out a shuttle, despite the raging winds. "I hope you find your father. Be careful out there." He sent Orticon out with a brief spiral salute.

The genetics lab was quiet. Orticon moved on toward the ruins and found a small group of Free-minds arguing about the ahlork and the approaching Earth ship, disorganized and leaderless. Each varok had his own idea of what should be done, but all were convinced the humans posed the greater danger.

"I have news from Vior, my friends," Orticon spoke in as calm a voice as he could manage. "Global Varok is in contact with the human space vehicle. They will land at the Ahl Vior Space Station at first light. They have claimed to be students of our steady state and want to experience it first hand. We have no reason to believe that they are hostile."

Angry denials washed over him. "First, please listen to what I have to say. There is fear and guilt in many minds here," he called out. Immediately there was silence.

"Yes, I read your moods, as naturally as I see your faces." Orticon let the protest filter through the crowd, as he knew it must. Then he spoke again. "Our patch contact is a natural part of our being. We can deny it no more than we can deny that our eyes see."

"You are no longer a Free-mind."

"That is not true. Mood reading is not the deep probe; privacy and respect remain intact. I still oppose the deep probe in legal proceedings, except when sufficient evidence provides strong reason to suspect guilt. We can help define those boundaries, but we must be clear in our purpose as Free-minds."

"We must be prepared to defend ourselves. We don't know what the humans really want here."

"I believe my family and their colleagues when they say Earth is no threat. I have seen no reason for doubt in their minds, which they willingly open to me. Please hear me. We have thought that the varokian sense of reading moods and touching minds was a vulnerability. But it is a strength—freeing us from the terrifying uncertainties of not knowing each other's true mind.

"All is known between us. It is a gift that has always bound us together—made easier the consensus needed to maintain Varok's steady state. When I left here, I traveled across Vior to understand the changes happening with Mahntik's economic growth. I saw Varok's consensus split apart by greed for addictive berries and material goods. Mahntik has destroyed Varok's faith by lying to us all. Yes, *lying*.

"If we don't move quickly, the fabric of Varokian society—that society built on the inherent trust that lies between us—will fall, not to invaders from Earth, but to our own ill-considered appetites, and to the manipulations of one hidden mind."

"What are you saying?" The Free-minds were confused. Orticon had always been well-respected among them. "Mahntik has led us toward strength!"

"Mahntik has led us to illusions," Orticon stared them down, one by one. "We Free-minds have an important purpose. We have awakened the councils of Varok to the need for restraint in the use of the deep probe. Now we must face what we have rationalized away—that the genius of Varok lies in consensus, restraint and local control. Mahntik would break that for her own gain—not for the defense of Varok."

"She cares deeply about Varok's safety!"

"Mahntik can tell us so because she has perfected the mind-block."

The response was more disbelief than anger. "Mind-blocks are for children's stories."

"My uncle Orlah has seen it. Mahntik can close her mind at any level. She must be stopped. We must not support the mind that lies."

"You are asking us to believe the impossible, to take an old myth as truth."

"Think about what I have said. We don't have to agree, but please think about what you see, what makes sense—consider for yourselves how it compares to Mahntik's words."

Orticon got no argument. A few heads nodded in assent.

"I am searching for Gitahl—he can best show the truth about Mahntik. When we meet at the Earth landing, look with your own eyes for any threat from the new arrivals. Judge for yourselves."

Without fully realizing what they were doing, the Free-minds joined together in a silent affirmation.

Tandra—arriving on L'orkah with Conn, later that same light-period

"I'll check out a sturdy four-wheeler as soon as we land at the station, Tandra," Conn hollered over the hovering airshuttle's motor as it strained against the violent winds. "We'll check Mahntik's house first."

I could barely hear him over the storm. The small airshuttle bounced on the waves of the acrid gale like an ilara caught at sea. "Is the radio working? I'm going to try to find out if anyone at the station knows where Nidok is. His ahlork should be able to find Gitahl."

We had caught the last shuttle from Harallahn, urging the pilot to make one last trip. For more than a light-period we had circled west, keeping the disturbance in sight. The storm now covered half the northern hemisphere of Varok.

We had had lots of time to talk. As we reviewed our thoughts, we avoided speculation about Orram and Lanoll's fate. We had scoured the shores of the Unbounded Sea where Artellian last saw Lanoll. Three ahlork recovering from battle there said they had seen the varok Gitahl drag an elll into a shuttle, and fly out across the ocean. *So here we are. Now what?*

Conn nodded to me as he spoke on the radio. "Yes, I understand.

Have you had any word from Orram—Oran Ramahlak?"

I was surprised at the ambivalence I felt. Sharing Orram's attraction to Mahntik had been a strange experience, I admitted, but it had opened new, deeper channels between us. *We are—were—half the other's mind. And now what? Is that gone because he may be with her? Surely she is guilty of treason and murder.*

As we came over L'orkah, Conn turned off the radio. "Nidok defeated most of Sartak's flock at Harallahn, but Sartak himself has escaped and is expected to attack again, with larger flocks from the western web fields here on L'orkah."

"Is there any news of Orram?"

"Nothing."

"Lanoll?"

"No. But Orticon has been to the station. He took out a shuttle in search of Gitahl."

"I hope he's alright."

A howling downdraft nearly threw our own shuttle to the ground. We skimmed erratically over the dry beach of L'orkah's lowlands and turned with some difficulty away from the cascade of orange mist flowing down from the northern heights. When we emerged from the mists, we saw Mahntik's house standing against the gray slopes above, its silhouette swarming with tiny black dots—ahlork, scrambling to rise into the wind as we landed.

We wasted no time. The storm battered our pedal-powered four-wheeler as we fought our way from the station to Mahntik's house. The front entrance stood open. Broken ahlork lay all around.

"Oh, Conn. Why has Nidok's flock indulged in such violence? They are risking everything—all legal status. What chance has Nidok to repair a Greater Flock torn like this?"

"The Greater Flock will heal," Conn said. "Nidok has forged some kind of alliance with the majority. By opposing Sartak's germ threat and treason, they've earned themselves a place among the sentient species that write the laws of Varok. But first we've got to let them punish and redeem their own."

I nodded and swallowed hard. "What do we do now?"

"We find a Free-mind willing to lead us to Gitahl."

We entered Mahntik's house and found several Free-minds

arguing passionately with their fellows. "The ahlork are mad," one said. "Mahntik was right; we must follow them to the reactor to stop Sartak."

"That can wait," another interrupted. "Nidok is keeping Sartak busy. The Earth ship is now orbiting Varok and will land soon. We must be ready to defend ourselves."

Conn couldn't contain himself. "Don't be ridiculous. The humans are coming to visit and learn, nothing more."

"Who is there?" They had not realized they had company.

"Orticon's family," Conn said. "We are looking for Oran Ramahlak."

"We haven't seen him," snarled a tall Free-mind with a boyish face.

"Master Ramahlak often visits here with Mahntik," another volunteered, "but I haven't seen him in several light-periods."

I took Conn's arm, and he gave my hand a comforting squeeze. "What about the elll, Lanoll?" he asked.

"We don't know her." The first Free-mind took a menacing step toward us. "Look at the reactor. Security is dismantling it. There are many strangers there."

"Has anyone seen Gihn Tahlor?" Conn risked pressing them further.

"No." All agreed this time.

"If you do, please report his location to someone in security. Gitahl is wanted for questioning in Leyoon's murder. Hiding him could make you accessories."

"Protecting the humans when they arrive will make you accessories—to Varok's invasion by Earth! You had better stay with us."

Four young varoks moved toward Conn and me. I couldn't believe they would try to hold us, but Conn was not so naive. Before I realized what was happening, he grabbed my hand, shot a laser pen at the varoks' feet, and dragged me out the door. We jumped into our four-wheeler and sped downhill, southwest toward the ruins.

LANOLL AND GITAHL FOUND

Orticon—the Ruins of Tahkin

Orticon aimed his shuttlecar for the ruins where Gitahl had been producing rhenium, enjoying a respite from the storm where the tall buildings blocked the winds. Running along the dune-filled streets, he avoided heaps of rubble and thick growths of bramble.

Turning west, he passed through a stand of windowless towers that stood mutely in rows, empty of landing platforms. The business sector, he assumed. He left the anonymous hulks behind as he came upon the scattered remnants of ancient hotels overlooking the Misted Ocean. The air was white with spray from the angry waves below.

The ruins were different here. The ages-long process of burying and uncovering, of growth and decay and re-growth that gave the rest of the ruins a semblance of quiet dignity, was disrupted. Here the pattern of the ancient city was torn apart, the few standing buildings stripped of material, the unusable scrap thrown aside, forming a chaotic jungle of chemically tortured beams and laser cut slabs, scarred with ugly burns. This was not mining by ahlork; they left few signs of their efforts.

Orticon left the shuttle near one entrance to the tortured area. The mining of rhenium was larger than any operation he had ever seen. It must have expanded at a great rate very recently.

He hadn't gone far through the rubble when a small group of ahlork passed overhead, then landed noisily a few hundred meters away.

The varok ran through the plasti-steel jungle and soon lost himself in the many passages around the heaps.

The angry noise of disturbed ahlork erupted just to Orticon's left. As he eased closer around a pile of alloy beams, he saw three of them arguing excitedly with a varok, whose throbbing nerves ran across his skull in lacework patterns.

"No!" Gitahl interrupted the beasts. "I will have nothing to do with cultures taken from the labs. You probably spilled them already. Your wing-tips could be swarming with germs right now. Take them away!"

"You take them!" an ahlork screamed. "Nidok won't dare come close, if you have them."

Orticon saw the white markings on his neck. Sartak.

The ahlork pressed the culture tubes onto Gitahl. Several fell to the ground, as the ahlork rose into the air and fled toward the coast. With a cry of disgust, Gitahl kicked the tubes away, ran to a large field collector, and doused himself with water from a tap rigged in the side.

Orticon made a dash for the cultures, ripping off his jacket as he ran.

"Watch out, Orticon. They could be deadly."

It was Lanoll, calling back to him as she disappeared into the piles of debris.

"Wait. Lanoll!"

Orticon kicked the cultures into his jacket and tied the deadly bundle together by the sleeves. As he turned to run, two laser beams cut into the duff at his feet. Orticon held out the cultures to Gitahl, who stood aiming laser pens directly at his face.

"Is this what you want? Come and get them." He dropped the jacket, and the varok fired at the cultures.

The jacket burst into flames.

"Now," Gitahl said, easing up to the cultures and kicking them out of the flames. The culture tubes were still intact. "I would like a ride in your shuttle. Lead me to it. I don't want to waste time looking for it." He scooped up several of the tubes and ushered Orticon ahead of him.

When they arrived at the shuttlecar, Gitahl threw the cultures into the vehicle and climbed in after them, keeping his laser aimed steadily at Orticon. The shuttle's hydrogen packet came alive, and the varok careened through the rubble toward the heart of the storm.

Orticon called and searched for what seemed a long time before he found Lanoll between web fields and the ruins, frightened and too dry.

"Can you walk?"

"Not much farther."

Orticon ripped the sash he wore and tied the pieces around the elll's feet. "Where have you been?" he asked. "I found Conn and got him home. We're not far from the coast. It would be safest to follow the cliffs back to the shuttle station."

"Conn is alive?"

"Mahntik had him imprisoned. Nidok rescued him. I took him home a long time ago. Tandra nursed him back to health."

Lanoll erupted with a joyful whoop. "Conn. Alive. He's well? You're sure?"

"By now they should be here on L'orkah, looking for Orram and for you."

"Thank Harrahn, Orticon. Thank Whatever! I saw Orram only briefly at Harallahn. Is he here on L'orkah? I've seen some awful things, when Gitahl held me at Harallahn. Broken ahlork everywhere and Gitahl . . . such cruelty, Orticon."

"We need to find Conn and Tandra. We do not know where my father is. He has not answered calls. We'd better get to help as quickly as possible."

Moving carefully through the mined ruins, they soon emerged onto the cliffs lining the shore of the Misted Ocean. The storm was clearly visible now, hovering over the eastern slopes of L'orkah like a Jovian current orphaned and gone wild. Its western edge was expanding at a noticeable rate, driving before it a small flock of ilara that had failed to make the crossing to Vior.

A narrow trace of a path led them through the line of ruined towers framing the shore of tumbled rock, then it turned out onto a narrow shelf overlooking the ocean. Acrid red tongues of mist were lapping hungrily at the lower slopes.

"There are ahlork out there." Lanoll pointed above the lower currents to a break in the storm, where many tiny square silhouettes bounced eastward in recognizable syncopation.

"Coming or going?"

"Going, I think."

Orticon strained to keep his eyes on the tiny figures amidst the changing streams of vapor. "Yes. It's a huge flock. It must be

Nidok. Why couldn't they wait out the storm?"

Lanoll pulled the sash from her feet and waved it in the air.

"I think they've seen us."

Three ahlork banked on the high winds, rolled with the toss of a violent stream of yellow mist, then sank quickly toward the ocean like overloaded cartons. At the last possible moment, their wings folded. They disappeared below the cliff edge, then shot upward with full wing spread, gained the high ground where Orticon and Lanoll stood, and landed with a final tilting of their wing-plates.

Nidok folded his wings and sniffed the air.

"Yes, we're Oran family," Orticon said with a laugh.

Nidok harumphed with a gargle. "We were hunting Sartak when we saw a varok flushed from here. If it is Gitahl, my flock will take him to security."

"I'm sure you'll do what you can, Nidok," Orticon said.

"Or do you have a taste for blood?" Lanoll did not trust him. "You have done foul work on Sartak's flock."

Nidok's square face lengthened with the rebuke. "Satak corrupted Greater Flock. Path of True Flock is not blood. We must fight to stop Sartak."

"Understood," Orticon said, "but right now we need your help, Nidok. If we can get Gitahl to the courts at Ahl Vior, your work will be well done. His mind holds the key to both Mahntik's treason and Sartak's conspiracy. You must not destroy him."

"Our path is not stained by murder of varoks."

"And be careful. He has the cultures from the genetics lab—the ones Sartak stole. They must be taken unbroken."

"We correct this shame—ahlork tainted by stolen germs."

"Orram is missing," Lanoll said. "It will take us several light-periods to walk back to the shuttle station. We must find Conn and Tandra."

"We fly there now. Varoks will send a shuttle for you."

"Good idea. I'll call ahead to Security. We'll ask them to notify the courts in Ahl Vior that your flock may come. And please have your flock keep watch for Orram. He may be in trouble." Lanoll touched the ahlork's scarred lip. "I am also part of Conn's family."

"Also? How do you know *also*?"

"I have taken the family ring." Lanoll raised her hand to show Nidok.

"Lanoll, Conn has taken Nidok's scar," Orticon said. "We are all family."

Lanoll startled, but quickly the idea slipped into place. They joined limbs as best they could, then Nidok flew on to his work.

Nidok—moments later, over the Ruins of Harin

"There," Nidok cried to his flock, as they flew over the northern edge of the ruins. "That is him, the ugly one. Face like dried hoats gone bad. Take him before he gets to reactor cave. Remember, take tubes unbroken. In circle, drop and snare. Lock wing tips. One on each limb. One flyer support head. Change in fives. I go alone to other business."

Tandra—moments later near the ruins east of the reactor

"Well, what do you think, Tandra my dear?" Conn said, looking dry and tired. "Shall we go swimming? My favorite lake is just over that hill, and the storm is beginning to calm."

"We might as well." I felt as worn as Conn looked. *He often visits here with Mahntik.* The Free-mind's words echoed through my thoughts, draining my energy. *At least he is safe, at least for now.* "Orram has not been here, and the reactor is nearly closed down. I'm convinced that Orram does not want to be found. He won't answer any kind of message. I think you're right. Mahntik's got him by the—"

"Hush, cynical lady. Don't let Mahntik throw you off Orram. He's not human, you remember, probably blinded by his patch organs, but Varoks don't have the kind of testosterone that humans do. They've got some kind of methyl group that dims their—"

"I'm just so lost, Conn. I gave up my life on Earth for what? I have to do what is needed for Varok. That's the only way my being here will mean anything for Earth. And what does Shawne have if the family dissolves?"

"You and she will always be stuck with me, whatever happens. You know that, Gentle Face," Conn said.

I sat down on a bit of rubble and willed away angry tears. "Maybe I should send her home with the humans. I came here to model Varok's ancient steady-state and present it as an example to Earth. Mahntik is tearing that apart, and if Orram is defending her, if he is so blind . . ."

Conn wrapped his long arms around me and held me close. "He's just trusting his patches. It may take some time for him to recognize—"

"Surely you are not defending him now. How can he miss the evidence we all see? You said the same thing when you gave up your ring—if Mahntik has become part of Orram—I can't bear it, Conn. I am too human. Sex matters to me, too much, and so does Varok. I can't share Orram. I can't be part of him, if she is part of him. She is a traitor to all I believe, to all I hope for Earth and Varok. I'll have to choose. It's Orram or Varok."

FINDING ORRAM

Orticon—moments later

While Orticon and Lanoll stood on the platform, waiting for the next airshuttle to Vior, they tried to contact Orserah on Orticon's communicator.

"The eastern edge of the storm must have touched Mount Ni by now; the locale should be clear," Lanoll said. "If you keep trying to transmit with full-option signals, you'll get through. Eventually the emergency cable network will give you space, at least across the valley."

After several attempts, Orticon finally heard Orserah's voice.

"I understand you are safe. I can't make out what you are saying. Have you found Orram? Tandra and Conn?"

"Orserah, I am with Lanoll. She is fine now, but haven't seen the others. Conn must be told—Lanoll and I will be at the landing, the human spaceship landing. We're going after Mahntik. Free-minds will be there. There could be trouble."

"Not everything is coming through," said Orserah. "There are reports of a crowd gathering at the landing site, Orticon. They don't sound friendly. You must come home. Can you hear me? You must come home and get Conn's ring. It must come from Orram. Find Orram."

"I got most of it, Orserah. A ring? I don't understand. Contact Jesse and Killah. Tell them we will see them at the Earthship landing." He shut down the transmitter. Time was their worst enemy now. "We'll have to take this next shuttle, Lanoll, if we are to get to the landing in time."

"I'd rather wait here for Conn and Tandra. Our best hope is that they will also plan to go back to Vior for the landing. Do we have time for a quick swim? I need to re-wet my sweater. The cliffs are not high over there toward the genetics lab."

"Of course. Let's take wheels over to the beach. They'll have a rack."

The elll and the varok selected two sturdy biwheels from the public rack at the shuttle station and rode the wide path that followed the cliffs west to the genetics laboratory. Leaving Orticon in the shade of a mineral tree on the beach, Lanoll enjoyed a long swim and a few live snacks in the tossing waves, then walked back to Orticon on her be-finned feet.

"Have a fresh snarl, Orticon. They're quite good raw." She handed him the small sea bug and looked up in time to see Mahntik and six young varoks board the airshuttle.

"We're going to be a little late, but we'd better wait for the next airshuttle, Orticon. I don't think we want to sail with that crowd."

He looked up and nodded agreement, then looked up again. An elll and another biped were careening down the path toward the shuttle station on a beat-up four-wheeler.

Tandra

I heard a familiar elllonian voice shouting, "Stop. Conn, Tandra, stop. That shuttle is full—"

"Of riff-raff, we call it on Earth. Hiho, Orticon. Fancy meeting you here." I threw down my wheels and ran to my adopted son, leaving Conn to soak Lanoll with the kind of joy ellls are so good at. "You have plenty of time until the next airshuttle," I hollered after the ellls, as they raced for deep water.

"Come sit with me, Orticon. I must talk with you." I sat down and leaned against the mineral tree, still breathing hard from our quick wheel trip from the lake.

Orticon folded himself next to me. "Want a nice juicy bite of snarl, Tandra?"

I took the slimy thing and chewed it up, not daring to study it first. "I'm glad we have some time to talk. I have not been able to contact Orram, and I have had no message from him."

"No one has, Tandra."

"But I am his mind-partner, his guide in navigating overwhelming tides—can't he trust me? Or has he shared minds with Mahntik? Has he been with her all this time?"

"We varoks don't jump minds, Tandra, as human males sometimes jump from wife to wife."

"Or vice versa," I said.

"May I read your mood? It is very different. I don't understand what you are not saying."

"Read away, Free-mind. Call it what you will—frustration, anger?"

"Cynicism?"

"Not really. It's more like confusion. I miss Orram so much I feel I could forgive him anything. Yet I feel deserted, and angry. I don't know what to do, which way to leap. How do I save the family? I can't put up with Mahntik, and I can't understand Orram's failure to respect the evidence that she is dangerous, if indeed that is his failure. But there is more to our problem, Orticon. I cannot agree with Orram's position on the mind-probe. I agree with you, with the Free-minds. The probe should not be used in routine investigations. The opportunity for abuse or oppression is too great. I've felt the pain of Mahntik's uninvited digging, and the investigations after Leyoon's death were excruciating for everyone involved. I hate to see it, but with mutants like Mahntik walking out of legend, Varok's legal proceedings will need greater reliance on physical evidence."

"Perhaps sufficient proof would merit the deep probe, as would cases that threaten extreme danger."

"Yes. That is what I have decided."

"Then we agree, Tandra. I use my patches now to read you, and I don't have to force my way in to know that we are in agreement. The open mind is not abused. It has made this society work for ages."

"Can Orram agree with us?"

"I'm not sure."

I went for the most frightening idea, needing to hear his denial. "Orticon, do you think he could possibly have joined with Mahntik's mind—or some part of it?"

"Where Mahntik is concerned, I can no longer imagine what may be possible."

THE EARTH SHIP LANDS

Conn—in Ahl Vior

Impressive landing, Conn thought, *coming in on the Ahl Vior field as if it were routine.* Five humans exited the Earth ship and waved to a small crowd of varoks, ellls and daramonts gathered across the way. They were met by rehab personnel with a wheelbus and a nervous set of officials from Global Varok. Before the visitors could enter the bus, Mahntik approached them with a group of thirty Free-minds carrying an odd assortment of tools and laser pencils. Conn, Jesse, Artellian and Killah emerged from behind the bus and blocked Mahntik's path.

"Bob Carliano," Conn hollered, pushing Mahntik aside and greeting the retired astronaut with a hug. "Good to see you again. Welcome to Varok." The elll turned to the confused crowd. "This is our old friend from the EV Science Observation Base on Earth's moon. Give him and his friends a noisy welcome—and put away that laser welding rig, Allantak. You could hurt yourself with that thing."

Conn faced the curious humans, threw his hand into a high spiral of greeting and ushered them onto the bus. The relieved crowd erupted with traditional welcoming expressions and followed the Global Varok officials and the visitors' bus toward the rehabilitation center.

As the exhausted young humans and their older escort were wheeled off the bus in recovery chairs, the Free-minds began to mumble to each other.

"There are only five of them," Conn overheard. "Their ship is so old—did you see anything that looked like a weapon?" Mahntik had lost control.

"We won't keep you long," Conn said to the humans, "but we would like you to tell us about your plans for this trip, Bob? Confirm your intentions and all that. I'll translate into Varokian for you."

Carliano eagerly explained that Earth needed to learn how Varok had managed to maintain a steady state for so many ages. "How does one try to convert to a no-growth economy? I hear that there are some unusual growth spurts here. We would like to see how you manage them. We are grateful to be received as guests of Global Varok. We will stay only until your beautiful planet . . . uh moon . . . comes under the shadow of Jupiter, out of sight of our shared sun—until the next deep dark, I believe you call it. We will touch nothing, leave nothing, and do nothing but take notes. Then we will fly home to share your advice and continue to fight for the transition to what we hope will ensure a healthy and sustainable future for all life on Earth."

Orram

Orram waited beside the rehab center, out of sight. Mahntik was not looking too happy with her Free-mind army. He saw her arguing with her young troops, then speaking urgently and gesturing with visible frustration.

"Be still, Nidok," Orram said. "Our journey will be over soon."

Nidok tried to flare his wing-plates against Orram's belt, which encircled him. "Nasty varok," he gargled.

"I am sorry the captain's loft on the hovershuttle was so cramped, my friend," Orram said. "Our trip across the Misted Ocean together will bear fruit, you'll see. You will have a fair hearing."

"I nest on dead acid plains before I enter trap of dark varok courtroom," Nidok said.

"Good. Here they come."

Mahntik led her group of young varoks toward the humans. Other varoks and ells crowded closer. *They seem more bemused than threatened at the odd assortment of weapons Mahntik's varoks hold*, Orram thought.

"Watch out for those portable laser welding rigs," he told Nidok, "and the varoks with battery packs on their shoulders. Lasers pens are visible in their hands."

Mahntik now appeared calm, in full control. *How beautiful she is.* Orram wondered at himself for noticing it now. *Her dark hair wild with loose strands of silver, her eyes flashing.*

The humans and the Global Varok officials began exchanging information. The Free-minds stared at Mahntik with some kind of bewildered hope evident in their faces, as she raised an arm to begin the attack.

Before she could give her command, Conn stepped out of the gathering and grabbed her, pinning her arms behind her back.

Orram nodded to Global Varok's security team and leapt to her defense. He relieved her of her laser pen in the scuffle, and aimed it at Conn.

The clueless young humans gasped, understanding too little Varokian, but sensing the drama. Bob Carliano, poor man, was utterly flumoxed, looking to Tandra for help and receiving nothing.

Orram did not dare read her, and had trouble putting down the concern he felt.

No one moved.

"It's good to see you alive, Conn," Orram said. It took every ounce of concentration for the varok to harden his mind against the familiar elllonian gaze.

"Where did you come from, Conn?" Mahntik asked, nearly irrational with anger. "Watch out, Orram. He's mad."

"Who is mad, Mahntik?" Conn asked. "Why are you here, Orram? To expose these human students to this varokian mutant?"

An ugly snarl curled Mahntik's face. "Varok welcomes no more humans. They bring dangerous germs and hidden weapons. Let me go, Conn. They will kill us all if we don't act now."

Orram gazed steadily at Conn, as if trying to read him. He concentrated on keeping his mind as empty of memory and suspicion as he could.

"I have taken Nidok," Orram said, keeping his eyes on Conn. "Trouble with his flock should be finished."

Mahntik hesitated, and Orram felt her begin an exploratory probe. Nidok struggled against his belt, lurching toward Mahntik. She pulled away, but remained firmly locked in Conn's grasp.

Gradually a wide, homely grin spread over the elll's green face. "When Tan and I were sneaking around L'orkah, looking for you, I told her over and over," he said in his slow tuneful accent, "that I would eat ahlork wing-plates for a solid Callisto Cycle, if I could just see you alive once more, Orram, my dear. You're going to cost me one hell of a bellyache."

A surge of emotion nearly washed out Orram's caution. Nidok made a timely lurch, angering Mahntik. There was no doubt Conn would hold her fast.

"Turn Mahntik loose, Conn." Orram's command hinted condescension. "Don't give in to your visions."

"Visions? I know what I've lived through, Orram. Move aside now. Mahntik has lived her last free moment."

Orram moved one step toward Conn. "We need her, Conn, to help us convict Leyoon's murderer."

"Now, how could you help, Mahntik?" Conn said. "What kind

of sewage flowing between your ears have you given Orram to taste?" The elll looked squarely at the varok. "Mahntik can put out whatever flavor and stench she wants, Orram. It's a remarkable feat—"

The elll's eyes narrowed as Orram slowly raised the laser pencil and armed it. "No, Orram. I am not damaged."

Nidok was baffled. He began to struggle more seriously against his leash.

"Conn? Where are you?" It was Tandra's voice. "Orram?" She stood facing him and Conn, to create a triangle. "So it is true. You are with Mahntik. Conn will not tolerate her treason in our family, nor will I."

She slipped the family ring from her finger and gave it to Bob Carliano, who looked at it and smiled sadly. "I know this ring. You three joined as family on Moon Base."

"I thought it could work, Bob. Now I see that I have to make a choice."

If Tandra saw Orram's laser pen aimed at Conn, she chose to ignore it. She gave it only a flicker of her eyes.

"Come home to Earth with us, Tandra," the human astronaut said. "We need you there to help us stay on track."

Tandra smiled at him and nodded in agreement, then spoke to Orram. "We humans here have sacrificed too much for the future for both our worlds. I cannot be a part of anything that supports Mahntik. She is traitor to Varok, to Earth and to all we believe. I choose Varok. Your attachment to her has dissolved the family."

Her tears spoke too true. Orram saw that she believed what she said. He stood tense and expectant. Had the game gone too far? "Tandra, I need your help."

"Orram, we are done," she said, but she moved to the varok's side and sought his mind. "Where have you been? Conn and I have looked all over L'orkah for you."

"I've been collecting elll plumes in the ruins." Orram pulled Conn's lost plumes from his pocket. "Interesting. What would an elll be doing in such a place, so far from water?"

"Very strange," Tandra said, "like you dropping out of sight for so long. Are you all right?"

Carliano and the humans listened, fascinated, but puzzled.

"I'm not a very good detective, but I'm fine, Tan. Conn is the enigma. Mahntik thinks he is dangerous, damaged by prolonged desiccation." Orram took Tandra's hands and looked for her ring.

"So it's true," he said. "The Family is broken. Conn? You both love Varok that much?"

Conn held out the empty finger where his web had been torn by the ring. "I won't be tortured to death and run down by rovers, only to have my memories doubted. No trust, no family, Orram."

"What?" Mahntik did not hide the spiteful joy she felt. Controlling her emotions was keeping her busy. "At last you have come to your senses, Orram."

"Conn is sick," Orram said to Tandra. "Nidok said that desiccation could have damaged his brain. Also, Mahntik's mind is clear of incriminating memory. Clear as Earth's proverbial bell."

Tandra turned from Orram's arms and faced Mahntik. "Look closer, Orram. Her mind is too shallow, too clear. Orlah saw her close it. Read her, Orram. You won't see much."

As he had done twice before, Orram tuned his patches to Mahntik's mind. There was no memory or thought to condemn her. He concentrated on the bewilderment he felt, in case she was reading him. "Her mind is clear," he said.

"Father!" Orticon came running, followed by several varokian security officers and Free-minds.

"Take the murderer," Mahntik shouted, indicating Nidok with a nod.

No one moved except Orticon. He took the leash from Orram and released Nidok. "Don't you need your belt, Father?"

As the ahlork settled noisily to the ground beside Conn, Mahntik struck out at him with her feet. Conn pulled her arms tighter in his grip.

"Mahntik lies. Focus on her," Tandra said. "The mind-block is real. All Varok needs to know of it, needs to know what trust is. Probe her deeply if you must."

The Free-minds recoiled from Tandra's command, but the security varoks and Orticon immediately locked onto Mahntik's closed mind.

"Don't you see how I am used? Get this ahlork away from me." Mahntik looked to the Free-minds, her voice shaking. "Orram believes I am in the right here. Read him. Take Conn."

"But do be careful," Conn said. He took both her hands in one of his and put a choking hold around her neck.

"We know you are the murderer, Mahntik," Tandra said, hoping the forthright accusation would catch her off guard. "Probe her. Probe her quickly, deeply. Orticon, help me. She is lying."

"There is nothing in her mind," several of the Free-minds agreed.

"Maintain the probes," a security officer insisted. "It would be helpful to see the block, to see if it can truly be done."

"We have no right to probe her like that," one Free-mind said. He bolted from the scene, disrupting the concentrated effort.

The diversion was enough to allow Mahntik to compose herself.

"Orram, scan me," Conn demanded. "Compare what you find in my mind with Mahntik's memory."

"Memory is very tricky, Conn. It must be called up willingly or dragged up to be read. It may also be warped in time—revised, without your knowing it."

"The mind-block must break on the paradox it creates in differing memories," Conn pleaded, "or Varokian society will grovel in doubts and suspicion from now 'til Harrahn rolls over in his grave."

"Maintain your probes," Tandra quietly reminded the security team.

"Tandra is as mad as Conn." Mahntik struggled against Conn's grip and nearly went irrational with anger. "Humans are not to be trusted."

"Are you to be trusted, Mahntik?" said Conn. "Did you know that Nidok's flock has already taken Gitahl in for questioning? Don't worry your sourness about him, Dearie."

"He—he is a traitor," Mahntik spat. "Gitahl has been working with the ahlork to—"

"To what, Mahntik?" Tandra looked at her quizzically. "Keep your probes focused," she urged the others.

"But she is totally free of any indication—" a security officer protested.

"It is too clear, too closed in. Watch every corner," Tandra insisted.

"I'm sorry," the officer said. "We have no right to continue."

"Watch every reaction."

Mahntik laughed. "You will never do it, Tandra," she said. "I am innocent."

"Never do what, Mahntik?" Tandra asked the question with a blank, puzzled expression on her face.

Orram's laser weapon shifted from Conn to Mahntik.

"You can let her go now, Conn," he said, with a burst of intense relief. "We have all seen it. Tandra, we have plenty of evidence to convict Mahntik of many crimes, including murder, but you were entirely correct to make your demonstration of the mind-block public."

"No!" Mahntik shouted. "No, Orram. My mind is clear."

"Yes, Mahntik. We all see the clarity of your closed mind. And pride—a pride that became transparent to us all for an instant. It revealed your thought as clearly as if you had spoken the words: 'No stupid human being will ever break down my mind-block.'"

Tandra

Conn laughed. "You saw Mahntik refer to her own mind-block? And Tandra set it up? Beautiful! Beautiful, my gorgeous, stupid human being." He pushed Mahntik away and wrapped his arms around me in a wiry hug. Tears of relief flowed down my face.

Mahntik paled at our jubilant expressions, only dimly realizing how I had sprung the trap.

"You are correct, Oran Ramahlak. We have all the evidence we need, both physical and mental. Thank you," a security officer said. "Mahnate Tikahn, you are charged with the murder of two ahlork and the great-fish Leyoon—and treason against Varokian society."

Two varoks stepped forward, but she backed away from them. In his wheelchair, Bob Carliano followed the scene, trying to make sense of it.

"No," Mahntik said, reaching into the pocket of the jump suit she wore, her face still and composed once again. "If you come toward me, I will release this culture. It is a deadly virus, a crude but very effective ally in clearing Varok of fools. Thank you for releasing my arms, Conn." With a dazzling smile she turned and moved away from the crowd. "I warn you," she called as she ran, "don't follow me."

"Right. Don't follow her. Cut her off," Orram suggested, as the security officers spread out to form their trap.

"Tell security to head Mahntik away from the shore," he called to Orticon, as the youth started off to follow them.

As they closed in on Mahntik, Orram shouted a warning. "We've got trouble! What ahlork are those coming out of the ruins, Nidok?"

"Those are last of Sartak's flock."

With a loud clacking of wings, the small flock dove for the varoks on the beach. Mahntik was holding off security with her cultures, backing toward the water.

Orram was alarmed. "Better stay back. Security can't take Mahntik with the ahlork getting in the mix." Orram reached for me in mind, and I responded. *Go to her. It may help.* Then, not sure what he intended, or how he could persuade Mahntik to trust Varokian justice, he set out across the sand to intercept her.

The ahlork flew in a tight circle above Mahntik, then settled to the beach and formed a fence of cocked wing-plates around her.

She broke out of the closing circle and ran toward Orram, screaming for help.

With a cry of rage, Sartak rose into the air.

Nidok scrambled into flight, his talons at full flex. "No more blood on the True Flock! No more," he screeched, leaping toward Sartak.

He was too late.

With a few powerful strokes of his enormous wings, Sartak reached Mahntik. "No one poisons waters of Greater Flock!" His maddened cry resounded over the beach. He dove at her, knocked the cultures from her hand, and took her by the shoulders with his huge talons.

Before Orram could reach them, two other ahlork helped Sartak contain Mahntik, and between them all, they carried her out over the lake toward the southern ocean, Ranarallahn, where lay the isolated rocks of Ahlnitahk. The orange-red sky graced the silver streaks of her hair with glimmers of warm light.

RENEWAL

Tandra—on the shore of Ranarnahrl

As Orram watched Mahntik and the ahlork disappear beyond the lake, he sank deep into my mind to find support, for his grief was real. The misdirection of Mahntik's genius was a tragic waste. I met his blue eyes, overflowing with love. *I understand. I grieve with you.*

"Gad, old buddy," Conn said as he joined us, "you're one hell of an actor."

"I think we have just experienced trust." Orram let himself laugh and cry at once. "I was terrified you'd believe my support for Mahntik." As we walked back to the landing area, Conn and Orram converged in a reunion they could no longer restrain. Bob Carliano met us in front of the rehab center, concerned about the fracas at the beach.

"You seem to have found yourselves," he said. "And Mahntik?"

"I think she will find poetic justice," Conn said.

"I seem to have forgotten something," I said, taking Conn and Orram's hands. "Bob, do you have both rings I gave you—Conn's ring, as well as mine? It's time for Orram to replace them. Lanoll, come join us."

"Are you sure, Tandra?" Orram asked. "I did experience a surge of testosteroid hormone around Mahntik."

"I know—I always understood why. I just didn't know how little it meant to you."

"And I won't forget how much is does mean to you, human lady."

Bob looked at us, apparently concerned and shaken from Mahntik's dramatic exit. "Tandra, are you sure you don't need to come home?"

"My work and my family are here, Bob. We will make sure you have a wonderful tour of Varok."

Orram took the family rings from Bob's open hand. "Tandra, you know I can only hope that my tame hormones will be just another wrinkle to smooth out between us."

"Of course," I said. Orram placed the smaller ring on my third finger, and the larger ring on Conn's broken-finned middle digit. "Love trumps all. Right, Lanoll?" he said, and our four hands went up into our high-five teepee.

The crowd quickly dispersed, as Varokian officials ushered the visiting humans, including a reluctant Bob Carliano, into space travel rehabilitation. Orram led Tandra, Orticon, Conn and Lanoll outside, along a rocky path to the nearby park.

Orticon walked beside his father and allowed himself a huge smile. "We were quite worried about you, Father."

"I couldn't stay in contact and keep my activities hidden from Mahntik. She probes all minds deeply, like some vicious insect, and without invitation. I had little contact with anyone, for how many light-periods? I can't say. But do I sense a change in mind, Orticon? I don't want to misinterpret you."

"I think you'll find us all in agreement, Father. I have seen Conn take the scar of Nidok. I have seen Conn and Tandra merge their consciousness with Orlah and save his reason. I have seen Mahntik's treason in the valley beneath Mount Ni. I long to know your mind. I am the son of Oran Ramahlak."

For a moment Orram and Orticon locked arms, riding the moment.

"Ouch." Lanoll tripped and fell, trying to save her webbed feet from the sharper rocks.

"Lanoll, are you all right?" I asked, helping the elll brush the sand and dirt from her plumes.

"I'm fine, though my feet are dry as a web-sucker and twice as prickly."

"We could go for a swim," Conn said.

"You could use some fattening up first," Lanoll said, then glanced at me. "I don't want to be greedy, or pushy."

"I've had some time with the Green Scab, thank you," I said. "Your turn."

"What I really need," Conn said, grabbing Tandra and Lanoll in his arms, "is lots of good, kinky sex."

It felt good to laugh, with no bitterness or reservation. "Now, off with you two," I said. "Enjoy the water."

They were no more than two steps toward the lake when Nidok returned, frantic with worry. He had been chasing Sartak, but lost him over the acid plains. He flapped dangerously close to Orram and Conn, and back to Orram—a bevy of emotions tearing at him as he tried to apologize for Sartak's latest atrocity.

"Gad, Boxface, I didn't know you cared." After several alarming misses, Conn caught the ahlork by a wing-tip and pulled him to the ground. "Sartak was not True Flock. He brings no shame on ahlork."

The elll's rough admonishment apparently shocked Nidok out of his hysteria, but he could not be consoled. "Sartak must be destroyed. I will send some of the True Flock—"

"To continue the war?" Orram asked. "It may not be slaughter this time, Nidok. I think Sartak has other ideas, heading south like that." He kneeled over Nidok, looking directly into the ahlork's impenetrable black beads. They told him nothing, but mirrored his own pain and exhaustion. "They'll stay busy trying to keep Mahntik's appetite satisfied."

Nidok's greater lip trembled, and he kept glancing up at the skies over the beach, wondering what he could do to right the many wrongs ahlork had perpetrated.

Orram reached out and grabbed Conn's wrist, exposing the prominent scar that crossed his tiles. "'To take the scar of an ahlork is to bind oneself to his nest and to his flock for life.'" It was a quote from the Pledge of Ancient Days. "I would know you better, Nidok—but since Conn has taken your scar, I claim a right to one, also."

"As do I," I said, kneeling beside Orram.

"No, Tan," Conn said, alarmed, "you've got too many blood vessels in your wrist."

Nidok glanced up into Conn's worried face, but I offered my arm next to Orram's. I was serious. "We all wish to be bound to the noblest of ahlork."

"Complete the seal of trust between the Oran-Grey-elConn family and the True Flock you represent," Orram urged.

Nidok lay a razor sharp wing-plate over our wrists, and the air exploded with the clacking rustle of his flock, as they settled on the beach to witness the historic exchange of trust. "The True Flock pledges . . ." Nidok began uncertainly, then his voice gained clarity and determination. "We ahlork pledge renewal of web fields. We pledge no more greedy, wide markets, no more lethal web-berries. We pledge not too many mines. We pledge protection for ilara and care for all daramonts. We pledge help to varoks and ellls who watch Varokian life."

"No longer simple scavengers on the fringe of Varokian law," Orram responded, "as Governor of Living Resources I declare that you are the noblest of friends—to varoks, ellls and great-fish, to daramonts and light-hoppers—guardians of the delicate balance of Varok."

With that, Nidok's wing-tip moved swiftly around Orram's wrist, then mine, leaving deep scratches that broke few vessels. He sealed the wounds with regurgitant. Then he backed away to a safe wing-span, stretched his wings to full length, took flight and soared over the lake. "Beware the True Flock," he hollered at us. "We come often to Orserah's house to keep your scars raw and ugly."

Tandra—at the Oran locale

It seemed as if an age of Deep Darks—filled with a thousand tasks never completed—passed over Mount Ni and the offices at Ahl Vior, before we were free to make our way back to Orserah's house.

While we were debriefing in the Global Varok offices, Bob Carliano and his human companions enjoyed their rehabilitation procedures and education. We checked in with Orserah and picked up Shawne, so she could meet the humans and join us for their grand tour. She immediately bonded with Bob Carliano, and I wondered if she didn't recognize him from their time at the Earth moon base.

"So how do you like living on Varok?" Bob asked Shawne, as we enjoyed fresh fish from the ellls' farm in the Forested Sea.

Shawne got up from digging her toes into the sandy beach and crawled into his lap. "I love it. Especially big old Jupiter up there in the sky. And I love the silly egg layers. That's my job, you know, at the locale. I feed them and pick up their eggs."

"Sounds like a great game of hide and seek."

She looked toward the water, where some elll tads were rolling in the shallows. "Right, but now I have to go." She jumped down and ran to the shallows, where she soon convinced the tads to tow her to shore-weeds that were ripe with sweet fruits.

The trip was more fun than work. Bob and his friends would face the truly difficult tasks after they returned to Earth, supporting the small but growing consensus that was needed to make change possible there.

"We must remind them that the longer you wait," Orram preached, "the fewer your options. You do not need to let nature make your choices."

We traveled across Vior, focused on solutions for Lake Seclusion, and made a quick trip across the sea to L'orkah. We visited web fields and ilara spawning grounds, talking with leaders at each locale about conditions there, and adjustments to help heal the lakes and soil. Within the next cycle, the humans made a reluctant exit, promising to coordinate our efforts to help Earth.

After seeing the human visitors leave for Earth, we made our way home and found the garden bulging with fruit and streaming with tender vines. In the center of neat rows of vegetables stood Orlah, his hands strong and steady. Shawne's weed-eating robot stood by his side, as he guided a hoe through the soil. When he saw us all riding toward him, he waved in greeting and called Orserah from the house to join the reunion.

"Re-forged in trust," Orram said. He took Conn and my hands

and showed Orserah that the rings were back on our fingers. "Re-forged in God-blessed good luck that Mahntik was too befuddled, thanks to Nidok and Tandra and Conn, to probe me deeply during my performance."

"What?" Orserah couldn't stand the suspense.

"Stay out of my mind, Mother, I want to embellish the story with words."

Orticon laughed. "You won't have much luck, Father." It was a wonderful sound, the first real laugh I had ever heard from him.

Epilogue: Varok

Tandra—at the Oran locale

As time put moss back on Conn's tiles and Orserah's stew put meat on his bones, we sank deep into the comfort of being together. Shawne grew into a sturdy little girl of nearly five Earth years. Every other light-period, she pulled Conn away from the algae pond or his office, and they combed the web-bushes by hand, looking for web-suckers. Too often they found too many. But more and more often, daramonts would approach and tease them, begging for a chase, and they would ride across the fields, defining web-bushes as hurdles to challenge the mounts.

At the waning of one beautiful light-period, as they rode under a horizon of delicate green, Lanoll rode out to meet them. "Hurry back to the house," she cried from atop her favorite daramont. "Nidok is here."

"I'll be fried." Conn reined in his mount. "I thought he'd never come back to us."

"Race you, Lanoll," Shawne challenged.

The daramonts agreed, and they took off in great arcs across the fields, only to be startled by Nidok's aerial antics as they neared the house.

"Hurry up, Fish Leather," Nidok called. "Orserah cooks us fine-smelling stew." He landed abruptly in the root garden, and tried unsuccessfully to tiptoe back to the path without trampling the plants.

"Still no manners. Didn't they teach you anything in Ahl Vior?"

"I learned nothing but pushing buttons—and what for? The flock destroyed Sartak and three other murderers before I got them to court. Gitahl in jail will eat crow. Right, Tandra?"

"Crow it is, Nidok," Tandra said. "You've been studying Earth slang."

Conn paced himself to the ahlork's slow waddle. "Enjoying Earth studies, are you? You sacrificed yourself for a wreck of an elll."

"Just one more ruin to salvage."

"How can we be sure Varok is salvageable, Clacker? Are we back on the right track?"

"Maybe half my flock is lost. How do I know? Nothing is sure. We live and do least harm. We steal no life-joy from others, as ellls say."

"How do you know so much about us?"

"I keep track who wears my scar. I'm glad to see you grow back ugly hexagonal sensor lines."

"Big words, Beady Eyes. You've been in Ahl Vior too long, trying to hatch books. You're supposed to read them, turn the pages and push the buttons, one page at a time. You're not supposed to lick the pictures and nibble the bindings."

"Rude elll." Nidok waited until they were inside to continue the fun. "When do you fatten him up, Orserah? He looks like skeleton walking on flippers. He doesn't survive the Forested Sea like that." He perched on the hearth. "I should take my scar back. I learn manners in Ahl Vior." With one swipe of his wing-tip, he stole Conn's bowl and hopped to a rock high on the hearth. See how much lunch you eat today, Brother Elll. No bowl is safe."

Once we had all finished eating we were reluctant to leave the hearth. When Nidok prepared to leave, Conn urged him to take the family ring.

He refused, but he did not respond with an insult. "Ahlork flocks have no loners. I can be no true member of your family, Conn. You honor all ahlork by asking. It gives us back our pride."

"Ahlork are respected for dismantling Mahntik's web-markets so quickly," Orram reassured him.

"There is no honor in our nests. We forgot the future. We forgot to leave no tracks in the sand, to leave behind our lives no trace but art and wisdom. That is what makes Varok last so long."

Orram looked as if he had been struck with a cocked wing. "Of course, Nidok, the steady-state is not just an economic ideal, it's an ethical system. It holds our responsibility to the future as top priority, above all other economic values. Those values prescribe what we do, as much as laws and limits. Ours is a balancing of choices between consensus and coersion."

I saw in Orram's mind how desperately he had wanted Shawne and me to know stability and to be secure. He had assumed Varok would provide that security automatically. In practice, its laws had proven to keep all resource levels constant. But no level of life quality could be sustained long-term without the underlying shared ethic. Until Mahntik challenged Varok's fragile balance, Orram had not understood the true cause of its vulnerability—it depends on consensus, shared belief in the commandment, "Secure for all future lives what you would like for yourselves."

"For that insight I owe you more than all the retribution your flock can pay," Orram said. He startled the ahlork by clasping one wing-tip between his hands. "You have shown me the face of Varok as Leyoon saw it. I respect your wisdom and ask you to take the ring, on my behalf, as well as Conn's."

"Call me brother. Treat my flock like Nidok. That is all." The ahlork hopped to the great porch, stretching his wings to full length, scattering everything in their wake. Then he lept into the air and disappeared.

Tandra—one Jovian year later

Nidok returned to his flock, but as the Jovian year passed, he and his nestlings were never gone for long. Eventually their visits extended beyond light-periods to encompass whole Varokian cycles around Jupiter.

It was a long Jovian year of difficult work for Orram and the family, as Varok adjusted to the replanting of old webs. Addiction to Mahntik's berries persisted, and we watched aghast as Lake Seclusion was forced to a population dispersal. It was also a year of joy, with the hatching of Conn and Lanoll's chosen egg—a schooling elll born of two loners. We called him Stringer.

It was a year in which we humans—Jesse and I—became fully integrated to Varok. As Jupiter rode once around the sun, Shawne grew into a lovely girl of sixteen Earth-years, an expert trainer of daramonts and a musician of talent maturing under Conn's complex tutelage.

It was a year saddened by the loss of Orlah, who completed his last deep dark in the restful channels of Conn's mind. Orserah gradually grew frail, but she lived to enjoy the entire year.

It was a year of resolution, in which Lanoll's presence tempered Conn's instincts, in which Conn and Orram and I saw our differences grow deeper—and felt the gap between us grow too narrow to matter, as we opened ourselves to touch the alienness of the others and make it part of ourselves.

As the year progressed, Orticon finished integrating the information he had adsorbed at the Concentrate. He then went to L'orkah, intent on building bridges to the Free-minds who had worked to regulate the legal deep probe. Eventually, he was elected to be their representative to the councils of Global Varok, and all complaints of mind-abuse were referred to him.

He wrote to Shawne more and more frequently:

> *Our family deserves the highest respect possible*
>
> *1) because of varoks like Orram, who have faith in knowledge and the understanding it spawns,*
>
> *2) because of ellls like Conn, who have faith in their God-given senses,*
>
> *3) because of ahlork like Nidok, who understands what science is—the art of trying to prove how wrong you might be,*
>
> *4) because of humans like Tandra, your mother, who is not afraid to stand on good evidence while leaping to faith in what evidence cannot prove, and*
>
> *5) because of great-fish like Leyoon, who see the future in the present, where tiny wings can generate hurricanes over time.*

Shawne

"Hop on, Conn," Shawne laughed from atop a huge black daramont. "Free rides for red plumes! Free rides for red plumes!"

"That's no free ride you're offering. I have no plumes to spare."

Conn set aside the robot's plow and walked up to the daramont, who presented his mane for combing. Obligingly Conn ran his fingers through the long silk hanging over the great neck. With a powerful leap, he mounted the daramont behind Shawne.

"You should do more walking. That's what we Varokians do."

"That rule applies to everyone but me."

"No exceptions! Ellls had better learn to grow longer toes," Shawne scolded.

"No way." Conn shook his head and scowled darkly. "How would we catch the wild Harrahn of the Misted Ocean if we had toes?" The elll nudged the daramont into a gentle lope, and when they reached the house, he slid off the mount and helped Shawne down. "Now, you would do well to help your Orserah clean the hearth dishes, as you are supposed to, before riding daramonts. I'll be in the orchard."

When she had finished her chores in the house, Shawne escaped happily to the orchard, where she found Conn perched in a broad-leaf fruit tree, cutting away crossing branches and crowded growth with a lever-activated hand cutter. He called a greeting to her in a sonic code that made sense only to them. Delighted, the young woman repeated her version of the code, then busied herself by dragging the cut branches to one corner of the web field and stacking them for mulching and cooking fuel.

The light-period was at its warmest, and the lightning sent a continuous glow over the land, while the auroral mists retreated to display the full glory of the Vahinorral. Suddenly the crest of the mountains broke through the mist, showing off dramatic cliffs of red above a rich gray collar of soft slopes.

Shawne fixed her gaze on the colorful scene. Her delicate torso, devoid now of its baby roundness, lengthening in preparation for womanhood, was a thin twig swallowed by the heap of branches she pulled.

"Hey, Blue-eyes, you're leaving a trail of brush behind you,"

Conn hollered from atop his ladder.

"Oh!" She laughed and looked behind her, then threw down her burden and went back to pick up the dropped branches. The mountains caught her eye again and she slowed her pace. "Isn't the Vahinorral beautiful, Conn? When can we go across the mountains again? I want to visit the ellls in the Forested Sea. It's been such a long time."

"Maybe next year, Shawne."

"But next year never comes on Varok." She threw the re-gathered sticks into the larger pile and sat on them.

Conn came down the ladder, and settled himself in the soft earth beside her. "We've had to work very hard this year, Shawnoon. We've had no webs for many seasons, and the stalks have been full of web-suckers. But things are getting better. Soon we'll have fish from Lake Seclusion again. The old webs are coming back strong in the valley now, so you'll be able to weave new cloth and make new clothes for your first term at the Concentrate."

"Still, it seems like forever since we've gone anywhere," she said as she dug absently in the dirt with a stick. "And we'll probably never get back to Earth for a visit."

"Not for a while. Not until its safe. We're all working on that. Maybe you can go back when you're finished at the Concentrate."

"I would like that."

"Shawne, look." Conn whispered. He pointed toward their beleaguered web field. Three small flying creatures were settling on the bushes, while two others dove at the web-suckers that threatened the valuable stalks. "Ilara. They're back!" His voice rang with an intensity that gave Shawne a chill. "Now we'll have that trip across the mountains. It won't be long, Shawnoon. Everything's going to be all right."

The child and the elll eased closer together, slowly, so they would not startle the small creatures. Green auroras painted dancing sprays of light on the swirling mist as they huddled together and watched the tiny ilara take their fill.

Epilogue: Earth

Bob Carliano—in a message to Global Varok

> *On our return to Earth, we soon realized that education about steady state possibilities would have to wait for an end to poverty and hunger. Then the population could reach a stable level, as it had in Europe years before. If needed, replacement certificates could be issued in tenths to even out the pressure to have more children.*
>
> *Localization of economic activity with no mobility of money and labor would be imperative, as would eliminating the connection between regulation and politics, between government and business. No more subsidies.*
>
> *Some efforts could be made only on a global basis, like the estimate of non-renewable resources and the percentages to be auctioned for development each year.*
>
> *The most difficult decision or vote would be choosing a standard of living, deciding the safe level of resources to be used per capita per year, what would provide a good life for all members of an optimum population of humans. That optimum should no longer threaten other species on Earth with extinction.*

"First on our list of priorities," Carlilano said to Conn over the maser radio, "should be water management, through efficiency, reuse, conservation, desalinization, every means possible to preserve its quality and fair distribution. It must be regarded as a right, not a commodity to be bought and sold. Renewable sources of energy and high taxes for overuse are next on the list."

Conn added his advice in very direct language. "Shorten your work week and share jobs. Use less machinery and more labor. Create local currencies and put a tax on any exchange across locales. Pay no subsidies or unearned incomes. Period. Count all environmental impact costs to set realistic prices."

The conversation would continue and spread as Varok's example illustrated the real possibilities for Earth's future.

Appendices

Detailed regulations from top-down authority
can have unintended consequences;
rules alone will not enable the steady-state to emerge.

Long-term sustainability depends on universal
commitment to its key principles.

—Orram, in a message to Bob Carliano

A. CONN'S RECOMMENDATIONS FOR EARTH

1. The most efficient thing to do is to cap energy use—lots of luck. But be sure to cap off specific resources, based on known reserves. Be sure the use of non-renewables does not exceed their waste. The no-brainer is to be sure renewables are one-hundred percent regenerated before you use them up.

2. Population numbers should be stabilized—all of them, region by region. Everyone gets to replace themselves. Of course, they can buy up someone else's replacement certificate, or sell theirs. Use incentives to encourage replacement only. No nasty coercion allowed. Education, women's rights, and birth control help—a lot.

3. Inequality leads to revolution, which usually doesn't work unless someone has a real plan—like letting workers determine wages and salary differentials. No more than fifteen percent difference in income; that's enough for needed incentive. Employee business ownership and co-ops help. Everyone, that's *every sentient being*, gets a Citizen Income, an automatic unconditional payment from the government, funded by inheritance and luxury taxes or something more inventive.

4. For goodness sake, stabilize the money supply. Encourage localization with local currencies. Print just enough to run the global government, which should be busy counting resources and not much else. Banks can mediate loans but must keep one hundred percent reserves, i.e, loan ony what others have saved. Loans should require collateral—remember that word? Banks could also stash jewels in rented safe deposit boxes, but do little else.

5. Forget the gross domestic product (GDP). Try Bhutan's GPH or the GPI+—something that measures well-being. Just don't count the cost of cleaning up someone's nasty pollution as great economics. Separate the ends like well-being from the means.

6. To insure meaningful and full employment, shorten work times to distribute jobs where needed and increase leisure and

creative time. The government, like the city council, might do some job guaranteeing in the fields of education and medicine, or fixing bridges, but no subsidies on polluters, please.

7. Set prices, business revenue, to include all capital costs, environmental and disposal or recycling costs. Think social benefit, not profit. Tax away excess profits, income and harmful practices, like intrusive advertising (junk mail).

8. Localize. Localize. Localize all goods and services. Raise tariffs if necessary to protect local business. Free trade is just another example of "Winner Take All," so keep money and labor at home. Institute a Tobin Tax on exchange of currencies. Hire locals. Finance local businesses locally. Quit shipping tasteless apples all over the world, and eat more local kumquats. Share appliances. Cluster ventures that need a large infrastructure.

9. Revise lifestyle ethics to emphasize "enough is enough," cliché though it is. You don't need a new one, a prettier one, a shorter one, an uglier cool one. Share appliances. Fix what's broke and require manufacturers to take responsibility for their products, all the way to the junk or recycle heap—like some Europeans do. Spare parts businesses will boom. And no producing gewgaws for gewgaws sake. Encourage art and games instead.

10. Print this on your forehead: the economy is a sub-system of the environment. It's not the other way around. The human population is already too big for Earth to absorb its wastes, much less produce new cell phones for everyone. Everyone needs clean water to drink. Now! Invent more new ways to explore how to stabilize, not grow, the economy.

—Love and good luck, Conn*

*Conn's recommendations are based in part on the economic theories of Herman Daly and CASSE (Center for the Advancement of the Steady State Economy).

B. A Reader's History

3631 *ir* **(Earth 5000 BCE)** - Events recorded in *The Unheard Song*.[1]

3634 *ir* **(Earth 4962 BCE)** – Amanok writes his memoirs.

4225.8 *ir* **(Earth 2020 CE)** – Tandra Grey born on Earth.

4228 *ir* **(Earth 2047 CE)** – Shawne Oran-ElConn-Grey born on Earth.

4228.3–4228.4 *ir* **(Earth 2050–2051 CE)** – Events recorded in *A Place Beyond Man*,[2] revised as *The View Beyond Earth*.[1]

4228.4–4229.5 *ir* **(Earth 2051–2064 CE)** – Events in *The Webs of Varok*.

4229 *ir* **(Earth 2059 CE)** – Aman Telariahn (Amantel) publishes Amanok's memoirs as *The Unheard Song*.

4229.8–4230 *ir* **(Earth 2068–2070 CE)** – Family events recorded in *Conn: The Alien Effect*.[3]

4229.8–4409.7 *ir* **(Earth 2068–4202 CE and beyond)** – Biological Events recorded in *Conn: The Alien Effect*. (See above.)

4230 *ir* **(Earth 2070 CE)** – Events recorded in *Shawne: An Alien's Quest*.[3]

1. Coming from Penscript Publishing House in 2014.
2. Charles Scribner's Sons, 1975; Author's Guild Backinprint.com edition, 2011.
3. Coming from Penscript Publishing House in 2013.

C. Bibliography

Completing the Picture—
Adding Ecological Economics to Complexity Economics

Enough Is Enough: Building A Sustainable Economy in a World of Finite Resources (to be released in January 2012 by Berrett and Koehler, bkconnection.com) by Rob Dietz, former executive director of the Center for the Advancement of the Steady State Economy and Dan O'Neill, lecturer in ecological economics at the University of Leeds and the chief economist for CASSE, describing with precise clarity the *why* and *how* of converting to a steady state economy like Varok's, complete with notes for source information and index.

The Gardens of Democracy by Eric Liu and Eric Hanauer. An overview of problems with classical economics, economics as a complex system, and the role of government, leaving the *how* of solving problems to citizens. Sasquatch Books, Seattle, WA, 2011.

The Center for the Advancement of the Steady State Economy's top policies for achieving a steady state economy. For tending the economic garden that has become overgrown—how to get over our obsession with growth and its cause, uncontrolled debt. Available online at steadystate.org/discover/policies/.

Gaian Democracies by Roy Madron and John Jopling. Complexity in society and sustainable economics. Schumacher Society Briefing #9, Green Books Ltd., Devon, UK, 2003.

Hot, Flat and Crowded by Thomas L. Friedman. As a reminder that nothing real can grow forever. Farrar, Straus and Giroux, New York, 2008.

Plan B, Lester R. Brown, New York, WW Norton and Co., 2003.

For the Common Good: Redirecting the Economy Toward Community, the Environment and a Sustainable Future, Herman E. Daly and John B. Cobb Jr. A scathing critique of classical economics and the moral implications of its faulty premises. Boston: Beacon Press, 1994.

Thinking in Systems by Donella Meadows. Covers policy resistance, tragedy of the commons, low performanc drift, escalation, success going to the successful, addicitons, rule dodging, and wrong goals. Chelsea Green Publishing, Vt., 2008.

D. The Archives of Varok Online

Visit http://ArchivesofVarok.com for:

> Varokian and Ellasonian Glossaries
> An extended history of Varok
> "Deleted" scenes
> Free previews
> Sequel news and release dates

Follow the series on Facebook:

> www.facebook.com/ArchivesofVarok

Find Author Cary Neeper online:

> Blog: www.caryneeper.com/blog.htm
> Twitter: twitter.com/CaryNeeper
> Goodreads: goodreads.com/Cary_Neeper
> Library Thing: librarything.com/author/neepercary

Cary Neeper lives in the US Southwest with her husband and a friendly menagerie of dogs, fish and fowl. An avid proponent of sustainability and steady-state economics since the 1970s, she studied zoology, chemistry and religion at Pomona College and medical mi-crobiology at the University of Wisconsin–Madison. Cary paints landscapes in acrylics, including the cover art for *The Webs of Varok*. She blogs about sustainable economics and hen house life at CaryNeeper.com/blog.htm.

18549340R00203

Made in the USA
Charleston, SC
09 April 2013